ISLES OF
STORM&
SORROW
TRILOGY

'Hogan builds a vivid world, and her descriptions
of life aboard ship evoke the taste of salt
in the air … visceral battles and bristling prose'

SFX

'A rip-roaring, swashbuckling adventure
that left me breathless from the
first page to the last'

Kat Dunn, author of *Dangerous Remedy*

'Every line held me captive.
Bex Hogan is a master storyteller!'

Menna van Praag, author of *The Sisters Grimm*

'Pulse-pounding fantasy pirate adventure …
full of romance, hand-to-hand combat,
bitter revenge, terrifying sea monsters
and magic – I loved it'

Kesia I   *Thunder*

ORION CHILDREN'S BOOKS

First published in Great Britain in 2020
by Hodder and Stoughton

1 3 5 7 9 10 8 6 4 2

A CIP catalogue record for this book
is available from the British Library.

ISBN 978 1 51010 585 0

Typeset by Hewer Text UK Ltd, Edinburgh
Printed and Bound in Great Britain by Clays Ltd, Elcograf S.p.A

The paper and board used in this book are made
from wood from responsible sources.

Orion Children's Books
An imprint of
Hachette Children's Group
Part of Hodder and Stoughton
Carmelite House
50 Victoria Embankment
London EC4Y 0DZ

An Hachette UK Company

www.hachette.co.uk
www.hachettechildrens.co.uk

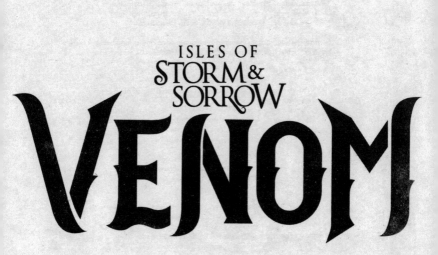

ISLES OF
STORM &
SORROW
VENOM

BEX HOGAN

Orion

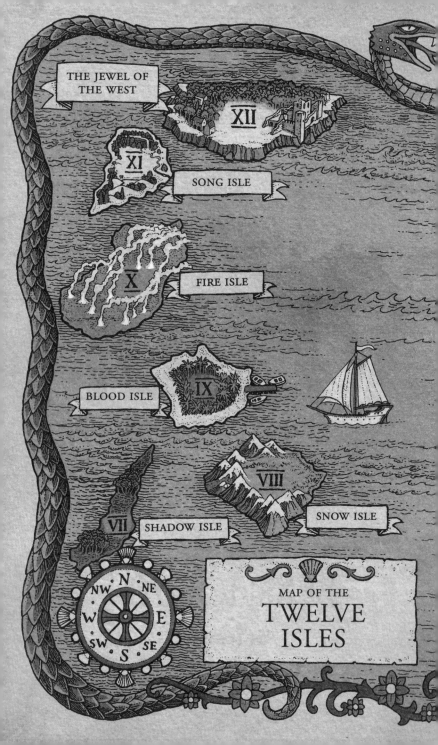

THE JEWEL OF
THE WEST

XII

XI

SONG ISLE

X

FIRE ISLE

BLOOD ISLE

IX

VIII

VII

SNOW ISLE

SHADOW ISLE

NW N NE
W E
SW S SE

MAP OF THE
TWELVE
ISLES

KING'S ISLE

I

FALLOW ISLE

II

BLACK ISLE

III

FLORAL ISLE

IV

MIST ISLE

V

ROCK ISLE

VI

For Joe.
My eternal north.

PART ONE
EAST

1

It's a beautiful night for a wedding. The moon is radiant, offering its shimmering light as a blessing on the union, and the stars shine bright in celebration. The gentle breeze scatters delicate pink petals from the trees like confetti.

The room I'm in looks down over the gardens of the summer palace, and I rest my head against the cool glass of the window. Not moments ago I was surrounded by people, fussing over me, preparing me, filling the air with laughter and excitement. Now I'm alone. Waiting.

I am dressed for midnight. The only colour on my person is the scarlet thread woven through my corset. Otherwise I'm entirely in black as befits the Viper, though for one day only I'm in an elaborate gown, rather than my fighting garb. I slide the dagger gifted to me by my crew into my boot and immediately feel more myself. A bride I may be, but I have plenty of enemies who would love to use this day to their advantage.

There's a soft knock on the door. It's time. A flock of nerves takes flight inside me, fluttering in my chest. With a deep breath, my chin up, I meet my future head on. Two chambermaids greet me with a smile, before placing a heavy velvet cloak on to my shoulders and fastening it with a bejewelled brooch at my throat. The hood is lifted carefully over my hair and I'm escorted from my chamber.

The ceremony is taking place outside, in a courtyard lit by a thousand candles and filled with islanders who have congregated to watch this historic event unfold. A hush descends over the crowd at my arrival, every head turning to watch me make the long walk to where the priestess waits to mark our vows. My heart is beating fast – too fast – though I'm comforted to see members of my crew standing either side of the aisle.

And then there he is. My eyes lock on him like a needle on a compass. Bronn. My eternal north.

His face remains as impassive as ever – he's had years to practise concealing his feelings – and though I'm still not always able to read him, today I have no doubt what's going through his mind. Reluctantly I pull my gaze away from him, moving my focus to the man waiting for me just feet ahead.

Torin. He is dressed in the finest cloth, trimmed with velvet and sparkling with fragments of crystal. He has never looked more handsome. He smiles at my approach – a wonderful, genuine smile because Torin can't give anything less – but even so I glimpse his conflict. I'm not the only one forsaking love in the name of duty today.

In a few steps I'm beside him, trying to block out the rest of the world as I listen to the priestess's words, making my vows with as much honesty as I can. I promise to honour Torin, swear to defend him with my life, and pledge to remain true to him above all others – until death parts us. This last oath is by far the most difficult to make, but I force the words out. At least both of us know the truth. And as I'm not deceiving Torin in any way, there's no guilt.

Behind Torin, standing just close enough to be in my peripheral vision, is his new bodyguard, Braydon. I'm not used to him yet; he seems to trust me as little as Sharpe did to begin with. But while I eventually won Sharpe round, I suspect Braydon's dislike for me might be harder to overcome. I can sense him scowling even as I become his princess.

My eyes dart over to Sharpe, standing off to one side. The loss of his sight meant he had to be reassigned, and though he remains Torin's aide, his misery these past months has been obvious. He looks as though he wants to be here as much as Bronn does.

Our vows made, Torin and I are instructed to place our wrists together, as we did during our binding ceremony so long ago. But this time, rather than red-hot metal, silk is wrapped round our scarred skin, and we turn to face all those who have assembled to witness such a momentous occasion.

The crowd cheers, and my crew salutes us, before Torin leans over to kiss me gently on my lips. It's all part of the act, I know, but I can feel the blood rush to my cheeks. His skin is soft where Bronn's is rough; his touch is ice where Bronn's is fire.

He is my husband. I am his wife.

When we walk back down the aisle, still bound together with the silk, I manage to avoid looking at Bronn. It takes me a few moments to realise I'm holding my breath, and I exhale. The worst, after all, is over. I force myself to relax, even going as far as to acknowledge the crowds of people who are cheering our departure.

It's then I see him. The stranger. There's nothing extraordinary about him but that's exactly what makes him stand out. He's dressed a little too normally. He's blending in a little too much. He stands exactly like a man who doesn't want to be noticed.

I look away, to avoid rousing his suspicions, but keep him in the corner of my eye – I don't want to lose sight of a potential threat. Torin must feel me tense, because he looks over, concerned.

'What's wrong?'

I give him the brightest smile possible, so that to the crowd I will seem merely like a happy bride talking with her new husband. 'Behind me, towards the wall. Black hair, tied back. Tall. Do you see him?'

Torin returns my false smile with one of his own and leans towards me, giving the impression of whispering sweet nothings into my ear, while really looking past me to see who I mean.

'Yes. Who is he?'

'I was hoping you might know.'

'Want me to have him removed?'

I shake my head. 'The last thing we want to do is cause a spectacle.' But I make a mental note to ask one of my crew to keep an eye on him the first chance I get.

When we reach the end of the aisle, Torin searches my face. 'We did the right thing, didn't we?'

I squeeze his arm with my free hand. 'Of course we did.' Though I do already wish the night was over. I would rather not have to endure the coming celebrations.

I've had no say in this wedding. I didn't want it here, in the summer palace, deep in the heart of the First Isle. Set atop a mountain peak, the palace is bleak and isolated and a long way from my ship, which makes me feel vulnerable and uneasy. I didn't want an extravagant feast and dancing when the islanders are still struggling to fill their bellies. But it's all been arranged by someone else.

The King.

The very thought of the man makes my anger rise. I hate that he still has the crown, but by the time I returned from the West, Torin had already struck a deal with his father. Torin had given him two choices: abdicate or be overthrown. Ever the coward, the King did not relish a fight with his son and the new Viper, and so in order to protect his reputation and legacy, the King agreed to abdicate quietly. But he had one condition: that he remain on the throne until this marriage had taken place, so he could use the excuse of royalty and Viper allying as his reason for stepping down. For the sake of the islands and to avoid further bloodshed Torin agreed, but when I found out the King's request a worm of suspicion burrowed into my stomach. Trusting the King isn't something that comes naturally to me, and I feared he'd only agreed to whatever would delay his abdication, giving him time to squirm his way out of his promise. So I'd paid him a visit, not long after I arrived back in the East, to add a little incentive. It was just like old times, climbing through his window in the dead of night, to make him wake to a living nightmare. I told him he would announce his abdication during the wedding feast, and presented him with a document to sign. His word was not enough for me; I wanted it in writing. And if he refused? Well, I had no qualms about threatening the royal neck.

I killed my father. I will not hesitate to kill someone else's.

They were words he understood, threats and violence being the only language the King will listen to, and he had done as I'd asked. But even now I feel a sense of unease. The King has betrayed me before and I have no doubt he'll try to again.

And while we sit beneath the stars, in the open air, that feeling only grows stronger, as I watch my new father-in-law tearing strips of roast suckling boar from the bone.

The King has invited everyone of importance throughout the Six Isles to celebrate the wedding. Distant family, governors, chief merchants, captains of the Fleet – they're all here, and I was happy for them to come, to witness his abdication, but I can't help suspecting the King's motives were quite different. For him, they're here to be impressed by his lavish display of wealth. The King does love to be admired.

Still, at least the atmosphere is warm – the courtiers are full of smiles for me, and no one seems displeased with the Prince wedding the Viper.

Finally it's time for speeches – another ritual that requires only my silence – and my breathing turns shallow with nervous anticipation. Either the King is about to relinquish his hold over the Isles or he's going to prove he's as untrustworthy as ever. I fear I know precisely which it will be. And if he forces my hand, then tomorrow all memories of a happy wedding will be forgotten. The silent war for power that's been raging between us will come to an end one way or another – and whether it's peacefully or with violence is now in the hands of the King.

The King is the first to speak, and he begins by waffling insincere words about how glad he is to see everyone, how grateful he is to them for making the journey here. He draws everyone's attention to the feast, boasting of the quantity, noting the quality of the wine brought up from his cellars. But when he moves on to state how happy he is that, at last, the royal family and the Viper will be united by marriage, his tone changes. He goes to great lengths to insist no one should be in any doubt that the covenant between land and sea has never been stronger. It sounds more like a threat than a wedding speech and – judging by the looks on the watching faces – I'm not the only one who thinks so.

He talks about the days to come, the great power of his kingdom. He does not address his people's suffering, the hardships they bear. He says nothing about Adler, the monster who raised me; nothing about the fall of one Viper, the rise of the next. There's no praising his son for the part he played in defending the East.

And there is not one word about him abdicating the throne.

When he raises his glass of wine, toasting a long and happy partnership, he looks directly at me and smiles. A smile filled with a thousand challenges. A smile that tells me he intends to go nowhere.

Just as I feared.

I hold his gaze unflinchingly. Because if he thinks for one second that I'm going to let him go unpunished for all he's done, then he is very much mistaken. He's had

9

his chance and squandered it. The hard truth is this: I have to use the signed document to insist he abdicate, and if that fails, then I'm going to have to do what I should have done all along. I'm going to have to kill the King.

He looks away first, much to my satisfaction. Deciding it's time to remind the King who he's dealing with, I stand up.

I can feel disapproval from every side. It's not tradition for a princess to speak at her wedding. But I am the Viper, and I will not be silenced.

'Today is an historic moment, it's true,' I say, my voice firm and clear. 'But it's more than that. This alliance is a new beginning. For too long the islands have suffered, have been left to fend for themselves through terrible adversity.' I pause. 'Well, not any more. This is my vow: I will never stop fighting for you. From this day forward, the power of land and sea belongs to the islanders, to serve you above all else. And, I swear to you, peace will be restored.'

I've run out of words, and when an awkward silence falls I glance down at Torin.

My break with tradition wasn't exactly planned, and his jaw is clenched with tension. But in a show of solidarity Torin gets to his feet and raises his glass. 'To a new era!'

It breaks the spell and everyone joins in the toast.

And now I look at the King and give him my own smile. One that promises I will gladly destroy him if he continues to pursue this path.

I take my seat, allowing Torin his chance to speak. He has only kind words for his people, and he reaffirms my pledge that we will work tirelessly to end the dark days plaguing our lands.

But while he talks I can't help thinking how hard it will be to keep my vow to the islanders. Because the truth is – I have been fighting relentlessly since I came home, and yet I've hardly begun to make a difference. The carnage created by Adler is not easily undone, and several notorious and violent groups of bandits continue to elude me and my crew.

I take a deep breath. In such a public setting I must remain calm. Looking around the crowd, I try to gauge their reaction to our speeches.

My eyes fall on the stranger from the ceremony. I'd forgotten about him in my fury at the King's betrayal but now my unease comes rushing back. He is leaning against a stone wall, not sharing in the feast and he is certainly not clapping. He simply stares at me. Intently.

I look away and shuffle my foot, reassured by the sharp scratch of the knife blade still resting in my boot. Every instinct tells me I'll need it before the night's end.

Finally the feast is over and the music begins. Torin escorts me to the open floor where we dance together for the first time. He must sense all my misery, because he holds me firmly but with great tenderness and I rest my head on his shoulder, endlessly glad that he is nothing like his father.

I'm obliged to dance with several more members of the court, but eventually I'm able to make my excuses and leave the floor. Desperate for a moment's peace, I move to the edge of the courtyard, choosing a vast stone pillar to hide behind, and leaning my forehead against it. I close my eyes and wonder if this will ever end. If I'll ever be able to undo the suffering, because if not—

'You look beautiful.'

I hadn't heard him approach and, with the first true smile I've given all day, I turn to face Bronn.

'Thank you. So do you.'

And he does, in his full Snake blacks, his raised hood casting a shadow across his brooding features. Dark, fathomless eyes peer through long lashes, eyes that I have lost myself in many nights.

Bronn steps closer, the pillar shielding us from view, and he leans to brush the hair from my forehead. The merest graze of his touch is the sweetest fire and I close my eyes, remembering the last time we were alone together. How we'd held each other, never wanting to let go, yet knowing we must, wondering if every kiss would be the last. I would have stolen all the time in the world to stay there in his arms a bit longer: two bodies, two souls bound as one. Instead I'd wept once he fell asleep, mourning the life we could never have.

'Are you OK?'

I make a noise like a strangled laugh. 'No. Are you?'

'No. But I will be.'

He's so close now; I can feel the warmth of his breath on my skin and my heart beats faster, crying out from inside my chest, begging him to stay here with me. But I can feel him slipping away already. A distance that has nothing to do with proximity is growing between us.

In the few months since we left the West we've both thrown our energy into hunting down bandits. Carrying the guilt of surviving when we've lost those we love and knowing the price paid by so many for the sake of the Isles, we've attempted to dull our grief by fighting fiercely, not allowing their deaths to be in vain. After raids or battles, when blood had been shed, we always found our way to each other, stealing precious moments to feel alive when surrounded by death. We have sought comfort in each other's arms, and though we knew it couldn't last, it was easy to pretend.

I was selfish. I didn't want to lose him so soon after finding him again. But now, as I stand in my wedding dress longing for a man who isn't my husband, I see all too clearly that *everything's* changed. This marriage will tear us to shreds, will open wounds that will fester – not heal. It's already started. Today has cut into Bronn as surely as any blade, and I am the one holding the dagger.

I move slightly away from him, steeling myself to do what's necessary. 'I have a job for you.'

Bronn frowns. 'A job?' He doesn't sound impressed.

I peer round the pillar and point to the long-haired man still lurking in the shadows.

'Find out who that is.'

Bronn follows my gaze, before looking back at me. 'Doesn't Torin know?'

I shake my head. 'If he's not a guest, I don't know how he got past the guards. I don't trust him. He watches too closely. I would feel better if you could follow him. Question him.'

My concern is real, but the truth is that I'm also trying to put some distance between us, and assigning Bronn a mission is the best way to do that. The look he's giving me suggests he knows my motives. Knows I'm saying goodbye.

It's a while before he speaks and when he does his voice is colder. 'Consider it done, Captain.'

And, giving the curtest of nods, Bronn walks away. It's as if he's extinguished all the candles and stolen the stars. My world has never felt so dark.

The celebrations last too long, but eventually Torin and I are escorted to our wedding chamber, high up in the east tower, with bawdy laughter and coarse jokes being thrown at us the whole way.

Once the door is mercifully shut, Torin leans against it and exhales, while I kick the empty chamber pot across the room.

'That lying, cheating, conniving piece of scum!' I can no longer contain my rage towards the King, and it spews out of me in an uncontrollable stream. 'Rotten, scheming hagbreather!'

'Yes, my father never fails to disappoint,' Torin growls.

'Backstabbing, treacherous wartwhale! We should never have trusted him for a minute.'

Torin sighs, rubbing his jaw. 'You mean *I* shouldn't have trusted him.'

His frustration with himself tempers my fury. 'You wanted to try the peaceful approach first,' I say, collapsing backwards on to the bed, flinging my arms out wide. 'It was the right thing to do.'

Torin comes to perch beside me, removing his boots. 'I should have known better. My father will do anything to cling to his power.'

'No, it's my fault. I was too lenient on my return.' Worn down from fighting, I allowed the King to feel safe. I should have poured fire on his agreement with Torin, forced him to abdicate immediately. And now, because of my weakness, things are going to get ugly.

Torin lies back next to me and for a moment we just

stare at each other, too weary for anything else. 'Let's not dwell on it any longer,' he says eventually. 'Let's have just a few moments of the day untarnished by his presence. Tomorrow, the fight can resume. We'll insist he keep his word and give up the throne as agreed. You have the document he signed, don't you?'

I nod. 'In my room. But he could argue it was signed under duress.'

A knowing smile spreads across Torin's face. 'Was it?'

'There may have been some coercion,' I say with a shrug.

'All right, well, if he decides to argue its validity, then we overthrow him. We hold all the cards.'

More conflict. Just what the Isles don't need. But in my heart I know this is where we're heading. And though it won't pain me one bit to rid us all of the King, I wonder how far Torin's willing to go to be free of his father. Overthrowing him is one thing. But would Torin let me kill him if it came to it?

'It's funny,' Torin says, nudging me with his elbow. 'Of all the ways I imagined my wedding night, I didn't think I'd spend it talking about my father.'

I smile. 'Me neither. We have far more important things to do.'

'Sleep,' we say at the same time, and it feels good to laugh together, after the strain of the day.

Torin helps me undo the laces of my corset, but then averts his gaze while I slip out of my gown and exchange it for my shift. Once he's in bed, I lie beside him and hold his hand.

'It's sad,' he says, 'that no one but us knows how momentous today actually was. East binding to West. The start of a new reign. Our reign.'

Something unpleasant stirs in my stomach. The reminder of my duty to the West is unwelcome. I can barely help the East.

'We're not the only ones,' I say quietly. 'Bronn and Sharpe know.' Immediately I feel bad as pain flashes in Torin's eyes.

'They understand why we had to go through with today,' he says.

I smile by way of apology, not wanting to infect him with my misery. Torin's hopes for the future match my fears for the present, and it is why we need each other. Together we are balanced.

'We can do this,' he continues, squeezing my fingers. 'We will do this.'

I lean forward and kiss his forehead. 'I know.'

'Good night, wife,' he says, his eyes sparkling with affection.

'Sweet dreams, husband.'

I watch with envy how quickly sleep claims him. Though exhaustion prickles through my bones, for a long time I just lie there, my head too crowded with thoughts. The air is thick in here, suffocating, and I feel the walls closing in on me. Leaving Torin alone in our marriage bed, I move to the window and push it open, desperate for air. It's as if the night is crushing my chest and I cannot breathe. I have to get out of here. Without even bothering to dress, I wrap my cloak round my shift and slip my dagger back into my boot.

When I appear at the door, three surprised guards look up at me. I raise my hand for them to be quiet.

'The Prince is asleep,' I say, ignoring their suggestive glances. 'I left some things in my old room and wish to retrieve them.'

'Allow me to escort you.' Braydon stands up, and then adds as an afterthought, 'Your Highness.'

'There's no need; I can find my way.'

'I insist.'

'Very well, if you must.'

There is no concern in his offer, only mistrust.

We walk through the castle, the only light coming from the candle I hold. It's quite a way to go to my room in the west tower, and all the while Braydon is several paces behind me, his eyes boring into my back.

When at last I reach my door, I turn to him. 'I think I might stay here for the rest of the night. I don't wish to disturb my husband. Thank you, Braydon.'

The bodyguard is clearly not happy to leave me, but what can he do? He bids me a frosty good night and at last I'm alone. The quiet is a balm to my troubled spirit.

18

So much of my life has been spent in isolation that now I find hours surrounded by others leaves me itching for solitude.

I move to the other side of my room, pausing as I pass the desk to check the drawer remains locked. Satisfied the scroll signed by the King is safe, I push the doors open on to the balcony, drinking in the cold air of the early hours of morning. The moon beams down on the castle, illuminating the delicate nightglow flowers that weave through the stone wall beside me like stars, and for a moment I allow myself to believe that things will fall into place as we hope.

I haven't felt much peace since I left the West. And it's not just the fighting. A quiet dissatisfaction is growing inside me like a weed. I don't know what it is, but it climbs and snakes, spreads and suffocates. Maybe it's just part of adapting to my new life. Or perhaps it is simply frustration clawing at me from within. But it's always there, an ever-present reminder that something is not right.

A sharp wind whips my cloak about me, stinging my skin, and as I brush the hair from my face an unexpected movement catches my attention. Leaning forward slightly, I try to identify what it is.

Scaling the ivy-covered walls of the east tower is a figure dressed entirely in black. The moonlight glints off the blade he holds between his teeth as he climbs swiftly upwards. Whatever his intentions, they're definitely not friendly.

Only one person sleeps in that tower – Torin – and so I don't hesitate. Moving as soundlessly as the intruder, I remove my cloak and take my dagger from my boot before climbing on to the balustrade and reaching for a foothold on the castle wall. Running through the palace would take too long – this is the only way I'm going to reach him in time.

My hands glide easily over ancient stones, urgency causing the blood to pulse through my body so that even my fingertips tingle. My blade grazes my tongue and sweat runs down my back. I don't even let myself think of the drop beneath me. A single thought screams through my mind.

Hurry.

I'm closing the distance between us, but then I lose the intruder as he disappears through the bedroom window I opened not long ago. I climb faster. If I don't get there quickly, it'll be too late. When I'm close enough, I push off the wall and leap towards the window ledge, only just making the distance and hanging precariously for a moment before I scramble up into the room.

Before my eyes can adapt to the gloom, my hair is grabbed and my head slammed against the wall. Pain streaks through my skull and I drop the blade from my mouth as I gasp for air. He knew he was being followed.

20

He's swinging his knife round now, aiming for my guts, but I recover quickly and bring my fist down hard on to his arm, so that now he's the one who drops his weapon.

I don't wait for him to collect himself, bringing my hand up into his chin, and causing him to stagger backwards. But he avoids my next blow and lands one of his own, sending an explosion of pain through my shoulder.

I wish it weren't so dark, because all I can see of the intruder is that he's wearing a mask over his nose and mouth, his hood concealing his hair. I need to know who would be brave enough to steal into the Prince's room so brazenly, and I reach forward, hoping to remove the mask. But again he evades me. He's fast, and it's like he knows what I'm planning before I do it, because he's able to dodge every move I make.

He's good.

But I'm better.

Changing tactics, I kick him in the stomach, knocking him off balance. It's all the edge I need, and now I'm able to make my strikes count: a punch to the face, a jab to the ribs. And as our silent dance continues, the moonlight catches on his striking amber eyes, which blaze with fear.

'Who are you?' I have to know.

His response is to lunge for my neck, his hands seeking to crush my bones. I manage to grab his wrists

21

before they can do their damage, and for a moment we're frozen in a deadlock.

There's only one thing to do – I snap my head forward into his. He falters in pain and, with his balance compromised, I kick him again. He lurches away from me and falls on to the bed where Torin has been sleeping, oblivious to the danger.

But the weight of an assassin landing by him is enough to wake him, and Torin groggily sits up. 'Marianne?'

He's still half asleep.

The attacker hasn't fully recovered from the headbutt, but it won't take him long. I have to be quick. Racing to where my dagger still lies on the floor, I pick it up, and aiming directly for the man's heart I fling it with all the strength I possess.

Only for him to catch the blade between the palms of his hands.

Such skill, such a reflex, momentarily stuns me and before I can gather my wits the assassin turns and plunges my dagger firmly into Torin's chest.

2

My breath leaves me as if the wound is my own. I race towards the attacker but he's already sprinting to the other window, and I have to make a choice: pursue him or save Torin.

Cursing, I run to where Torin lies, his blood rapidly soaking the sheets.

He's wide awake now and confused as I pull him into my arms.

'Marianne?' He's clutching his chest, and I move his hand away to see how bad it is.

'You're all right; let me look,' I say as calmly as I can, despite the panic roaring in my ears. The knife has missed Torin's heart, but he's losing a lot of blood.

I start to tear one of the sheets, pressing the material hard against his chest. 'Nothing I can't fix,' I say, giving him my most encouraging smile, but I realise his eyes are closing as consciousness escapes him. 'No, no, stay awake.' And then I'm shouting to the guards, unable to stem the tide of fear rising in me. 'Help! Help us!'

'Torin, look at me.' I speak with my most commanding voice, daring him to disobey. 'You're not going to die, do you hear me? Don't you dare die.'

I can see him fighting, but he's losing the battle, and when he tries to raise his hand towards me it only lifts a few inches before it falls back to the bed.

I could save him with magic.

The idea comes from nowhere. Magic is something I haven't allowed myself to think about since I turned my back on it in the West. But I'm desperate. Could I reach inside myself once more for the power to save him?

The door bursts open, shattering the thought, and the guards stare at the scene before them, open-mouthed.

'Call for the healer.' I'm shouting again, angered by their inaction – and my own. 'And raise the alarm. The intruder can't have gone far.'

One of the younger guards runs off, screaming murder and waking the castle from its drunken slumber. Another hurries over to us and even through my panic I'm aware of the suspicious look he's casting over the situation.

'Pass me that bottle on the chest,' I say. It's a weak tonic, and not one I'd normally ever use for a wound like this, but it's better than nothing and Torin's running out of time.

The guard doesn't move. He's staring down at me and it's then I realise how this must look.

Me, still in my shift, which is now drenched in blood, and my knife protruding from my new husband.

'Please.' I force my voice to be softer this time. 'He's dying; let me help him.'

For a moment I think it's hopeless, but perhaps the guard senses my despair because he walks over to the chest and picks up the tonic.

I exhale. 'Thank you.'

But as he stretches to pass it to me a voice cuts through the air.

'Don't you dare give that killer her poison.'

The guard sheepishly steps back from me, bowing his head as the King strides into the room, and my heart falls when I see Braydon with him. He clearly went to fetch the King the moment he saw what had happened.

'Get her away from my son,' the King says.

Braydon and the other guard move towards me.

'If I let go of this, he'll bleed to death in seconds,' I warn, and they hesitate. Torin's turning a frightening colour and it's not hard to believe death is imminent for their prince.

'You.' The King points to the older guard. 'Take her place.'

The man swallows nervously as he stands beside me. I position his hands down on the blood-soaked sheet.

'Press hard. Don't let go.' My command is laced with threat. Torin's life depends on it.

Braydon grabs my arm and pulls me off the bed.

'I didn't do this,' I say to the King. 'But I can save him, if you let me.'

The King ignores me and turns to Braydon. 'You say you left her in the west wing?'

'Yes, Your Majesty. She must have climbed through the window.'

'I followed an intruder! He fled out of that window,' I say, gesturing to the far wall, where the open window swings in the night breeze. 'You can still catch him.'

The look the King gives me says everything. They're not searching for anyone else. They have their suspect.

'Arrest this traitor.'

Braydon wrenches my hands together and clamps irons round them. I don't fight, but only because the last thing I want is for the guard to move from Torin's side. So for now I'll let them do this. As long as he lives.

The sight of the King's healer finally arriving does nothing to lessen my dread. Old, frail and looking worryingly dishevelled, the healer is barely awake, until the sight of the Prince seems to shake the sleep from him, and he hurries to his royal patient.

'Add silverbud and swampnettle to your poultice,' I say as I'm dragged from the room. 'And lace your tonic with whiterust.'

I doubt my advice will be heeded but I don't trust the old remedies the healer uses. They're largely ineffectual.

Torin has only slightly more chance of surviving under his care than with no care at all.

Braydon is joined by another five guards to escort me and despite the circumstances I feel a shard of satisfaction. They've remembered who I am after all. Not just some woman who happened to marry their prince, but the Viper. They should be worried. If I wanted, they'd be dead in minutes. Fortunately for them I don't want them dead. I'm not leaving this castle until I know Torin's going to be all right.

I'm taken down to the dungeons and thrown into a cold cell. The summer castle isn't often used, so the dungeons are mostly empty with only a few neighbours to witness my arrival – a relief since I'm the one who's been catching most of the prisoners in the Isles recently.

As Braydon pulls the padlock through the chain, I grab his arm. 'I didn't do this,' I say. 'The man who did is still out there. He might come back. Whatever you think of me, promise you'll keep Torin safe.'

Braydon rips himself free from my grasp and spits in my face. 'Viper bitch. You'll hang for this.'

I give no reaction outwardly, but inside I'm raging.

Alone in my cell, I take a moment to consider my situation. Shivering in only my thin shift, the immensity of what's happened begins to sink in.

Someone tried to kill Torin. Someone exceptionally skilled. And the King is framing me for the crime.

I sit down.

This is bad. On so many levels. Who could want Torin dead? Who would benefit from his death? The most obvious person is the King, but for all his many faults I can't believe him capable of this. Of having his own son murdered. If not him, though, who? I didn't recognise the would-be assassin, but it's possible he was working with the stranger who shadowed the evening's events.

But then, apart from the three guards, there was no reason for anyone to suppose I wasn't in the bedchamber with my new husband. Surely the presence of the Viper would cause most people to reconsider an attempt? Unless the assassin was there for me. I can easily believe more people would wish me dead than Torin.

The war I've waged against the bandits has been bloody and it's been brutal. My aim always was – and remains – to take prisoners, to bring them to justice for their crimes, but the reality is they're prepared to fight to the death and my crew are the best fighters there are. Though I've lost a few Snakes, it's been nothing compared to the losses of the bandits, and while my crew celebrate our victories, they leave me unsettled and uncertain. Bronn thinks it's because I'm still afraid of becoming like Adler, but it's more than that. It's not quite the justice I imagined bringing to the East.

Regardless, there are many bandits still to catch, including the most deadly and notorious group, led by a brute named Karn. They have managed to elude our every attempt to find them, so strong is their network of terror. The closest we got was discovering a stash of their weaponry and taking it for ourselves. It wouldn't be too difficult to believe Karn would send someone to kill me – I'm sure he'd love the Viper title for his own – but what is harder to believe is that any of his men would be skilled enough to catch a blade like that.

I slide down on to the cold ground, my foot tapping nervously as I try not to think about Torin. Did the healer get to him in time? Or is it already over? Burying my head in my hands, I bite back tears. I've already lost Grace, my sister in all but blood. I can't lose him too.

Should I have used magic to help him? Could I have done? Since I left Esther on the Eighth Isle, I haven't had time to think about that side of myself, of all the possibilities I gave up when I turned down her offer to teach me to become a Mage. Or maybe I just haven't allowed myself to dwell on it. I made a choice to leave the West, to focus on bringing peace to the East instead, and there has been no place for magic in that fight. I buried that part of me, the wild, uncontrollable force that I fear so much, that I desire so much.

I bang my head hard against the wall, desperate to free my mind of these maddening thoughts.

No, my urge to use magic was simply a foolish impulse. I wouldn't have known where to start – a truth that claws at my guts. If I'd allowed Esther to teach me as she offered, could I have healed Torin?

There are no answers. I can only wait. I will do nothing until I know Torin is going to live.

When dawn breaks, I hear footsteps approaching.

The sight of my visitor causes my heart to pound, but I don't move.

'You can have five minutes,' the gaoler says to him, before leaving us alone.

And I run to grasp Sharpe's hands through the bars.

'How is he?'

'Alive.' Sharpe squeezes my hands tightly. 'For now.'

My relief is palpable. 'Thank goodness.'

Sharpe shakes his head. 'He's unconscious, Marianne. He's not waking up.'

'Don't worry, that's fine. His body needs time to rest – probably the healer gave him something to keep him asleep.' I can feel the weight of the night lifting from me and am keen to reassure Sharpe that all is now well.

But his face remains like stone and he won't stop shaking his head.

'You don't understand,' he says. 'I'm certain the healer *is* keeping him asleep. But not just so he can heal.'

I finally realise what Sharpe's telling me. 'They don't want him to clear my name.'

Sharpe bows his head. 'I'm sorry. The King wants the trial to happen immediately. He already has every

30

important advisor here for the wedding, every ally at his disposal. He's making his move to be rid of you.'

I can't say I'm surprised.

'There's more,' Sharpe says. 'He had your chambers searched.' And his fingers tighten round mine.

'He took the document, didn't he?' Of course the King would have wanted to destroy the evidence that he was willing to step aside for Torin.

Sharpe nods. 'He will not want you left alive, Marianne.'

No, he won't. But what will he do about his son?

'And Torin?'

'I don't know,' Sharpe says, his voice clipped with worry. 'Maybe the King hopes without you Torin poses no threat. Perhaps he'll wake him once . . .'

'Once I'm dead.'

'I fear for him,' Sharpe says. 'But I don't think the King would murder Torin.'

And yet I'm beginning to suspect that he may have already tried to.

'You know I didn't do this, don't you?' My question is barely a whisper; the answer matters so much to me.

'I wouldn't be here if I thought for a second you'd done it.' And he actually gives me the smallest hint of a smile, the first I've seen from him in months, and if he's offering it as a sign of friendship and comfort, it works.

'Thank you.'

31

'I will do anything I can to help you,' he says, though we both know there's little that can be done.

'Sharpe, can you get word to my crew? I don't know how they're going to react to this, but tell them to sit tight. The last thing the Isles need is us declaring war on the King the day after our alliance.'

The gaoler is returning now, so Sharpe just nods. 'Be safe,' he says and squeezes my fingers one last time before dropping them.

'Look after him,' I call out as Sharpe walks away and then he's gone, leaving me alone once more.

My blood runs white-hot with fury. Could it really be true? Is it possible the King hired someone to murder Torin just to keep his power? All it would have taken was a nod from Braydon that I wasn't in the room and he could have sent an assassin to ensure there was no one left to force him to abdicate. Or did he intend to have us both killed? To turn our wedding bed into our death bed?

I see no one else for the rest of the day. No food or drink is brought to me, and by the following morning it becomes clear that none will be. Perhaps this is the King's tactic. Starve me, weaken me. What he's forgetting is that I've been on rations for months – as have most people. While he commandeers far more than his fair share of supplies and continues to keep his belly full, the rest of us have grown used to surviving on very little. I can withstand a few days' fasting. It won't be the first time. And as for being alone – well, I almost prefer it.

But after I've watched the moon rise and fall four times through the cracks in my wall, my isolation is disturbed. The gaoler approaches, accompanied by three other guards. The way their eyes greedily devour my body tells me instantly what they're here to do, and though I'm tired, I'm also angry.

I don't move from my corner, where I've been huddled for the past two days, making the most of my own body heat, and watch as they come into my cell, locking the door behind them.

I say nothing as they haul me to my feet and then circle me, as if I'm a mere object for them to play with.

My hands are still in irons, and this is making the men foolhardy. Believing me to be restrained, they inch closer.

'Not so tough now, are you?' It's the gaoler who speaks first. 'Without your men to make you look strong and keep you safe.'

'And there's nothing safe about us,' another says.

The youngest of the guards reaches to grab my chin and pulls my face towards him to inspect it. 'She's just a girl.' He sounds surprised and a little relieved. Perhaps my age and gender reassure him that I can't hurt him, despite the fact that I'm the Viper. Perhaps he thinks that I earned the title by way of cheating or lying. As if just anyone could claim it. Or perhaps he simply thinks I slept my way to the top.

'Please,' I say softly, playing up my apparent vulnerability. 'Don't do this.'

They laugh and the gaoler comes nearer. 'There's no point begging,' he says, his voice suddenly devoid of humour.

I raise my eyes to meet his and this time when I speak, there's no hint of weakness. 'I wasn't. I was giving you a warning.'

And I make my move, before they have a chance to make theirs.

With the flat of my hand I smack the gaoler hard in the forehead, throwing him backwards. In the split second he's dazed, I spin to duck the blow coming from the guard on my right, and land a punch of my own into the chest of the man on my left, which, with the weight of the irons behind it, cracks his sternum, making him drop to the floor with a shriek.

The first two are coming back for me now. I lunge at the gaoler, lifting my shackled hands over his head and using his body as an anchor to raise myself up so I can kick the other guard hard in his throat, rendering him unconscious. It's all happening too fast for the gaoler, and he has no time to react as I fling my body round so I'm on his back, pulling the irons hard against his neck. While his hands flail wildly to try to stop me,

I pull harder until he can't breathe any more and passes out.

That leaves the youngest guard, who's standing in the furthest corner and looking like he might wet himself.

I untangle myself from the body now lying on the floor and make my way to him, grabbing his collar to slam him against the wall.

'You tell the King he continues to underestimate me,' I say, my voice sounding more like a growl than anything human. 'Tell him the next time he sends men to my cell, they'll be carrying them out dead, understand?'

The guard nods, his brow dripping with sweat.

'Good.' I release him. 'Now get these pigs out of here.'

Broken-sternum-man is already crawling towards the door, and the young guard drags the other two bodies out, nearly forgetting to relock my cell in his haste to be away from me.

It's only after they've gone and the blood stops careering round my body that the pain starts to make its presence known. Somehow, during the fight, I managed to dislocate the shoulder that the assassin struck earlier.

Damn.

I'm going to have to pop it back in.

Resting the palm of my hand against the wall, I take a deep breath, before forcing all my weight towards it, shoving the bone back into place.

I pass out for a moment and wake up on the floor, shivering and in pain, but I've done it. I make no effort to get up, exhausted. The agony was worth it: in the midst of the chaos I stole the key from the gaoler's belt without the young guard noticing and I don't even have to move far to conceal it in one of the cracks in the wall.

Though I don't imagine the guards will try that again, it's hardly made the arrival of food and water more likely. Their humiliation won't go unpunished, so I can expect to continue starving until such time as the King decides to make his move.

And when he does, I'll be ready.

3

Two weeks after my wedding day, the court is assembled in the palace's central marbled hall, a space usually reserved for summer balls.

It's taken the King far longer than I would have expected to pull this sham of a trial together, and I wonder what's happened to cause such a delay. Perhaps the King had less support than he supposed and had to resort to blackmail and other threats to get the testimonies he required. Whatever the reason, I knew things weren't going well for him when water started being delivered to my cell. He wants me weak, not dead. Not like that anyway – it has to be public. Official.

I haven't heard from Sharpe since I saw him that first day, and I can only assume his silence means he's been unable to leave Torin's side. And so I've bided my time, wanting it to appear as if I've given up, all the while waiting, safe in the knowledge that no one has discovered the stolen key yet. Once I've found out what the King is up to, I will be ready to escape.

He had me dragged into the hall early this morning, still wearing the blood-stained shift that I wore the night of Torin's near-death, and the murmurs of disgust were audible. I'm filthy and I stink. I can only imagine how I look, but it certainly isn't imposing, threatening or any of the things the Viper should be.

Half the First Isle seems to be congregated in the hall; my once cheering wedding guests are now a jeering crowd.

I've been made to wait, sitting on my solitary chair, positioned so that everyone can gawp at me, which they do relentlessly, until eventually the King arrives and the show begins. It quickly becomes clear that this is going to be quite some performance.

'My dearest Islanders,' the King begins. 'Thank you for coming today, though I deeply regret that such attendance was even required. My son . . .' He trails off, his voice breaking with false emotion. 'Forgive me,' he continues, his hand pressed against his chest, eyes swimming with crocodile tears. 'Prince Torin is gravely ill, fighting for his life, and all I want is to be with my child.'

Oh, please. I doubt the King's been to visit Torin even once. Nevertheless, a spike of fear shoots through me. Is he telling the truth? Is my husband's condition still so serious? Or is this another part of the King's act? Perhaps I should just stand up, flee this hall, and fight my way to the healing room, leaving a trail of bodies strewn on the floor in my wake.

Only the knowledge that such an action would jeopardise everything we've all fought for – the stability of the East – stops me from doing exactly that. Instead I sit and force myself to listen to the utter bilge pouring from the King's mouth.

'It breaks my heart,' he's saying, 'that this woman –' and he pauses to point at me – 'whom I embraced as my own daughter, should have betrayed us all in such a fashion. That she could be responsible for the possible death of my boy.'

Our eyes meet and I see no sorrow in his. Just a steely determination to destroy me. Whether or not he intended to have me killed that night is irrelevant now. This is my assassination.

The King looks away and resumes his attack on my character. 'I wouldn't have believed her capable of hurting Torin if I hadn't seen it with my own eyes. The memory of her looming over his body, her knife in his chest . . .' Again he pauses to collect his composure. 'Well, you can all see his blood on her clothes.'

There's a murmur of horror and disgust from the crowd, and I glance over at the jury to gauge their response. The King has assembled quite the council to judge me – it's made up entirely of his advisors and governors from the other Isles. Men who belong to him. And from the look on their faces I'd say they're enjoying the King's performance as much as he's enjoying giving it.

'It grieves me to say this,' the King continues, not sounding in the least bit aggrieved, 'but our Viper is far from what she seems. She has deceived us all, and today it is sadly my duty to reveal to you her true nature.'

The proceedings continue with Braydon, which is to be expected seeing as he can give evidence that will align with what the King wants everyone to believe.

The King stands him opposite the jury, which means I'm looking almost directly at him, though Braydon avoids making eye contact.

'Would you please tell the court what happened on the night of the attack?' the King asks him, looking supremely confident before his council.

'The accused left the wedding chamber in the early hours of the morning, wishing to return to her former quarters.'

There is a hum of surprise in the room at this, for why would a bride wish to leave her new husband on their wedding night? Instantly this is cause for suspicion.

'And did she go alone?' The King seems to be enjoying this rather too much for a man whose son's life is hanging in the balance.

'No, though she wished to. I insisted upon accompanying her.'

'Why was that?

Braydon now looks over at me. 'Because I've never trusted her. She's a Snake.'

There's a general nodding of agreement through the congregated court, and I fight not to roll my eyes given that these same courtiers were fawning over me not that long ago.

'Indeed,' the King says. 'And what happened then?'

'I escorted her back to her old room, where she insisted she would remain, for fear of disturbing the Prince if she were to return. I was reluctant, but it was not my place to question her, and so I bade her good night.'

'And when did you next lay eyes on her?' The King is coming to his triumphant climax now.

'When I burst into the Prince's chamber and discovered her crouching over him, her knife sunk deep into his chest, the window still open from where she'd climbed in.'

The cry of outrage that echoes through the hall brings a small smile to the King's lips and a blow to my heart. They're all so willing to believe me guilty and, this time, the pang of fear I experience is entirely for myself.

When the room settles down, the King addresses the jury once more.

'This testimony on its own may seem evidence enough to condemn the accused, but I implore you to listen to the remaining witnesses to truly grasp the lengths this girl is willing to go to for power.'

I bristle at his use of the word 'girl'. I'm the Viper. I did what no other dared do – stood up to Captain Adler and won. The King's choice of words seeks to undermine that, to diminish who I am, and, despite my fear, I seethe.

Braydon is excused from the stand, and in his place the King parades person after person to besmirch my name. He starts with guards, most of whom I've never seen before, who reel off fictions revealing my 'constant abuse of power'. I'm not sure anyone listening really believes that I flounced round, flinging glasses of wine into guards' faces for the sheer fun of it, but it doesn't matter. The King is clearly just warming the crowd up.

Next, the chambermaids who dressed me for the wedding are brought in and testify that I shared with them my reluctance to be married. That I was the most joyless bride they'd ever seen. How I admitted I was only marrying Torin for his throne. They look at the floor as they repeat words they've been told to speak, and I feel sorry for them. I don't believe they are here by choice, and hate to think what threats have been made against them. And the fact is, though I never said such things to them, there is some truth to their accusations. I *was* a reluctant bride. Just not for any of the reasons they might imagine.

When the chambermaids are done, it's the turn of the senior advisors. The first to take the stand is Lord Pyer, Royal Overseer of the Mines on the Sixth Isle, and cousin to the King. Though I've never spoken to the man before – hadn't even heard of him before the wedding – he manages to give me a look of pure disgust as if we're mortal enemies.

'I have long counselled the Prince not to marry this woman,' he says, as if he disapproved of the marriage and hadn't been laughing and drinking with everyone else to celebrate it just days ago. 'But she bewitched him out of all sense.'

The King nods sagely, as if he has always shared such an opinion. 'Tell me, why was that? Wouldn't you want a powerful match for your nephew?'

'I wish my nephew nothing but happiness, and it is my fervent hope that he wakes soon from the sleep this witch has sent him to. Because he would be the first to point the finger of blame straight at this she-devil.'

He's not holding back with the venom.

The King frowns, his exaggerated display of surprise still captivating the crowd. 'She-devil? They are strong words, cousin. Do you have a reason to call her such a thing?'

Lord Pyer nods. 'Her father used to bring her with him to the Rock Island. His secret weapon, she would move through a crowd like a huntress, and when she found her prey she would swoop. Strong men would fall for her honeyed words, husbands would leave wives. But a kiss from her lips marked you for death. Adler stole much from the people, from the Sixth, from the Crown by using her to seduce – then kill.'

43

The King glances at me and wrinkles his nose. 'I'm sure many of you, like me, would struggle to believe this woman capable of seducing anyone.'

There are sniggers of amusement round the room, because, yes, I look far from my best. But I stare at the King with particular loathing. He once tried to seduce me, and I wonder how much of what he's subjecting me to now is to punish me for rejecting him.

'Can you perhaps give an example of her wickedness?'

Lord Pyer swells up with self-importance at the King's question. 'I certainly can. Captain Adler hoped that with a diminished supply of crystal, the worth of his own stockpile would increase. I happen to know for a fact that she was tasked by Adler to sabotage the mines on my island. Her actions are the direct cause of the incredible hardship the East has been suffering.'

The gasps are audible, including mine. He's just blamed me for everything, *everything*, the Isles have endured. How dare he? I want so desperately to defend myself, but keep my mouth shut. Anything I say here will be used against me – if I'm angry, it will be evidence of my violent nature; if I cry, it will confirm my weakness. And so for now, silence is my best weapon.

The King is shaking his head, ostensibly with disbelief, but honestly, he looks pleased with this revelation. 'She is the cause of the very suffering she claims to want to end? Perhaps there are no bounds to her villainy.'

No one asks Pyer how he knows this as 'fact', or for the slightest bit of evidence to support his words, and he's excused from the proceedings.

The King has many more witnesses like him. Men of high status who lie about corrupt deals I have offered them since I became Viper: extra crystal in exchange for their loyalty, assassinations of enemies for the promise of power. Bribes I can imagine Adler happily making with all of them, but nothing I would ever do. In fact, the more I listen, the more convinced I am that they are the ones guilty of these crimes against the crown, and the King has forced them to skewer the truth, or else be imprisoned themselves. I guess it's reassuring that he's had to make up attacks against me, rather than there being endless injured parties offering to come forward on their own to send me to my death.

But when the Ambassador of the Fourth Isle begins his grievance against me, I find it harder to hear. Because this time, I do feel responsible. Since Adler burned the island to punish me, nothing has grown there. What little magic lingered in the earth has entirely gone and the land has died. It's a truth I struggle to bear, having loved one corner of it so very much, and there is nothing I wouldn't do to restore the island to its former beauty.

The Ambassador blames me. His charge is that it was

my fight with my father that brought the fire of destruction to his island, my lust to steal power from the Viper. I cursed the land, and killed hundreds.

Of course, the King has conveniently decided to overlook the fact that Adler was betraying him, so I end up being portrayed as an evil daughter, so determined to have power that I murdered the man everyone still believes was my own father.

A she-devil indeed.

At this point the King calls for a break, to allow the jury the luxury of food. I am returned to my cell where I have nothing to do but evaluate what's happened so far.

One of the things I wanted to gain from this trial was to learn who my enemies are. It's fair to say I've made some new ones today, and I can pretty much conclude that the entire jury are willing to sign my death warrant; they're all in the King's pocket. But I suspect most of those giving testimonies aren't against me – just trying to save their own skins.

If Torin were to wake up and exonerate me from the crimes of which I'm accused, I believe support for my death would slide away. It's a bold move to try to eliminate me in this fashion. And it makes me fear that the King will do anything to prevent Torin from coming round.

Oh, please let him wake up. Let him live.

By the time the gaoler returns with the guards to

escort me back to the makeshift court room, I'm ready for whatever else the King has to fling at me. I can withstand the lies. After all, this day has already been brutal. How much worse can it get?

But the gaoler doesn't come alone. Beside him, clearly pained to be in such unsavoury surroundings, is the King. In this filthy place he looks unnaturally clean, his skin glows bronze from the sun, his hair shines with oil. And yet there is no disguising the look of victory he wears and my heart tightens beneath my ribs.

'Leave us,' the King says to the gaoler, whose face falls with disappointment as he bows and slips away.

The King and I regard each other through the bars, our hatred equally matched.

'You know,' the King says, about to touch the cell bars, before thinking better of it, 'I would have kept my word.'

I laugh humourlessly. 'And abdicated?'

He smiles and shakes his head. 'No, that was never going to happen. I mean, I would have married you. Do you remember all that time ago, when you came to me for help? I would have made you my queen, and all this unpleasantness could have been avoided.'

'Then Adler would still terrorise the islands and he would be coming for your neck.'

The King shoots me a vicious glance. 'Instead it was you who came for it. For my son's.'

I falter, trying to search his expression for any sign of

the truth. 'What do you mean? I've told you: I had nothing to do with what happened to Torin.'

'You are a liar, just like your father. The moment you had the royal alliance you needed, you tried to kill the Prince, and I have no doubt you would have come for me next, had you not been caught.'

My mind is racing. He honestly believes that I was responsible. He's not framing me; he's punishing me. And if that's the case, then I've been wrong too. It wasn't him who sent the assassin. Which means I have no idea who did.

I step forward, so the only thing separating me and the King is cold steel. 'I am telling you, I didn't do it. Whatever you think of me, however much you want to remain on the throne, you must keep Torin safe.'

For a moment I think maybe he believes me, but then his mouth curls into a cruel grin.

'Your tricks won't work on me,' he says. 'Your desperate grab for the throne has failed. And I thank you for it, truly. You've made it far easier for me. Let me tell you what will happen now. Tomorrow you will be executed for your treachery. Torin will remain perfectly safe, his wound is mending and the draught the healer is giving him keeps him adequately nourished, and more importantly unconscious. One day I may allow him to awaken, but not until I'm certain he cannot steal what is not his. And I will remain King long after your name is lost on the wind.'

I try to grab him, but my shackles slam into the bars so that my fingers barely brush him as he steps back, triumphant.

'You're the only treacherous one here,' I shout at him as he walks away. 'I will make you pay for this. Your blood, not mine, will be spilled!'

The gaoler approaches me with a smile and I meet his gaze. He holds up a key, and all hope drains from me. 'You think I didn't know you took this?' he says. 'I wanted to retrieve it immediately, but the King insisted it would be more fun to let you believe you could really escape. And he was right.'

My heart starts to race as his grin widens. He unlocks the door and a dozen guards sweep in to grab hold of me. Then the gaoler hangs the key on a hook far, far out of my reach.

'There's only one way out of this for you and that's at the gallows.'

And for the first time since I was imprisoned a hot flush of panic spreads across my skin before being absorbed into my very core. Without the key my cell is impossible to escape from; I've tested every corner of it. And I'm too heavily guarded to put up a successful fight. The guards push me out of the cell and we begin our journey back through the dark tunnels towards the spiral staircase that takes us up into the main castle. With every step despair flickers a little higher, a little brighter – I'd felt so confident that I could outwit the King, that this trial was only happening because I'd decided to let it. What a fool I've been. I've given him everything he wants, and now I'm not entirely sure what I'm going to do.

The King thanks both the jury and all those gathered, welcoming their attendance with far more enthusiasm than he did during his wedding speech.

'I think you've all come to know our Viper a little better during the course of this morning,' he says, as if the revelations have hurt him. 'But I fear the worst is still to come: tales of her true nature from those who know her best.'

He claps his hands and the double doors are pushed open.

There's a collective intake of breath from the crowd as Bronn enters the hall and I can't blame them. He cuts a far more impressive figure than I ever could. Every muscle, every contour reveals his strength, while the mysterious aura that surrounds him is only heightened by the dark hair falling over his face. He is beautiful. He is deadly. He mesmerises all who see him.

My heart can't decide whether to stop or race faster as he strides towards the King and stands to face me. I have no idea what he's doing here, but betray no hint of emotion at seeing him, though I want to run to him and disappear into his arms.

Bronn sweeps his hair back as he glances up at me, his eyes narrowing ever so slightly at my ragged state, and as I glimpse his anger I know that, despite sending him away, I've not lost him yet.

'Please,' the King says to Bronn, 'would you tell the honourable chosen who you are?'

'I'm Bronn, first mate aboard *The Maiden's Revenge*.'

'And do you acknowledge this *girl* . . .' The King points at me and spits the word with contempt. 'Do you acknowledge her as your captain?' He says it as if this was the most ludicrous notion in the world.

Bronn looks at me, and to all in the room it would seem as if he hates me. 'No.'

There's a murmur of shock at his declaration and I realise I'm holding my breath. I have no idea how this is going to play out.

The King, however, is loving every moment. His audience is reacting exactly as he'd hoped.

'No?' The King acts surprised. 'Why ever not?'

'Because she has done nothing worthy of being Captain. She isn't even a Snake, not technically. She failed her Initiation.'

The King bows his head, as if this is gravely disappointing to him. 'Failed. Her. Initiation.' Just in case anyone missed that little announcement. 'The very reason her father disowned her and cast her out, is it

51

not?'

'Yes,' Bronn says. 'She couldn't do what was required of her.'

'So this girl, who's not even officially in my service, murdered her father, stole his title and now masquerades as the Viper?'

'Actually, she didn't murder Adler.'

'I beg your pardon?' The King feigns shock, but there's nothing insincere about mine.

'Marianne didn't kill Adler. He fell. Slipped on the rigging and died as he hit the deck.'

Well, this is an interesting strategy.

The King is trying to hide it, but his glee at having persuaded Bronn to spout such lies is obvious enough to me. 'You mean there's no legitimacy to her claim at all? How does she get away with this on board your ship?'

Bronn sighs. 'Because I let her. The crew accept her merely because I tell them to, and they are loyal to me.'

'And why do you tell them that?'

Bronn addresses the jury directly. 'Because she paid me to.'

The King looks disgusted. 'Paid you? When times are so hard?'

'Yes, she promised me that when she became Queen, she'd make sure I'd have all the power and riches I could ever wish for. I took the deal.'

'When she became Queen.' The King really is

enjoying repeating his favourite passages of this damning account. 'So you believe she had her sights on the throne all along?'

'Yes. She manipulated your son into marriage, even though she doesn't love him, and planned to overthrow you once he was cold in his grave.'

'You speculate?' The King raises his eyebrow.

Bronn stares directly at me with such ferocity it burns my very being. 'No, she told me.'

The roar of outrage echoes through the hall, and the King's eyes gleam with satisfaction. Bronn has done a thorough job of discrediting me and painting me as a true enemy of the crown. I search his face for any sign of his intent, but see nothing. I just have to trust him.

When the room settles, the King turns to Bronn once more. 'You have just confessed to accepting blood money against the crown, which I'm sure you're aware, is a serious crime. Tell me, why shouldn't I lock you up with this traitor?'

'Because I regret what I did. And have returned all the money to you. I hope my testimony today goes some way to making amends.'

The King gives a first-class impression of appearing lenient. Forgiving. 'I have to ask you. Where do your loyalties lie?'

Bronn looks him dead in the eye. 'With you, Your

Majesty. I always have and always will serve the Eastern Isles. I am sworn into the King's service and am bound to it.'

The King nods his approval. 'And for the sake of those who don't know, can you confirm you did complete your Initiation?'

Bronn's jaw clenches tight. 'Yes, I did. Without hesitation or question.'

He's won over every person in the hall. They love him; they admire him. And so the King finally says the words this has been leading to all along.

'I think we can all agree that the accused is little more than an illegitimate usurper.' The King pauses for the inevitable hum of agreement. 'And so I motion that with immediate effect she is stripped of the title and instead bestow it upon this man, who has demonstrated unfailing fealty to his king and people.'

He strides over to shake Bronn's hand. 'Congratulations, you are now my Viper. You're excused to return to your duties with immediate effect.'

'Thank you, Your Majesty.'

And then he's gone, without a backward glance, leaving me with nothing but the sense that I will never see him again. Never have the chance to tell him I shouldn't have pushed him away that day. Never be able to say I'm grateful for what he just did, despite knowing how much he must have hated it.

Because Bronn is a master at hiding the truth, at

making people think what he wants them to think. I'm certain that he just stood up there and apparently betrayed me to protect the lives of all those on board the *Maiden*. He knows as well as I do that if the King and Viper were to become enemies, then all the work we've done so far to restore the Isles would be undone in an instant, so he's also protecting the people. He's trusting me too – trusting that I have a plan beyond this trial.

And yet.

There has always been an unspoken truth between us. That Bronn was Adler's true heir. And though he's never once said so, I know Bronn's always longed to captain the *Maiden*. To be the Viper.

Now he is. And my own insecurities raise their ugly heads.

There isn't time to dwell on them right now, though, because the King announces he has one last witness to call. One final knife to bury in my back. I can't think who else he could possibly find to hurt me worse than Bronn.

Until Sharpe is escorted in.

It's immediately clear to me why I haven't heard from him since the day he visited me – he's been tortured.

His injuries are hidden, so to everyone else in the room there's no evidence of the abuse, but I know the signs. The way he shuffles hints at broken toes, multiple bruises, possibly cracked ribs. He winces as a guard touches his back and I can only imagine the lacerations deep in his skin from where they've whipped him.

It takes every shred of strength I possess not to launch myself at the King and break his cowardly neck. Instead I harness my hatred, feeling it spreading through me like a poison.

How I want to make them pay for this. How will I ever make them pay for this?

'Would you please tell the honourable gentlemen who you are?' the King says to Sharpe as if they were the closest friends.

'I am the former bodyguard to Prince Torin.' His voice rasps, like he's done nothing but scream for days.

'You've known each other since you were boys, have you not?'

'We have. Protecting him was more than just a job to me; the Prince is my family.'

'And could you please tell us why you are no longer his bodyguard, given your devotion to his safety?'

Sharpe gingerly raises his arm to gesture at the cloth over his eyes, and the pain it clearly causes him breaks my heart. 'I lost my sight.'

The King is getting impatient now, wanting Sharpe to hurry up with his account. 'And how did you lose your sight? In the line of duty?'

'No. Because of Marianne.'

I swallow hard. This isn't going to be pretty.

The King steps closer to Sharpe and rests a hand on his shoulder. To most it will look like an act of comfort. To me, it is a clear threat that Sharpe should toe the line.

'I know this is difficult for you,' the King says. 'But please try to tell us exactly what happened.'

Sharpe doesn't speak for a moment, and the longer he's silent, the worse I know this is going to be.

'I never liked Marianne,' Sharpe says eventually. 'When she became engaged to Prince Torin, I tried to speak up, and warn him of the dangers of allying with the Viper. But the Prince has a generous heart and would hear nothing against her. She knew, though, knew I was a threat to her marriage, to her plans. And so she removed me from the equation.'

'She did this to you?' The King sounds horrified.

'Yes. She tricked me into being alone with her, and then she took my eyes.'

There it is, the final nail in my coffin. People are on their feet, chanting for my immediate death, demanding my execution. I fight back the tears, wondering if this is it. After everything I went through, everything I lost, is it all going to end in failure now?

'Why didn't you tell the Prince?' the King asks when order is restored. 'Reveal her true nature to him before they wed?'

'I tried,' Sharpe says. 'But love is a powerful thing.

People will do whatever is necessary for the ones they love. To protect them at any cost.'

That last sentence is solely for me. Sharpe's telling me that what he's just done is to protect Torin, and I understand. The King has always disapproved of the love between his son and his close aide, and has used it to blackmail Sharpe. Between torturing him and threatening Torin, the King had given Sharpe no choice but to voice these lies, and I don't blame him one bit. He did the right thing.

Now it's time for the King to wrap this farce up while the people are baying for blood. He moves swiftly to request the jury consider their verdict and it takes them only moments to confer.

I am found guilty of treason. Of attempting to murder my husband. Of plotting to overthrow the King. I am to be hanged at first light.

I'm escorted out of the courtroom under heavy guard in a state of shock. The curses from the watching gallery barely penetrate my skull because all I can hear clamouring in my head is *What now?*

I could protest my innocence, point out that if I was the heartless killer I've been portrayed as, Torin wouldn't still be breathing, but who would listen? The King has utterly succeeded in destroying me. If I don't find a way out of this, I'll be dead in hours.

Think, Marianne.

If it were Bronn in this situation, he would have a plan. Would already know every exit, every possible way out of the palace. I was here several days before the wedding took place, but never thought to map out escape routes. Some assassin I am.

Perhaps if I only had a handful of guards I could fight them and slip away. But considering what happened the last time they underestimated me, no one's taking any chances. A dozen strong guards surround me. That would be a challenge even at my best – in my weakened state it would be impossible.

By the time I'm thrown back into my damp prison, it all becomes irrelevant anyway. Without the key I'm trapped here until they come to take me to the gallows.

I slide down the wall, fighting away despair. This trial has taught me nothing other than that the King loves power above all things, including his son.

Torin. Every time I think of him, my heart squeezes too tight, fearing the worst. What fate awaits him now? Will his father keep him asleep for ever? Or just for many years? Can his body even survive such an unnatural sleep when already weakened from his injury?

My mind drifts to my own fate. I imagine the rope against my skin ... coarse, clawing, how it'll tighten until it steals the life from me. For a moment I wonder if Bronn will storm the execution, rescue me before burning the palace to the ground. I almost smile at my own foolishness. He wouldn't risk the lives of his crew for such a futile endeavour. And he wouldn't attempt to save me alone. No point in us both being dead. Maybe he will come and watch so his face could be the last thing I see before the darkness claims me?

No. I will never see him again and my sob is a lonely echo in the night.

But if I am to die, then I will not let my sorrow show. I am the Viper, whether the King likes it or not, and I will be strong to the end. Silently I remember the names of all those in the jury who signed my death warrant. One day they will regret choosing the King's side. Even if I can't return from the grave to haunt them, then I'm certain Bronn will eventually find a way to avenge my death.

The sound of someone approaching brings me to my feet. It's not dawn yet, and I can't think of any good reason why I'm getting a visit.

A guard I don't know strides up to my cell, a plate in his hand. 'Last meal,' he says, his voice gruff and clipped.

I frown at him, but walk over to take a closer look. 'Why would the King waste food on a dead woman?'

'Not sure I'd call that food,' he says with a smirk, and I reach to pick up the bread roll he's brought me. I bang it against the iron bars and it makes the same noise a rock would.

'I can hardly wait,' I say, moving to return it to the

plate, but he steps away.

'Don't choke,' he says, turning to leave. 'Or it'll spoil all the fun tomorrow.'

And then he's gone, before I can ask the questions building inside me. There's something about the way he cautioned me, something unnatural, that makes me suspicious, that almost gives me hope . . . and if there's ever been a time to act on such feelings, it's now.

I tear into the stale bread, which is no easy feat, until I stab my finger on what is concealed inside it. A needle.

Sharpe. He must have found a way to get this to me, that's why the guard was unfamiliar. Silently I thank him. He's given me a chance and I'm not going to waste it.

The gaoler and his two other guards are at the far end of the prison, sitting around a table, gambling. They've been drinking, eating, trying anything to stay awake through these long night hours, and are paying no attention to what's happening in the cells they believe are safely locked.

Crouching, I stretch my fingers until they reach the padlock on my prison door, and as I do so a memory of Grace freeing herself from the King's dungeons comes to mind. She picked the lock with a hairpin that day, but the needle works just as well, and her presence is so strong I can almost believe she's standing beside me as the lock springs open. Slowly, quietly, I unravel the chain from round the bars, and loop it into my hands. It's a

61

better weapon than nothing.

I creep up on the guards from behind, taking advantage of the element of surprise, and swing the chain hard across the back of the gaoler's head. He instantly slumps forward. The other two guards scramble to their feet, but they're drunk and disorientated. I bring down the chain over the nearest man's knuckles and his sword clatters to the ground as he cries out. Before he has time to think, I've whipped the chain back up and this time slash him hard across the face, knocking him to the floor. The third man is watching all this, frozen with fear, and now he looks at me with pleading eyes. I could let him run, but then he'll raise the alarm. There can be no mercy. I stoop to pick up the fallen sword, ready to fight, but he raises his arms in pitiful surrender. I press the blade against his chest.

'You have keys?' I ask, gesturing to the irons still clamped round my wrists.

He nods.

'Then free me.'

He fumbles as he searches for the right one, before eventually finding it, inserting it into the lock and letting the irons fall away. A swift blow to his temple with the sword's hilt and he no longer presents a problem. I look at the three of them, so easily overcome, and shake my head. How much have they had to drink?

Still, their utter incompetence worked in my favour.

Swapping the sword for a dagger from the gaoler's belt, I think about my next steps.

Before I do anything else, I need to find Torin, to see him, help him if I can. The castle is asleep and it's easy to slip through the shadows undetected. The passageways in the depths of the castle aren't frequently used, even in the busiest hours. It lures me into a false sense of security, thinking that I'm the only ghost roaming the halls at night. But the moment I reach the steep spiral staircase that connects the main castle to the dungeons, I hear voices. Lots of them. Creeping up, I take a look and my heart sinks. While the King may have felt confident leaving only three guards on duty outside the cells, he apparently wasn't taking any chances for the rest of the castle. No amount of stealth will get me past the regiment assigned to this doorway, and if I try to fight my way through, I'll meet my death earlier than scheduled.

Cursing to myself, I flee back down the stairs. There has to be another way out. I hastily retrace my steps, but every door I try is locked, so that the only path to take is the one that leads back to the cells. And then I see it, right before the entrance to the gaol: a narrow hallway off to the left. There are no torches on the wall this way, but I can see a sliver of light like a beacon in the distance, and so I run towards it. It's only when I reach the end that I understand why the King hasn't bothered to waste guards down here. Moonlight shines through a small window on the west side of the castle. Beyond it is nothing but a sheer drop down a perilous mountain. It's not a way out; it's certain death.

'Prisoner on the loose!' The words bounce down the stone walls to reach me and I swear under my breath. I should have killed those guards rather than just knocked them out. They know I'm here somewhere, like an animal in a trap. I look again at the window. If I don't want to be captured, this is my only chance.

I'm dead anyway. I'd rather die free. And so I pull myself up on to the stone ledge and push open the window.

4

It would be raining. Within minutes of lowering myself out of the window I'm soaked through, my shift plastered to my skin, my fingers turning to ice as they cling to the slippery rock surface.

Lodging the dagger in thin cracks provides me with precarious handholds, but they're few and far between and my progress is slow. Still, down is the only direction I can go, and so I persevere, knowing it won't be long before the whole kingdom is looking for me.

And yet I can't shake the feeling I'm going the wrong way. Away from Torin. To save my own neck I'm abandoning him to his father's questionable mercy. I swear that if we both live long enough, I will return for him, but it does nothing to assuage my guilt.

The wind is whipping up now, and I'm seriously regretting not taking the guard's cloak as well as his blade. Chilled to the bone, I shiver as I struggle to grip the dagger, blinking away blinding raindrops.

It happens in a split second. My foot slips, and the dagger isn't secure enough to take the sudden jolt of weight, and then I'm sliding, falling, falling fast, so fast that I gasp for breath. Desperately I try to find something to grab hold of, but the rain has left the rock like glass, and momentum is spinning me out of control. I'm dimly aware of pain shooting through me, as my skin is torn off, as my bones are battered against the rock face, but all I can think about is saving myself. I stab the rock with my blade, frantically searching for any gap I can take advantage of, but it's too hard, too unyielding.

When the dagger eventually lodges in a crevice and abruptly stops my fall, I'm barely expecting it and only just manage to cling on, my recently dislocated shoulder practically torn again from its socket by the jolt. I hang there, one hand clutching the dagger, pain shooting through me, my feet dangling. For a moment I'm too shocked to do anything, but then I look down and panic grips me once more. I may have fallen a long way, but there's still an enormous drop beneath me. I try to pull myself up, hoping to secure myself, but my strength isn't what it was after rotting in that cell.

I don't know what to do.

Exhausted, and wondering how much longer I can hold on, I allow my body to press close to the rock and for a moment I'm still, feeling its cold surface against my cheek. Despite everything, the very immediate peril I'm in, I close my eyes. How I've missed being outside, missed the smell of the air, and I breathe slowly in and out, allowing nature to soothe my soul until the fear starts to subside.

Through the howling storm I notice a softer noise. A gentle hum that's coming directly from the mountain. I strain to listen, for the sound is sweet and familiar, like a friend calling out in greeting. It's been so long it takes me a while to realise what I can hear – the fragile whisper of magic.

And as I drink in the buzzing warmth of the mountain, which nourishes me more than food ever could, I finally understand the dissatisfaction that's been growing inside me since I left the West. Denying the part of me drawn to magic has created an emptiness within. A cold, dark void that has spread every day. I hadn't known it until now, as the space refills and causes a glow of pure joy to swell inside, even here in the direst of circumstances.

The traces of magic in the East are all but gone, only forgotten fragments lurking in the deepest, darkest parts of the land, but now, somehow, I'm drawing it out of the stone. The problem is I don't have the knowledge to harness it or utilise it in any way. Esther would know what to do. All I can do is be aware of it.

Or is it?

The last time I tried any kind of summoning it was in Western waters when desperation and a thirst for vengeance had enabled me to rouse water raptors from their slumber. Now my life is in jeopardy again, and if I don't try *something* I won't make it down this mountain alive.

'*Veitja.*' My lips brush the rock as I breathe the ancient word into the mountain. I wonder if the stone will remember this long dead language; certainly I recall very few words from the dusty tomes I read long ago in a dark room on the Sixth Isle. But I remember this one. *Help*. And, as this archaic tongue belonged to the Mages, I'm hoping it might work for me now.

Nothing happens. The rain runs down my face, melting my hair against my skin, and reminding me that if I don't fall down the mountain, then I shall certainly freeze to death.

'*Veitja.*' This time I don't just whisper the word with my mouth; I speak it with every fibre of my being, through every part of my flesh touching the mountain, willing the rock to answer the plea from my very core.

And I hear its reply.

The hum grows louder, a great roar spreading through the granite until it reaches my fingertips and vibrates through my bones. I am utterly connected to the mountain; it awaits my command. The thrill of this magical binding almost makes me forget the danger I'm in – almost – and cautiously I test the cliff face with my foot.

Immediately I find a foothold. Then another. Wherever I move my hands or feet, the rock seems to shift, allowing me enough ledge to grasp hold of, reshaping itself once I've passed. I'm able to move fast now, gliding as easily as a raindrop down glass. The moon is obscured by cloud, and so, under the cloak of darkness, I pass safely to the bottom of the ravine. I do not allow myself a moment to marvel at what is happening, not until my feet are firmly on the ground once more, at which point I laugh out loud with relief and astonishment, leaning against the staggeringly vast rock face and spreading my arms wide to embrace it.

'Thank you.' I do not know the ancient words of thanks, but hope the sentiment at least will be understood.

The connection is fading, the magic dying away, and I'm painfully aware of the loneliness that slips back in its place. For those brief, intense moments I'd felt oddly complete, a part of something immensely powerful. I can barely believe it just happened. The rock moved. For me. At my request.

I've felt the powerful seduction of magic before, but never like this, never without fear and anger tainting it, and as I sprint across the ravine floor, grateful for the cover of shadow, I wonder again if I made the wrong choice turning my back on magic. Given that I'm fleeing for my life, stripped of my title, and further than ever from restoring peace, the decision to become the Viper isn't looking so much like the right one.

Once I reach the forest that lies west of the mountain, I allow myself a moment to catch my breath. Two weeks in a cell and my fitness is definitely not what it was. But soon this forest will be filled with guards searching for me, so I press on, weaving in and out of trees, their gnarled branches appearing to point the way to freedom.

I need to get to a harbour, need to get off this island, and then I need a plan. First things first, though. I'd better find some warm, dry clothes or I won't make it at all.

The sound of horses storming in my direction reaches me before I find shelter. The King's Guard are searching for me. There's only one place to hide in a forest and so I scale the nearest snowbark tree, climbing the pale white trunk as high as possible to disappear among its dense copper leaves. Perching in a fairly precarious position, lying as flat as possible, I wait, hoping my pursuers will pass through the forest quickly, hardly daring to breathe in case I give myself away.

There's a rustle in the leaves in front of me and my heart forgets how to beat. Prowling slowly towards me, perfectly camouflaged and far more balanced in this environment than I could ever be, is a timber bear, his eyes liquid black as they meet mine. His claws wrap elegantly round the branches, razor-sharp to catch his prey, and I try hard not to look at them, uncomfortably aware of how easily they could rip me apart.

I've never seen one before, but Grace told me about the tree-dwelling creatures, hunted so mercilessly for their russet pelts that they're close to extinction. They're beautiful but unpredictable, capable of savagery if threatened – and I imagine finding me in his tree would be considered a threat.

I hold his gaze. There's no way I'm going to be the one to break it, to show fear. But I'm mentally trying to figure out how I can reach my dagger if he strikes.

His nose starts to twitch, sniffing the air, and then I hear what he has already smelled. They've released hounds. My spirits sink. My chances of escape are getting worse all the time, but now I've led the guards to the bear and possibly endangered his life too.

Still I don't blink, staring deep into the soul of the animal before me, and I think he sees my fear, the widening of my pupils as danger closes in on us, because everything about him softens. We are not enemies; we're united by a common foe. We are the hunted.

The hounds are close now, having easily locked in on my scent, and the pack rushes up to the tree, clawing at it and barking for all they're worth. They'll draw the guards here in no time. So long as there's no more than a handful of soldiers, I still stand a chance, though the hounds will make it significantly harder. And though I have the height advantage, they'll be on horseback. Not to mention they'll be warm and well fed and not an exhausted bag of bones, which is what I feel like right now. The best I can do is go out fighting. And hope they don't discover the bear.

A group of guards gallop up beneath us, praising the hounds and looking to see if they can spot me through the foliage. To my relief they don't seem able to detect me, but there are at least a dozen of them and that's going to be a challenge in my diminished state. I smile sadly at the timber bear. If I am to die, I'm glad I don't have to face the moment alone, even if my only companion is a bear.

They're calling out now, demanding I show myself, and one even fires a bolt from his crossbow up into the leaves, missing both me and the bear by some margin. The hounds bark louder and something stirs in the beast's eyes, a wild anger that simultaneously terrifies and excites me. He makes his move before I even realise what he's doing.

The bear lowers himself down the trunk, his massive claws sinking into the wood with ease to keep him steady, and he takes a swipe at the nearest hound, lifting it from the ground and flinging it into the neighbouring tree. Its limp body crashes back to the forest floor and the other hounds whimper and shrink back, as do the guards who cower when the bear lets out a deafening howl.

One of the guards gives a nervous laugh. 'Damn dogs found themselves a bear. Come on, we need to keep looking for her, or the King will string us up instead.'

The hounds are reluctant to leave, but the snarling bear helps persuade them to follow their masters, who spin the horses round and head deeper into the forest.

The bear climbs back up to where I'm still lying and licks his paw.

'Thank you.' I'm in no doubt the bear just saved my life.

The animal lifts his head towards me and nuzzles me with his amber snout. He's telling me to go. To keep running.

I rest my hand gently on his fur, trying to communicate my gratitude through my touch. 'Stay safe,' I whisper to him and he makes a grunt in reply. I'm as certain as I can be that we understand one another.

When I move, I move fast. I lower myself cautiously down the branches and drop to the ground. Pausing for a second to listen for any sound of company, I run, away from where I saw the guards go. I want to find water quickly; it's the only way to break my scent, and so I sprint as fast as my weary legs will carry me, tripping and stumbling over rocks and roots, towards the stream that, if I've remembered rightly, runs parallel to the forest in the south. It's not the direction I wanted to take as it leads me further away from the coast, but right now that's going to have to wait. Long-term plans will have to give way to immediate survival.

When I finally crash into the icy water of the stream, the force of the current snatches at my legs so I struggle to stay upright. But now all I have to do is follow the water for a while and the hounds will cease to be a problem. As I'm already soaked by the rain, wading through the river doesn't make much difference, although I'm very aware that I need to find shelter soon.

It's when dawn is about to break that I catch sight of a dwelling – the first I've seen since I escaped. Emerging from the stream, my extremities so cold I can no longer feel them, I drag myself in its direction. I've not seen any sign of the guards since I fled the forest, and though I've heard the hounds baying in the distance, so far I've managed to elude them.

The household has not yet woken for the day's labour, and so I slip unnoticed through the rooms, searching for dry clothing and food. I help myself to an outfit, a satchel and a chunk from the loaf of stale bread, leaving the rest for the family. I don't want them starving on my account. Then I head for their barn, where I remove the filthy, drenched shift and wash myself as best I can in the horse's trough. I've deliberately picked a dress to wear, hoping to pass unnoticed as a peasant girl, rather than the Viper, and then I take my knife to my hair. I can't cut it all off, for fear of revealing the birthmark on my neck, but I can shorten the distinctive mess I've always had, and once it's gone it's easier to place the simple linen coif over my head.

It's the best I can do to disguise myself, and the warm

woollen stockings and boots are coaxing life back into my toes and feet.

Once I've eaten half of my chunk of bread, I set off again, desperate to keep moving, knowing the King's fury will mean he'll stop at nothing to have my head. I run for hours, staying off the roads, trailing through ditches and weaving in random directions to confuse anyone tracking me. My mind is sharp, focused only on survival, but behind that focus is a barrage of thoughts and questions clamouring to be heard. When I'm safe enough to allow them room, I'm going to have to process everything that's happened, but there just isn't time for that now.

It's the horse that attracts my attention first. From my concealed position in the ditch, which runs alongside the highway that stretches from one end of the island to the other, I can see him pawing the ground uneasily. His head is held oddly high, his eyes wide, his mouth foaming, and as I get closer it becomes clear why he's so terrified. The wagon he was pulling is on its side and going nowhere.

Though I know I should turn away and keep running, I cannot ignore the poor animal trapped in his harness. Checking there's no one around, I climb up the embankment, and once I take in the sight properly, I almost wish I hadn't.

It was no ordinary wagon, but a cross-island

stagecoach carrying travellers. It's been attacked, plundered for any valuables carried, and recently by the look of things. There are bodies strewn on the ground: innocent men, women and children who'd been going about their business before they met a sudden and violent end. A brief wave of fear sweeps me as I realise the perpetrators could still be close by, but it's soon quashed by a tsunami of anger. By challenging me the King has practically invited the bandits to continue their rampaging, because who other than me has dared stand against them? Under his command the King's Fleet have been rendered impotent, and the King's Guard useless. Once Torin took the throne, he planned to change that, but, as it is, all opposition to the bandits has been removed, and it's clear that in only a matter of weeks things have deteriorated quickly. I almost will them to return to this scene of carnage. I want to remind them I still live and they shouldn't forget it.

The frightened horse demands my attention with stomping hooves and stops me from drowning in my fury. I speak calmly as I approach him, soothing him with words he cannot understand, but which I hope reassure. Beside him, another horse has collapsed, blood still fresh on his flank where he's been shot.

His whole body tenses when I rest my hand on his withers. 'It's going to be all right,' I say, as I run my fingers down to the harness and start to unstrap it. 'You'll

76

be free soon.'

The horse snorts, but doesn't put up any resistance when I pull on buckles until he's eventually released from his prison. For a moment he seems frozen, unwilling to trust what I've done, but then he bolts, galloping down the road and putting as much distance between himself and this butchery as possible.

Which is what I intend to do.

Until I feel it. The unmistakable prickle of magic, hot like a rash across my skin. I glance behind me, running my gaze over the dead, moving towards the sensation. And then I see her.

The woman is lying slightly further away from the wagon than the others. Maybe she was trying to run before she was beaten, her body broken.

But she's not dead yet.

All around her I sense the threads of energy. They weave and shimmer, the hum of her life departing for ever, and I run to see if I can help her.

She's deeply unconscious, death imminent, and instinctively I reach my hands up towards the life force leaving her. But then I hesitate. A small boy I loved fiercely once warned me not to try to bring back the life of a she-wolf this way. Maybe Tomas was right. Maybe there's a line with magic that shouldn't be crossed. I certainly learned plenty of other hard lessons on the Fourth Isle. But that was an animal. This is a person, and she's not entirely dead, just on the fringes. I've never felt this so strongly in a human before. Never. It's as if talking to the mountain has awoken the magic inside me, and I'm not sure I want to ignore its tempting call. Though perhaps that's the very reason I should.

A tiny mew interrupts my dilemma. I move closer, searching for its source. Wrapped beside the woman, small and helpless, is a baby.

What choice do I have? Leave them both to die? Take the child and raise it as my own, as Adler once did? Though the last thing I need is to be slowed down by other people, it's never been in my nature to abandon those in need, no matter how hard Adler tried to beat the impulse from me.

And so I reach once more for the energy around the woman's body, now understanding why it's so strong. She doesn't want to die; she's clinging to life for the sake of her baby. She's fighting the way my mother once did to stay with me. My mother failed – no one helped her. I won't let the same happen here.

I have no idea what I'm doing, but it's like net that must be untangled and I've spent many hours doing that, methodically teasing strands to return to the right place. I fall into a trance, barely aware of my surroundings, focused solely on repairing what should be irreparable, and letting what can only be described as magical instinct guide me. My blood runs hot, the magic flowing through my veins pulsing with my heartbeat, slow at first but then in a rush, the heat almost burning me from the inside out.

But before I can finish, I'm torn from the spell I've fallen under. Because someone's screaming.

It's the woman.

5

My first thought is that I've killed her, but her lungs are too strong for that to be true. Immediately I fear I've done something worse, altered her in some horrific way by incorrectly weaving a magic I have no understanding of. It takes me a moment to realise she has simply regained consciousness and the horrors of her previous waking moments are flooding back.

'It's OK,' I say, wanting to steady her, to comfort her. 'You're safe now.'

I'm trying not to think about the fact that I've brought her back from the brink of death using nothing more than magic. The power fluttering through my bones is intense and I do my best to ignore it, to give all my attention to the terrified woman in front of me, but it's hard. After months of avoiding magic, the past few hours have done their damnedest to remind me of its existence.

'My baby,' she says, clawing at my arms. 'My baby?'

'Is right here.' I'm speaking in calming tones, as if handling a wild animal, because, honestly, she's scaring me.

At the sight of her child the woman sobs in relief, clutching the baby to her. Then a wave of confusion passes across her face followed by fear as she looks up at me.

'What happened?'

'Your coach was attacked,' I say, reaching out to reassure her, but she flinches away. 'I found you here. You were unconscious.'

The woman frowns and she is definitely afraid.

'Were you trying to escape?' I hope to coax some information from her.

'I don't ... I don't remember.' She looks panic-stricken.

'That's all right. You're probably just in shock.'

But her eyes are wide as she stares into mine. 'Do I know you?'

'No,' I say. 'I just found you.' She's beginning to concern me. 'What's your name?'

She opens her mouth, but then closes it again, her brow knitting tight together. 'I don't know.'

A horrible sick feeling stirs in my gut. 'How about your baby? What's their name?'

The woman glances down at the child now sleeping in her arms. 'I . . . I have no idea.' Her eyes are wild as she clutches my arm. 'What's wrong with me? Why can't I remember anything?'

I have an awful feeling I know exactly why she can't, but I'm not about to tell her. 'Don't worry,' I say, avoiding the question. 'I'm sure your memories will come back.'

Internally I'm beginning to panic. This is a disaster. I'm supposed to be stealthily escaping the island, but now I've given in to temptation, arrogantly attempted something powerful that I didn't understand and caused a whole world of mess. I can hardly leave her here now when I'm the cause of her broken mind.

'I don't suppose you know where you were going?' I ask, though I'm fairly certain I can guess the answer.

Her sobs are the only one I get.

'Right.' I haven't got time to waste, not with guards hunting me. 'Let's have a look through your things. Maybe there'll be something that can help us.'

The woman nods and seems relieved to have a suggestion at last. But her bag is all but empty, the bandits having taken anything there might have been of value and everything else besides. We search through her pockets and find nothing to help us, but then we feel the rustling of paper beneath her skirts and realise something has been stitched into the fabric. With my dagger it's easy enough to reopen the pocket to reveal a letter. It's tattered and well read, the ink smudged in places from what might possibly have been teardrops. It's a love letter. Most of what the note contains isn't useful and is none of my business besides, but the writer speaks of a ship: *The Black Nightshade*. I haven't heard of it before, but it could be something to go on. I skim to the end, hoping for a clue in the sign-off, but it's simply signed with the initial R.

'Do you know what it stands for?' I ask, though I suspect the letter means as much to the woman as it does to me. My suspicion is confirmed when she shakes her head.

'OK,' I say, after a moment's thought. 'There's a harbour several miles south-west of here. I think we should go there, see if anyone's heard of this ship and maybe then we'll find someone who knows you.'

The woman's eyes widen further, which I didn't think was possible. 'You'll come with me?'

'Of course. I can't exactly leave you on your own now, can I?'

To my surprise she throws her arms round me. 'Thank you, you're my saviour.'

I say nothing and hope my cheeks aren't burning too much. I'm no saviour.

Gathering up her things, I offer to carry the baby, but she refuses to be parted from the child for even a moment. Instead I take her arm and support her weight, for her body is battered and bruised and walking is clearly difficult.

Until now she's had her back to the scene of the attack, and she cries out when she sees the corpses of those not as fortunate as herself. I guide her away from them, avoiding the blood that's both pooled and spattered across the ground.

We don't talk much on our journey, and I'm glad of the silence. The guilt I'm experiencing is unbearable.

Because of what I achieved descending the mountain, I grew overly confident. Thought I knew more than I did. And when I tried to weave magic I can't control, I only succeeded in damaging this poor woman. My guess is that the strength of her love for the child meant that the minute I'd restored enough of her life for her to survive, she broke free of me and returned to her body – before I could finish the spell. Not that there's any guarantee I could have even finished it properly. I should have listened to Tomas – he always was wiser than I.

Now my arrogance has left her mind empty and I have no idea whether she'll ever recover those memories.

I try hard to silence the voice whispering that even without any knowledge I was still able to bring someone back from the edge of death, that such power was within my grasp. I try to ignore that my body feels oddly hollow now the magic has subsided, that I want more than anything to feel that heat again.

We reach the harbour by early evening, and I'm instantly wary of any guards. The good thing about travelling with another woman, though, is that I don't look so much like a fugitive, and the handful of guards who are stationed at the town's entrance barely give us more than a cursory glance.

Still, the last thing I want to do is draw too much attention to us, and so I take the woman directly to the harbour itself. The quickest way to find information is to ask someone, but there's the chance of being recognised. I target an older woman selling fish. She's more likely to take pity on my injured friend than anyone else I can see, and less likely to know my face.

'Excuse me,' I say with as much warmth as possible. 'Can you help us?'

Her eyes instantly narrow with suspicion. 'That very much depends.'

I keep my smile bright. 'Have you heard of a ship called *The Black Nightshade*?'

There's nothing friendly in the shift of her features. 'Who wants to know?'

I change tactic and drop both my smile and my voice. 'My friend was attacked on her way here. She has no memory of who she is. The only item on her person was this.' I hold out the worn piece of paper and the old woman considers what I've said.

'What's your part in all this?'

'I found her on the road. I'm just trying to help.'

The old woman fixes a hard gaze on me. 'Why?'

I raise my eyebrows. 'I could hardly leave her to fend for herself, could I?'

'You don't want money?'

I shake my head.

'Good, cos you won't get any. That's Raoul's ship. He'd more likely skin you than pay you.'

'Raoul?' The mysterious 'R'.

'You'll find him in the tavern. And you best be as honest as you say you are, missy, or he'll have your head.'

Great. Though her warning doesn't scare me, the last thing I need is another problem.

I thank her for her time, then guide the woman and child towards the inn.

Before we enter, I squeeze her arm. 'Does the name Raoul ring any bells?'

She shakes her head; she's like a rabbit caught in a trap.

'Don't worry. Just let me do the talking.'

I'd rather not venture into a tavern, which is likely to be as full of bandits as it is sailors. I hope I look as far from the Viper as I think I do.

No one glances up at our entrance and I feel some tension slip from my shoulders. I scan the room for someone who might be a captain that commands such respect and fear. Seated in a far corner are a group of men and women who, while laughing and drinking, are alert. One man stands out from the rest. From the way he holds himself and the way the others act round him I can tell he's important – and dangerous. His skin is as black as his clothes, thick hair runs like ropes down his back, and the fire in his eyes blazes so fiercely I can see it even from this distance. Raoul.

'Stay here,' I say to the woman, who's hovering nervously by the door. 'If anything bad happens, run.'

This is possibly the wrong thing to say because she looks ready to flee right now, but I give her arm a pat and then head towards the table where the group is sitting drinking.

When I approach, several of the men stand up, hands on the hilts of their swords. Raoul waves them down, deeming me no threat.

'Gentlemen, that's no way to greet a lady,' he says, flashing me a smile that has no warmth in it. 'What can I do for you?'

'Are you Raoul?'

'Seems to me if you're asking, you already know the answer.'

'Does this mean anything to you?' I hold out the letter and watch as his face changes, real emotion replacing his façade for a moment.

He's on his feet with his knife at my neck in a heartbeat.

'Where did you get this?'

'Let's all just calm down, shall we?' And I press my own blade firmly at his guts, just so he knows I'm no pushover.

He releases me and we both hold our hands up to show willing.

'Tell me where you got that.'

'It belongs to my friend.' I gesture towards the door. 'Do you know her?'

Raoul's face lights up now, and I see a look I recognise. Love. He starts towards her. 'Lilah!'

But the woman, whose name is apparently Lilah, steps back, cradling the baby close to her. Raoul hesitates, turning to me with uncertainty.

'She's had an accident,' I say, and gesture for Lilah to join us, which she does with some reluctance. When we're quietly seated, with Raoul's crew surrounding us, I resume the story.

'And you don't remember anything? You don't remember me?' Raoul sounds hurt as Lilah shakes her head.

'I don't even know the name of the baby.' Her voice trembles.

'Bay,' Raoul says. 'Our child is called Bay.'

Oh, this is messy.

Raoul turns to me. 'She was supposed to meet me here this morning. We've been waiting for her.'

'She's your wife?'

'Not yet. She's running from her family. They don't approve of me.'

'I'm sorry.'

'How do I know you didn't do this?' It's all too clear Raoul wants to make someone pay for hurting Lilah, and though I suspect she'd be dead without me I'm hardly an innocent in what's happened to her.

'She saved me,' Lilah says, her voice soft but firm. 'I

wouldn't be here without her. And she's the only person I know.'

The look Raoul gives Lilah almost breaks my heart. It would destroy me too if Bronn looked at me like that, like he had no idea who I was, like all that bound us together was lost.

The thought of Bronn is unwelcome. I don't want to be distracted by him right now. Did he locate the stranger from the wedding? Does he know I'm alive? Is he searching for me? Or has he been seduced by the role of Viper as I was seduced by magic?

One of Raoul's men has been staring at me a little too closely, and now he leans down and whispers into Raoul's ear.

His gaze lifts sharply towards me, his eyes narrowing. I think he's about to ask me something when the tavern door opens once more, only this time it's half a dozen of the King's Guard. I lower my head and Raoul smiles.

'So it's true then? You're our treasonous princess?'

I shrug. 'Something like that.'

'You looking for a way off this island?'

'Honestly? If it wasn't for Lilah, I'd already be gone.'

Raoul clenches his jaw. 'You put yourself at risk for her?'

'Look, I know no one believes me, but I became the Viper for a reason. I wanted to help people. And though that plan is going spectacularly wrong, I couldn't leave her and the baby for dead.'

The guards are getting closer now, searching every table, and my instinct to flee intensifies.

'Say nothing.' Raoul has apparently made a decision about me, because he turns his chair so that he more or less blocks me and I lower my head down away from prying eyes.

'Good evening.' Raoul greets the guards as long-lost friends. 'To what do we owe the pleasure?'

'Looking for someone,' the tallest guard says and thrusts a piece of paper with my likeness scrawled on it towards Raoul. 'Seen her in these parts?'

Raoul blows air out of his mouth and makes a display of thinking. 'Can't say as I have.' He turns to his crew. 'Any of you seen her?'

The men follow Raoul's lead and shake their heads.

'You sure?' The guard is insistent. 'There's a price on her head.'

Raoul tilts his chin up. 'How much?'

I hold my breath, wondering what sum he'll sell me out for, furtively looking around for an escape route in case it comes to that.

'Enough crystal to keep a man like you happy,' the guard says.

Raoul's eyes narrow slightly and his pretence of friendliness is gone. Perhaps he doesn't like the guard telling him what kind of man he is. 'Afraid I can't help you.'

'We'll be posted here for a few days,' the guard says, realising this is a lost cause. 'Find us if you see anything.'

Raoul tips his head but as they leave he spits on the floor. He turns to his men. 'Think we're ready to leave, don't you?'

Lilah looks scared as everyone gets to their feet. 'I don't understand.'

'I'm going to take you home,' he says to her, and I see her eyes flick over to me. 'She can come too,' he adds before looking at me. 'If you want.'

I consider him closely. 'Where are you going?'

'Does it matter? It's not here.'

He has a point, but I'm not going to go blindly with these people.

'It matters.'

'Fine.' And he flashes a wicked grin at me. 'Ever been to the Third Isle?'

6

The Black Nightshade is a stunning ship. Made entirely from the same nightheart wood as the *Maiden*'s figurehead, she truly is a daughter of the Black Island.

Though she's a relatively small trading vessel, a two-masted brig, our journey is quick and smooth, and I wonder how I've never seen her like before.

When I ask Raoul what waters he favours, he gives me a sly smile. Like he knows what I'm really asking.

'She's special, isn't she?' He's clearly very proud of his ship. 'Built her myself. With the help of my brothers.'

I'm impressed, but not surprised. I'm fast realising Raoul is a man of mystery.

We slipped unnoticed from the tavern to the harbour, and once we boarded the *Nightshade*, which was camouflaged so well as to be almost invisible against the black water, we were soon underway. Lilah and I were taken to the hold, which was serving as makeshift quarters, but, not one to trust easily, Raoul had men positioned on the other side of the spare sail strung up for privacy. 'To show you around,' he'd said, but we both knew it was a precaution. I was, after all, on the run for attempted murder and treason.

But despite the distance growing between me and the King, the mass of worries crushing my chest isn't easing.

I continue to feel sick with fear for Torin. And guilt for leaving him behind at the mercy of his power-hungry father. Maybe I shouldn't have left the castle without trying harder to help him. Was I selfish to run? The fact is, though, it's too late to go back now, and so I can only hope the healer is gifted enough to keep Torin alive, and the King is smart enough to let him.

My other problem remains the same. The Eastern Isles are no closer to peace than before, and the King is a far greater threat than either Torin or myself had anticipated. The trial demonstrated one very important thing to me. He has strong allies throughout the Six Isles. With Torin out of the picture the Fleet will once more answer to the King, and I no longer command anyone. The war has never seemed bigger and my army never smaller.

I'm going to need more help.

If I'd hoped that might come from Raoul and his men, the thought is quickly extinguished when he invites me to his cabin for dinner. I expect that Lilah will be there, but apart from his guard positioned at the door, we're alone.

When I ask why the privacy, he hands me a mug of rum. 'Because I think we need to have a chat, and I don't particularly want anyone else privy to that.'

I take a long swig of the golden liquid, and nod my head. 'I see. So what can I do for you?'

'I want you to fix Lilah.'

I suddenly feel so tired. Rubbing my face, as if somehow that can wipe away all the responsibility, I say, 'And what makes you think I can do that?'

Raoul gets to his feet and starts to pace the room. 'Do you think I don't hear things? Whispers of what you once did?'

I'm not entirely sure what he's referring to, so say nothing.

'Is it true that you summoned water raptors? That magic flows in your veins?'

How the hell does he know that? No one on my ship would have betrayed me. Unfortunately the same can't be said for my face, which gives Raoul his answer.

'So it is true.'

'It was a lot more complicated than it sounds.'

'But you do have magic? Like the Mages?'

I can hear his desperation. How much he wants this to be true for the sake of the woman he loves. And so I answer him as truthfully as I can. 'Yes. But I have little control of it, and I lack the skill to do what you ask.'

'Or perhaps simply the motivation.'

And taking a step towards me, he raises his pistol and points it at my forehead. At the same time his man moves behind me and presses his pistol to my back.

'You *will* fix her,' Raoul says, and his tone leaves me in no doubt he'll kill me without a second thought if I refuse.

'I told you, I can't.' My voice is equally forceful. 'Threatening me won't change that.'

He pushes the barrel hard against my skin. 'I've heard all the rumours about you. You say you want to help, but you're no different from the father you murdered. Or pretended to, depending on who you believe. Vipers are all the same – violent, cruel and selfish. I'm giving you a chance to redeem yourself.'

Doesn't *anyone* have anything good to say about me?

I've had enough of this. With lightning reflexes I strike Raoul's hand and snatch the pistol from it when his grip falters. Instantly I spin round and thrust the pistol to the other man's throat, while simultaneously grabbing his wrist and pulling it to my hip, so that his pistol is now aimed directly at Raoul. I've disarmed them in the time it took them to blink.

'You shouldn't believe everything you hear,' I say to Raoul, enjoying the look of disbelief on his face, as I slowly manoeuvre my prisoner so that I'm in front of them both.

'And perhaps some things I should pay more attention to,' he says, raising his hands in surrender.

Cautiously I lower the weapons.

'Get out,' Raoul says to his companion, who is more than happy to flee the room. I don't offer to give Raoul his pistols back.

'I told you,' I say. 'I can't help Lilah. I wish I could. I'll talk to her, but once we reach the Third Isle, I can't stay.

'Oh, you're not coming to the Third Isle.'

I frown. 'I'm not?'

Raoul considers me closely. 'What do you know of my island?'

'Very little,' I say. 'It has beautiful forests, and its people are reclusive – present company excluded.'

'Have you ever been there?' he asks, and it feels like a loaded question.

'Once.'

'And what did you think?'

In my mind I see Adler standing over the hooded figure, demanding I kill him to complete my Initiation. I remember my fear. I remember my decision. I wouldn't become an assassin, not for him, not for anyone. That day changed my life for ever.

I meet Raoul's expectant gaze. 'I think it felt deserted. I didn't see one inhabitant. In fact, you are the first person from the Third I've ever met.'

I'm not sure what answer Raoul hoped for, but mine seems to please him, because this time his eyes light up. 'All right, Viper Princess.'

'Marianne will do.'

He raises his eyebrows, but nods. 'Marianne. It would seem I was wrong about you. And so, I'm going to tell you a little something about my people that they wouldn't want you to hear. What do you know about the Seers?'

I'd seen them mentioned occasionally in the old books back in Torin's library on the Sixth, but to be honest I'd been paying far more attention to the magic side of things. 'Not much.'

Raoul sits down at the table, and gestures for me to join him. After a moment's consideration I do – after all, I'm still holding two pistols and he has none.

'The role that the Seers played in our islands' history has been forgotten by everyone beyond the Third Isle.'

Raoul reaches for his rum and drinks before he continues. Perhaps he isn't as comfortable sharing his people's secrets as he claims. 'Because they don't want anyone to remember. You see, all the Seers came from the Third Isle, and long ago they used to pass their knowledge gained from foresight to the Mages, who would then, in their great wisdom, advise the royalty. The Mages rarely gave the Seers any credit for disasters that were averted. When it was prophesied that a war was coming, one that would either unite the Isles for ever, or bring about their permanent destruction, the Seers decided they'd had enough. They wished only to protect their people, and preserve their trees. And so they removed themselves from society, leaving the remaining five Isles to their fate.'

'That's why no one ever sees the Third Islanders?' I don't bother disguising my anger. 'Because of a war they saw coming? The one I'm losing now?' And he had the nerve to call Vipers selfish. 'Who are you, Raoul? If your people are in hiding, why aren't you?'

He doesn't answer for a moment, but then seems to make a decision. Reaching into his pocket, he removes a small pouch and pulls it open, scattering stones on to the table between us. Small and perfectly round, they have engravings scratched into their surface, lines and patterns that hold no meaning for me, but mesmerise me nonetheless.

Raoul takes the stones into his hands. 'These are rúns. My father taught me to carve them, my mother to read them. For years they've given me a prophecy of my own.'

I look at him expectantly.

'To live,' he says simply. 'I don't agree with my people's decision to hide in isolation, which is how you find yourself on my ship. I didn't want to hire couriers to move my precious cargo round, I didn't trust anyone, and so I disobeyed my father and built the *Nightshade*.'

An interesting story, but I've become good at hearing lies buried in the truth. 'So you're a courier?' I don't hide my scepticism. 'A simple tradesman delivering goods?' I snort. 'You're a smuggler, aren't you? Let me guess, the Third Isle grows more than just beautiful trees.'

The smile returns to his eyes. 'You've seen the black flowers that carpet the forests? Well, let's just say they have a pleasing effect when dried and burned.'

I raise an eyebrow. 'I imagine the tax would be high on such goods too, am I right?'

Raoul shrugs. 'Such luxuries shouldn't only be for the rich.'

'You're quite the hero.'

He ignores my sarcasm. 'I don't think the Viper has any authority to judge my morals.' He sighs as he puts the stones back into the pouch. 'Recently the stones are saying something different to me, though. Not just to live any more, but to fight.'

'You want to join me?'

He laughs. 'Not even a little bit. No, I'm prepared to fight – to the death – for one thing only. My family. To protect them, keep them safe.'

And just like that everything starts to make sense. 'The problem is Lilah doesn't remember you.'

'Exactly. Which is why I asked you to help her.'

Now it's my turn to laugh. 'If that's you asking, I'd hate to see you demand anything.'

Raoul simply shrugs, saying, 'Don't know why you're complaining. You're the one with the pistols.'

'I was telling you the truth. I don't know how to help Lilah. Yet.'

Raoul looks up sharply. 'But you want to learn. That's what you're doing?'

I nod. A plan has formed in my mind since leaving the First Isle. A way to win this war. A way to save Torin. It's far-fetched, dangerous and highly unlikely to work, but it's the only plan I have. I think there may be one person left in the Eastern Isles who can help me, if she's still alive. And I have a feeling she is. 'I can't make you any promises. But if I'm able, when I'm able, I'll come home and do what I can for Lilah.'

He bows his head, and presses his hand to his heart. 'You are nothing like the rumours would have me believe. Apart from perhaps one of them.'

I doubt I want to know. 'And what would that be?'

'You know how to fight.'

With a smile I slide his pistols back over the table to him. 'Best you don't forget it.'

After that Raoul lets me help out on the ship. Whenever I'm with Lilah I try to coax out some memories from wherever she's buried them, with no success.

But while my attempts fail, I can't help but notice that as Lilah spends time with Raoul, a closeness is beginning to form. Though she has no memory of him, though she's scared and far from home, Lilah is being drawn to Raoul again, whatever brought them together in the first place doing so once more. Love is a magic far more powerful than any I can ever hope to weave.

Watching them makes me ache for Bronn. Every day I search for a sign of the *Maiden* but the waters are practically deserted. We barely pass a fishing vessel, let alone traders. Fear is making everyone wary of venturing far from home.

On the fifth day, when the black silhouette of the Third Isle comes into view, Raoul joins me where I'm pitching the deck.

'It's time for you to leave,' he says, throwing an arm round my shoulder.

I lean against my mop as I look up at him. 'So what, are you going to throw me overboard?'

'That depends. Can you swim?'

I laugh, and shake my head. 'I'm going to miss you, Raoul.'

'Somehow I doubt that.' He pauses. 'Before you leave, may I read for you?'

It takes me a moment to realise he means the rúns. The prospect of having my future read makes me feel more than a little uneasy and Raoul notices.

'No fate is set,' he says. 'The stones don't rule you. But sometimes guidance can be beneficial.'

I'm hardly in a position to turn that down and so I agree. We sit on the deck and Raoul takes the rún stones from their pouch. He scatters them before me and frowns.

'What?' My heart sinks. 'Is it that bad?'

He doesn't answer, just picks them up and throws them again. His frown only deepens.

'What, am I going to die?' I'm only half joking.

But when he looks up at me he's not laughing. I see doubt in his eyes. And fear.

'There's another ancient prophecy, one we've all grown up hearing on the Third Isle. *A storm is coming. A wild fury that will devour night and day, earth and sea, until all that remains is sorrow. Fear her, face her, destroy her.* But no one ever knew who or what it referred to.'

A shiver passes through me. 'What do the rúns say, Raoul?'

'Fear her. Face her. Destroy her.'

Our eyes meet, and a fatal sense of destiny claims me. 'What does that mean?'

Raoul shakes his head. 'I don't know.' He hesitates before saying, 'Are *you* the storm, Marianne?' For the first time since I've met him he sounds truly afraid.

'Raoul!' The shout comes before I can answer, and we both turn to where his first mate is standing, pointing out to sea.

'What is it?' Raoul runs over to look. 'It's the King's Fleet. It's time you were gone.'

He's grabbing my arm, and leading me towards the back of the *Nightshade*. 'I've put some provisions in your boat, but it's not much I'm afraid.'

I glance at the small dory. 'There's no way I can outrun the Fleet in that.'

Raoul reaches round his neck and removes a cord with a circular black pendant. Made of wood, there's an intricate carving of a forest on the front, which I glimpse briefly before Raoul places it over my head.

'This is a talisman I made. It will hide you from your enemy's gaze.'

I must look stunned because he chuckles to himself. 'How do you think I've managed to avoid detection for so long?'

'I can't take this.' It's too much.

'Take it. Live. And come back to us when you find a way to help Lilah.'

Lilah. 'I haven't said goodbye.'

Raoul pushes me towards the dory. 'There isn't time. Unless you're after a family reunion with your father-in-law.'

I'm really not, and so I climb down into the boat, untying the rope and throwing it back up to him.

As I take the oars and start to pull away, I call, 'Why are you helping me?'

Raoul flashes that brilliant smile. 'Because you're the girl who didn't shoot.'

And when my mouth drops open, he starts to laugh.

I can hear it long after the ship disappears from view.

7

The last time I rowed from the Third Isle to the Fourth, I had to commandeer a sailing vessel to make it there alive.

But I'm not the same person as I was then. And I don't have a choice – there simply are no other ships. I'm going to have to get there the hard way.

This dory is not designed for the open sea, nor do I have a compass, and so I know it's going to be a tough journey. Thanks to the meagre supplies Raoul was able to give me at least I won't starve, and the sun isn't as hot as the last time I took this route, so I definitely have better odds.

The days are filled with the endless rhythm of pull, release, backwards, forwards. Sleep is a luxury I can't afford or I'll drift, so I only allow myself short naps during the day, making full use of the stars at night to guide me. My hands are bleeding, rubbed raw from the friction of the oars, the muscles in my arms and back screaming for relief, but I force my mind not to dwell on it. Distraction from pain is the only way I'm reaching the Fourth Isle, and so I focus on what lies ahead, all the while doing my best not to think about what's behind me.

I wish I'd had more time with Raoul, learned more about his people, although I wasn't disappointed that his uncomfortable reading of the rúns was cut short. I don't want to spend too long wondering why the words of an ancient and dark prophecy would attach themselves to me. I'd rather speculate as to how he knew I didn't kill the man at my Initiation. It's possible that news from the trial travelled fast enough to reach his ears, but somehow I don't think that's the source of his knowledge. I'll ask him one day, if I live that long. But, in a way, setting off on my own is for the best. While I certainly would have liked to revisit the Third Isle, the Fourth Isle was always my intended destination.

I once met a woman there who saw straight to the truth of me, who knew secrets she shouldn't. Though it's entirely possible the savagery of Adler killed her, I suspect Old Tatty would survive the end of the world. It's more going to be a case of finding her.

It rains on the fifth day after I leave the *Nightshade*, and while at first the water is welcome as it replenishes my diminishing supply, I'm soon soaked, and by nightfall am frozen to my core. My already slow progress grows ever more laboured. When I feel close to giving up, however, I think of Torin and of Sharpe, and how every minute I journey further away from them is another until I can return with help, and that keeps me going.

Worse is to come, though. Just as my journey is nearing its end, the tantalising shadow of land visible on the horizon lowering my defences, I get some company. Not soldiers this time, or indeed any kind of person. The threat now is from beneath me. A young giant serpentshark decides I look interesting and circles my boat aggressively. Even though he's far from fully grown, his sleek body is twice the length of my boat. He starts banging the hull with his long snake-like head and all I can do is hope he'll get bored and move away. Even if he intends me no harm, one swipe from his strong tail could capsize me and though I've been working hard to overcome my fear of the water, I have no desire to find myself in the ocean's grasp. But perhaps he smells the blood on my hands and the sweat on my skin, because he soon identifies me as food.

He charges towards my boat, slithering through the water like a giant eel. My little dory will fold like paper against even a young serpentshark's jaws so I know I have to act fast. Wielding an oar in one hand, I attack first, smashing it down into the open mouth of the approaching shark, which fortunately hasn't yet dislocated, otherwise he could devour me and my boat in one mouthful. His teeth viciously clamp down on the oar, devouring chunks with every bite, but as he does so I'm able to draw him towards me, close enough that I can plunge the knife in my other hand deep into his skin, gliding it between the silver armour-like scales.

Instantly he recoils from me, his blood staining the ocean.

Despite how quickly the water turns red, I know I've not delivered a fatal blow, and I wait for him to rally for a second attack. But whether he wasn't expecting such a fight or just isn't that hungry, he decides I'm not worth the effort and to my great relief he swims away.

Not wanting to hang about to see if he changes his mind, I grab my remaining oar and use it as a paddle, alternating sides as needed, my journey even harder than it was before. But, to be honest, I'm feeling lucky I still have two hands after having them so close to the serpentshark's razor-sharp fangs.

The shark doesn't reappear, and it isn't too long before I finally reach the Fourth Isle. I beach the battered dory, and a quick inspection shows how close the hull was to breaching after the serpentshark's attack. Leaving it where it is, without bothering to hide it, I grit my teeth and press on, though I desperately want to rest. No one will care about a little wrecked boat on the sand, but seeing me would be a different matter.

Up ahead a flock of gulls are screaming on the sands, others circling above. I think nothing of it until a rotten smell carries on the wind and I cover my nose with my arm to stop from gagging. As I make my way up the beach I see the cause: dead fish carried in on the tide and left to decompose in the sun. I frown at the sight. It's not unusual to see the odd lone carcass dropped by a passing bird, or unwanted by a scavenger. But this must be a whole shoal, and I cannot think of a reason for them all to have died at the same time.

Keen to escape both the smell and the noise, I hurry further on to the island.

When I first arrived on these shores all that time ago, my overwhelming impression was of beauty, endless meadows of colour and life. Now it is ash. A barren and dead land. I swallow back my pain as I take the path inland, accompanied by ghosts. I want to confront them, *need* to confront them, and so, despite my exhaustion, I head for the place I once called home.

The ground isn't too dissimilar to the Third Isle now, but while the forests and plants there thrive on the black earth, here it repels life. The smell of smoke lingers on the air, a constant thickness clawing at my throat.

But it's only when I approach the cottage that the devastation truly hits me. The babbling stream is dried up, the house nothing more than a burnt-out shell. I clamp my hand over my mouth to hold back the sob that's quick to rise as I force myself to keep walking to where the grave is.

The mound of earth I raised is practically the only thing the fire didn't destroy. Tired and alone, I drop to my knees and lie down on top of the grave. Though I'll never forgive myself for what happened to Joren, Clara and Tomas, I can't help but wonder if it's a good thing they never witnessed this sight. It would have broken their hearts as it breaks mine.

I don't know how long I lie there, but soon the earth is wet with tears I hadn't realised were falling. Pressed against the ground, I listen for any trace of magic, something deep and salvageable, but hear nothing. The hum of the mountain on the First had given me hope, but the magic seems to be truly gone here.

I clench my fists, crushing the dusty ash between my fingers, and I whisper into the earth.

'I'll find a way to fix this,' I say, knowing that my family can't hear me, yet longing for them to. 'I promise you. Somehow I'll bring your island back.'

I roll over and look up at the sky, drained of all emotion. My grief has caught me off guard; I thought I'd said goodbye to these people a long time ago. I hadn't realised how much I missed them, hadn't understood that grief never really leaves, only fades. I've been so determined to look forward, desperate to atone for Adler's sins, that I've not allowed myself to feel the losses along the way. But if you forget your people, then what's the point?

When I'm ready to say goodbye, I stand up, dusting off the ash as best I can from my clothes. There really is nothing left to stay here for and so I head towards the settlement.

I pass no one. People either died on this island or fled. And yet despite this, I sense I'm not alone. Someone knew I'd come and is waiting for me. Though the settlement had hardly been bursting with life the last time I was here, now it's little more than embers. It's hard to tell where the main street once was, but I make my way through the wreckage, my heart as heavy as my legs, searching for anywhere that someone might find shelter.

I needn't have bothered.

Old Tatty is sitting in the dirt, huddled in rags, her frame little more than paper-skin on bones, and when I see her she starts to laugh.

'My magic girl,' she says, spreading her arms wide. 'You've come at last.'

'Hello again,' I say, settling myself down on the ground opposite her. 'So you survived then?'

She waves her hand dismissively. 'As if you doubted it.'

The old woman may be alive, but I doubt it will be for long, judging by the frailty of her body, if not her mind. I reach into my bag and offer her some bread. She looks at it like it's a personal insult.

'Keep it,' she says. 'Your need is greater.'

I'm not sure I agree with that, but I'm not going to force it on her, though I don't put it away either. She may yet change her mind.

'You know why I'm here?' It seems reasonable to imagine she does, given she was waiting to greet me.

'You want to know about the magic.'

I nod, strangely relieved. 'I need to know how important it is. Whether I should follow its pull, or forget it for ever.'

'It all depends why you're asking. Do you ask for yourself, or for others?'

I frown. 'Does it make a difference?'

Old Tatty grabs a handful of black dust and throws it at me. 'Of course it does. Don't you understand yet what you're dabbling in?'

I refrain from spitting the dirt from my mouth, but wipe my lips. 'Is magic the only way to truly restore peace to the Isles? That's why I'm asking, why I'm here.' But even as I say it, I know I'm lying. It's not the only reason I'm here. I'm asking for myself too. Seeking permission to give in to temptation and answer its call.

Old Tatty surveys me. 'Who are you?'

I frown with confusion but before I can reply she continues impatiently.

'Are you the Viper? A princess? Eastern, Western? Do *you* know who you are?' She sees the hesitation on my face and pounces on it. 'You *need* to know. You *must* know. If you don't possess that strength, you will never master magic.'

She's hit on several nerves and I can feel myself getting defensive. Even before I knew the truth of my heritage, I wasn't entirely sure who I was, and I've just fought on, not allowing myself time to dwell on where my place really lies. 'I don't see why it matters.'

I'm prepared for the shower of dirt she throws at me this time, but not for her venom. 'Foolish girl. Don't you know why the Mages died out? They didn't need a king to eliminate them. They destroyed themselves. What is magic if not power? And nothing corrodes more certainly than power. To truly understand magic you must be willing to risk everything, sacrifice all, be prepared to give yourself up to the power – without *losing* yourself to the power.' She gives a sad shake of her head. 'They all lose themselves in the end. If you don't have the strength, you'll lose yourself too.'

I stare at the old woman and wonder when she became lost.

Her words make sense. I've always been afraid of my desire for magic, of the overwhelming urge to abandon myself to it. I've glimpsed its power and tasted its sweetness. I long for it – I always have – and that terrifies me. Because I know there's darkness in me. I know it would be easy to lose myself to it for ever.

'Can the Isles ever be at peace without magic?' I ask my original question again.

Old Tatty reaches for my hand now, running her bony fingers along my palm in a manner that I think is

112

intended to be reassuring, but is decidedly not. 'No. Without magic there can never be true peace.'

I sigh, feeling the weight of inevitability settle over me. 'But how? How does someone even bring back the magic?'

She gives me a knowing look. 'Someone? Or you?' Then she scoffs. 'Only a Mage has the ability to restore the magic here, to let the islands flourish once more. As for how? I lack such knowledge. Everyone does.'

Exasperated, I say, 'And what of the West? There's magic there, but still unrest.'

Old Tatty pulls away from me now and spits in the dirt, stirring the two together into a mucky paste. 'Without magic there can't be peace. But the existence of magic alone doesn't ensure it. Have you not listened to all I've said?'

'So I need to learn magic, but not be corrupted by it?'

Now she smiles, and it stretches wider and wider until she starts to cackle. 'You've got it, Viper girl. Do you begin to understand? Do you begin to fathom what it is you're asking?'

It's an impossible task. No wonder she's gone mad. To have the solution but know it's unattainable is enough to drive anyone to insanity. And yet . . . what can I do? I've vowed to protect these lands, these people. I have to try. For Bronn. For Torin. I have to try.

Old Tatty shakes her head like she can read my mind.

'You know I have to do it,' I say. 'You knew it before

I came. So help me. If there's anything you can tell me, please. Help me.'

Her finger continues to swirl patterns in the pasty earth. 'Magic comes from nature. It is either given or taken. It is rarely given – to command nature you must earn its respect. If it is taken? Then you are nothing more than a thief. A powerful thief, but a thief nonetheless.'

She pauses in her pattern making and frowns. I realise now that the motion was not random; she was casting some spell and it's told her something. Something that worries her.

'What is it?'

Old Tatty looks up at me, and for the first time she looks scared. Just like Raoul did after reading my rúns. 'Time is running out for you. For all of us. Your enemy will destroy you and everything you love. We will all be destroyed.'

Her fingers clutch me now, digging in tightly, pulling me closer to her face, her eyes bulging wide with fear. 'I have seen your death, Viper girl.' She releases her grip and I spring away from her. Old Tatty looks sadly at the ground and wipes the pattern away. 'And I am sorry for it.'

It's as though someone's kicked the wind out of me. I came hoping for aid, and hear only prophecies of doom? It's hardly encouraging.

'If the King wants to kill me, he'll have to catch me first.'

But Old Tatty shakes her head. 'Not the King. You have had this enemy since before you were born.'

An image of Adler forcing me to bleed myself flashes into my mind. Of him slamming my head against walls. Of his blade sliding into my guts. I have to blink the fear away. He's dead. He can't hurt me any more. 'Who?'

Her eyes shine with sorrow as they meet mine. 'A thief. That's all I know.'

There's nothing more for me here, and I get to my feet. 'Thank you,' I say to her. 'For talking with me. But I'm going to try anyway.'

She chuckles wryly. 'Of course you are. But you must hurry. The two men you love? One will be dead by the next blood moon. The other? Well, his fate is entirely in your hands. As all of ours are.'

Cold panic trickles over my skin. Blood moons are rare but every one brings with it fear and death. I was a child when the last rising occurred, and was forbidden to go outside for its duration or to take part in the Snake rituals to guard against its evil influence. But Grace had told me all about it. How they had hunted the silver seals who bask in moonlight on rocky islets that jut from the ocean. How the beautiful, gentle creatures were dragged on board and slaughtered, the Snakes painting their skin with the seals' blood to ward off the bad luck they believed the crimson moon would bring. I hadn't minded being excluded after hearing that.

But I have no idea when the next one will be.

'How long do I have until the blood moon?' I ask Old Tatty with more than a trace of panic.

But she merely shrugs as if such a detail is of little importance.

Taking a deep breath, I lean down and place the crust of bread into her lap. 'We're all going to die one day, so I may as well die for the people I love. And if this new enemy is going to destroy us all anyway, then what have I got to lose?'

'More than you know, Viper girl. More than you know.'

Her misery slices into me like a blade. I dread to think what she's been through, and what's worse is I know she won't tell me. I sense it's the kind of pain you can only learn by suffering it, and I'm set on a path that will carry me there.

'Goodbye,' I say to her, and throwing my bag on my back, I start to walk away.

I've only taken a few steps when she calls after me.

'Sacrifice, Viper girl. You must learn the true meaning of sacrifice.'

My blood runs cold but I keep walking. Between Raoul's unsettling reading of the rúns and now this prophecy of death and sacrifice, a new weight of foreboding has settled in my chest, and so I do the only thing I can – leave this desolate place as fast as possible.

* * *

116

I head south-east towards the coast. The journey takes several days and I don't see a single sign of life among the wastelands as I travel. I'm glad of the solitude after my time with Old Tatty. There are two things I'm now certain of: one is that magic is dangerous and will lead me towards darkness and potentially my death; the other is that I have to learn magic if there's to be any hope for the future.

It's not ideal.

When a situation seems overwhelmingly awful and hopeless, I find the best solution is to take things one step at a time. And my first step is to make my way to the Sixth Isle. Though I haven't been back to Torin's fortress since Adler massacred those innocent people and stole Sharpe's sight, it's the only place I know where there's a library full of magical knowledge. And I'm clearly going to need all the help I can get.

I've had enough of rowing through oceans on unsuitable boats that take forever to get anywhere, and so I resolve to find another way to reach Rock Island. Though most boats were used when people fled for their lives during the fire, I have a horrible feeling that in some places there simply wasn't time. There should be some ships abandoned round the Isle and if there are, I'm going to find them. After only a few hours tracing the coastline, my instincts pay off. I spy a perfect little sailing boat – small enough for me to manage alone, but big enough to make my journey comfortable. I scramble down the dirt track towards the cove where it's anchored. The tide is out and so I only have to wade up to my waist to reach it. Painted on the side, in a childish hand, is the name *Little Vixen*. I silently thank its previous owner, hoping that they escaped the island another way. After checking the *Vixen* is still seaworthy, it isn't long before the Fourth Isle is just a shadow on the horizon. I vow that I'll either return there to restore magic, or not at all.

The weather is kind, the wind favouring my direction, and I'm relieved. Tiredness has been my most bothersome enemy for some time, and the chance to rest is very welcome. A search of the *Vixen* for anything useful isn't hugely forthcoming, but I do find a small notebook and chunk of lead, and so, while we glide contentedly through gentle waters, under the caress of a soft breeze, I begin a herbal – a list of all the plants and herbs I know, their descriptions, their medicinal properties, their toxicity. I describe what concoctions I've used them in, illustrating where I can, though I lack the talent to do anything real justice. There should be some documentation of these medicines in case . . . Well, in case I die. I don't want all my knowledge to be lost when it could help someone.

But as I write down the tonics, noting what combinations achieve maximum potency, a tingle of excitement passes through me. If I'm to truly learn magic, I will undertake a huge step from remedies to potions. It's a scary but wholly welcome prospect and I think deep down I knew that this was always going to happen. I was never going to resist the call to magic and was stupid to think I could.

I'm almost feeling a sense of hope, of purpose, as I enter the mists around the Fifth Isle. Until it starts to rain. At first, it causes me no concern, for though the visibility is poor, I know these waters are deep and free of rocks, and a little inclement weather isn't enough to bring alarm. But then something hits me on the shoulder, making me jump. When I look at the deck, I'm astonished to see a dead skyweaver, a small red bird that lives in the cliffs around the island. Poor thing must have died mid-flight and fallen where it flew. But then the next body falls. And the next. I can hear splashes in the water and hurry to the side of the boat. Even through the mist, I can see floating red bodies all around, the sea turning to feathers.

It's as unnerving as the dead fish on the Fourth Isle, and leaves me with the same uneasy sense of dread. Like something bad is coming that I don't even understand.

By the time the Sixth Isle appears, I'm more than ready to escape the ocean, and begin the next part of my journey. Though Rock Island has never done anything to make me like it, I'm feeling desperate to find Torin's books, to have another chance to learn from them. Old Tatty said time is running out and I believe her.

But I'm also on edge. While the Fourth Isle was abandoned, the Sixth Isle is more densely populated than ever, brimming over with refugees displaced from the Fourth, and if I don't want to be discovered, I'm going to have to move with caution.

I bring the *Vixen* in carefully through the labyrinth of deadly rocks that surround the Sixth, avoiding any harbours or coves where I might attract unwanted attention. Instead I angle her up towards the uninviting cliffs and grab hold of the rock. It would instantly rip the flesh from my fingers if I hadn't wrapped rags round my hands, but as it is I'm able to secure the rope round the jutting stone without too much difficulty. Throwing my bag over my body, I then take a deep breath and start to climb. The jagged surface is lethal, cutting through the material to draw blood, but it also has many handholds and foot supports, making it relatively straightforward to scale.

When I reach the top, I untie the rags from my hands and pull up my hood. The castle is east and so that's where I'm headed.

The wind is brisk and as I walk I think about the last time I was here, fighting with my crew in a violent skirmish to oust bandits from a settlement they had taken over, rendering the people dwelling there little more than prisoners. The terrain, and the position of the settlement in an enclosed valley, had made the fight particularly difficult and innocent people had lost their lives despite my best efforts. Always it seems my best just isn't good enough. The cold air that whips up my skirt is nowhere near as icy as the memory. In an attempt to distract myself from unwelcome thoughts, I try to focus on the bounty I've come here for. The books bewitched me when last I read them, but back then I wasn't ready to fully hear what they had to say. Now I'm hoping to understand them in far more depth.

Up ahead an abandoned mine looms in the distance. The path I'm taking passes beside it and, as I approach, I can't help but remember what Lord Pyer accused me of at the trial. Of personally sabotaging the crystal supply for my own nefarious gain. It was a genius way to turn people against me. To see this once striking mine now reduced to a ghostly shell is devastating. The beating heart of the island's industry has been ripped out. I suppose it's easier to believe an assassin guilty of such an atrocity than to confront the real reason the crystal mines are defunct: the terrible accidents that took place due to appalling conditions – a result of negligence that Lord Pyer himself was probably responsible for.

Not only do I need to find a way to restore magic, but I have to heal the economy, and I almost choke on the weight of it all. It's too much for one person. I don't want it. It was meant to be all of us: me, Bronn, my crew, with the King's Fleet at my command, and Torin, the new King. How can I possibly do this alone, an outlaw wanted for treason?

A cry from the mine cuts through my growing despair. I pause, wondering if I've imagined it, because surely no one can be down there, not in the state it's in. I strain to listen, and then I hear it again, a noise that could be a call for help. Damn it, the last thing I want is to be sidetracked, but what is the point of me acting the hero, if I ignore the plight of someone in need?

The mine is situated at the top of a steep incline. The wind is even stronger up here and there's more than a little eeriness to the place. But nature doesn't scare me. I learned a long time ago that it's people you need to fear. I detour off my path, climbing over piles of discarded rock brought up long ago from the mine. Maybe someone strayed up here from the nearest settlement and fell in – for the abandoned mines here are far from safe.

Now little more than a vast open pit in the rock surface, the mine would have once been surrounded by timber scaffolding and ladders for workers to climb down into the darkness. The only part of the external structure still standing is the wooden platform and pulley system protruding from the centre of the hole in the ground, which would have once carried up buckets of mined crystal and ore. It would be incredibly easy to fall in here by mistake at night.

When I reach the edge, I peer down into the shaft. At first I see nothing but darkness, but eventually my eyes adjust to make out the lingering structures of platforms circling the mine wall, walkways and ladders joining them together. Ropes and pulley systems that haven't been used for a long time hang there, redundant. They seem the safest way in. In fairness they may well be the only way in.

With a deep breath, I take a small run-up and leap into the mouth of the mine. For a second I'm not certain I'm going to make the rope, but then my hands clasp round it and I swing there for a moment, listening to the clanking of chains, the creaking of wood.

It holds.

More than a little relieved, I shimmy down, my eyes adjusting to the gloom, until I reach a platform and jump lightly on to the planks. Even alone it's oppressive down here, and I try to imagine what it would have been like to work in such a place, day in and out, surrounded by thousands of miners, all sweating, all afraid. The fatal drop in the centre is certainly enough to give even the bravest of people pause.

Now that I've been swallowed by the darkness, I listen again. At first I hear nothing, but then there it is.

Drawing my dagger from my belt, I make my way along the rickety wooden planks, precariously held up by wooden beams that disappear vertically into the black abyss of the pit.

To my dismay I realise the noise came from further in the mine, and eye the ladder down to the next platform with suspicion. I don't trust those rungs one bit and so position my hands and feet either side, my blade between my teeth, and slide to the next level.

This time I make for one of the many tunnels leading off from the main pit, where miners have burrowed deeper into the island in search of more precious materials. I follow the rocky path, taking care where I tread, the natural light growing dimmer the further I venture.

There's something up ahead and I squint, seeing what looks like someone slumped on the ground.

'Hello?' I call. 'Are you all right?'

No answer comes, and when I get closer I see why. The person is far beyond any help, barely more than a skeleton in rags, though some decomposing flesh still clings to the bones. I crouch beside the body, and sigh with sadness. What a lonely place to die. I wonder about his story; was he seeking shelter here from bandits? Or was he injured when the mine was still operating and unable to escape? As I stand up, something catches my eye. Squatting back down, I lean in, ignoring the smell of the rotting flesh, hardly believing what I'm seeing.

'You crafty thing,' I say to the skeleton. Because lodged in an empty tooth cavity, towards the back of the jaw, there is a little chunk of crystal. Even a piece this small would be incredibly valuable and I can only assume my dead friend here was stealing it for himself. Who would think to check there? I reach my hand into the skull, pushing the jaw wider open, and dig the crystal out of its cavity. Taking a small pouch from the bag Raoul gave me, I tuck the treasure safely inside, before another thought occurs to me.

I read once in the old manuscripts, that ground crystal, more informally known as diamond dust, could be used in potion making. The theory went that if added with good intentions, it would have a positive effect. But if added with ill intent, it would render the potion a poison. Such a powerful ingredient would be worth far more to me than the crystal itself and I glance at the cavern walls, wondering. Standing up, I run my fingers along the sharp stone, wincing slightly as it cuts at my flesh. When I remove them, my skin is coated in sparkling dust. Smiling to myself, I start to brush the residue from the wall into the pouch. If this works, then it'll make healing tonics all the more potent. I'm thinking of Torin. Such a tonic could save his life.

A flicker of light in the darkness up ahead stops me in my tracks. I came down here because I thought I heard someone in trouble. But if they have a lantern, they're not likely to be in any desperate peril and as the sound comes again, louder this time, I realise I've made a mistake. What I heard wasn't a cry for help. It was the sound of raised voices, echoing out into the night and deceiving my ears. And whoever is living down here, they've heard me calling and I have a feeling they won't welcome an uninvited visitor. I'm about to make an inconspicuous retreat when I realise the flickering is already getting closer. I've got company.

Moving as swiftly and silently as possible, while trying to avoid rotten planks of wood, I race back towards the main pit. They know there's an intruder in their midst, and there are a lot of them.

Still, if I can get back to the pit and up the rope before they reach me, then I'll never be more than an apparition to them. I'm all confidence until I arrive back at the central walkway and skid to a halt.

Bandits have emerged from every tunnel leading off this pit. They're all armed. They're all angry. And they're all staring at me.

'Get her!' someone shouts, and from both directions men charge towards me.

There's nowhere to run. The men on my right are closest, so I focus on them first. I scan my surroundings and with only a split second to make a decision, lunge towards an axe lying redundantly against the wall, and swing the massive blade down into the rotten wood at my feet.

The impact causes the weak planks to fall away, decimating a chunk of the walkway and cutting them off from me. The furious mob turns about to get to me from the other direction.

I'm already thinking of the other flank of attack, and use the axe once more to slice through a wooden beam, yanking it free and brandishing the long spike as a weapon.

It's only as I stand there, positioned to fight, that I realise I've made another mistake. A big one.

The structure supporting these walkways was already frail and I've just smashed a huge hole through it. By the sounds of creaking timber, the beam I've just removed was also fairly vital.

The bandits hear it too – the ominous sound of destruction. From below us the intricate framework of the mine is collapsing and suddenly catching me is no longer their priority.

We all scramble at the same time. Bandits push and pull to reach the nearest ladders first; men are flung down the deep drop in the middle in an attempt to clear a pathway. There's no loyalty among them, so I know they won't hesitate to crush me for their own survival.

I get to my ladder just before one of the bandits and leap on to it as high as I can. Instantly the rungs give way beneath my feet, as I'd suspected they would. I fall slightly, and the bandit grabs my ankle, trying to pull me off. I kick him hard and manage to break free, hauling myself up the side of the ladder with my arms. Others are trying to climb up behind me, which makes the ladder wobble precariously, but I focus solely on going upwards. I make it to the next walkway moments before the deafening crack explodes from beneath us and, like a house of cards, the walkways collapse, each one giving way to the next.

I know there are only seconds before the ground disappears beneath my feet.

More desperate bandits have reached the walkway and are storming towards me to vent their fury.

There's a tied rope to my left, and it's my only hope. Grabbing hold, I slice through it just beneath my hand and cling on as the rope sends me shooting up at high speed, leaving the bandits behind. As the mine implodes in on itself, the rope reaches the pulley and jolts me so violently that I let go, hurtling towards the edge of the collapsing mine. I dig my fingers into the rock, disregarding the pain and pulling myself up. As the remainder of the structure crumbles, I manage to scramble to the surface, and with an almighty crash the mine blows up a cloud of debris, its final breath.

That was close.

Brushing the dust from my clothes, I turn to put as much distance as possible between myself and this scene of chaos, but stop in my tracks.

Three people stand watching me, and I forget to breathe.

'You're a hard woman to find,' Bronn says. 'Captain.'

8

He called me Captain.

Tension I didn't even know I was carrying falls away at the sound of that one word – I hadn't realised quite how deep my insecurity ran.

'What took you so long?'

Bronn takes a step closer. 'We had to make sure the King wasn't following us, all while tracking your route. Being duplicitous isn't easy, you know.'

I allow him a small smile. 'I think you're a lot better at it than you realise.'

He bows slightly. 'Best compliment I ever had.'

And then his arms are tight round me, not caring who's watching.

'It's good to see you,' he mumbles into my hair, and I can tell by the way he says it he had his doubts he ever would again.

I tighten my grip on him. I have missed him so much.

Eventually I move slightly away and narrow my eyes. 'I *paid* you?' I remind him of his words at my trial.

Bronn shrugs. 'What? You told us to play along and trust you, so I did.' Now he beams at me. 'Fooled them all, didn't I?'

I shake my head a little as I laugh. 'You certainly did. You almost had me too.'

His smile disappears, replaced by a sudden seriousness. 'I hated saying every word of it.'

'I know. I'm sorry you had to.'

Reluctantly I tear myself away from him and go to greet my other friends, noticing as I do that my loyal sea vulture, Talon, is circling above us. Harley, the indomitable and outspoken sailing master who has become one of my most trusted friends, comes forward and pulls me into a mama-hug, squeezing the breath from me, but warming me at the same time. Holding my arms, she leans back slightly, surveying me. She looks at my wispy hair, my thinning frame, my bruised skin and she tuts.

'I'm OK,' I say to her. 'Really.'

'I know you are,' she says, her fingers tightening on my arms. 'Tougher than you look.' But when she winks at me it's full of love and support and I have to swallow hard not to tear up.

Then Toby greets me and I swear the boy has grown another foot since I last saw him. The quartermaster's son has blossomed on the ship following Adler's death, though he still lacks true sea legs. 'You all right, Captain?'

His concern is so genuine that I reach to hug him. 'I am now. Where's your father?'

'Ren's back on the *Maiden*, with the rest of the crew.' It's Bronn who answers. 'I'm assuming you have a plan, because we need to do something fast.'

'I do. Sort of.' I scrunch my nose. 'But you're not going to like it.'

Harley laughs. 'Well, you know me, the madder the plan, the better.'

'Tell us on the way back to the *Maiden*,' Bronn says, but I catch hold of his arm.

'No. I'm not leaving this island yet.'

He frowns, but doesn't voice the question in his eyes. 'It's not safe to talk in the open. There's a cave just south of here that I used to smuggle crystal into for Adler. We'll be safe there.'

The four of us set off, Bronn staying close to my side, and I tell them about the bandits I discovered in the mine. If they're using the mines as hideouts, then it's possible Bronn's cave might not be as safe as he thinks it is, but when we get there it's clearly undisturbed, the entrance barely visible among the dark cluster of rock. We scramble down into the hole and do our best to crouch on the spiked ground.

'So tell me everything. Have you had word of Torin?'

The three of them exchange glances. Harley takes a deep breath and reaches for my hand. 'Your husband is still alive. Sharpe is at the castle with him, but other than that we have very little idea of how he's faring. Politically, everything's worse than ever; bandits are taking advantage of your incarceration and rampaging. There have been many deaths. Many attacks.'

Though it's pretty much what I was expecting, it's still tough to hear.

'And the islands themselves grow weaker,' Harley continues. 'Wildfires have been spreading across the Fallow Isle, and it's not only the crops we're losing. It's the black brambles.'

My heart lurches at this news. Medicinal supplies were already diminishing after losing so many ingredients to the flames on the Fourth Isle. If we lose the main ingredient for second-salve, we're soon going to struggle to heal anything or anyone.

Harley is still talking, though. 'The grazing land on the Fifth Isle isn't regrowing, so the animals are starving. It's almost like . . .' She pauses, and her reluctance to continue unnerves me. What is Harley afraid to say? 'It's like the islands are cursed.'

I think of the fallen birds I saw, the dead fish washed up on shore, and sense it's all connected. Could the scorching of the last traces of magic from the Fourth Isle have sparked the slow death of all the islands? Has Adler doomed us all?

My stomach knots. Because if I'm right, I don't just need the magic to restore peace in the islands. I need to restore the islands themselves. And how can I possibly do that?

'We have to find a way to protect Torin,' I say, pushing such a nightmare aside. First things first. 'He lives at the mercy of his father, and should the King feel threatened in any way . . .'

'It's already taken care of,' Bronn says. 'I have men on the inside who are keeping a close watch and have orders to take whatever action is necessary to keep the Prince safe.'

I stare at him for a moment, as his words sink in. '*You* have men on the inside?'

The atmosphere in the cave alters, the air growing a little colder.

'Yes,' he says, folding his arms as if bracing himself for my response.

My eyebrows raise in disbelief. 'Would you mind telling me how long you've had spies at the palace?'

The shift in his weight suggests he would really rather not. 'Since before Adler died.'

Irritation burns at my throat. 'They're Adler's men?'

'No, they're loyal to me. To us,' he adds just a little too late. 'I sent them there once your engagement was made, to—'

'To what, Bronn? Spy on me?'

'No, to protect you.'

He can't understand why I'm upset, and *I* can't understand how he can fail to.

'Why didn't you tell me? I've been the Viper for months, I deserved to know where my Snakes were.'

Harley and Toby are looking firmly at the ground, probably hoping it will split open and drag them away from this quarrel. But I don't care how awkward it is. I want an answer.

Bronn looks reluctant to give one. 'Because, honestly, I thought if I told you there were Snakes in the palace, you would order them to leave.'

'You're right, I would have. Torin is our ally.'

'And as soon as Torin took the throne, I intended to withdraw my people.'

'That wasn't your decision to make.' My voice is sharper than the rock cutting into my feet.

'But it's a good thing I did, or you wouldn't have escaped.'

It takes me a beat to realise what he's saying. 'That was a Snake?' I thought it was Sharpe who had sent me the needle. But it was a member of my crew – one I didn't even recognise.

'Of course,' Bronn says. 'How else do you think you got out of there alive?'

He's unbelievable. He's taking credit for my survival? 'Oh yes, because once I opened that cell, I just breezed out the front gate.'

Bronn shakes his head in confusion. 'Yeah, well, you're welcome. And now those same Snakes are making sure your husband stays alive, but I can withdraw them if you wish.'

I glare at him. Unfortunately, whether I like it or not, his spies are invaluable to us. And they did, technically, enable me to escape, so I suppose I should be grateful. I just hate that he kept that secret from me. What others does he have?

I force myself to meet Bronn's eye, swallowing back the anger that was quick to rise. 'Leave them. They're probably Torin's best chance.' It takes me a moment before I'm able to add, 'And thank you. I *am* grateful that you sent me help to escape.'

He nods in acknowledgement and the tension eases a little.

'What of the assassin?' I ask, deciding to move on from the topic. 'Do you have any leads on who he might have been?'

'None.' Bronn pauses. 'Do you think the King himself could be behind it? He certainly seems to have benefitted the most.'

'That's what I thought, but no. He came to see me during the trial and he genuinely thought I was responsible. Which means we're clueless.'

We all fall silent for a moment.

'And what happened with the stranger at the wedding? Did you catch up with him?' I'm surprised Bronn hasn't mentioned him before now. In all honesty he is the man I'm most suspicious of, his mysterious presence at the palace the most likely connection to the attack.

But to my disbelief Bronn looks embarrassed. 'I lost him.'

'What?' Bronn is the best tracker in the world. He doesn't lose a target. No one outruns him.

The stranger has secured his place as number one in my suspect list.

'I'm sorry,' Bronn says. 'I followed him as far as the coast where his trail disappeared. Then I heard about what happened with you and forgot about it.' Now he looks uncomfortable. 'You think he was the assassin?'

I remember the amber eyes staring back at me as I fought Torin's attacker. I would recognise them anywhere, and they didn't belong to the stranger lurking in the shadows. 'It wasn't him in the room, but I wonder if he's behind it. The assassin had a style of fighting I didn't recognise, and was incredibly skilled.' I tell them about his ability to catch my knife.

'So,' Harley says in her usual matter-of-fact way, 'we don't know who tried to kill the Prince, or why. The King is clinging to his throne irrespective of the cost to his islands. And you're wanted for treason. What are we going to do about it?'

'We need help.' It's all so clear now. The answer is obvious. I need magic and I need an army. Where else could I possibly go? But I know they're going to hate it. Bronn is going to hate it. 'We can't win this war alone.'

'And who are you going to ask? There's a small number of the Fleet ready to stand with us, but other than that? You're not that popular right now.' Harley voices what she and Toby are thinking but I can see Bronn is ahead of them. He knows what I'm suggesting and is already shaking his head.

I face Harley squarely. 'I'm going to go back to the West.'

'No.' Bronn's resistance is expected, but more animated than I'd imagined. 'We're not going back there.'

'You're right. We're not. I am.'

Bronn leaps to his feet, pacing the cave and rubbing his face. Harley looks from him to me.

'What am I missing?'

'They won't help you, Marianne,' Bronn says. 'Don't you remember what it was like over there? We barely made it out alive.'

'That was different.'

'You'd have to reveal yourself to them even to have a chance,' he says, and he's pleading with me. 'They won't care about us. Why would they?'

Toby looks confused, but Harley is irritated. 'You mind telling us what you two are on about?'

I take a deep breath. I should have known this wasn't a secret I could expect to keep for ever. 'You both know Adler wasn't really my father. But what I haven't told you is who my real parents were. I'm sort of –' I pause in embarrassment – 'sort of descended from the royal family.'

Toby's mouth drops open and Harley closes her eyes, holding one finger out for me to pause.

'I'm sorry, do you mean the Western royal family? The ones who were all wiped out?'

I nod. 'That'd be the one.'

'I need a drink.'

Bronn passes her his flask and Harley draws deeply from it.

'Who else knows?' Toby asks, and he's looking at me in a whole new way. Like I'm more important than he realised. I don't like it.

'Only Bronn and Torin. Grace knew.' Every time I speak her name, something goes wrong with my throat. It tightens in on itself like it doesn't want to exist any more.

'And you want it to stay that way?' Harley raises her eyebrow.

'For now. Can you imagine what the King would do if he found out?'

'Probably murder his own son and force you to marry *him*,' Toby says, and we all turn to look at him. He's right. That's exactly what the King would do. For Torin's sake he must never know.

Which is another reason I have to act now. I take a breath, knowing that once I say it out loud, there's no going back. 'I'm going West to raise an army.' There, that's my plan. It's the only way I can think of to save the Eastern Isles. To save the Twelve Isles.

'It's one hell of a long shot,' Harley says, but I can hear she's impressed.

She's right of course, but my bloodline isn't the only thing I'm relying on.

'You know nothing about the West or the people there,' Bronn says and it's a fair point. 'For all you know they'll kill you on sight. They may not want a royal family.'

'Grace's people will know how to help,' I remind him quietly. He has no answer to that.

Harley looks between us, sensing there's much we're not saying but she doesn't press us. 'So, we're going West then?'

I can't help but smile – she always did love bad odds. 'No. We can't leave the East unprotected. The *Maiden* has to stay here. You have to keep the King from doing anything rash, and above all make sure Torin remains alive.'

'You're not going alone,' Bronn says, and though I love him for it, he's forgetting something rather important.

'Yes, I am. You're the Viper now, not me. You have to stay with your ship.'

Bronn faces me with such intensity I forget Harley and Toby exist. 'We both know there's only one way for

140

that title to truly pass from one to another, and there's no way I'm ever going to do that. So enough with that talk. If you're going West, I'm coming with you.'

His eyes have never been easier to read. There is love, there is determination and such a fierce protectiveness that I lean forward and kiss him gently on the lips.

'OK then,' I whisper, my fingers lacing through his hair. 'You're coming too.'

Harley clears her throat, but she's smiling. My friends have never been under any illusions when it came to my true feelings. 'When you two are quite finished, may I make a suggestion?'

I smile as I nod.

'If you feel you can trust us, leave Ren and me in charge of the *Maiden*. We'll give the King the runaround, convince him we're looking for you, and keep an eye on your prince. Meanwhile you two can take a skeleton crew off West to raise the troops. How does that sound?'

I reach for her hand. 'There's no one I would trust more with my ship,' I say, squeezing her fingers.

'So how are you going to get there?' Toby asks.

'Do we have any of the Fleet still with us?'

'A few,' Harley says. 'But if you're thinking of taking one of their ships, think again. We need them here.'

Bronn turns to me. 'We'll steal a ship.'

'We will?' I raise an eyebrow.

'This island is crawling with bandits and I know the coves here. Trust me, we'll find something.'

I can't help but grin at him. Despite everything, the prospect of running off with Bronn to steal a ship is beyond appealing.

'Then we have a plan.'

I never thought I'd enjoy crossing the harsh terrain of the Sixth Isle, but alone with Bronn, walking hand in hand, I find myself surprisingly content. We've split up from Harley and Toby, who've returned to the *Maiden* to sort out our crew, and now we're heading to Torin's castle before embarking on finding a ship.

'So you've decided then,' Bronn says as we navigate our way over sharp rock.

'Decided what?'

He gives me a sideways glance. 'I'm not stupid. There's only one reason you'd be willing to return to this castle and that's for the books. You want to talk to Esther, don't you? You want to become a Mage.'

I sigh. I'm not sure Bronn really understands my pull towards magic. He's never heard its call and is grounded in a world where, to him, it doesn't exist. And yet he knows, or is at least starting to realise, how very important it is to me.

'You saw what magic could do,' I say to him, the image of two magnificent and terrifying water raptors flashing into my mind. 'And I'm beginning to think that Torin was right, that there can never be true unity without it. I'm not sure we can bring peace to these islands unless I find a way to harness it.'

I tell him about my conversation with Old Tatty, and of my encounter with Raoul. Bronn's very quiet when I speak of the prophecy, and so I decide he doesn't need to hear everything. I don't mention the foretelling of my death.

'I'm certain of very little,' I say when I reach the end of my tale. 'But what I do know is we're losing. And at this point I can no longer afford to ignore my heritage or my ability. Not if either brings with it the possibility of winning. Can you understand that?'

Bronn stops walking and reaches to stroke my cheek. 'Of course I can. I just don't know how to protect you against things I know nothing of.'

I lean up to brush a soft kiss on his lips. 'You don't need to protect me. Just be with me.'

He nods and I see him fighting to put his doubts aside. 'I can do that.'

We carry on walking but both of us are quiet now, keeping to our own thoughts. For myself I'm trying not to think about all the problems in our relationship we're ignoring, how much there is we're not speaking about. Like the fact that I'm married. Other than Harley referring to Torin as my husband, we've skimmed right over that. And the fact that I pushed him away at the feast after my wedding. But the truth is – no matter how hard I try not to think about it, it's there – and I can feel the barriers coming up between us. We may love each other but some obstacles are just impossible to overcome.

My wedding day fresh in my mind, I turn my thoughts to the stranger I sent Bronn after. The stranger I was certain was an assassin. The stranger who outsmarted Bronn. Nothing about him makes sense.

'You said I was hard to find,' I say, and I can see Bronn taken slightly by surprise at the change in conversation. 'Did you mean that?'

'Yes,' he says. 'Surprisingly so. Probably wouldn't have found you if it wasn't for Talon. He'd find you anywhere.'

I pull out Raoul's talisman and hold it up. 'Raoul gave me this. He said it would shield me from my enemy's gaze.'

Bronn frowns. 'I'm not your enemy.'

'No, but it still might have made things harder. The point is, could the stranger from the wedding have had something like this? It would explain how he managed to disappear from sight.'

The smallest glimmer of a smile lights up Bronn's face. I think he's grateful for the suggestion that there would have to be some sort of magic at work for him to be outwitted. But then the smile fades as he takes the talisman in his hand.

'What?' I ask, thrown by his sudden change of mood. 'What is it?'

'Where did he get this?'

'He made it. Why?'

'It's nightheart wood.'

'So?' The wood is rare, but it's no secret the Third Islanders carve it.

Bronn rarely looks unnerved, but he looks it now. 'Someone once told me that the roots of the Black Forest trees were still laced with magic. That anything carved from their wood was a talisman. That's why their carvings are so desirable, so expensive. I never believed it, always thought it was just a story made up by the traders to push up the price. But what if it's true?'

'Who told you?'

Bronn isn't listening. 'It would mean the *Maiden* was more than just a figurehead.'

I understand what he's saying. 'Do you think it would explain why she's impossible to defeat?'

'Maybe. And it would explain why he commissioned her.'

'Adler? He told you this?'

Bronn nods. 'I never took Adler as one for believing in magic, so I thought he found the story as ridiculous as me. But what if he knew there was some truth to it?'

I don't want to think about the man who raised me in any capacity, but it makes sense. Adler would want every advantage over others, would chance it just in case. Raoul told me how his people wanted to protect the trees – if they're a fragile link to the magical past, then no wonder. 'The question is, if the stranger had something like this, where did he get it? Who was helping him?'

'Maybe Raoul isn't on your side as much as you think.'

It's possible, but I'm not convinced. Raoul seemed to care only for Lilah, the child and their safety. It'll have to be added to the list of mysteries I need to solve.

We don't talk much more before we reach the fortress. You wouldn't know it was there if you didn't know what to look for, even after being empty for so long, but unfortunately I'll never be able to forget where the entrance is to this desolate place.

The merest smear of blood staining the rock face is the only hint of the massacre that occurred inside, and I pause, needing a moment before I revisit the scene of such horrors.

It takes both of us together to prise the door open, and when we finally manage it a blast of stale, dank air hits us, like a swarm of souls was locked inside waiting to escape. There is no light, and so Bronn sets about scraping a piece of flint against his knife until the sparks catch on a rag, while I wander slowly into the dark tunnel. The sorrow hangs heavy in the air, as if the rock itself mourns the tragedy it witnessed and now offers its cold condolences. I press my hand against the wall and offer mine back. We all saw things we shouldn't that day and the memory of Sharpe's empty eye sockets floods back like a nightmare I've tried in vain to forget.

Bronn gently touches my shoulder, a lantern now lit. 'Which way?'

I'd forgotten he's never been here, that he wasn't part of the atrocity – and I envy him.

'Down here.'

We pass the great cave, where the twelve standing stones dwell. I'm more than happy to keep walking, but Bronn's drawn to their splendour.

Reluctantly I follow him into the space and he walks among them, staring at the dried blood that stains them still.

'Twelve stones. Twelve Isles?' And he raises an eyebrow.

I sigh. 'Yes. Torin and many others believe reuniting East and West is the only way forward.'

'Reuniting them with magic?'

'Possibly.' I shrug. 'Who knows? But the Mages did once exist, even you can't deny that.'

'I always assumed they were power-hungry narcissists, who said whatever the royalty wanted to hear.'

My laugh rings hollow. 'Maybe they were.' I've had

enough of being in here. I can't bear to look at the stones any longer. 'Come on, it's this way.'

Part of me had been worried I might not remember how to find the small room hidden down twisting tunnels, but there was no need. It's as if there's an invisible thread guiding me towards it – I know exactly where I'm going. I don't even need Bronn and his lantern. I could close my eyes and still find my way. And despite the sadness here, I start to smile. The books are waiting.

The wooden door is open. No one ever thought to return and shut it after Adler's attack and so it's remained in the exact same position it was as when Sharpe flung it open to fetch Grace and me. For a moment I'm lost in the memory with ghosts, weighted down with their sorrow, but then I walk into the room, and the atmosphere soothes me.

Bronn holds the lantern up, shines it round the room, and whistles. 'That's a lot of books.'

'I know.' And I smile.

He doesn't. 'How are you expecting us to carry all these?'

'Why do you think I brought you along?' Now I've managed to coax a smile from him and it lights up the room more than the lantern ever could. 'Don't worry, I just need to find the most important ones. For now, at least.'

He rests the lantern on the stone slab and sits beside

it. 'And which ones are they?'

I run my fingers across the dusty covers. 'I'm not sure yet.'

His frustration is palpable, but to his credit he says nothing. He just waits while I breathe in the air and circle my prey. The truth is, I have no idea which ones to take, but I don't have the luxury of time, so I'm going to have to do my best to remember. Fortunately, as no one's been in here since I was, most of what I was reading is still spread out over the table.

After an hour or so of stacking books into different piles, Bronn's impatience is beginning to irritate me.

'Why don't you go back up to the great cave?' I suggest. 'If you go straight through and follow the tunnels, you'll find a storeroom. Maybe you could find some sacks or something for us to carry these in?'

Not one to enjoy sitting idle, Bronn heads off immediately, leaving the lantern with me. Even in the dark, I have every confidence Bronn will find his way. A skilled assassin can always find his way.

With him gone the atmosphere settles and a stillness returns. I sort the main books I've returned for, the ones I'd read in the past and struggled to understand, but there are whole shelves and piles brimming with undiscovered information. I cast my eyes over them all, several times, and with every glance certain ones stand out from the rest. If Bronn were to return and ask me in what way they stood out, I wouldn't be able to say. But they do. And I know they are the ones I have to take.

Some are easier to reach than others. When Bronn appears with two large hessian sacks, he finds me balancing on top of a precarious and wobbly pile, stretching to reach a small tome tucked into the gloomiest corner of the room. But it had shone out the brightest to me. It's the one I feel most excited about.

'Steady,' he says, rushing to help me, but my fingers have curled round my bounty and I pull it free before leaping to the ground.

'I'm done. Let's load them up.'

'Which ones?'

I point to the two piles and Bronn sighs. They are pretty big.

Slapping him on the back, I take one of the sacks. 'Come on, you're a strong lad. It'll be fine.'

He mutters something under his breath, but I know he's not really cross, especially when he places the books into the sack with surprising care. When they're full, we heave them over our shoulders. I immediately wonder if I've been too greedy.

'You're mad. You know that, right?' Bronn says to me, groaning slightly under the weight. Ever the gentleman, he's taken the heavier one.

'Then what does that make you, for helping me?' My

voice has gone slightly high-pitched under the strain.

'A fool.' His voice is suddenly serious after the light teasing and I'm surprised to see him looking at me in a strange way. Sad and happy all at the same time. 'There's nothing you could ask me to do that I wouldn't.'

I drop my books and rush to wrap my arms round him, kissing him deeply. 'Then I'll try never to ask too much.'

He nods his thanks, but as we weave our way out of the tunnels, stooped under the weight of our heavy burdens, I can't shake the look on his face out of my mind.

Bronn is a warrior. He has been trained to be utterly ruthless, to carry out whatever is asked of him and never to fail. An assassin must not have vulnerabilities and Bronn has always been the very best assassin. But as we escape from the darkness of the mountain back into the open air, Old Tatty's words ring in my ears. She spoke of sacrifice. Of losing all I hold dear. The fate of the man I love rests in my hands and the mere thought causes an impending sense of doom to tug at my guts.

Bronn does have one weakness. One that could cost him dearly.

Me.

We hurry across the island towards the south coast, where we hope to find a ship. It's the bandits' favoured side of the island, as it has the most hidden coves to lurk in. The sacks over our shoulders are heavy, but we push on. Even without Old Tatty's warnings still reverberating in my head, I know time is not on my side. I'm a wanted woman, hunted by the crown. My husband is a wounded animal caught in a trap. If he dies because I take too long . . .

The unbearable thought is interrupted by the sight of smoke rising over a jagged ridge up ahead, close to the coastline. Bronn and I exchange a glance.

'Please tell me there's not a settlement beyond there,' I say, fearing I know the answer already.

'One of the few non-mining communities on the island,' he says. 'Mostly taverns and inns for tradespeople and smugglers.' Simultaneously we draw our weapons, letting the books fall to the ground. I hastily wedge them in a cleft in the rock, hoping they'll still be there when we can return for them later. Keeping low, we run towards the brow of the hill and then lie flat, ignoring the sharp pain of the rock as we try to assess what's going on.

Whatever has happened in the settlement, we're too late to be of any help. There's no sign of fighting, or people at all, only a handful of buildings on fire. The worst of the damage is already done, and little more remains than stone carcasses.

We make our way towards the steps that lead down into the natural crater where the settlement is nestled, our movements silent, not wanting to make a sound in case anyone else is still here. The air is thick with smoke, and I can tell from the smell that it isn't just wood burning. Charring flesh has its own unmistakable stench.

The first building we reach seems to have once been an inn, and though it's not on fire it's been ransacked. A quick inspection reveals it's been stripped of everything of worth. And there's not a soul in sight.

Bronn splits off to check out the back, while I explore the rooms upstairs, but though I find nothing Bronn shouts my name after only a few moments.

I run downstairs, bursting through the back door to where he's standing.

'What? What is it?' I ask, looking around for danger.

But Bronn just gestures behind me, and I turn to see what made him call.

The innkeeper is pinned to the wooden door, his wrists and ankles spread out wide and pierced with spikes of rock, a larger shard impaling him through the middle. His tongue has been cut out and nailed beside him. A warning perhaps? Did the innkeeper try to defend himself? Did his words offend his killer?

Together we release the body from its grotesque position and rest him on the ground. Bronn covers him with an old blanket and looks up at me as he kneels beside the body. 'What do you think?' he asks.

'I'm thinking the bandits have grown bolder,' I say. 'They fear no retribution.'

Bronn doesn't say anything. He doesn't need to.

'We should check the rest of the settlement.' I have a feeling this won't be the only grim discovery we'll find.

The absence of bodies as we move about bothers me. There should be more evidence of a fight, people cut down where they made their final stand. A whole settlement doesn't just disappear. Is it possible they escaped?

When I find them, my glimmer of hope fades. What brought them all to be inside the stone building at the far end of the crater, I'll never know. But whether they fled here to hide, or were rounded up like cattle to be slaughtered, what I do know is it's here they met their grisly end. Charred remains fill the space, families huddled together, parents trying to shield their children from an unstoppable force. The air is foul and I'm breathing in death.

Bronn comes into the building behind me, and for a moment we just stand in silence. After a while he puts his hand on my shoulder.

'The smoke probably killed them before the flames touched them,' he says, as if this brings some kind of comfort.

Covering my mouth and nose with my hand, I step closer to the bodies. The one slumped nearest the door, on top of another person, has a blade protruding from his back. I pull it out and turn to Bronn. 'Or maybe they were already dead.'

Bronn frowns. 'You think they were cut down while

running?'

I shrug. 'Maybe. Some of them at least. What does it matter how they died? They're dead and there's nothing I can do about it.'

And with a scream of frustration I fling the blade across the room and storm out. Without a backward glance at the settlement, I hurry to retrieve my books, my heart growing as sharp and unyielding as the rock I walk on.

For so long I have fought for justice, for peace. But right now, I want only one thing. Vengeance. The magic in my blood calls for others' blood to be spilled. Retribution. Maybe it's time I listened.

9

The cove is tucked into the south-east side of the island, a wretched, desolate place, and it's home to only one ship today. But one is all we need.

Three men sit on deck, basking like terrorturtles in the sun, with a barrel for a makeshift table where they gamble, smoke and drink.

'Excuse me?'

At the sound of my voice they all spin round, pistols raised, but when they see it's just me – just a woman – they all relax.

'What do you want?' It's the oldest of the men who speaks, and I assume he's the Captain.

'I'm looking for passage off the island. I'm willing to work for my place.'

The men exchange glances, and their leader gets to his feet, wobbling slightly with intoxication. 'What work could you possibly do on a ship?'

My dress is blinding him to who I am, a fact I was relying on. If he looked beyond, to the scar Cleeve carved on my face, to the steel in my eye, he might suspect more of a trap. 'You'd be surprised.'

He sniffs. 'Don't take women on board. They're bad luck.'

'Please,' I say, giving the perfect impression of a desperate soul. 'I really need to get away from here.'

He doesn't even dignify my plea with an answer.

I try a different tack. 'Let me play. If I win, I get to be a part of your crew.'

This causes them all to fall about laughing, as if such a notion is beyond ludicrous.

I pull out the small piece of crystal I took from the mine and hold it up for them. 'And if I lose, you can keep this and you'll never see me again.'

The sight of the crystal sobers them up quickly enough. 'Well now, perhaps we were too hasty,' the man says, wiping his nose with the back of his sleeve. 'What is it, husband problems?'

'Let's just say, there are certain people I'd rather not see again,' I answer, walking over to the table.

'I'm Jed,' the man says, and pulls over a keg for me to sit on. 'This here's Arnold, and this is Larry. He's losing, aren't you, Larry?'

Larry is young, and seems particularly glad that I've arrived, presumably because he thinks his luck has changed. Poor Larry.

'You ever played knucklebones before?' Arnold asks with a sceptical gaze, turning a bone over between his finger and thumb.

Adler taught me to play knucklebones before I could walk properly, when he was my father and I his child, and he had great hopes for me. By the time I was ten, no one on the *Maiden* would play with me because they knew they would lose. When Adler entertained rivals, or even comrades, he'd pull me out like a secret weapon to win their treasure and – perhaps more importantly – to humiliate them.

'Once or twice,' I say, and notice the smiles of smug satisfaction on the men's faces. They're blissfully confident that the crystal is theirs.

'I'll go first,' Jed says, taking a long swig of rum. 'Show you how it's done.' And he takes the five bones and throws them in the air, flipping his hand over to catch them on the back. Only two land securely. Then he throws them again, this time catching only one in his palm. This is now his 'taw', his main throwing bone. It's not a bad start considering how much I reckon he's had to drink.

'We're playing no sweeps,' Larry says, and I'm not sure if the reminder is for me or for Jed.

'I know,' Jed says, but I can tell he was hoping Larry hadn't remembered, because now he has to throw his taw in the air and pick up one of the other bones before catching his taw, repeating this until he's picked them all up. Sweeping would mean he could brush the bones closer together. No sweeps means it's considerably harder.

He makes it through all the ones, and cheers himself at his victory. 'Now,' he says, pointing at me. 'If you make it this far, you move on to twos.' And he demonstrates by throwing his taw up and snatching two bones into his fist before catching the taw.

Arnold and Larry roll their eyes, unimpressed with Jed's showing off. But it doesn't really matter to them. As long as they beat me, they get the crystal.

Jed makes it to fours, but there his luck runs out. Though he scoops all four bones into his hand, he drops his taw. His go is over.

'All right,' he says, throwing the bones at Arnold, who's laughing. 'You do better.'

Arnold starts the proceedings again, while Jed drinks more.

'Where'd you get that crystal, anyway?' Jed asks me, eyeing the bag that rests in my lap.

'From the mines.' I flick my eyes up to meet his and see his suspicions dancing there. 'Or rather, my husband did. I took it from him.'

'Poor bastard,' Jed says with a chuckle. 'What's he gonna do to you when you go home empty-handed?' When I say nothing, he smiles. 'Yes, nothing good, I'd imagine.'

'Where's the rest of your crew?' I ask, watching Arnold struggle to make it through the first round of the game. He's battling with his coordination, probably because of the rum.

'Fetching supplies. We got ourselves a commission, so once we've stocked up, we'll be on our way.'

'Oh?' I keep my interest fairly neutral, but my ears have pricked up at this morsel of news.

It's Larry who answers. 'Would have been gone a lot bloody quicker if Ferris hadn't torched the nearest settlement just cause he could.'

I feign ignorance, but my heart is spiking. Ferris is one of the particularly elusive bandits we've been failing to capture for months. He's among Karn's closest allies. And is apparently the cold-hearted killer responsible for the massacre we just stumbled upon. If we could catch Ferris, I could make him pay for what he did. Right after he tells me where I can find Karn.

Jed looks like he would kick Larry if he could reach him, so I diffuse things quickly. 'Who's Ferris?'

'No one,' Jed says, glaring at Larry.

The distraction is too much for Arnold who, having only just started twos, drops his taw.

It's Larry's turn. 'Like she's gonna care,' he says, defending his loose tongue to Jed. 'It's not as if she's coming with us.'

'Unless I win,' I say, which causes him to snort.

'Whatever.'

Larry's as useless at the game as Jed suggested he was. He fails even to make it through ones, which means it's my go.

'So, what, I throw them like this?' I say, doing a poor job of catching them on the back of my hand. The men laugh, sensing that the crystal is almost certainly within their reach now.

'Something like that,' Jed says, shaking his head. His thoughts are transparent. Women are idiots. If I'm this stupid, I deserve to be taken advantage of. A sudden image flashes into my mind, of me sticking my dagger into his guts to wipe the smug grin off his face, and the venom in the thought takes me by surprise. A part of me wants to act on it, the anger I feel towards him fast to rise, and I have to take a deep breath to calm myself. I thought I'd defeated the darkness I know I'm capable of, but now I see it's only been dormant. It has awoken, fierce and strong, and the magic that quietly dances through me seems only to whisper its encouragement.

I've had enough of being patronised. I've bought us enough time. And I need to pull away from dark thoughts now, before they take root.

My taw selected, I race through ones. My hand is lightning-quick, moving faster than their drunken eyes can follow. My reflexes aren't hampered by alcohol and are sharp from years of every kind of training. I say nothing as I blitz my way through twos, then threes and by the time I reach fours, the men are sweating.

'I thought you said you'd only played once or twice,' Jed says, shifting uncomfortably on his keg. I don't think he likes being shown up by a woman.

'That's what I said.' It just so happened to be a lie.

I throw up the taw, scoop all four bones into my hand and catch the taw instantly. I've won.

'So, when do we set sail?'

Larry looks up at me, confused by what's just happened. 'You can't come with us.'

'But I won. We had a deal.'

Jed shakes his head in disbelief. 'No, you cheated. Deal's off.'

'How did I cheat?'

'You distracted us. With your . . . you know.' He gestures at my person, so I can only assume he means my femininity.

'Tell you what,' I say. 'New deal. I'll throw all five bones in the air. If I can't catch them all on the back of my hand, I'll leave as agreed, giving you the crystal.'

Jed narrows his eyes. 'And if you do?'

'Then I get your ship.'

They're silent for a moment, before they burst out laughing. 'Take our ship?'

'Yes.'

'You're on,' Jed says. 'No way you're gonna catch all those on your hand.'

I shrug. Then promptly prove him wrong.

'Now, gentlemen, it's time for you to leave my ship.'

It's hardly unpredictable that they draw their pistols now. They were never going to let me take what I fairly won. But that's OK. I just needed to distract them long enough.

'Come on,' I say to them. 'You think you can fight me? You're so drunk you didn't even notice the ship was moving.'

They all immediately look up, only to see Bronn smiling at them from behind the wheel.

'What the—' Jed starts to say, but I make my move.

I push the barrel into Arnold and Larry – who are so inebriated they just fall over – and easily disarm Jed, before bringing his arm up behind his back, and pointing his pistol at his two useless comrades.

Bronn is striding up to us now.

'Did no one ever tell you men not to underestimate your opponent?' Bronn says, looking with undisguised contempt at our prisoners.

At his approach the three men visibly cower and I'm not sure whether it's because they recognise him, or because his presence is so striking that it would make anyone afraid.

'What do you want to do with them?' Bronn says, and when he sees the men's confusion that he's addressing me for orders, he adds with emphasis, 'Captain?'

'These men are trespassing on my ship. Time for a swim, I think.'

With a nod Bronn picks Arnold and Larry up by their collars and drags them to the side of the ship.

Despite their pleas, Bronn hurls them over and I shove Jed against the foremast.

'Where were you going to meet Ferris?' I say, pressing the pistol against his neck.

Jed's eyes scan my face, lingering for the first time on my scar. 'Who are you?'

'Who do you think?' I virtually spit the words at him.

Finally I see comprehension dawn, the magnitude of his mistake becoming clear.

'You? You're the Viper? But you're just a girl.'

I'm getting so sick of hearing that. 'Well, if you don't tell this "girl" where Ferris is, then she'll be the last thing you ever see.' And I thrust the pistol deeper into his flesh.

'All right, all right,' he says, holding up his hands. 'In my pocket, there. There's a map.'

Bronn does the honours and fishes a scrap of material out, casting his eye over it before handing it to me.

'What's Ferris going to do to you when you go home empty-handed?' I taunt him the way he taunted me. 'Nothing good, I imagine.'

To my satisfaction his face melts with dismay.

'Next time you make a deal with someone, don't try to weasel out of it,' I say, releasing him to Bronn. 'Hope you can swim.'

And despite Jed's protests, Bronn hauls the Captain off his own ship.

Now it's mine.

When Bronn turns back to me, I look away. I don't want to talk about my violent outburst, and I know it won't have gone unnoticed. All I want to do now is go and catch myself some bandits.

My new vessel is called *Storm Promise*, and I feel like this is a good omen. The mood I'm in, I'm ready to whip up a tempest. My enemies would be wise to cower right now.

We rendezvous with the *Maiden* to pick up crew and supplies before sundown. When her silhouette first darkens the amber skyline, my breath catches in my throat. It's been too long since I saw my ship, my home, and I've missed her creaking sides, steady motion and open sails. Bronn expertly steers the *Storm* alongside the *Maiden* and Ren throws over a rope for me to tie us together. Then he offers me his hand and escorts me on to the deck.

My crew – my family – salute me, and tears spring to my eyes. Above me, Talon screeches and swoops down with such speed, I barely have time to lift my arm for the vast sea vulture to land on. I have missed them all more than they'll ever know. Far more than I would have expected to.

I had worried that being away for so long things might have become a little messy on board, but the deck is impeccable, not a rope out of place. And my crew

165

seem relaxed and at ease. It's a relief to see my absence hasn't caused any problems here at least.

'Nice ship.' Ana, the boatswain who joined the crew after surviving the battle against Adler and the water raptors, is casting an admiring eye over our bounty. 'Any problems?'

'Not with getting the ship,' I say, as Bronn leaps over to join us. 'But we do have a problem.' And shuffling Talon to perch on the rigging, I explain to everyone about Ferris, about what he's done, and about the map that could lead us straight to him.

'What do you want to do?' Ren says when I'm finished, and for the briefest of moments he looks to Bronn first. Straight away his eyes flick back to me and I pretend not to have noticed, but the sting remains. Perhaps I've been away too long after all.

'I've had enough of Ferris,' I say, shifting my position ever so slightly to stand in front of Bronn. It's possible my crew need reminding who their captain is. 'We can't let this opportunity pass.'

'And what of your mission?' Harley says. 'There's a reason you just got yourself another ship.'

She's right of course, and for a second I hesitate, torn between two paths.

Bronn's hand rests on my shoulder. 'Why don't you leave Ferris to Harley and Ren? The *Maiden* is a far better ship to take into battle and they're more than capable. Trust them to protect the Isles while we fulfil your quest.'

Just like Harley, he's right, and yet I find myself bristling. Maybe it's because I should have been the one to make the decision, or perhaps it's because as soon as he's said it the crew nod as if Bronn's word is law. A very real spike of envy is impaling my chest.

'If you're happy to take on that burden?' I raise my eyebrows at my two stand-in captains, who both look a little hurt that I've even asked.

'What we're here for, Captain,' Ren says.

'Then it's decided.' I turn to Bronn. 'Can you begin preparations?'

'Yes, Captain. We'll be ready to sail within the hour.'

'Very good.'

While Bronn and the crew set to work, I walk across the deck, trailing my fingers along the rail. I don't want to leave my ship, not again. A gnawing in my guts warns me that if I leave her, I may never see her again.

Forcing dark thoughts away, I smile at the Snakes working on deck, greeting them, asking how they are, wanting to reconnect with my family before I'm forced to say goodbye. I invested so much time and effort to unite the crew after Adler died, to change our ethos, inspire a new role for us in the Isles. But old habits die hard, especially among assassins, and I can only hope the hard-fought harmony isn't too fragile, or it may not withstand losing both me and Bronn.

After touring the lower decks, inspecting my ship thoroughly and finding nothing lacking, I find myself at my cabin.

When I push the door, I'm hit by the escaping stale air, and I'm unexpectedly relieved. No one has been using the Captain's quarters in my absence, and though I wouldn't have minded if Bronn had, there's something reassuring about knowing he didn't.

Since I killed Adler, I've tried my best to purge this room of him. Gone are the foul jars filled with body parts, along with all the other gruesome trophies the man had collected. The smell has improved with endless cleaning, burning herbs, and copious amounts of fresh air. There are only two real lingering remnants of his presence here. One is Talon, although today his perch is empty, as he keeps a watchful eye on proceedings outside. The other is Adler's desk.

Perhaps I should have ripped it from the floor, and thrown it overboard, let it sink without a trace. But it's so beautifully crafted, I couldn't quite bring myself to.

And there's something about sitting where he sat that reminds me of my purpose. Who I mustn't become.

I lower myself into the chair behind it, and glance down at the drawer, at the four small words etched in the wood. I saw them for the first time when I became

Captain and sat where Adler sat. I had never before known Adler lived by a motto or a code.

Fight dirty. Kill fast.

Sounds about right.

I look away and let my gaze drift around the room. It still doesn't feel like mine, this cabin. And not just because of all its associations with Adler. It's more a sense that I'm not really meant to be here. That I'm just treading water.

That I'm not the rightful Captain.

After all, what Viper would allow the bandits to run such rings around her? Far from destroying my enemies and bringing peace, the Isles are more under threat than ever. Images of flesh scorched black flash into my mind. How afraid must those people have been in their final moments? How alone? The need to hunt and hurt my enemies is an almost physical pain, the desire to make them pay overwhelming. Frustration and hatred mingle together into a bitter bile and with my dagger I angrily scratch out Adler's words for ones of my own.

Strike first. Die last.

That is what this Viper wishes. To sink her fangs into her enemies, bite deep until the venom spreads. To stay in this fight to the very end. To be the last to fall.

Once I've etched my vitriol into the wood, my anger subsides and I look at the words with sadness. What is happening to me? I used to want only peace. To protect.

To defend. To unite. That should be the legacy I leave behind for my successor should I not return. When did I become so cynical?

The moment a man plunged his blade into Torin's chest and snatched that future from our grasp.

There's a knock at the door, and Bronn's face peers round it.

'We're ready whenever you are,' he says.

I nod. 'I'm on my way.'

When he closes the door, I stand up and take a breath. It may be a long time until I'm back in these quarters, back with my ship. If ever. I change into my own clothes, glad to finally be free of the filthy dress I stole on the First Isle, and gather a few belongings into a bag with a heavy heart. There was so much I wanted to achieve as Viper and it's hard not to feel I'm leaving as a failure. Torin and I thought we had all the power, but I see now how quickly such flimsy advantage can be snatched away. But even through my sadness I can feel the magic humming quietly inside me, reminding me it's an altogether more immense force that no one can steal from me – a comforting thought.

When I emerge back on to the deck, I'm greeted by Harley, who comes and puts her arm round my shoulder, turning conspiratorially towards me so no one else can hear her speak, and placing something into my hand.

'Thought you might be wanting these,' she says.

My mother's brooch and my compass. Precious items I'd left in her safekeeping when I went to my wedding, not wanting anyone to see the Vultura crest and recognise it. If I hadn't left them with Harley, they would be lost now back at the palace and I close my hand protectively round them.

'Thank you,' I say.

'Not just trinkets, are they?' she says, and I can tell she's pieced more parts of my life together. When I shake my head, she adds, 'Then you might be needing them, where you're headed.'

For a moment I daren't speak, for fear of my voice shaking and tears spilling. 'I might well,' I say when I can manage.

'And I thought you might want this too,' she says, pulling a necklace from her pocket. The necklace Torin gave to me so long ago, as a symbol of our partnership. I stopped wearing it because such jewels are far from practical on board ship, but now I'm glad to see it, and fix it round my neck. I clutch it tightly in my hand, as if somehow it can summon Torin to me. I wear it now as a reminder. That whatever happens next, I must hurry. For the man I married. If Old Tatty is to be believed, he has until the blood moon and I have no idea when that is.

'We'll watch over him as best we can,' Harley promises me with a warm smile, but then it fades away. She has more to say. 'You'll notice we're not giving you much in the way of food,' she says and there's concern in her voice. 'Things are worse than when you left, and our barrels are emptying. Reckon if you're careful, that'll be enough to last you there and back, but don't expect any more feasts.'

'I can barely remember what food tastes like,' I say, though my heart's sinking at the news. How quickly things have deteriorated. The islands aren't strong enough to survive further suffering.

'Here,' I say, and I take the piece of crystal from my bag. 'Use this to help where you can.'

Harley's eyes widen at the sight of it. 'That's worth a fair bit. You sure you won't be needing it?'

I shake my head, and press it firmly into her palm. 'It's needed here.' But I'm keeping the diamond dust for myself.

She tucks the crystal safely into her pocket. 'You have my word it'll be used wisely. Though if the crops keep failing, even crystal won't be able to help anyone.'

'Thank you. And, Harley? Make sure you get Ferris,' I say to her under my breath. 'He's a parasite and must be stopped. But take him alive. He might be useful in tracking Karn down.'

'I know,' she says with a look that reminds me she's no fool. 'Don't you worry about us. You just get yourself safely West and do . . . whatever it is you're going to do.' And, squeezing me tight, Harley reminds me that nothing escapes her attention. 'Don't worry, I'll make sure your ship is waiting for you when you come back.'

The smile I give her is somewhat sheepish. 'Thank you.' I glance at Bronn, who's busy organising the changeover with his usual efficiency. 'Bet he made a good Viper, though.'

Harley shrugs. 'He's Bronn. Of course he did. But he has no interest in replacing you, you know that.' When I say nothing she says, 'Don't you?'

'Yes. But I sometimes think he would be the better choice.'

Harley takes a deep breath. 'He would be a different choice. But it's irrelevant. You killed Captain Adler, not him. The title is yours. The only way for Bronn to earn it is . . . well, like I said, it's irrelevant. That man wouldn't hurt a hair on your head, let alone take your life. So stop thinking on it.'

She pulls me to face her square on. 'Now go raise us that army. And when you return, bring hell with you.'

'I will.' And I throw my arms round her, the sudden thought that I might never see her again too powerful to ignore. 'Goodbye.'

My affection knocks the hardness from her for a moment and her whole person softens. 'I'll see you soon.'

I nod and smile, but as I take my leave, pausing to briefly hug Ren, Toby and Ana, the sensation only grows stronger, Old Tatty's words haunting me. She said she saw my death and right now every fibre of my being thinks she is right. The chances of me seeing my crew again, or my ship, feel very remote.

As the space between the two ships grows, I have to fight the impulse to change my mind, to abandon this journey. There's still time to forget the whole thing, to stay here and fight the King alone.

Instead I watch the *Maiden* disappear into the gloom of nightfall. My fear isn't going away, but I won't let it rule me either. It'll just have to be my companion, because I've made my choice. I choose magic. I choose my heritage. I choose to try to bring peace for one and for all, or die in the attempt.

But as darkness wraps its cold arms round me, I can't shake the certainty that what I'm about to embark on is a one-way trip.

10

To start with, I deal with my sense of impending doom by throwing myself into work. I've missed being on a ship, and with only a small crew there's plenty to be done. I'm also keen to recover my fitness after being imprisoned and on the run. It's invigorating to scale the rigging as the sun breaks the darkness, the salt clinging to my lips and the sea breeze sweeping over me like a wave. It's good to be on an adventure again, to have a purpose.

At night I keep to my cabin, poring over the books Bronn and I heaved around the Sixth Isle. Though my death may have been prophesied, though the odds may be stacked heavily against me, I'm not about to give up, so I do the only thing I can. Improve my odds.

Magic is the key. I have no idea how but I do know that I need to learn as much as I can if I'm to stand any chance of figuring it out.

But as the days pass, the lure of the books grows stronger and I spend more time alone and less time pitching in with the crew. Soon I don't want to be disturbed at all, and so I put Bronn in charge of the *Storm*, while I read till my eyes want to bleed. As I discovered months ago when Torin introduced me to the books, there is more information in these pages than I could ever hope to absorb, but this time at least I understand more of what I'm reading. The small tome that called out to me from the top shelf is written entirely in the ancient language of the Mages and every word causes the magic to flutter inside me, like a baby bird testing its wings. I spend hours trying to decipher it, writing down any mention of a word and its translation from other volumes into a book of my own. The language seems to be half the incantation, half of any spell and vital to harnessing the magic itself. The memory of how one word coaxed the mountain to my aid still stirs excitement deep in my belly and drives me through my tiredness to discover more.

Bronn joins me in the evenings, bringing small scraps of food and water, though I take very little. The crew who are doing physical work need it more than I do. Mostly we sit in silence, Bronn tired from his labour and me buried in dusty pages.

'Why don't you have a rest?' Bronn says on the second week after parting ways with the *Maiden*. 'We've barely spoken these past few days.'

'Did you know, in the West, there are plants so filled with magic that in the right hands they can be used to bring life back even to someone beyond all other help?'

'Really? And do you know which plant that is? Or how to use it?' Bronn doesn't sound impressed.

'No, it doesn't say. But I'm going to keep looking.' I look up and the sparkle in my eyes fades. Bronn isn't sharing my excitement. 'I'm sorry. I'm not trying to ignore you; it's just important that I know as much as possible.'

'Can't Esther teach you all this when you get there?'

I extricate myself from the pile of paper I'm buried under and move to sit beside Bronn on the floor. 'Maybe. But time isn't on my side. Who knows how long Torin has left before the King decides to be rid of him? Or how long the islanders will survive once the food runs out entirely? I can't waste a second.'

He leans over to kiss me lightly, sighing when I pull away. 'All right,' he says. 'I understand. I just miss you.'

His words soften me, and I rest my head on his shoulder. 'Do you think we'll ever have peace? To just be alone together without the rest of the world demanding things from us?'

Bronn presses his lips into my hair. 'I hope so.'

A sharp bang on our door makes us both sit up.

'But not today,' he says with a wry grin.

'Come in,' I call, and a young Snake called Gretchen walks in.

'Sorry to disturb you,' she says, and she's blushing. 'But you need to see this, Captain.' Her eyes dart from Bronn to me. She doesn't know which one of us she's supposed to address.

I leap to my feet a little too quickly, wanting to assert my authority, but Bronn's close behind as we follow Gretchen on deck.

The light almost hurts my eyes after so long hidden away in my cabin, but I soon see what the problem is.

'Is that . . .?' I squint hard, wanting to be sure I'm seeing what I think I'm seeing.

'That's Ferris's ship.' Bronn doesn't sound impressed.

'But he's supposed to be somewhere else,' I say, thinking of the map Jed gave us, where the *Maiden* was headed.

'That weasel must have found a way to warn him,' Bronn says. 'Should have killed him when we had the chance.'

'Well, we can't let them get away.'

Bronn doesn't conceal his surprise. 'What are you suggesting? That we fight them in this?'

'That's exactly what I'm suggesting.'

We stand glaring at each other for a moment. Apparently Bronn is unconvinced.

'We can take them,' I say, determined they're not going to elude us once more. I hate the thought of them laughing at us, thinking they've outrun the *Maiden* yet again. 'This ship's got guts, and so do her crew.'

'Her skeleton crew,' Bronn reminds me.

'And I'd take a few of us over an army of them any day.'

We're back to our stand-off once more. But there's only one Captain on the ship, no matter what confusion some people might be experiencing.

'What are your orders?' Bronn knows when I've made my mind up.

'We can get close without arousing their suspicion,' I say, though once they see the name of our ship, they'll know it's the one we stole from Jed. 'Then we attack.'

'We can't use the cannons,' Bronn says. 'There's virtually no gunpowder on board.'

'Assassins don't need weapons.'

'You want us to get close enough to board?'

I nod. 'Hand-to-hand combat. It's the only way.'

To my dismay Bronn doesn't appear to share my confidence. 'Are you sure this is the best idea? We can send word to Harley, tell them our coordinates. Maybe we should focus on our mission and leave this to the others.'

He might be right. He usually is. But I can't bear the thought of Ferris getting away with what he did on the Sixth Isle. The vengeful voice inside me drowns out all others. I have to make someone pay before it drives me mad.

'No. We have an opportunity and we're not going to waste it. Change course and prepare for battle.'

I think Bronn sees it: the flash of doubt in my eyes. His own expression is grim as he nods obediently and sets to rallying the crew, while I run back to my quarters.

This is going to be brutal, I know that. But I'm sick of my enemies slipping through my fingers. I'm being thwarted at every turn. Now I have a chance to claim a victory, and I need one so badly right now.

I grab my dagger and ready my pistol. And then I secure the manuscripts in chests, hoping to keep them safe from any intruders.

When I return to deck, armed for the fight, Bronn comes to stand beside me.

'I'm guessing they'll have a crew double our size. Not great odds.'

Irritation burns through me. 'Are you afraid?'

My words cause the intended anger. He tries to suppress it, but I see it nonetheless. 'I don't like to lose good men unnecessarily.'

'What have we been doing all these months?' I say, my voice rising. 'Stopping bandits. This is precisely what we have been trained to do. You used to attack spontaneously all the time under Adler.'

'Yes, under Adler. Not under you. This isn't like you.' He pauses. 'You don't have to prove anything.'

His opposition causes me to waver for a moment, but then, steeling my resolve, I stare at him hard. 'Yes, I do.'

'Fine.' It doesn't sound fine at all, but Bronn knows how stubborn I am. 'I assume you want Ferris alive?'

I nod.

'Let's do this then.'

The *Storm* is only slightly smaller than Ferris's galleon, and we close in on them with ease. As we get near, Bronn signals for the mainsail to be furled while I shout for the crew to prepare for close quarters. But already a cold disquiet is growing inside me. Something's not quite right. They should be emptying their cannons at us by now.

Bronn stands beside me. 'It's too quiet.' He echoes my own thoughts. 'Ask for surrender?'

I exhale. 'Think it's a trap?'

He nods. 'It's a trap.'

'Right, let's go see what they've got.'

I hail the galleon, requesting their captain surrender and it isn't long before the white flag is raised.

It's far too easy. I turn to my crew, checking they're ready. Several of them will stay on the *Storm* to cover the deck of Ferris's ship with a fusillade of fire, creating a blanket of smoke to give us an advantage once we board. I hope it's enough.

Once the *Storm* has come alongside the galleon, we throw over some grappling hooks and I lead the way on to the other deck.

'Hello?' I call out, all of us keeping a pretence that we're uncertain about what's happening, when really we know that they're hiding, ready to strike.

And strike they do. All at once Ferris's crew come screaming up from below deck, pistols firing and swords drawn.

We duck for cover before the shots can reach us and my crew start firing their own pistols from over on the *Storm*. Using the distraction, we come out blazing and launch our attack. Bandits are thugs – their fighting is brutal, but without skill. My crew, on the other hand, are lethal. Cutlasses slash through bellies, axes plunge into skulls, and blood is flying everywhere. I make for the galleon's ropes, targeting the ratlines with my blade, while I search for Ferris. Instead my gaze falls upon a familiar face – Jed. Angrily I hack through the ropes once and for all, releasing the mainsail on to the deck like a cloud of confusion.

My crew were expecting it. Ferris's weren't, and I seize the opportunity to run towards Jed, who sees me coming and flees. I give chase, effortlessly cutting down a bandit who leaps into my path. The delay gives Jed time to find another sword, though, and he faces me with a victorious grin. He thinks he's already won.

'Found a way to warn Ferris then?' I snarl at him.

'Your mistake for not silencing me,' he says.

'A mistake I won't repeat.'

He laughs. 'You're outnumbered. And outarmed.'

'And you still think any of that matters to me?'

I attack fast – wielding two swords takes a lot of training, and I'm willing to bet he's not that skilled. I may only have a dagger, but bringing it hard against the blade in his left hand is enough to send it clattering to the ground, his grip too weak. Before he can adapt, I lunge forward, sweeping my blade across to sever his other hand.

He screams, dropping his second sword, and clutching at the wound spurting bright red blood.

'Where is Ferris?' I demand, grabbing him by the shirt.

He whimpers, a coward to the last, but his eyes betray him, flicking to his left. I follow their direction and see a man decorated with trinkets and oozing authority.

'Goodbye, Jed,' I say, and plunge my dagger deep into his chest. I don't even wait for his body to drop to the deck before I'm running towards Ferris, crashing into him and throwing us both down before he can empty his pistol into Gretchen's back.

He's strong and tries to push me away, but I'm small and nimble and duck under his arm, smashing into the arch of his back and manoeuvring so that I'm sitting on top of him, pinning him down with my blade at his neck.

'Ferris, I presume?'

'And you must be the child Viper,' he says with a laugh. 'How does it feel to be continually thwarted by bandits?'

I shrug. 'I'm not feeling too thwarted right now.'

His laugh grows louder. 'We outnumber you three to one. It is I who shall be claiming you as a prize.'

My anger rises dangerously high and I pull my pistol from my belt.

'Bronn?' I shout his name loudly and in the corner of my eye see him locate me. He takes in my situation and follows the direction of my pistol's aim.

'Get back to the ship!' he screams at our crew, running as he does so.

I glance down at Ferris and see his confusion, before he too realises what I'm about to do.

Fear clouds his face. 'You wouldn't dare.' He doesn't sound too sure, though. 'You'll kill yourself.'

I smile at him. 'I'm not dying today.'

And I shoot.

As soon as I press the trigger, I'm on my feet, pulling Ferris with me, and as the blast detonates, we're thrown from the ship into the water, my shot reaching the barrels of gunpowder I'd seen stacked at the far end of the galleon. Splinters of wood rain down from the sky and I see the *Storm* moving hastily away, putting as much distance as possible between itself and the sinking, burning ship. I'm still holding on to Ferris's arm, which is just as well because he's been rendered unconscious by the impact of the water and would drown if I weren't keeping him afloat.

Despite everything that's just happened, it's being in the ocean that makes my heart begin to race too fast.

Though I've spent the past few months trying to overcome my fear and forge the connection with it that my parents wished for me, the sea still sparks a panic unlike any other.

And as the fear spreads it carries with it a cold undercurrent of uncomfortable truth. *What did I just do?* It's as if the water has restored me to my senses, washing away the darkness that had gripped me. I struggle to understand what possessed me to make such a succession of foolhardy decisions. I could have got my crew killed. And for what? Just so that I could be the one to administer revenge?

But unless I wish to drown along with Ferris, I can't dwell on my mistakes now. It takes a while to swim towards the *Storm* dragging Ferris's dead weight with me, but eventually I'm helped back on board along with my prisoner.

'Take him straight to the brig,' Bronn orders, as he lifts me to my feet. 'Are you hurt?'

I shake my head. 'Did we lose anyone?'

'No,' Bronn says, but despite this he doesn't sound pleased. 'A few injuries, but nothing you can't tend to.'

'Any other prisoners?'

'Just a couple. I'll interrogate them in a moment.'

'Leave Ferris for me.'

Bronn turns to look at me in surprise. 'Really?'

I bristle slightly, guilt making me defensive. 'Yes, really. And question them, Bronn. There's no need for anything more at this point.' He knows what I mean.

'Five minutes ago, you were blowing up their ship. Now you have a problem with me interrogating them?'

'Battle is different,' I say, not wanting to admit the truth to him. I know I'm being inconsistent, but I cannot account for what came over me. Now I'm keen to make amends for my previous bloodlust. 'They're our prisoners now. And I'm not a big supporter of torture.'

I'm not certain I've ever seen Bronn look so agitated. 'Who said anything about torture? I simply want to provide them with some incentive to talk.'

That was what Raoul said as he thrust a gun to my head. There are some incentives I'm not willing to permit. Even for scum like Ferris. 'Please, Bronn. Can you just do as I ask?'

He looks at me confused, like he can't understand my erratic behaviour. I don't blame him. Eventually he sighs. 'As you wish.'

I watch him as he walks away and hate the rift I can sense widening. All we seem to do these days is disagree, approaching every problem, every choice, from polar positions. But there's little I can do about it now. My priority is to make my decision to attack Ferris worthwhile. I want answers only he can give me.

Once I change into a dry outfit, I make my way straight to the brig, to the further of the two cells, where Ferris has been put by himself, his fellow survivors all sharing the other. Bronn isn't to be seen, so I'm guessing he's taking them one by one. To question.

Ferris is shackled to the hull of the ship and is going nowhere. He's regained consciousness but looks like he wishes he hadn't. At the mere sight of him a rush of hatred flares up inside me, the same desire to punish him that led me to risk all our lives. I fight it back. Killing people was Adler's way. I won't let it become mine. Not again. I took Briggs's life while lost in vengeance. It's a path that leads nowhere good.

'Sorry about your ship,' I say without a trace of remorse.

Ferris raises his head slightly and glares at me. He says nothing.

'Looks like a nasty cut,' I continue, gesturing to the gash above his eye. 'I could give you some medicine if you want? Maybe some rum for the pain?'

Ferris narrows his eyes. 'Your price?'

'I simply want to know where I might find your friend.'

He curls his lip, revealing several rotting teeth behind it. 'I have lots of friends. You'll have to be more specific.'

I know damn well that he knows who I'm talking about.

'It's Karn I want,' I say. 'You're only here as a substitute, and a poor one at that. Tell me what I want to know, and you'll be free to leave.'

Ferris clenches his fists, and fights against his chains, longing to hurt me. I don't flinch. 'I will tell you nothing.'

'That would be unwise,' I say, taking a step closer, wanting him to know I don't fear him. 'Do you know where this ship is headed? The West.'

There it is, the flicker of fear shown by all sailors at the mention of Western waters.

'If you tell me everything you know about Karn, then I might be able to arrange for you to leave us before we cross the divide. If you don't . . .' I let the thought hang in the air for a moment. 'Did you hear the rumours about water raptors?

The look on his face tells me he did.

I lean forward to whisper softly in his ear. 'They weren't rumours. And they have quite an appetite.'

I move back, and for a long moment we hold each other's gaze, neither one of us blinking, or wanting to be the first to break.

Ferris folds before I do, and a spark of victory ignites inside me. 'You're better than I gave you credit for,' he says. 'Not quite the child everyone thinks you are.'

'Then talk. Give me information and win your freedom.'

'But there's something you're not good at,' he says, and I can feel my victory slipping away. 'You're a terrible liar.'

Trying to keep the upper hand, I say, 'I'm not lying; we are going West.'

'I believe you. But I don't think for one second you'll be feeding me to any water raptors. Not your style.'

Frustration makes my temper flare. 'And what exactly is my style?'

His horrid, sneering smile returns. 'You're just a bit too bloody honourable for the likes of that.'

'I just destroyed your ship and most of your crew,' I growl at him. 'Don't tell me what I will or will not do.'

But it doesn't matter. I've lost him. Rightly or wrongly, he's simply not afraid of me.

The urge is undeniable. I want to take my dagger and strike him with it. Carve my name into his skin and brand him as my enemy. Let the air shiver with his screams as I bleed him into subservience.

I swallow it back like bile. 'You will tell me,' I say. 'Maybe not today, but you will.'

I swear it as much to myself as to him.

Later, Bronn seeks me out to ask how it went.

'He's keeping his silence,' I say. 'For now. How did you get on?'

'Same.' He sighs, and I can tell he's wrestling with whether to be honest or not.

'Spit it out,' I snap, not in the mood for playing games with another man.

'I can get them to talk,' Bronn says. 'Milligan wasn't the only one on the *Maiden* who knew how to loosen tongues.'

Milligan. The mere mention of the old surgeon's name sends shards of alarm to spike my chest. She wasn't trying to coerce secrets from me when she tortured me. She just wanted to hurt me. She succeeded. There is a reason I don't want to resort to her methods.

'No,' I say a little too fiercely, curling my fingers into my palm. The nails she removed still haven't fully grown back. 'We do it my way.'

'Your way won't work,' Bronn says, and he's as frustrated as I am.

'You don't know that.'

Bronn runs his hands through his hair and turns to leave, but I hear what he mutters under his breath as he goes. 'Yes I do.'

As much as it bothers me, what's worse is discovering he's right. Over the next few days I fail to extract a single piece of worthwhile information from Ferris. The mood on board the ship deteriorates and a dark cloud descends over my crew, maybe because of the obvious tension between Bronn and me, or perhaps because we're close to Western waters. No one really knows what to expect when the line is crossed, or what new nightmares we'll experience, and the mood grows ever more sour.

Days pass and eventually we cross the divide into the Western Sea. Bronn and I attempt to navigate, but we're struggling with the charts, finding it hard to decipher the route we should be taking to reach the Eighth Isle. The last time we made this journey, the ocean took us there without our say, but this time she doesn't intervene. Nothing seems to align with the notes we made when plotting our way back East, or the ancient maps we used the first time, and there's a growing feeling that we're lost.

Then the winds drop.

Suddenly and unexpectedly the waters still and our sails wilt. We're going nowhere.

To start with no one panics. It's hardly the first time the weather's let us down, and we wait for the wind's return. But as days pass without the slightest breeze unease spreads like a plague throughout the ship.

'It'll return eventually,' I say to Bronn one evening, as we stand on the still deck, desperately craving the merest hint of a storm.

'We'd better hope so,' Bronn says. 'And when it does? What course do we take? We're lost and we didn't have the food for even a day's delay.' And he smashes his fists down on to the railing.

I look up at him, wishing the friction between us would vanish.

'Are things that bad?'

He glances over at me. 'Not yet. But if this carries on? I don't want our prisoners to starve before they tell us anything.'

I can't mask my surprise. 'You're not feeding them?'

'Of course I am. But it's barely anything. I can't justify giving them too much when our own crew are barely surviving.'

Deep down I know he's right, so I say nothing. Especially seeing as we could have plundered Ferris's ship for supplies if I hadn't been overcome by revenge and blown it to pieces.

Weariness gnaws at my bones. This has all gone horribly wrong. I hoped this journey would be magical, filled with learning and time alone with Bronn. But all that's happened is we seem to have drifted further apart. And I don't know any tonics to fix us.

'The wind will return soon,' I say, feigning as much positivity as I can muster. 'As soon as it does, we'll bear north-west and I think we'll reach our destination. Meanwhile, cut my own rations in half and share the rest among the crew. I'll return to studying my books – I don't need much food to sustain me if I'm doing that.'

Bronn gives me a strange look, like he's reaching a decision of his own. 'If that's what you want.'

'What does that mean?'

He hesitates. 'Are you sure that magic is the answer? Can you not raise your army without it?'

We seem to be going round in circles again. 'Yes, I'm sure. Look, I know you don't like magic—'

'Can you blame me?' Bronn's face is creased with concern as he turns to confront me. 'Considering the effect it has on you?'

I stare at him in surprise. 'What effect?'

'You don't know?' He laughs humourlessly. 'Why am I not surprised?'

'What effect?' I repeat, my voice as cold as the night air.

'Name one single time when using magic hasn't led you to do something completely reckless. I mean, the water raptors? I was there, Marianne, I do remember the hell you unleashed. And . . .' He sighs. 'I don't know, since we got those books you seem like a blade freshly sharpened. Ready to draw blood at the slightest touch.'

My instinct is to argue, to tell him he's being ridiculous. But I hold my tongue, because the truth uncoils like a sleeping serpent in my chest. He's right. I did summon the water raptors with all the anger and hatred I possessed. And after using magic to descend the mountain, I became arrogant and left Lilah without a part of her mind. Always it seduces me with its power, always it calls to the part of me that I'm not proud of, the part of me that wants to hurt rather than heal. Is it possible that the closer I get to the magic I long for, the worse are the decisions I make? Have days of sitting alone, absorbing the books and their knowledge, warped my own sense of power and importance? Did Old Tatty not warn me about this very corruption?

Bronn takes my silence for hostility, though. 'Maybe I'm wrong,' he says, and he's as weary of our fighting as I am. 'All I'm saying is be careful. You may not yet know all the risks of magic.'

Once he's gone, I take myself to hide away in my cabin, his words echoing in my ears. Confusion draws in like clouds before a storm, feeding my ever-present frustration. I need the magic. I know I do. But I must be stronger, fight its control. And so for several days I'm drawn back to my manuscripts, searching for any potion that can draw the truth from my enemy, or even a spell that would summon a storm and move us closer to our destination, all while desperately trying to quench the alluring warmth every word brings to my bones.

I don't see Bronn in that time. Gretchen brings me my food and updates me on the obvious – that we're still not moving anywhere.

So when there's a knock on my door one night, I'm fully expecting it to be Gretchen bringing some message or other and am surprised to see Bronn standing there instead.

'Hello, stranger,' I say. It's good to see him.

He looks less pleased to see me, however.

'What is it?' I ask, my spirits already sinking deep into my stomach.

'Permission to speak freely?'

His formality shakes me, even causes me to laugh with disbelief. 'You don't have to ask,' I say. 'You can say anything to me.'

He's nowhere close to laughing. 'I interrogated Ferris.'

I'm so stunned it takes me a moment to gather my thoughts. 'You did what?'

'We were running out of time and we needed him to talk. I did what was necessary.'

I can't believe it. He disobeyed my orders. He went behind my back. Again.

'He sang a full song,' Bronn says, as if I care right now that he was successful. 'I know where we can find Karn.'

'I'm sorry, are you justifying what you did?'

'Yes, damn right I am.'

'You're unbelievable. Do you have so little respect for me that you would disregard my judgement?'

'We tried it your way; it wasn't working. You don't break your prisoners by talking to them. What was it Adler once told me? Bleed your enemy before your enemy bleeds you.'

'So now you're telling me you want to be more like Adler?' I want to scream. 'Who, by the way, you would never have challenged like this.'

'I'm doing everything I can to protect you from becoming like him.'

'What the hell does that mean?'

'You told me once you feared the darkness inside you, feared becoming what you hated. I keep trying to protect you from having to make decisions that would lead you there, but you resist me at every turn.'

Frustration bubbles inside me, hot like a cauldron. 'You have to stop this,' I say, turning away from him. 'I'm not a child who needs sheltering from all the horrors of life; I've seen plenty of them. I know you spent so long trying to keep me safe from a distance; it must be a hard habit to break, but there's no distance now.' I look back at him, my hand pressed against my chest. 'I'm here, with you.'

Bronn laughs. 'No distance between us? There's a gaping chasm!' He runs his fingers through his hair, trying to calm himself. 'Sometimes I wonder if you even want to be the Viper any more.'

The red virtually flashes in front of my eyes. 'Is this jealousy, Bronn? Are you mad at me because I'm the Viper, not you?' I regret the words as soon as they're spoken, because Bronn has never been anything but supportive. The jealousy is all mine.

I know that I've crossed the line as soon as the words are out. I see his anger rise like the clouds before a storm, a rolling darkness covering his face, and I know I'm not going to like what he's about to unleash one bit.

'Do you have any idea how hard I try *not* to be jealous of you?' His voice is quiet and far deadlier than if he was shouting. 'Do you know how many things I've done over the years I'm ashamed of? Terrible things in the name of the King and the Viper. I stayed for two reasons. One was you. The other was because I found somewhere I belonged. Adler turned a scared little thief into a warrior, and while I may have hated what he made me into, I also loved being good at it. What else was there for a man like me to aspire to, other than succeed him? What other place in the world is there for a killer like me? And yet I knew that was your path, not mine, so I stepped back. I accepted a long time ago that the future I wanted belonged to you, not me.'

His words hurt and I hate him for saying them. For tearing apart this wound between us, spilling painful truths out into the open where they can no longer be ignored and can never be forgotten. But, for now, I hold my tongue. Bronn's just getting started.

'Do you want to know how hard it was to watch you marry another man?' The issue of Ferris is now a distant memory. Bronn's fists are clenched, his muscles taut, every inch of his body holding back the force of the rage he's been fighting for so long. 'I have broken my body, been beaten half to death – hell, I've been tortured before – but never in my life has anything hurt quite as much as standing there while you vowed to love someone else.'

197

His anger has fully ignited my own, and all the fury that's been building inside me for weeks, for months, for years, spews out. 'It hurt *you*? What do you think it did to me? Do you think I enjoyed it?'

'How could you do it? How could you say those words, knowing you didn't mean them?' He's shouting now too. 'I know it was your duty, I know you don't love him, but it destroyed me. And I couldn't say anything, couldn't make things worse for you, because you were being so bloody noble. I can't be the bastard who makes you feel bad, who's eaten up with jealousy that the one person who matters to me keeps doing things that make me feel worthless. I don't want to be that man.'

His pain is devastating, but it also enrages me. 'Then don't be! It wasn't about you.'

'No, it's always about you. *Your* pain, *your* sacrifice, but you're not the only one suffering.'

'Fine.' I can feel the heat rising, the unravelling of my control as it gives way to rage. 'You want to talk about you? Why would you tell those lies about me at the trial?'

He looks astonished. 'Because you told me to trust you, to play along.'

'Play along, not destroy me!' The memory of his words claw at the inside of my mind. 'Admit it, you wanted to be Viper, and saw a way to make it happen without having to get your hands dirty.'

'You think I'd sink so low as to throw you overboard to get what I want?'

'Well, you've done it before!'

There it is, all the messy history finally laid out before us. All the resentments, the recriminations, everything that we've done to each other and had to brush aside, it can all be traced back to that one moment after Bronn's initiation, when I was still a girl in skirts clinging to our friendship and he pushed me into the sea and broke my heart. It hurts to realise that despite everything that's happened since, a part of me never moved beyond that day.

Bronn rubs his face with his hands.

'We can't keep doing this to each other,' he says, and the fight has left him. He sounds utterly defeated, his pain, his tiredness etched into every line of his face.

I'm hoping he'll walk to me, hold me and reassure me that we can overcome all this, that there's nothing so insurmountable that we can't face it together, but he doesn't. Instead he walks to the door.

Before he leaves, though, Bronn turns to me, his voice soft once more. 'I have made a lot of mistakes. But not today. I'm not proud of hurting Ferris, but it needed to be done. It worked. The truth is you're not the head of the King's Fleet; you're not a paragon of justice. You're the Viper. There's a reason it's called that. You don't have the luxury of doing the right thing – sometimes you have to do what's necessary. If you haven't got the stomach for it, then maybe I *should* be the Viper.'

And just like that he's gone, shattering my heart into pieces. Maybe he's right, maybe I did make the wrong decision – it wouldn't be the first time. But not for the reason he thinks. I can stomach it. In fact, I wanted to kill Ferris and his crew – all of them – slowly, painfully, brutally. The darkness that I've tried so hard to bury had surfaced with fresh intensity, and in the moment I'd fired at the gunpowder and blown the ship to pieces I didn't want to save the world. I wanted to destroy it.

I cannot learn magic if I cannot control my darkness. I cannot save the East if I cannot learn magic. But there it is, all the time. The desire to hurt, to punish, to control. And so I'm constantly trying to compensate for it, veering too far the other way and making mistakes.

Now my authority is challenged and my relationship is in tatters.

The truth has never been kind. But, deep down, I don't trust Bronn. Not completely. Though I know his reasons, though it was a long time ago, a part of me hasn't forgiven him for his past betrayals. For hurting me every day with his cold indifference. For pushing me into the icy water that he knew I feared. That's why I felt so jealous. I was scared. Of what he might be prepared to do to me again. And I'm punishing him unintentionally, afraid of my own insecurities.

This has to end; I see that now. In some way I've always known. The journey that lies ahead of me, I must take alone, for both our sakes.

Sacrifice.

The prophetic word that's haunted me has never rung truer. If I sacrifice him now, it may save him. It may save us both. Bronn will be free to live the life he's always longed for, away from my shadow.

It's time to let him go.

Once I've reached this conclusion, the wind miraculously returns and the charts seem to align with where we want to go, as if the waters had been waiting, delaying my journey until I made the right choice. The West wants me here alone.

When the Eighth Isle comes into view several days later, Bronn shows up at my cabin. Immediately my heart sinks, because I can see he's come to make amends, all his defences low to fix the distance between us. I'm going to have to crush him and it's more than I can bear.

'We're here,' he says, a relieved smile on his face. 'The crew are preparing to go on land.'

'Tell them to stop,' I say and watch confusion crease his face. 'They're not coming.'

'You want to take a small team over first?'

I sigh and rise to my feet. 'No, I'm going alone.'

Bronn's watching me carefully, and I know my

meaning isn't lost on him. 'I don't think so,' he says. 'That wasn't the plan.'

'The plan's changed.' And my voice has grown hard. Like my heart.

'I'm coming with you, Marianne.'

'No, you're not.'

For a minute we just stare at each other, opponents in a game without rules.

'Look, I know things have been strained between us recently, that it's been a difficult journey. The other day I said things I shouldn't have, that I didn't mean . . .'

'You meant every word,' I say, but there's no accusation in my voice. 'And you were right. I was wrong about how to question Ferris, I was wrong to think I should be Viper, and I was very wrong to expect you to stand by while I married Torin. I've been selfish, I see that now.'

His conflict is an open wound and I press into it hard, forcing the pain, driving it through him until he breaks. It's the only way to free him.

'There's nothing for you in the West, Bronn. Go home. Go East. Don't let what you did to Ferris be in vain. Hunt Karn down and destroy him. Be the Viper, just as you always should have been.'

'There's nothing for me in the West? What about you? You think I'm going to leave you here?'

'I have to do this alone.'

Bronn steps towards me now. 'We've come this far. Are we in this together or not?'

My heart is breaking, but I show no sign of my pain. 'Not.'

I see it then in his eyes, the hurt, the cruelty of what I'm doing. The doubt.

'Not?' His voice falters.

'You have a different path from me; you said it yourself. We can't pretend any more.'

'You don't get to choose my path.' His pain is turning to anger.

'Yes, I do. I'm your captain.' I fix my fiercest gaze on him. 'Go home. Keep Torin safe. Protect the East. They are your orders, Snake.'

That's done it, landed the blow with the same accuracy as if I'd knifed him in the guts. His jaw clenches as he withdraws into himself, a wall of cold hostility now separating us.

'Yes, Captain.' Never have two words held so much contempt.

And then he's gone, taking the air from the room with him. Only when the door is shut do my legs give way and I collapse to the floor, smothering my sobs with my fist.

PART TWO
WEST

I am alone. I am heartbroken. And I am lost.

Even the dazzling spectacle of the sparkling sands that welcomed me back to the Eighth Isle wasn't enough to lift my weary spirits. The tingle of magic that travelled up from the sand through my body may have been dizzying, but it only reminded me of the dangerous path I've chosen.

I have left everything I know behind for half a hope, a vain belief that perhaps I can harness magic and can then somehow rally an army behind me. But I've already shown I can't be trusted with magic. And to rally an army I will have to lay claim to a throne long left empty.

And for what? For people who would have watched me hang rather than rise against their king. For a husband I abandoned and who is probably dead. For a man whose heart I just ripped out and who certainly now hates me.

As I traipse my way through the marram forests, rain sluicing down the bamboo-like trunks and turning the sandy ground to sludge, I find one question dominates my thoughts.

Who am I?

Old Tatty said understanding that was the key to mastering magic, but I have no answers. Am I still the

Viper? Perhaps, but an absent one at best. Am I the girl fighting for peace? Sometimes I think she died long ago, crushed by cruelties inflicted upon her. Or am I simply the fool who just turned her back on all she loved for her own selfish gains?

I have no idea any more.

So I push on, determined to stick to the only plan I have. To find Esther and hope she can show me the way.

The problem is, I'm *literally* lost.

The *Storm* approached the island from a different angle than I did when I came before, and I am further south-west this time, leaving me in entirely unknown terrain.

My satchel contains only my essentials: compass, notebooks and a small supply of food and water. My dagger is lodged firmly in my belt, and the knowledge from the books planted deep in my brain. Anything else I might need, I hope Esther can provide once I find her.

If I find her.

All I know is the urgency to track north-east and reach the old woman before nightfall helps drown out the memories of leaving my crew behind. I left without saying goodbye, stowed away secretly under the moon's blind gaze, certain that at the sight of Bronn I would lose all my resolve and stay. But I fear I shall never see him again, never have a chance to explain why I had to leave, never have an opportunity to tell him that, despite everything I've said, I love him with every breath in my body, and that every step away from him is a fresh wound to my tattered heart.

The island is bigger than I'd realised from my limited experience of it, and I'm beginning to think I might not reach Esther's settlement today – or even tomorrow. Last time I was here, the island took me to her, but any hopes it might do the same again are slipping away.

Until a clearing emerges up ahead. For a moment my heart lightens, and I think I've made it, but I quickly realise my mistake. This isn't where Esther lives. This settlement is not only much bigger but is also shrouded in an unwelcoming atmosphere. Still, with the rain lashing down and the light fading, I'm running out of options, and so I cautiously approach the huts nestled in the forest.

I have only ever met one Western inhabitant before and that was Esther. But all my life I've been taught these islands are lawless, the people desperate. I have no idea what I might be walking into here.

Silently I creep through the trees, uncertain how my arrival might be received. But I see no one, the settlement quiet, the only sound the constant torrent of rain against the marram trees. The light is starting to dim, but I can still see well enough to notice a tall structure in the centre of the clearing, round which all the huts are positioned. Intrigued, I wander a little closer. It looks like an unlit pyre – bamboo branches of the marram grass woven together into a pyramid. A pit of ash circles the base of this monument, ringed by rocks that separate it from the sandy ground. At first I think perhaps it's a communal meeting place, a bonfire to keep the people warm while they socialise, but then I see what's attached to the pyramid and recoil.

What I'd mistaken from a distance as decoration are body parts. Fingers, toes, ears, they're all there. Clots of blood, not petals, adorn the bamboo. Clumps of hair hang from the branches, scalps torn from the living before they died. It is a shrine to despair.

'Who are you?'

The voice coming from behind chills me to the bone. I do not want to meet those responsible for such a construction.

Slowly I turn round, my fingers itching to pull my blade free, but my head warning me to stay calm. There are four men in front of me, all with blond hair and pale skin, and they look so similar that they must be brothers.

'I'm searching for a friend and lost my way,' I say, hoping to convince them I'm no threat.

'You shouldn't have come here.' The tallest of the four steps towards me.

'I'm sorry,' I say, standing my ground, though I want to take a step backwards to maintain distance between us. 'I won't stay.'

'No. I mean you shouldn't have *been able* to come here,' he says, and he's frowning. 'We have defences.'

My mind races fast. What kind of defences? I saw nothing. And why would they need them anyway?

'Are you one of them?' the tall man asks, while the other three stare on with cold expressions.

'One of who?' I'm stalling now, trying to decide whether to fight or flee.

'She can't be,' one of the other men says. 'We're protected.'

'But she's here, isn't she?' another argues. 'Maybe our protections have failed.'

'Or maybe we need more powerful shields,' the tallest suggests, before looking back at me. 'I do not think you're one of the Hooded,' he says. 'Are you?'

'No,' I say, wondering who the Hooded might be to inspire such fear.

'Are you a witch?'

'No,' I say again, this time not certain which answer would be the right one.

'You must have some magic to pass on to our land,' the youngest of the men says. 'Our offerings to the shadow demons have kept us safe from intruders for a long time, yet now here you are.'

Shadow demons? Offerings? I'm not liking the sound of any of this.

'I'm sorry,' the tallest man says. 'Truly I am. But we

will do whatever we must to protect our people, our land.'

'I mean no harm to any of you,' I say, sensing the shift in the air. I may not be a threat to them, but I can tell they most definitely are to me.

'Whatever magic you possess should please the shadow demons. Your sacrifice will keep us protected for some time.'

Sacrifice?

The prospect of being carved up as an offering makes my blood run cold, and now I pull my dagger free. 'Just let me go and we'll pretend none of this happened,' I say.

'We can't let you go,' the man says. 'Though we take no pleasure in it.'

And before I can strike, something sharp hits my neck, instantly spreading a cold numbness through my body. One of the men has blown a dart into my skin, and whatever poison it was dipped in is rendering me immobile.

They move in to catch me before I fall, and I want to fight but my limbs won't work properly, and my blade drops from my hand.

Their touch is rough as they hold me upright; I'm like a child's rag doll in a violent game. I have never been so powerless, so unable to defend myself – a fact that terrifies me almost as much as the knowledge of what's about to happen.

The tallest man approaches me. 'We'll make this quick,' he says, raising his weapon, a sharp arrowhead attached to a small handle. 'And we thank you for your sacrifice.'

One of the other men grabs a handful of my hair, holding it taut. Bloody hell, they're going to scalp me where I stand. I can't even close my eyes to hide from what's coming, can't ignore the dried blood still staining the weapon aimed at my head. But it also means I can't help but see the massive bird as it swoops silently from the heavens, sharp claws aiming for his target.

Talon is a deadly hunter, and he marks his prey, tearing flesh from the back of my attacker's neck, making him cry out in pain and surprise.

Shrieking a demand at the others to stay back, the sea vulture lands on my shoulder and removes the dart with his beak, before immediately commencing a fresh attack on the men who meant to kill me.

I watch with a mixture of awe, admiration and horror as Talon targets their faces, scratching at eyes, cheeks, ears – anywhere vulnerable he can sink his claws into.

With the dart removed my body is already beginning to return to normal. I can feel my blood flowing properly once again and will it to hurry up.

'Kill the damn bird!' The tall brother, now clutching at his neck where Talon attacked him, screams to one of the others, who stands watching in horror as Talon attacks his sibling, his fierce wings batting anyone away who comes close.

'You'll hurt him over my dead body,' I warn, as I struggle to my feet, picking up my dagger as I do so.

With all the strength I possess I hurl myself at the only uninjured brother, who's taking aim at Talon, and knock us both to the ground, where I land a hefty blow to his head, rendering him unconscious. Then I call to Talon, wanting him to leave the other brother before he tears him to pieces. The bird obediently flies to land on my outstretched arm, screeching at the men to keep their distance.

'I'm going to leave,' I say, as they stare, struck with panic and shock. 'If you try to stop me, or follow me, *you'll* be the ones in pieces.'

Before they can regroup, I stumble as fast as I can out of the clearing, allowing the forest to swallow me whole, Talon flying in front of me guiding the way.

With poison still in my veins my legs aren't functioning properly yet, but I don't stop moving, getting back up every time I trip and fall. Talon stays silent, protecting our location, but keeps close to me, and his presence offers all the reassurance I need. I don't know why he came after me, or how he found me, but I'm no longer in this strange place alone. It feels good to have a friend.

'Can you find the way to Esther's?' I whisper to him, and he nuzzles my hair in reply.

Through the night we keep moving, though the marram forest positively crackles with danger. But I know Talon's sight isn't affected by the darkness, and trust that he will warn me of any imminent threat as he leads me through the labyrinth of trees.

The rain has mercifully stopped now, but the ground is still squelchy, and the damp has caused the ring of wind through the hollow bamboo trunks to take on a deeper tone. I can't decide whether the sound is beautiful or eerie.

Dawn breaks and still we don't stop. I fear the brothers might be in pursuit or – worse – that whoever they're afraid of might discover me. The Hooded. I don't want to meet them right now.

My body is almost entirely recovered from the poison dart. I'm hungry and thirsty, but determined not to stop until I'm in the safety of Esther's enchanted clearing. Once I'm there, she can tell me what's going on, and what I need to do. I just have to get there.

It's twilight when I recognise a familiar fork in the path that I know will lead me towards Esther, and a wave of relief floods through me. I'm almost there. But it doesn't take long for that brief consolation to fade.

Something's wrong. The atmosphere is colder than I remember, the colours faded. The path that summoned me to Esther's clearing once before now says nothing and I already know what I'm going to find long before the huts come into view.

214

There is no one here.

Esther's absence is everywhere, from the withered leaves on the trees to the lack of birdsong in the air. I go to her house and peer inside. It's empty, all trace of habitation long gone. Gone too are her jars, her potions that filled the shelves. I wander around looking for any sign of a struggle, any hint that something bad happened to her, but find nothing. It's as if she simply disappeared from existence.

I drift back outside, clueless as to what to do next. This was my entire plan. Without Esther I'm stranded on an island I know nothing about, with no way to learn magic, and no idea how to find the Guardians, or anyone else who can help me. And I scream with frustration.

Talon flies to perch on the ground beside me, gently nipping at my leg. I open my satchel and take a small bit of sea biscuit out, breaking it in half for us to share. He swallows his piece whole while I nibble unenthusiastically on my half of the dry wafer. In the end I toss the last of it to Talon, who devours it in seconds.

'What am I going to do?' I say to him, stroking his feathers gently. The bird tilts his head at me, his gaze piercing. 'I shouldn't have left the others,' I say, finding it comforting to confide in someone who can't talk back. 'I should have stayed in the East and rallied an attack on the palace to save Torin and kill the King.' But even as I say the words I know it would never have worked. We'd have all died in the attempt, massively outnumbered by the King's Guard. And then there would be no way to restore the peace. I'd rather have broken Bronn's heart, and my own, than seen him dead.

Tired and despairing, the mere thought of Bronn brings tears to my eyes. I miss him already, though it's barely been two days. But it's the knowledge that the number of days without him will only grow that makes me forget how to breathe.

I shouldn't stay here. Without Esther's enchantments I'm sure it's not safe. But where is there for me to go? Exhausted I lie back in the dirt and close my eyes. Talon will wake me if he needs to.

When I do wake up, it's with a start. It's still early, the light weak as it struggles to stake its claim on the day, and my sea vulture is nowhere to be seen. Hoping he's just gone hunting for breakfast, I eat a little of my own.

I've awoken with a renewed sense of clarity. I'm where I'm supposed to be. It's only here that I can find magic, an army or both, and I must find them fast. I have to get home before the next blood moon – to save Torin. And then maybe together we can unite these islands as we longed to do in the first place.

Which means I'm going to have to try to find Esther. She's the only link I have to this land. I'm certain Talon can help me; sea vultures can find anyone. I just need to wait for him to return.

But he does not. I scavenge the huts for anything that might be useful – a fruitless task, but as I remember the many potions and ingredients that once filled the shelves I'm reminded of my love for the art of healing. It's been lost under the immense weight of needing to save the people, and the seductive power of magic. I must not forget who I was. Who I am. Someone more drawn to heal than to hurt. I've drifted a long way from that person. It's time to find my way back.

The sound of breaking twigs interrupts my thoughts. Someone's coming and it's not Talon. Perhaps Esther's returning, or it could be the brothers, having tracked me down, intent on claiming their sacrifice. I'm back out of the hut in a split second, and stand ready to defend myself against any attack, dagger drawn. My nerves rattle as the sound comes closer but then the marram grasses part and my breath catches in my throat. Ambling towards me with its head low is the most beautiful horse I've ever seen. Feathered feet, trailing tail, a shaggy mane – the horse is the colour of moonlight. Wise eyes peer out from behind the long forelock, staring right at me. I don't need to be a Mage to know it's no ordinary horse, nor this a chance encounter. It walks with calm confidence directly towards me and when it's an arm's length away, it stretches out its muzzle for me to stroke. When my fingers reach its nose, warmth spreads through them and into my blood; the reassuring, familiar whisper of magic binds us as we touch. The horse snorts contentedly and then, to my astonishment, it lowers its front legs and bows. I do the only polite thing and bow back.

Introductions made, I walk closer and pat the mare on her silken neck. 'You're a beauty, aren't you?' I swear she nods her head in response. 'Where did you come from? Do you know what happened here?'

I'm not actually expecting a response, but I almost wouldn't be surprised if she gave one. She doesn't speak, though. Instead she turns her head round to nudge me, nibbling at my sleeve. When I don't respond, she nudges harder.

'What?' I follow her gaze and smile. 'You want me to come with you?'

Now she makes a joyful whinny and I laugh. It's as if she knew I'd need a guide. I'm hardly overwhelmed with other options. Though I hate to leave without Talon, it just feels *right* to be with the horse. And Talon should be able to find me wherever I go. He's done it before.

'All right then,' I say, as I jump on to her back. 'But I should warn you, I'm not the best rider.'

The mare shakes her head as if to tell me it hardly matters. She's in charge. All I have to do is hold on. But she takes careful steps as we move out of Esther's clearing, moving slowly for me as I become accustomed to my position. I twine my fingers into her mane and begin to relax, sensing I can trust this horse to look after me.

She's taking me inland, away from the water, and north, in a direction I've never been. A flutter of anticipation tickles in my chest at the prospect of exploring more of the island. I've only ever seen the marram forests, and while their beauty is mesmerising, the chance to see beyond is exciting. The mare is certainly very purposeful; she knows exactly where she's going, and I feel sure we're headed towards Esther. Who else could have sent me an escort?

We travel for a long time, the day passing without any sign of Talon or anyone else, and it's after noon when the horse comes to a halt. I've allowed myself to relax and it takes me a moment to realise the atmosphere has shifted, that the horse is tense beneath me, and there is a specific kind of fear to be tasted on the air.

We're being hunted.

I lean down towards the mare's neck and whisper, 'What's wrong?'

She throws her head to the left, indicating that's where danger lies, and I turn slowly to look, simultaneously sliding my dagger from my boot.

To start with I can see nothing, just the darkness among the giant grasses, but then I glimpse it – the glint of eyes.

The she-wolf launches at us before I've even had time

to process what's happening. The horse rears up, and I clutch at her mane to stop from sliding off, but then the she-wolf is leaping at the mare's breast, sinking her fangs deep into the horse's flesh. I lean over to plunge my dagger into the she-wolf's neck as the mare screams. Immediately she releases the horse, who isn't waiting around for another attack and sets off at such a gallop it's all I can do to cling on.

She races through the forest, not slowing despite her injury, weaving effortlessly in and out of the trees for what feels like for ever, until she begins to stagger and eventually comes to a halt in a particularly dense part of the forest. There is no sound apart from my heart racing and the laboured breathing of my steed. I leap from her back moments before she falls to her knees and then collapses on to her side. She's dying.

Soothing her as best I can, I run my hands down her neck towards the wound. Fresh blood spills down her white hair, and I can see it's deep – too deep. I have nothing but the few items in my satchel and the clothes I'm wearing, so I tear the sleeve off my shirt and press it down hard to staunch the bleeding. The horse whimpers, and I stroke her head, desperate to help but not knowing how. I scan around us, searching for anything that bears a similarity to my remedies, and my gaze falls on a tall grass with blue seedpods balanced precariously at the tips. I recognise it from a sketch in one of my books but can't remember its exact properties. And yet I'm drawn towards it, something telling me this is medicinal rather than poisonous. Grabbing a handful of the pods, I split them open, sending plumes of sapphire dust into the air. Salvaging as much of the powder as I can, I spit on it, using the tip of my finger to mix dust to paste. Once it's thick and gloopy, I smear it over the horse's wound, pressing it into the warm flesh to plug the bleeding hole.

It's an act of instinct and only once it's finished do I wonder if I've done the right thing. For all I know I've just forced poison straight into the horse's bloodstream. When she fails to improve, my shoulders drop as low as my spirits. The mare can join the list of those I couldn't save, and I gently lift her head to rest in my lap, smoothing the forelock absent-mindedly as I wait for death to claim her.

But then the smell of burning reaches my nose, and to my horror I see the wound is bubbling, smoke rising from the damaged tissue. The horse pulls away from me, crying in pain, shaking her head in protest as she struggles to stand. Uttering a piercing shriek, she gallops off, swallowed up by the immensity of the forest.

I stare after her for far longer than is necessary because I have no idea what just happened. My confidence is shaken. If I can't trust my instincts, then what do I have left?

The horse brought me a long way inland, and I can

see the edge of the forest approaching, tantalising close. All that lies ahead of me is the vast mountainous range and that's certainly the direction the horse fled.

I have to know what I did to her, have to know what that plant was capable of, and so I decide to follow the trail of blood she left in her wake. If I'm being honest, I also have to know if she's lying somewhere in terrible agony, so that I can put her out of her misery if needs be. It's a thought I don't relish.

It's not hard to track her. Blood and hoofprints are enough for even the most inexperienced hunter to trace. I soon emerge from the cover of the forest and stare up at the climb before me. I'm woefully ill-equipped for a trek up a mountain, but what else can I do? And so I begin the journey, hoping I'll stumble across the mare before too long.

Hours pass. There's no sign of the horse, but as the path winds higher the temperature falls and my teeth begin to chatter as I slowly lose all sensation in my extremities. I'm confused. The droplets of blood have ceased and on this rocky surface there's no way to see hoof marks, but this must be the way the horse came. There's no other route apart from this worn-out old track. That I've not found her yet makes no sense.

I press on, fully aware of how aimless this search is becoming, and how it highlights my lack of direction and my woeful ignorance of this island. But perhaps she's returning to Esther – after all, who else could have sent her to me? And I have to find Esther, I just have to. Otherwise I've failed, and everything I've left behind, everything I've done – all those barbed words I used to impale Bronn's heart – will have been for nothing. So I keep walking, even as the snow begins to fall, searching for an invisible horse.

As night wraps its deadly cloak round me, the temperature drops even further and I know I'm in trouble. If I don't find some shelter soon, I'm going to die up on this desolate mountain. The path all but seems to have disappeared, and I'm climbing aimlessly. My feet are numb blocks at the end of my legs, and I've started to trip and stumble over rocks my frozen toes can't detect, when I hear something. The faintest sound of a horse whinnying.

Tired and freezing, I head towards the noise, wanting to find the animal it came from, hoping it's my mare. Tonight may be the last for both of us, but better we spend it together than apart. The wind is whipping up now, the blizzard near blinding me, but still I keep walking. Eventually I reach a copse of ice trees, their pale blue trunks shimmering even as their branches obliterate the light of the moon. This time when I fall to the ground I lack the energy to get back up, the strong gale buffeting me down, so instead I crawl on my hands and knees towards the sound.

The cold has coiled round me like creeping ivy,

binding my body with invisible ropes so that I can barely heave myself along, but as I reach the edge of the copse I see light. Fire. And a hut. A strangled cry of hope escapes from my mouth and I'm just about to attempt the struggle to my feet when a heavy boot crushes down on my shoulder and the end of a spear is thrust into my face.

'Stay there.' The voice is as harsh as the terrain. 'What are you doing here?'

I raise my hands as best I can in surrender, wishing I wasn't frozen into incapacitation. 'I'm looking for a horse.' Maybe it's not wise to have been honest, but my wits are dulled, my brain trapped in a fog.

There's a pause, and while I can't lift my head enough to see my attacker's face, I can sense fury spiking off her like razors.

'Rayvn!' Another voice is calling in the distance. 'What is it?'

The blow to my head comes swiftly and I black out. When I come to, I'm being dragged along by my left leg, which is doing a surprisingly good job of reviving me.

'Rayvn, what are you doing?' The other voice is closer now and I look up to see two women standing over me. They are undoubtedly sisters, with hair the colour of the ocean's depths and features that are almost identical yet entirely different. The woman holding my leg is all angles and edges, whilst the other has kindness smoothing

224

the steely glint in her eyes. They are both buried under heavy layers of cloaks and hoods – a stark contrast to my one layer, which is damp from snow.

'Found her on the boundary. She's come for the horses.'

The woman who is not Rayvn looks at me now and sees I'm conscious. Frowning, she steps over to squat beside me.

'Is that true? You here for the horses?' Her eyes burn into me, her lips set straight, and it strikes me there's something about her that seems familiar. Like somehow we've met before.

'Not horses, horse.' I'm struggling to speak my face is so numb. 'It was dying.'

Her squint deepens, while Rayvn's grip tightens on my leg. 'What are you talking about?' She turns to her sister. 'Let her go.'

My leg is unceremoniously released and I shuffle to sit up, wondering if the feeling will ever return to my fingers. 'Is Esther here?'

The woman frowns. 'Who?'

'I was looking for her . . . She sent me the horse, but then we were attacked and she was injured . . . the horse I mean, and I tracked it this way.' The stream of words is garbled and I'm dimly aware that my brain is slowing down. The woman is looking at me with such surprise I wonder if my words actually came out in the

225

right order.

'What's your name?' And the same kindness that softens her features is abundantly clear in her voice now.

'Marianne.'

'I'm Olwyn,' she says, and she shrugs off one of her many layers and wraps it round my shoulders. 'I think we need to talk. Let's get you inside.'

'Thank you,' I say, reaching for the hand she's extended. But as my fingers do their best to curl round hers, my heart stops entirely. Because on her wrist is a birthmark. It's faint, almost undetectable, but I'd recognise it anywhere.

She bears the mark of the crescent moon.

12

The hut is small, the fire that blazes warming every nook and cranny. Olwyn guides me to sit beside it, ignoring her sister's protests, and then covers me in blankets.

'Olwyn, stop this madness,' Rayvn says, her spear still firmly in her hand. 'What are you thinking?'

Olwyn ignores her sister. 'Are you hungry?' she says to me. 'Some warm soup perhaps?'

I nod as best I can, the heat from the fire causing a burning pain in my limbs as it defrosts them. Still, it's not quite as fierce as the stare Rayvn fixes on me, her gaze never lifting.

As Olwyn sets a pot over the flames, a small figure appears from a back room, a young girl with features finer than a bird's, who couldn't be past her twelfth year. Her face is the image of her older sisters', but more delicate and while their hair is blacker than jetstone, hers is bright white, just like the horse who led me here.

'Olwyn?' She's clearly nervous of my presence.

Olwyn springs to her feet and walks over to the girl. 'Pip, everything's fine, go back to sleep.'

'No.' Rayvn glares at Olwyn. 'It's not fine. You've brought a stranger into our home. You've put us all in danger.'

Pip's eyes widen with fear, but Olwyn just sighs. 'Calm yourself,' she says. The words are gently spoken but with enough authority to quieten Rayvn. 'Pip, why don't you come and meet our guest?'

And with her arms protectively wrapped round her little sister Olwyn brings Pip nearer me.

'Pipit, this is Marianne. Rayvn found her on the boundary, looking for one of our mares.' Now Olwyn looks at me, but it isn't suspicion in her eyes, more curiosity. 'Is that right?'

Again a nod is all my frozen body can muster, though I desperately want to ask her who she is how she has the same birthmark as me, and what that could possibly mean.

'Would you fetch our guest some soup, while I speak with Rayvn?' Olwyn asks Pip, who nods while the older sisters huddle in a corner and argue in loud but indecipherable whispers.

Pip nervously passes me a mug and I'm about to take it when I pause. I have no idea who these women are and have lowered my guard too far already. The last residents I met on this island wanted to drug and kill me. Who's to say these sisters won't do the same?

'Oh, for goodness' sake,' Rayvn says, striding over when she sees my hesitation. 'If we wanted to kill you, we'd stick you with a spear.' And she grabs the mug from Pip, taking a large mouthful of the soup to prove it's safe to eat. 'If you don't like our hospitality, you can always leave,' she says, and holds the soup out like a challenge. I rise to it, and the liquid slips like fire down my throat.

'Thank you,' I say after another few mouthfuls, the hearty broth reviving me from the inside out. 'And don't worry, I'm not here to hurt your horses.'

Pip looks reassured, but Rayvn is less easy to placate.

'So what do you want with them?' Rayvn says, and I sense that whatever Olwyn has said to her means she will tolerate my presence at least long enough to hear an explanation.

I tell them everything that's happened since I discovered Esther's abandoned home, leaving out some of the details of my failed attempt at healing, but hoping the rest of the story explains why I've stumbled on to their very remote land. 'But obviously I was mistaken,' I finish. 'Esther isn't here.' Though I'm beginning to suspect this might be exactly where the horse intended to bring me all along.

The three of them are all staring at me – Rayvn in confusion mixed with outrage, Olwyn in amazement and Pip in disbelief, her mouth hanging open.

'What?' They're making me suddenly uncomfortable.

'You rode the mare?' Olwyn sounds in awe, though it seems an odd thing to focus on in the scheme of the story. 'She let you?'

I nod, watching Olwyn and Rayvn exchange a very meaningful look.

'Pip, go wake up Mama,' Rayvn says, and for the first time she puts down her spear.

The girl obediently disappears into the back room, while Olwyn and Rayvn come to sit closer to me.

'Who are you?' It's the firmest Olwyn has been since I arrived.

'I told you. My name is Marianne.'

Her eyes narrow. 'You know that's not what I'm asking.'

We're both desperate to know more about each other, but neither of us is willing to be the first to take a step of trust.

'Do you know what you did?' When I look blank, she carries on. 'You rode a snow mare.'

I must still look blank, as Ravyn now speaks up.

'No one rides the snow mares,' she says.

'Oh.' I'm not sure what that could possibly imply. Have I broken some ancient law? A forbidden taboo? A protective order?

Pip returns, leading a frail old woman by the arm.

'Where is she?' The old woman's voice is far sturdier than I was expecting.

'Here, Mama,' Olwyn says, helping Pip guide the woman to the chair next to me. 'Marianne, this is our grandmother.'

Mama turns her head towards me and I see her eyes are misty, her vision impaired by the cloudy film over their lenses. She's reaching her hand out, and so I take it in mine, feeling my coldness soak away her warmth.

'Is it you?' she says. 'Is it possible?'

I glance up to Olwyn for an explanation but her face remains impassive. 'I'm sorry,' I say. 'I'm not sure what you mean.'

'You rode a mare,' Mama says. 'That hasn't happened in living memory.'

I'm reluctant to be the first to divulge much about myself so I try to turn things around. 'Your birthmark,' I say to Olwyn. 'Do you all have one?'

There's a perceptible shift in the atmosphere, and I recognise fear when I see it.

'What birthmark?' Olwyn fails to sound nonchalant.

'The one on your wrist. Do you know what it is?' When no one answers, I say, 'You bear the mark of the crescent moon.'

Mama's grip instantly becomes vice-like. 'How do you know of the mark?' There is both urgency and threat in her voice.

I hesitate for a moment. I don't know these people and I have no reason to trust them. Yet I trusted the horse who brought me here and I cannot shake the deep feeling of familiarity about them. I decide to take a chance.

I lift my hair and turn to show them the back of my neck. 'Because I bear it too.'

Once more the atmosphere shifts, the fear melting away to be replaced by sheer shock. Mama, though, starts to nod knowingly.

'I knew it was you,' she says. 'Who else could you be?'

Olwyn kneels beside her grandmother and rests her hand on her lap. 'You know who this is, Mama?'

Mama turns towards me, her smile wide now. 'Of course I do. She's our queen.'

Aware all eyes are locked on me, I try to think of something to say, but words are failing me fast. 'I'm really not,' I say, wanting them to stop looking at me like that, like I'm something special. 'But I am descended from the royal bloodline, so if you have the mark . . . I'm guessing that means we're related?'

Mama nods, squeezing my hands with real affection now. 'Only very distantly, but yes. We are. And you've returned to us finally. I thought I'd be in the ground before that day came.'

'*She's* our queen?' Rayvn sounds entirely unimpressed.

'Rayvn.' Mama only needs one word to scold her granddaughter.

'It's fine,' I say. 'Trust me, I haven't come with any expectations of claiming the throne.'

Mama gives a small smile. 'So why are you here?'

I sigh. 'It's a very long story.'

232

Their silence invites me to continue and when I don't, Mama says, 'Then it can wait for dawn. You must be very tired. Let us all return to sleep and we will talk when we are refreshed. The moon has already heard her fair share of revelations.'

Pip helps her grandmother back to bed, while Olwyn fetches me even more blankets to lie on beside the fire. Rayvn is the only one of us not settling down; instead she picks up her spear and strides out into the cold night air once more.

'She's on duty tonight,' Olwyn says when she sees me staring at the shut door. 'Don't take anything she says too personally.'

I smile at the young woman beside me, hardly daring to believe I've found someone I can legitimately call family, no matter how distant. 'I'm sorry I trespassed on your land.'

'You didn't.' She laughs at my confusion. 'What I mean is, if one of the mares came down the mountain to meet you, and brought you here, then it was no trespass. This land is their land as much as ours. If one of the mares wanted you here, you belong.' Her voice is giddy with excitement.

'Do you know if she's alive? Has she returned?'

Olwyn shakes her head. 'We don't own the herd; we're simply their protectors. But tomorrow we'll go and see if we can find your injured mare. Don't worry, they're warrior horses – far tougher than they look.'

'Thank you. For everything. You could have left me out there to die.'

'It's so strange,' she says. 'I just felt like we'd met before . . . that I knew you somehow and had to help you. Maybe it's because we're related?'

'Maybe. Whatever the reason, I'm glad of it.'

'Sleep well, Cousin,' she says, and then she leaves me alone with only the crackle of fire for company.

To say I feel overwhelmed would be an understatement. If I'd had any expectations of what might happen once I arrived in the West, they've been truly shattered. I've nearly died twice, and discovered I still have living, breathing kin. I've been unable to find a single trace of the woman I was relying on to teach me magic – and without Esther I can't train to be a Mage. Without becoming a Mage I can't return magic to the East, and peace won't be restored. And as for raising any kind of army? Considering the state I was in when they found me, I don't think this small family would be willing to lay down their lives to back me anytime soon.

Still, there's nothing to be gained from worrying about that now. Tomorrow will come soon enough and, perhaps with it, some answers. Or at least a way forward. And so I close my eyes and though I try desperately not to think of Bronn, his face is all I see before sleep obliterates everything.

*　　　*　　　*

A spider scuttling across my forehead wakes me. The fire has burned out, but the blankets have locked warmth round me so I'm nicely cocooned. The image strikes a chord in me, like a slipped memory of something important I've forgotten. Had I been dreaming about a woman in a cocoon? Delving into my fuzzy mind, I try to think what it might mean, but then the door opens, bringing Rayvn and a cold blast of air in, and blowing the thought out.

'You're awake,' Rayvn says. Not a question, just a statement. I don't quite know how to respond to her relentless frostiness.

So I peel myself free from the blankets and, though it's freezing outside them, get up to join her.

'I'm sorry about last night,' I say, rubbing my arms briskly with my hands. 'I hope I didn't startle you too much.'

She laughs a humourless laugh. 'I've seen rabbits more frightening than you.'

'You definitely didn't catch me at my best,' I say, but the look of disgust she throws my way suggests she thinks very little of what my best might be.

'Whatever. I need sleep. There's kindling outside.' And without a backwards glance Rayvn disappears into the back room, leaving me alone again. I'm not feeling confident about my chances of winning her round, and right now I don't have the energy to care.

Instead I grab the thickest of my blankets, and, wrapping it round myself like a shawl, I venture out into the crisp morning air to bring in wood for the fire.

Covered in fresh snow and bathed in early-morning sun, the mountain positively gleams. For a moment I just stand there, revelling in its unique beauty. I've never seen anything like this before. It's bleak, it's inhospitable and it's perfection all at once.

The hut is set high up in a clearing, and directly in front of me is the treeline that I emerged from last night. To the right the hut is flanked by rock, but to the left there is a flat stretch of white powder leading to a barn, and it's there that I head, sinking a lot further than I expect into the snow with every step. I'm going to have to ask Olwyn if I can borrow some more suitable footwear for the duration of my stay. As I gather an armful of logs from the neatly stacked pile I find in the barn, I wonder how long that might be. Obviously I can't linger here – I'm fairly certain Rayvn would have something to say about that even if I wanted to – but right now I'm clueless where to go next. I'm hopeful Mama might be able to help me; she must know the island well enough to give me some idea where Esther might have gone. Meanwhile I can't deny that the prospect of spending some time here, and getting to know these people whose blood I share, is appealing. There's a peace up on this mountain that's seductive, a solitude that makes the rest of the world feel far away.

But I remember all too well what happened the last time I sought to escape my reality with a loving family. What violence I brought upon them. Hiding from my life has never ended well for those around me, and I will not condemn these people to the same fate as Joren, Clara and Tomas. I will get what assistance I can and then I will leave them in peace. I take a deep breath and walk back to the hut, hoping that Talon finds me soon. I miss my feathered friend.

I have the fire nicely roaring by the time Olwyn comes through and she greets me with a pile of clothing.

'You'll need more layers if we're to go searching for the mare,' she says, opening a barrel and removing some preserved meat from a cloth. 'Snow hare,' she says, passing me some on a plate. 'Not the tastiest, but it keeps well.'

'Thank you.' The meat is bitter, but my stomach is glad for some nourishment no matter how unpleasant.

'Mama wants to speak with you and then we'll head out,' Olwyn says, and she sounds excited at the prospect. 'She's waiting for you in her room. Through there and on the left.'

She gives me some meat for Mama, and then I head, slightly nervously, to where Olwyn's directed.

Mama is sitting up in her bed, and when she hears me approach her face lightens with a warm smile. 'Marianne, you slept well I trust?'

'Very, thank you,' I say, placing the meat into her hands and sitting further down the bed.

'I shan't detain you long, my dear. I know Olwyn is keen to show you the herd. But I think you have questions that I might be able to help with, is that right?'

'Yes.'

'Then ask me, and if I can, I will answer.'

'I've come from the East,' I start, thinking it's best to be honest with her about my situation and my intentions. The last thing I want to do is give a false impression of myself. 'The Isles are at war with themselves, the people are suffering and I can't bear it any longer. Returning West was my last resort.'

Mama nods but looks confused. 'You came here to escape?'

'No, I came here for help. I came to seek my friend Esther, hoping for her guidance. But I found her gone. Do you have any idea what might have happened to her?'

Mama may be old in age, but her mind is fast. I can almost hear it making connections. 'You came for magic?'

'Yes.' I can almost feel my relief pour out of me. She must be aware of Esther, to know that I'd be seeking her in order to find magic. 'Do you know her?'

Mama shakes her head. 'No, but I have heard of her, though not for many years.'

My hope from moments ago fades. 'So you can't help me?'

'Not with finding your friend, no, I'm sorry. But if you live in the East, how did you meet Esther? Why were you here before?'

I take a moment. 'Can I trust you?'

She gives a wry smile. 'You strike me as someone who doesn't truly trust anyone.'

Her bluntness strikes a nerve. Perhaps it's true. I have plenty of reasons not to, the main one being that Adler lied to me my whole life. Maybe it's affected me more than I've realised. Maybe it's what fed my insecurities with Bronn. At the thought of Bronn a fresh sadness blooms around my scarred heart. But I realise in order to have any kind of meaningful dialogue with Mama I'm going to have to tell her the truth, and so I explain what happened to my parents, that I was stolen and raised by a murderer, and how I learned the truth last year. When I speak of Grace the words are accompanied by another crushing pain round my heart. I don't think I'll ever stop missing her.

When my story is told, Mama reaches for my hand, her fragile skin cradling my sorrow. 'I see your path has been a difficult one. I am sorry to hear of your parents' death.'

Her quiet sympathy disarms me and for a foolish moment I think I might cry. The weight of all the burdens I'm trying to carry seems too much, and suddenly I'm just a scared little girl, all alone, and heartsick with grief for those I've lost.

'I don't know what to do.' It's a relief just to admit that out loud. To myself. To anyone. And in the maternal presence of Mama, I feel perfectly safe saying it.

She squeezes my fingers, a weak movement, but enough for me to feel it. 'I'm afraid I don't either, nor do I envy you the responsibility that passed to you at your birth. But there are things I may be able to tell you. Things from long ago that seemed forgotten but have reawakened.'

'I'm listening.' The rawness of complete honesty is already a healing wound, my vulnerability being smothered in steely determination. I have to keep going, have to find a way.

'As you deduced from our faded birthmarks, we too are descended from the bloodline. But far more distantly than you. Long ago, when wise Kings and Queens ruled the Western Isles peacefully, our less-esteemed branch of the family was given the noble commission to protect the snow mares. They are magical beasts and must be kept safe at all costs. Only the King and Queen of the Western Isles were permitted to ride them – our job was merely to keep them protected. It has been an honour and a hardship, but our solitude meant we survived the war all those centuries ago, when the rest of the royal bloodline was all but wiped out. We were the only survivors – or so we thought.'

'Did your ancestors ever seek to claim the throne?'

Mama laughs. 'Never. Power is not something that interests my family. Our lives in these mountains have always been simple and isolated. You are only the second person ever to have come here.'

The loneliness of their existence is striking, but I know that's not the important thing she's telling me. 'Who was the first?'

'You're shrewd. I like that. I was a little girl when the visitor came. My mother welcomed him in and I listened by the door as he spoke of his mission. He called himself a Guardian of the Royal Bloodline, and told us how he was one of many committed to keeping the surviving heir safe. To start with my mother thought he meant us, and feared they had come to take me away, but he assured her there was another survivor, a direct descendant, and it was this line they would one day bring back to the throne. He simply thought we deserved to know the truth, that we were not the only remains of our kin.'

'And he never came back?'

'No, but we received word from him and then eventually his successor every few years by sea vulture, though the birds detest coming this far inland.'

Interesting. I wonder if that's why I've not seen Talon yet. 'When did you last hear from the Guardians?'

'The final message I received was almost twenty years ago, to say they'd lost your mother, though they continued to seek her, and if I were to hear word of her, to make contact.'

'Did you know that she was here?'

Mama shakes her head. 'But I wonder, was it coincidence she came to this island?'

I frown. 'What do you mean?'

'Have you never asked yourself why she was friends with Esther? Could it be for the very same reason you seek her?'

'You think she was becoming a Mage?' My pulse quickens at the mere possibility.

'Perhaps,' Mama says, though lightly, as if she knows I'm already leaping to all sorts of conclusions. 'But I will end by saying this. The only thing I know of magic is what I witness in the snow mares. I see its allure. And I see its danger. We may live an isolated life, but we hear things, whispers on the wind. Royalty and Mages walked hand in hand in the days before darkness descended, but though history would present the union as harmonious, ancient rumours should lead you to be cautious of that assumption. Those who find power do not like to share. Be mindful of that, Marianne.'

'I will,' I say. I have, after all, seen first-hand what being challenged has done to the King, what desperate acts he's been driven to.

'Now go and find Olwyn. Today, put all other cares aside and be reunited with the horses that have always been so synonymous with your family. It is a day to be cherished, not wasted on worry.'

'Do you want to come with us?'

Mama chuckles. 'No, I shall celebrate this momentous occasion by indulging in an early-morning nap – the first of many I shall have today. My bones are too old for such excitement.'

I smile, a rush of affection for this woman warming me from the inside out. 'All right, I'll check in on you when we return. And thank you for the advice.'

Mama's eyes are already closed as she lies backwards. 'Welcome home, child,' she murmurs before sleep claims her.

When I return to the front room, Olwyn is already waiting and passes me a fur to wrap over my many layers, and then a cloak. Finally she hands me a spear.

'Can you use one of these?'

I raise an eyebrow as I take it from her. 'What are we expecting to find out there?'

She shrugs. 'You never know. There's been an ice lion lurking around recently, but there are worse threats to the mares.'

Instinctively I know she means humans and wonder if she's heard of the Hooded, if the threat that makes people fearful in the forests below has reached them here high up in the mountains. I have so many questions about the Western Isles, but as we venture outside, our feet crunching in the deep snow, I ask instead about her, needing to understand this isolated existence.

'I don't mind it up here,' she says, as we traipse round the back of the hut, where a flat white plain stretches out like a moonlit ocean before the plateau meets the rocks once more. 'It's all we've ever known, and all we ever will know.'

'You've never left the mountain?'

Olwyn shakes her head. 'I'll only leave to find a mate.'

'What?' I fail to mask my surprise.

'How do you think we survive? Once the first of the youngest generation reaches her twentieth year, she must prepare to head down the mountain with the snow mares to find a mate.'

I'm confused. 'I thought you said the snow mares didn't leave the mountain.'

'They don't – apart from in the mating season. When the sea stallions roll in to shore, the mares go to meet them.'

My brain tries to absorb this information. 'Sea stallions?'

'Water horses. Once they came every year to visit the

mares, but since the royalty disappeared, they've come less frequently. They last came eleven years ago, and who knows when they'll next return.' Olwyn glances at me. 'It's possible now you're here, they'll be back sooner.'

'And when they come, you'll go to a nearby settlement and find someone to impregnate you?'

Olwyn nods.

'And you're OK with that?'

'It's my duty,' she says, but her split-second hesitation has told me everything I need to know about how she truly feels.

'Maybe the sea stallions won't return?'

Olwyn's sadness is palpable. 'Maybe. But then, eventually, the snow mares will die out. And we'll have failed in our service.'

Always duty enslaves us. Whether it be my responsibilities, Torin's, Bronn's, or Olwyn's, there's always some external force binding each of us to paths we did not choose. Would it really be so terrible if we all just walked away? Turned our backs on what we ought to do, and embraced what we wanted?

Isn't that what you've done? The small voice in my head has a point. Whatever my reasons or justifications, I've come West to pursue the art of magic. It may be the only way I could see of saving the East, but it is also a magnificently selfish act. A worm of discomfort stirs in my belly, and I remember all the warnings I've gathered on my way so far. Giving in to my own desires and wishes will lead to madness and corruption. I must fight magic's tempting call, which is coming ever more frequently.

I'm about to ask Olwyn why Rayvn's taken such an instant dislike to me, when she grabs my arm.

'Look.'

She points ahead of us and, though the mare is expertly camouflaged, I can see her unmistakable outline descending the sheer rock face towards us as though it was the easiest thing in the world.

Olwyn's reverence for the horse is immediately clear as she takes a step backwards. 'We're not supposed to get close to them,' she says in a whisper.

'I don't think we're getting a choice,' I say, as the horse canters across the plateau. It is undoubtedly the same mare I rode, and she dances with excitement to see me, throwing her head round in greeting as she draws close. I can hear Olwyn gasp as the mare slows to a walk, but I'm not really paying attention because I'm looking for the mare's injury and struggling to believe what I'm seeing. She comes to stand within arm's reach of us and then with all the grace in the world, once again she bows.

'Hello,' I say to her, and, ignoring Olwyn's sharp intake of breath, I stretch out to pat the mare, my hand running down her neck to where last night there was a burning mass of agony on her breast.

I can't believe it. There should be an injury, a nasty one. At best there should be a cauterised wound. But there's no sign of any recent trauma. Only the faintest of scars.

Somehow – and I don't know how – I've healed her.

'This was the horse?' Olwyn can't believe it either.

'I know,' I say. 'You can hardly see anything ever happened to her.'

'No, I mean, she's the leader of the herd, the dominant mare. You have no idea how amazing this is.'

But though I'm sure that's important, it's not as immediately mesmerising to me as the immense healing properties of the plant.

'Describe it to me,' Olwyn says when I share my disbelief with her. I do my best to recall the structure and shape, but it's when I mention the colour that Olwyn says, 'Firewort. It must be.'

'Yes, that's right,' I say, the memory of seeing the name in my books coming back to me now. 'You know it?'

'I've heard of it,' she says. 'But I've never seen any. It's incredibly rare.'

'Then we were lucky,' I say to the horse, running my fingers through her silken mane.

Olwyn's looking at me strangely. Almost suspiciously. 'How did you know what to do with it?'

'I have an interest in remedies,' I say, intentionally vague. But Olwyn's no fool.

'Potions?'

'I'm still learning.'

Her eyes are wide once more. 'You can do magic.'

'No,' I say, quick to dispel her excitement. 'I would like to, but I have lots to learn. That's why I came here.' And I explain to her who Esther is, and why I was seeking her teaching.

'So you're not going to stay?' she asks when I've finished, her disappointment unmistakable.

'I can't.' I'm disappointed too. 'Believe me, I wish I could.'

'The horses want you here.'

'One horse,' I point out. 'One horse brought me to meet my family. And I'm very grateful. But my other family needs my help.'

Olwyn's about to protest further, but then her attention is caught by something over my shoulder and instead a smile spreads across her face. 'Not just one horse.'

I follow her gaze and hold my breath. Descending the treacherous rocks are hundreds of mares, young and old and in between, coming to join their leader. They canter across the plain together, a white wall, like the surf rolling in on the ocean, until they reach us, and as one lower to bow before me.

Heat rises to my cheeks – such a display of respect from these magnificent beasts could not be more undeserved. I return the gesture, but when I look to Olwyn for guidance, I'm shocked to see her face damp with tears.

'What's wrong?'

'Nothing,' she says, half laughing. 'I've just never seen anything like this before. They've all come to greet you. Their queen.'

I swallow hard, floundering in these strange new waters. My eyes run over the herd, admiring how many there are, and how their pure hair blends into their surroundings. Several have darker muzzles than the rest and I'm wondering if that represents youth or maturity when I realise that there are foals among the herd. Not many, but definitely some.

'I thought you said the sea stallions hadn't been in eleven years?' I sound rather too accusatory.

'They haven't.'

'Then how are there foals? They can't be more than a few months old.'

'Actually they can.' Olwyn seems to be recovering from the overwhelming situation. 'Snow mares are magical. They don't have the lifespan of ordinary horses.'

'So how long can they live?'

'For ever – if they're not hunted or killed in battle. That's why protecting them is so important; it's why we live up here. Please, Marianne, stay. Find out why they brought you here.'

I look from her to the ancient horses and know I'm going to give in to temptation – for now at least. There is too much beauty to walk away from with nowhere to go. A few days' rest can't hurt.

'All right,' I say. 'I'll stay.'

Unsurprisingly Rayvn isn't thrilled to learn that I'm staying.

'We don't have enough food for an extra mouth,' she says when Olwyn explains what happened with the horses.

'I'm only going to be here a few days,' I promise. 'And I've been on rations for weeks – so I'm used to not eating much. Anything you can spare me will be gratefully accepted.'

'The frost-roots are nearly ready to harvest,' Mama says. 'They will see us through the next few months, with or without a guest.'

And as Mama has said it, the argument is settled, though it's not enough to stop Rayvn scowling at me.

I spend the next couple of days largely with Mama, looking over some old maps she has of the island, and asking as many questions as I can. I'm trying to figure out where Esther could have gone – as well as trying to familiarise myself with the island I was born on.

One evening, when Pip is out on patrol and no one is bickering, I decide to risk asking about the Hooded. But when I mention the name, I'm met with blank looks.

So, I tell them about what happened when I first arrived on the Eighth Isle and watch as their expressions darken with concern.

'Human sacrifice?' Olwyn says, glancing at Ravyn, who looks equally unsettled.

'They've always been a superstitious lot on that side of the island,' Rayvn says.

'Why's that?' I ask.

'Because that coastline faces the Shadow Island.'

Now it's my turn to look blank.

'The Seventh Isle is known as the Shadow Island,' Olwyn explains. 'Partly because our mountains cast a gloom over it.'

'But some say the shadows are more than that,' Rayvn adds. 'Spirits, demons, shadow creatures once summoned by Mages that never returned to their resting place. The old stories warn that they lurk in the waters between our islands, looking for a way to breach our boundaries and spread their evil. So people who live on the west of this island have long made offerings to these spirits, some requesting their protection, others beseeching them to stay on the Seventh.'

'But it was always gifts of flowers, food, art,' Olwyn says. 'What would make them turn to such violence?'

'Fear,' Mama says, and though her voice is quiet she commands full attention. 'Whoever the Hooded are, they must inspire a terrible fear.'

'Then we must be vigilant,' Rayvn says, clenching her fists.

'So human sacrifices aren't common here?' I say.

Olwyn looks at me with a confused smile. 'No. What exactly do you Easterners think we do over here?'

I can feel heat rise to my cheeks.

'You think us savages?' Rayvn is less amused.

'Not at all,' I say. 'I mean, there may have been the odd mention of how lawless and dangerous it is here.'

'And whose fault is that?' Rayvn snaps.

Shame sweeps over me. I know better than most that the blame for our fractured history lies with the East.

'Do the Eastern Isles suffer without us?' Mama asks, and there is no malice to her question, just simple curiosity.

'I wouldn't be here if there wasn't suffering,' I say. 'Between the King, his old Viper and the bandits, violence is all too commonplace.'

Mama shakes her head. 'The East did that to itself. What I mean is, without the West, is the East incomplete, as we are?'

I have no idea what's she talking about.

'Do you know anything?' Rayvn says, her tone acidic enough to strip flesh from bone.

'Shall we mock her or educate her?' Mama says, *her* tone sharp enough to silence her granddaughter. Then she turns to me. 'I sense the East has been sparing with the truth about the past we share.'

I smile. 'That's a polite way of putting it. They remade the past to frame themselves as heroes and you as the villains.'

'How sad that one awful moment in our history has wiped away all that came before it,' Mama says. 'The Eastern and Western Isles have always been two halves of a whole. The East was the practical, steady half, with their industry and trade ensuring we all functioned and survived, while the West was the creative half, blessing the islands with art, music, vibrancy. Together we brought balance, each half nourishing the other in a way they maybe didn't appreciate they needed. After the war, we were the more obviously deprived, the lack of our main trade suppliers leaving us deficient in everything, and nothing makes people more desperate than empty stomachs. But the East lost too. Not just magic, but the beauty of our ways, our culture. Is the air not thinner without our songs? Is the world not greyer without our colour? Our differences made us stronger, but one King could not see that simple truth, and tore us apart. He, and anyone who thinks like him, are blinder than me.'

And though she's talking about the Twelve Isles, and teaching me vital fragments of a lost past, all I can think about is Bronn. The other half of me. We let our differences tear us apart too, when we should have celebrated them, embraced them, accepted them.

Olwyn takes my hand in hers, mistaking the tears welling in my eyes for sadness over our divided lands. 'But *you* are special,' she says. 'Yours is a story of both East and West. Maybe your return brings hope of reconciliation?'

Rayvn snorts her contempt and Olwyn rolls her eyes.

'You'd rather centuries more division?' Olwyn asks.

'No, I just can't imagine her mending a broken seam, let alone restoring the Twelve Isles.'

I raise my eyebrows but say nothing to defend myself. Rayvn doesn't have to like me, though I do find her venomous reaction to me curious. She reminds me of a wild animal trapped behind bars, the life she's been born into not one she would have chosen for herself. Duty binds her, but always she is fighting, punishing those who remind her of her cage. Perhaps she hates me because I can leave these mountains when she cannot.

Later that night, as I lie on the floor waiting for sleep to come, I think over what Mama told me about the islands and how they used to exist together. I feel sure the key to bringing peace lies in their shared history – that the answers are there if I can just uncover them.

My dreams roll in like a storm, surrounding me with suffocating darkness. I see a woman cocooned. She's alone, she's afraid, she's hiding. I hear her ragged breath, I sense her fear. She's speaking but her words are inaudible – though I strain to listen through the thick fog of my mind. Her face is hidden from me, but I watch her lips move, try to decipher their message, until finally they form one urgent word.

Run.

I wake with a start, hot and sweating, when by rights I should be cold in this night air. I leap to my feet, race through to the room where Rayvn and Olwyn sleep and shake them hard.

'Get up, we have to hurry,' I say, throwing their clothes at them.

'What's wrong with you?' Rayvn says, groggy with sleep.

'It's Pip,' I say. 'She's in trouble.'

'How do you know?' Olwyn says, but they're both rushing now.

The truth is, I don't know how I know. I just woke with the strongest sense that she was in danger out there, the warning from the cocooned woman echoing in my ears.

Within minutes we're running out into the night, each of us armed with spears, me with my dagger tucked in my boot as well. The only sound is the crunching of snow beneath our feet; our breath floats like mist in the crisp air.

Then we hear the clamour: the horses' cries of fear, the shout of a brave young girl and the roar of a fearsome beast.

'An ice lion,' Olwyn says and we all run faster towards the noise.

The sight is one to behold. The herd of snow mares is trapped, the cliffs creating a natural corral round them. Facing them is an ice lion. Only a small girl stands between them, her spear raised.

The ice lion is massive. Twice the height of the tallest mare, it towers over Pip, its steel pelt shimmering in the moonlight, its lacy mane like a silver spiderweb glistening with diamonds. The open mouth is a dark cavern, teeth like lethal stalagmites and stalactites, its roar like a summons to the depths of the ocean. It's beautiful, it's deadly, and it's about to strike.

I think we all realise we've made a mistake at the same time. Because beside the ice lion, sprawled on the ground, is the body of its mate. Pip doesn't need our help; she's already single-handedly dispatched one beast, and was poised to finish the job.

But our sudden appearance has interrupted everything and both girl and lion turn to look at us in surprise.

Rayvn acts first. Her spear flies through the air and pierces the ice lion through the flank.

It rears up in reaction, and lashes out with a mighty paw, its razor-sharp claws slicing through Pip's leg. She retaliates by sweeping her spear through his, so that their shrieks of pain mingle into one.

'Pip!' Olwyn shouts, as her sister falls to the ground.

'Rayvn, get the horses away,' I shout, throwing my cousin my spear. She catches it easily and runs towards the herd, ushering them out of the enclosed space while we distract the ice lion.

He charges at Olwyn and me, and I pull my dagger from my boot, ready to stand my ground. But to my surprise, Olwyn makes a charge of her own, running straight at the beast. For a moment I can't help but stare, mesmerised at the attack she launches at the massive predator. Her spear is like an extension of her arm, and she swings it swiftly, deftly, driving the ice lion backwards as he struggles to understand what is happening to him.

'Marianne, help her!' Rayvn shouts angrily, waking me from my reverie. I'm not sure Olwyn actually needs any help, but I run towards her anyway.

As I approach them, Olwyn forcefully thrusts her spear at the ice lion's chest and I think for a moment that this is the strike that will fell him. But he manages to twist his body just enough to avoid a fatal blow, the spear instead landing in his shoulder. He swings his body hard, and Olwyn, still holding the end of the spear, gets flung into the air and tossed to the ground where she lands with a thump.

Then the ice lion looks at me. Our eyes connect, hunter and prey, and I see the glimmer of determination there. He means to kill me. Swiftly and without mercy. He starts to run, spears still sticking in his flesh, but I stand my ground, focusing. I'm only going to get one shot at this.

I wait as he approaches, closer and closer, his growl a deep thunder that shakes the very mountains. I hear Rayvn scream at me to move. I see her spear fly towards the beast and miss as he ducks out of the way.

When he's close enough for me to see the whites of his eyes, I throw my dagger. It lodges deep into the ice lion's heart, and he collapses even as he runs, his body sliding through the snow until he comes to a stop right in front of me, empty of life.

Olwyn is already staggering back to her feet, and so I run straight towards Pip, whose blood is being greedily consumed by the snow.

'I'm sorry,' she says, her voice weak, her already pale skin turning deathly white,

'Are you kidding me?' I say, shaking off my top layer of fur. 'You didn't flinch in front of that lion.'

'But I didn't kill it.'

'You killed the other one.'

Rayvn's joined us now, and she stares in horror at the blood gushing from her sister. 'It's my fault,' she says. 'My shot wasn't accurate enough.'

I press my clothing hard against Pip's leg. 'Rayvn, hold this here.'

She does as I ask, while I tear a strip of material from my cloak and fashion a tourniquet round Pip's thigh. There's no way this girl is going to bleed to death on my watch.

Olwyn has reached us now, a deep gash on her forehead spilling blood down her face.

This time I take off my cloak altogether and throw it at her. 'Use that to keep pressure on your wound,' I say. And then I scoop Pip into my arms.

With great reluctance Rayvn stays to keep watch over the herd, most of whom have fled now up the mountain, while I run as fast as I can back towards the hut, reassuring Pip the whole way, even as she fades in my arms.

Once we're inside, I start barking orders. 'Get the fire burning brighter, and heat water. I need clean cloths, as many as you can get me, and a needle and thread.'

When I realise that Olwyn is struggling, still applying pressure to her head as she tries to fuel the fire, I call her over.

'Let me look,' I say, and examine the cut. It's nasty, but not life-threatening. Already the bleeding is beginning to cease. 'Here.' I tie a strip of material round her head to keep the wound clean until I can deal with it. 'I'll stitch it up for you later.'

Olwyn gives me a strange look, but doesn't argue. She lets me turn my attention back to Pip, and fetches me all I've asked for.

Pip has passed out, the blood loss too much for her. 'Do you have any tonics?' I ask Olwyn. 'Any herbs?'

'I'll wake Mama, she'll know.'

'I'm already here.' Mama is hurrying into the room, still in her nightgown and carrying several bottles in her arms. Without preamble she says to me, 'I have mistshade, wormfoot and crystal-leaf, which do you want?'

I've not heard of any of them before, and ask to inspect the plants.

'Mistshade is good for fighting infection,' Mama says.

'And the others?'

'Crystal-leaf wards off a fever. Wormfoot aids digestion.'

'Mash some mistshade and crystal-leaf with a little hot water until they make a paste.'

Mama nods, and staggers over to the pots in the kitchen. Olwyn goes to help her, and while they're preparing the mixture I start to clean the wound left by the ice lion. It's deep, but not down to the bone. As long as I can keep the cut free from infection, Pip should recover well.

I work through the night. Once Mama's prepared the paste, I smear it over and into the cut, wiping away blood as I go, until I'm ready to stitch the wound closed.

'This is going to hurt worse than anything so far,' I warn Olwyn, who comes to sit beside her sister. 'She will wake up. And I need you to keep her still.'

Olwyn nods, clenching her teeth, while I heat the needle in the fire's flames. And then I get to work.

Almost immediately Pip rushes back to the horrors of consciousness, her scream consuming the air. But I don't flinch, just focus on repairing the damage done, though Olwyn begs me to stop, and Pip's screams turn to sobs. I hate to hurt her, but it's the only way to save her.

When it's over I take Olwyn's hand. 'Fetch some snow and wrap it in cloth. It will help the pain.'

Mama comes to comfort Pip, gently wiping her brow, and whispering soothing words.

'The worst is over,' I say to Pip. 'Sleep now and rest.'

She manages to give me a weak smile before she closes her eyes, and leans into her grandmother.

When Olwyn brings me the cold compress, I arrange it round Pip's leg, hoping I've done enough to keep infection away. Only time will tell.

Once I'm finished with Pip, I turn my attention to Olwyn's head. She swears under her breath a few times as I stitch it together, and when I'm done she rests her hand on my shoulder. 'I don't know about you, but I need a drink.'

She returns with two mugs, and passes me one. I take a sip, and almost choke on the strong liquid that sears my mouth and throat. By the time I've finished coughing, my nerves have already started to settle.

Olwyn grins at me. 'Good, right? Icefire. That's made from the sap of the ice trees.'

'It's lethal,' I say with a smile, but take another sip.

'Thank you,' she says after a while. 'For everything.'

'Don't thank me yet,' I say, suddenly very tired. 'Pip's still not out of danger.'

'She's a lot safer than she would be without you.'

But as I take another longer sip of icefire, I wonder how true that really is. Without me raising the alarm, Pip would surely have killed the ice lion on her own. All I did was make things worse.

It is, after all, what I seem best at.

14

At first I think Pip is going to be lucky, but when the infection arrives it strikes fast.

If there had been any thought in my head of continuing my search for Esther, it's soon extinguished. I simply cannot leave her to die. And so my stay in the mountains extends. I tend to Pip during the day and patrol the horses at night.

I experiment with different poultices, vary quantities of herbs, roam the land for any other plants that might heal. I keep Pip's temperature low with damp cloths and snow compresses. And I wish that I knew enough magic to heal her with a single touch.

One afternoon, as weariness threatens to consume me, Olwyn brings me a bowl of frost-root stew.

While I eat, she takes my place, freshening the cloth draped over Pip's forehead, and stoking the fire. After a while she gestures to my necklace, which has fallen free from its hiding place beneath my shirt.

'That's beautiful,' she says. 'Where did you get it?'

I reach for the stone, and hold it close to my chest, before tucking it back under my clothes. 'It was a gift.' I don't want to think about Torin, though the truth is every moment I've sat tending to Pip I've felt guilt that it is her bedside I'm at, and not my husband's. Every symptom I've treated, I've wondered how he is, whether he still lives, and willed him to keep breathing until I can return to his side.

'From someone dear to you?' Olwyn gently pries for answers.

'Yes, very.'

She watches me closely, and I try to give nothing away.

'Someone close to your heart, but not the one who possesses it.'

When I look up at her in surprise, she smiles back at me. 'You hide your emotions well, but not entirely.'

'What does it matter?' I say a little too sharply. 'I left them both behind.'

'And now you're stuck here.' Olwyn says what I cannot.

'I didn't mean it like that.'

'But that's how you feel?'

'I left to help them. Instead I fear I'm failing them.'

Olwyn says nothing for a moment. 'Maybe you're too hard on yourself. The fate of the Twelve Isles can't rest on one person alone.'

Why then does it feel that way?

'At least you can leave,' Olwyn says. 'You may be weighed by duty, but you're not a literal prisoner to it.'

I glance up at her. 'You're not happy here?' I had sensed that Rayvn wanted to break free from the mountains, suffocated by her life here, but Olwyn always seemed so steady, so calm; it never occurred to me that she might want to leave too.

'It's not that I'm unhappy,' she says quickly. 'But the thought that I might never learn the beauty of the other islands? Might never get to see all the world has to offer? It saddens me.'

She stands up to take my empty bowl away. 'You are many things, Marianne. And you bear many burdens. But to me one thing is very clear. You are a healer. Of people, yes. But maybe of the lands too.'

Olwyn walks away, but her words stay with me. I know she meant healing the division between East and West, but what if it's more than that? When Adler scorched the Fourth Isle, the magic bled away from the land entirely. And now the Six Isles are sick. The symptoms were all there, I just didn't pay enough attention. But I finally understand.

The land needs to heal. Magic is the cure.

If I don't find a way to restore magic, it isn't simply that peace can't return. It's far worse than that. If I can't bring the magic back, the sickness will spread. The islands will die.

And so will everyone who lives there.

*　　*　　*

For all Olwyn calls me a healer, still Pip does not improve. The wound is festering now, and I know that unless something changes soon, I'm going to lose the battle for her life. One morning, when I've returned exhausted from my night patrol, I slump into the chair by the fire, and start to remove my layers of clothing.

'I think I should go back down the mountain,' I say to Mama, who has been up all night with Pip.

Rayvn, who's preparing the breakfast, turns to look at me, a knife still raised in her hand. 'You're going to give up?'

I'm too tired for her relentless distrust. 'No, of course not. I want to try to find some more firewort. It healed the mare, it can heal Pip.'

Rayvn frowns 'You know how rare it is. Even if you were able to find it, Pip doesn't have the time.'

'I wonder if you should search for a death asp.' Mama speaks so quietly I almost miss it.

'Why would she want to do that? You used to warn us to stay away from caves in case one was lurking about.' But Rayvn's abandoned the food and has come to join us.

'Yes, they're lethal, their venom toxic enough to kill with one bite, but my mother once told me something else about them. A myth that their venom could also heal. That the snake itself decided whether to kill or cure. Maybe now's the time to start believing in myths.'

I leap to my feet with such force that they both jump. I can't believe I've been so stupid. The diamond dust. It's been in my satchel all along, and I'd forgotten about it until Mama's story of the snake jogged my memory. A venom that could serve for good or ill. Like the dust.

Without offering them an explanation I run to fetch my bag, which I'd thrown under the bed I share with Olwyn to keep it out of the way. Delving to the bottom and hunting about, my hand finally closes around the small pouch filled with the ingredient I had intended to take back for Torin.

For the briefest moment I hesitate. If I use this to help Pip, I'll have to think of something else to help Torin.

If he's even still alive.

The fact is Torin isn't here. Pip is, and this is the only thing I haven't tried.

I run back out to the kitchen and start putting together the ingredients for a poultice.

'You know I made a new one not even an hour ago,' Rayvn says, but her tone is tinged with curiosity.

'Not with this.' And I hold up the pouch. 'I forgot I had it, but Mama reminded me. It's dust from the crystal mines back home. Supposedly it makes a potion more potent. It's your intentions that dictate how it works. If I wished it to poison, it would. And if I wish it to cure . . .'

'You think it'll work?' Rayvn doesn't sound convinced.

'No idea, but do you have any other suggestions?'

She doesn't, and so I focus on what I'm doing. I only have one chance at this. Once the paste is prepared, I sprinkle the fine, sparkling powder over it before stirring it in.

Let her live, let her heal.

A plea from my heart poured into the remedy. I just hope it's enough. That what I read in the books was true.

When it's ready, I carry the bowl with great care to where Pip lies, deeply asleep in the grip of the fever. After I've wiped away the old paste, I apply my potion, still willing it to save the small girl lying before me.

I don't know what to expect, but apparently we were all hoping for an immediate reaction because when nothing happens, Rayvn raises a dubious eyebrow.

'Is that it?'

Biting back a snappish response, I simply say, 'Be patient.' But inside, panic is rising. What if nothing happens?

Time will tell. For now, we can only wait.

We don't have to wait long. Only an hour later, Pip's temperature drops. By midday she awakens from her fevered dreams, and by the time Olwyn returns from patrol the wound in Pip's leg is forming a scab.

None of us can really believe it, but our eyes are not deceived. The diamond dust has been almost as miraculous as the firewort, and I'm simultaneously elated and furious. Why had I never heard of its effects until I read an archaic book in a hidden library? Surely this would be an invaluable ingredient to healers? In fact, something so desirable would be beyond the purse of all but the very richest. Yet among the many treasures Adler obtained for the King, I never heard tell of diamond dust.

It takes a little longer for Pip's strength to return, her body weakened from the prolonged incapacitation, and so I make her daily tonics in an effort to fortify her.

And all the while my need to leave builds. I will not go until Pip is fully recovered, but my dreams are tortured by images of Torin dying – alongside the islands he was born to rule – in the light of the blood moon, as Bronn lies trapped behind flames, beyond my reach. All the while the cocooned woman haunts the background, telling me over and over again to run, so that every time I awake I'm exhausted and terrified and desperate to flee.

My only peace is in the stillness of the night during my patrols, when I find a connection to the mountains. To the mares. To the magic.

Alone in silence, I listen to the gentle song of the island, a lullaby I can't hear during the day, and though the view is little more than white and grey, the land never seems more vibrant.

It allows me to breathe. It's the only time I can think clearly, without being consumed by panic. The magic of the land reaches to embrace me, and I bask in its quiet energy, feeling at one with nature. Here, Old Tatty's warnings and Raoul's prophecies hold no fear for me; here, I don't seek to harness magic, or control it. I just draw comfort from it.

Often the mares seek me out, quietly revelling in the moon's glow with me, and I like to walk among them, knowing our time together is drawing to a close, and making the most of what remains.

After one particularly long day, I'm lying in the snow with the horses surrounding me, looking up at the blanket of stars illuminating the night sky, when the mare besides me nudges my arm with urgency. I'm so tired that I hadn't noticed the horses' agitation but now I'm instantly alert. The horses are nervous, rising from the ground and edging away. I'm on my feet in a second, my spear in one hand, my dagger in the other.

It happens quickly. One minute the air is still, the next the intruder is charging at me; in a heartbeat I am a warrior once more. The man comes straight for me, but I easily dodge his advance. Protecting the mares is my only concern and so I instantly launch a counter-attack, but he easily evades my blows. His speed matches my own, and though my reflexes are lightning-fast, he seems to anticipate my every move as if he knows what I'm going to do before I do it.

This ability to read my thoughts serves him well, and he manages to knock me off balance, sending me hurtling into the snow. I leap back to my feet, expecting him already to be chasing the mares, but he isn't. He's still facing me, bracing for my next attack. And that's when I realise he isn't here for the horses. He's here for me.

I don't waste a second, bombarding him with an even more vicious assault, but again he's one step ahead of me, and I can't get the upper hand. But then something strikes me. I've been so busy trying to outmanoeuvre him that I've failed to notice the obvious. He's not fighting to kill me. He's fighting to defend himself. Who is he? Wanting answers, I adjust my tactics, hurting him no longer my priority. Shifting my weight backwards, I flick my spear under his feet and send him hurtling to the ground. Once he's on his back, I straddle him, pinning him down and resting my knife at his neck in warning. He's going nowhere. I reach to pull his mask down. And I freeze.

It's like looking at a ghost. The features, the shape, every contour of the face is identical to Grace's, just slightly more masculine. There's only one person this can be.

'Jax?'

Grace's twin frowns. 'How do you know my name?'

My mind is racing. If Jax is here, then the Guardians have found me. How?

Ignoring his question, I grab his collar and ask one of my own. 'How did you know I was here?'

I think he would have answered, were it not for the blade that suddenly slips against my throat, causing me to freeze.

'You're outnumbered. Let him go.'

I don't recognise the man's deep voice, but if he thinks I'm frightened, then the Guardians haven't been watching me long enough. 'You think two of you is going to be a problem?' I scoff.

'I said, let him go.'

I look at Jax, who doesn't seem afraid either – in fact, I can almost hear his mind turning over, still wondering how I know who he is. By the look on his face he's reached an accurate conclusion.

He's about to say something when another voice cuts across the night air, this time one I do recognise.

'No. You let *her* go.'

I've never been so pleased to see Rayvn, even if the only reason I can think of for her being here is that she's been spying on me during my patrols.

The four of us remain frozen in a peculiar tableau, all blades and spears raised.

'We just want to talk,' Jax says eventually, raising his hands in surrender.

'Then why did you attack me?'

'Your reputation precedes you, Viper,' the man behind me says, and my skin prickles. They really do know who I am.

It's not like I'm actually going to hurt Grace's brother, so I decide to make the first move and lift the blade away from Jax's neck. Once I've done so, the dagger quickly disappears from *my* neck and eventually Rayvn reluctantly lowers her spear.

I step away to stand nearer Rayvn, and eye the Guardians warily. 'All right then, talk.'

The man beside Jax pulls his mask down, and instantly my goodwill vanishes. The last time I saw this man he was at my wedding, a stranger lurking in the shadows. My main link to the man who nearly killed Torin.

I launch myself at him, and so unexpected is my attack that he's knocked to the floor. The only reason I don't seriously hurt him is because both Rayvn and Jax are there in seconds, pulling me off him, shouting for me to calm down. They hold my arms still while the man gets to his feet, wiping the blood away from his lip where I managed to land at least one good blow.

'You recognise me then.'

I can't believe it. He's smiling.

'You're a dead man, but if you give me the name of your accomplice, then I might consider killing you swiftly.'

His smile falters. 'What? Who are you talking about?'

'The man who tried to kill Torin. He was yours, yes?'

Now the smile is entirely gone. 'No.' Like Jax moments ago, he too raises his hands as a sign of no harm intended. 'I have no idea what you're talking about. I didn't know the Prince was attacked.'

'Liar.'

He shakes his head. 'I'm not lying. My name is Mordecai. I'm a Guardian of the Royal Bloodline. I came to your wedding simply because there were rumours that the remaining survivor we'd been searching for was still alive, and was the Viper no less. Once I'd seen you, I knew our search was over, and came home to report to my superiors.'

I have no reason to trust him, and yet the sincerity of his words is clear. Though I really don't want to, I believe him. Grudgingly.

'So how did you know I was here?'

It's Jax who answers. 'Our advisor felt a shift in the air. He sent us.'

That has my attention. 'Your advisor?' There's only one kind of person who could detect such a thing, and my thoughts leap instantly to Esther. 'A Mage?'

Jax hesitates. 'Perhaps these are conversations best left for the journey?'

I frown. Since the moment I recognised Jax, I knew that my stay with my family, with the mares was over, that my duty had come to reclaim me, and yet his assumption rankles me. 'What journey?'

'Why, to the Twelfth Isle, of course,' Mordecai says. 'It's time to take you home.'

15

Olwyn throws extra logs on to the fire, but no heat they provide can warm the cold atmosphere in the hut.

Jax and Mordecai, now standing in the small room, haven't been afforded the same welcome I received. Rayvn woke her sisters and Mama, knowing they needed to be part of this conversation, and Pip was sent out for the first time since her injury to resume the patrol. The rest of us are now settling to a discussion I fear won't end happily.

'So you really had nothing to do with the attack on Torin?' I know they want to talk about my future, about taking me away from this hallowed place, but right now I want assurances. And Mordecai has to answer some questions before I'm going anywhere with him.

'I swear to you, I know nothing about it. I travelled East alone, witnessed your marriage, and once I was certain of your true identity, left to return here. After I threw off that man you had follow me.'

I bristle at the thought of anyone describing Bronn as 'that man', even as my heart aches to think of him at all. 'Yes, and how exactly did you manage such a feat?'

'I have exceptional skills.' Mordecai is all smiles.

Jax rolls his eyes. 'He had an enchantment from our Mage, to make him invisible from any pursuit.'

Mordecai nudges his arm, but Jax only shrugs.

'It's not like I needed it. Even without it I would have got away,' Mordecai says a little more defensively than is needed.

'I wouldn't bet on it.' I fold my arms and stare at him, hating him for using magic against Bronn and making him doubt himself.

Jax seems less inclined to annoy me and shoots his companion a look to shut him up. 'I am sorry to hear about what happened to your husband. But what made you think Mordecai was involved?'

'Because from the moment I saw him at my wedding, he stood out as trouble. I knew he wasn't there to celebrate. That's why I sent –' I stumble, not wanting to say Bronn's name out loud here as if somehow that would make all that happened between us more real – 'that's why I sent someone after him, to find out his intentions. Meanwhile the assassin came for Torin. And he was skilled, far more than any mercenary. Two strangers seemed too much of a coincidence, so I assumed you were working together.'

'Well, if he was skilled, I can see why you'd think of me,' Mordecai says and everyone stares at him. 'What?'

'Someone tried to murder her husband,' Jax says. 'Maybe you shouldn't speak for a while.' He turns to me

278

apologetically. 'Forgive my friend, he's an insensitive, arrogant ass, but his heart's in the right place.'

'And what place might that be?' Mama's voice is dripping with suspicion. 'What is it you young men want with our Marianne?'

'She is our queen,' Mordecai says, serious now. 'We've devoted our lives to finding her so that she can be restored to her throne. It's time for Marianne to return home.'

'She is home.' Rayvn's defence is unexpected and from the look on Mama and Olwyn's faces, they share my surprise. If Rayvn notices, she ignores us. 'This is her home.'

'With respect, her place is at the palace.'

'With respect,' Olwyn says curtly, 'this isn't your decision to make.' She rests her hand gently on Rayvn's arm. 'Or ours.' She turns to me, not quite managing to hide her sadness. 'What do you want, Marianne?'

Dear Olwyn, always brushing her own desires aside to do what's right. I'm so grateful for her asking. I only wish I had an answer.

'Who is your advisor?' I ask Jax rather than Mordecai. I still can't bring myself to trust him entirely. Or like him. 'Are they a Mage?'

Jax glances at Mordecai who gives a subtle nod. 'Yes, we have a Mage working with us,' he admits. 'It was him who sensed your presence once more.'

Simultaneously my heart falls and rises. It's not Esther

then, and the mystery of her whereabouts continues to worry me. But also, there is another Mage, waiting to meet me, who could teach me everything I need to know. I hadn't dared hope there were others.

Then it dawns on me exactly what he just said. 'What do you mean "once more"?'

'You've been here before, yes?' When I nod Jax continues. 'He sensed it then, which is why Mordecai went east to find you. Believe me when I say we mean you no harm. We've sworn to protect you.'

He holds my gaze and I see him silently begging me to come with them. I can tell he has many questions for me about Grace and my heart aches just thinking of how I'm going to crush his hopes. He doesn't know it yet, but any reunion they could have had was stolen by the same man who stole my life from me.

Of course I'm going with them. Once I learned of the Mage, there was never any question. There's nothing more I can do for Pip now; her recovery will continue perfectly without me, and going to the Twelfth Isle is better than aimlessly searching this island for Esther. This Mage of theirs may be able to instruct me in magic, and the Guardians may be willing to help me fight back in the East. It's my best chance of returning to the islands, to Torin, before it's too late.

I move to crouch beside Mama, and take her hand in mine. 'I have to go with them,' I say, not wanting to hurt the old woman. 'I need to try to save the East, to save my friends.'

Mama pulls my hand to her lips and presses it there tightly. 'I know you do,' she says, her voice trembling with emotion.

'I know I said I'd stay until Pip was fully recovered—'

'The child is going to be fine. You saw to that. It is right that you go.'

'I'll come back,' I say, meaning every word. 'I won't be gone for ever.'

The smile she gives is so sad it breaks my heart. 'You'll be gone long enough.'

'Will you be safe?' Olwyn says, her eyes flicking coldly towards Mordecai and Jax.

'Oh, don't worry, she's more than a match for those two,' Rayvn says with her trademark reluctant admiration.

'In fairness we weren't trying that hard.' Mordecai sounds offended.

'You didn't need to fight me at all,' I say, pointing out the obvious.

'Actually, you started it,' Jax says. 'I was just defending myself.'

I'm about to object, but then I wonder. Was I so quick to attack first that I misjudged the situation? 'I thought you were here to hurt the horses.' I'm not going to apologise to them.

'Just like a Snake – hot-headed.' Mordecai says it with a smile, but it still annoys me. They may be my Guardians, sworn to protect me, but they know nothing about me, or who I am.

Olwyn ignores him too, pulling me into a tight embrace. 'I will miss you,' she says softly.

'You too.' And I hold her even closer before releasing her.

There's an awkward moment where Rayvn and I regard each other, wondering if enough has happened in the last few minutes to thaw the frost in our relationship, but we're interrupted before either of us can decide.

'You girls should go with her.' Mama's words are so quiet I almost miss them at first. She's reaching her hands out, and her granddaughters take them. 'You two were not made for the mountains,' she says, though the words clearly pain her. 'I believe Marianne came here to take you away as much as anything else.'

Olwyn and Rayvn look at me, their mouths slightly parted, a shared conflict obvious to anyone.

'We can't leave you, Mama,' Olwyn says.

'I'll still have Pipit,' she says. 'That child was born to this life, she lives and breathes it. And she's strong enough now to resume her duties. But you two have never truly been happy here, and though I love you for trying I wouldn't be doing my duty as your grandmother if I didn't release you from your obligation and set you free.'

They are both frozen, seemingly reluctant to seize the opportunity for fear of what they'd leave behind.

Though it's far from my place to interfere in this family's business, I sense Mama's desire for me to speak up. Because I agree with her. They should come with me – I want them with me. And so strong is their sense of duty that without a little encouragement, neither will be willing to leave.

'Nothing is for ever,' I say, echoing Mama's words to me and gently urging them to take this chance. 'You can return home whenever you want.' Though my instincts tell me their roads lead far from this place, to new and dangerous adventures.

Olwyn and Rayvn look at each other, silently communicating, a sisterly conversation comprehensible to no one else. Eventually Rayvn smiles and Olwyn reaches to hold Mama once more.

'Are you sure?' she asks.

Mama's cloudy eyes blink tears away. 'I don't need sight to see that both of you are ready to leave. It's time, my dears. It's time.'

Rayvn goes outside to fetch Pip and what follows is an emotional blur of packing, tears and farewells.

When it's my turn to say goodbye to Pip, I lift her chin up and force her big, scared eyes to meet mine. 'Are you going to be OK?' I keep my voice low, so no one else can hear us.

'I don't know.'

'They'll come back to see you,' I say, hoping to encourage her. 'And maybe one day you can join us?'

But Pip is shaking her head. 'No, you don't understand. I will miss them, of course, but that's not what I'm worried about. Without them there's only me to protect the mares.' She pauses, her fear clear for me to see. 'What if I'm not good enough?'

I squat down so our eyes are at the same level and I fix my most earnest gaze on her. 'You are more than good enough, Pip. Never doubt it. That night with the ice lions? You stood and defended those horses with your life and you would have succeeded if we hadn't interfered. You are kind, you are loving and you are brave. Believe in yourself, like we all believe in you.'

She nods and then leans over for one last embrace. 'Come back one day,' she whispers in my ear.

'I will, I promise.' And I mean it with every fibre of my being.

Mordecai and Jax patiently wait until we're ready to go, and though I wonder at one point if we'll ever tear Olwyn away from Mama, Rayvn is desperate to leave now she has permission. I look at her, fierce and wild, and think, not for the first time, how well suited she'd be to life at sea. On the *Maiden*. I turn away, not wanting to think of my ship, and more specifically the people sailing her.

Finally, when there are no more tears to be shed and no more words to be said, we head off into the early hours of the morning, with a backward glance from Olwyn and me, and none from Rayvn.

Fresh snow has fallen since we came inside, and the ground crunches satisfyingly beneath our feet. Mordecai and Rayvn lead the way, with Olwyn directly behind. I walk between her and Jax, who is bringing up the rear of our little party. It's only as we reach the treeline that I hear the whinny. We all turn our heads to the left to see the dominant mare trotting towards us.

She's come to say goodbye.

No one else in the group moves, Jax and Mordecai visibly transfixed by the beauty of the mare, but I step forward, knowing she's here for me. I press my hand to her muzzle and she brushes it with her lips as we rest our foreheads together, breathing in each other's air.

'Thank you,' I whisper. 'For finding me.'

The horse nuzzles me in response.

'I'll come back,' I say, scratching her chin. 'But look after Pip and Mama, won't you? They're very special to me.'

I pat her soft neck, buried beneath the tangle of mane, and kiss her lightly on the nose before I turn back towards my friends. They're all giving me that strange look that makes me uncomfortable – the look of awe and admiration. If they really knew me, not one of them would feel that way.

We continue our journey, starting the difficult trek down the mountain. The sun is rising now and the light washing the terrain is almost purple in colour. It's far more welcoming than the weather was when I climbed up this way and for that I'm incredibly grateful.

The direction Mordecai is taking us isn't the same as the way I came; we're heading further north, presumably to where their boat is anchored. To start with the ground is treacherous with loose stones, but eventually the incline reduces and something akin to a path emerges, and when it does I drop back a little to fall alongside Jax. As we've been walking I've sensed his desire to talk to me, to ask questions, and I decide to put him out of his misery. I can't bear to make him wait any longer.

We walk a few strides together before he speaks.

'So you know my sister.' He doesn't ask, just states the obvious.

'Yes, I knew Grace.'

Jax tilts his head towards me, his eyes filled with resigned sorrow. 'Knew?'

I rest my hand on his shoulder. I can tell he's known for a while that I had nothing good to tell him, my silence speaking the words for me. But now he wants explanations.

'She was my family, the closest thing I'll ever have to a sister,' I say, wishing my throat would stop retracting whenever I mention her. I take a deep breath. 'She was murdered by the man who raised me. I'm sorry.'

Jax's eyes glisten, but no tears fall. 'I thought as much. I've felt no connection to her for a long time, and feared . . .' He stops, his voice now tight with emotion. 'But when you saw me, recognised me . . . well, I hoped . . .'

He turns his head away from me now and I reach for his hand, though I barely know him. But he's Grace's twin and we share the loss.

'Tell me what happened.' He still doesn't look at me, which makes it easier. Because it isn't a short story and I want to do Grace's life justice. So I tell Jax how Grace saved me, so many times over – how she took me from being a scared little girl afraid of her own shadow and trained me into a warrior. How she taught me to stand up for what was right. How she loved me simply for myself. I explain how she came to live on the *Maiden*, and how, once she realised who I was, she stayed to raise and protect me. I tell him everything about Captain Adler and how he put a bullet through Grace's beautiful head without a second thought. That her body rests on this very island.

By the time I finish the story both Jax and I have shed a few tears. The rest of our group have distanced themselves from us, understanding our conversation is private, though I know I'll need to share it with them in the fullness of time.

'She was successful then,' Jax says finally, once he's collected himself. 'The first of the Guardians to find the true heir to the bloodline.' He sounds proud, before his confusion breaks through. 'So why didn't she want *us* to find you?'

I hesitate. 'Grace was afraid you'd force me to take the throne, and we both knew that wasn't what I wanted.'

Jax looks sharply at me. 'You don't want the throne?'

'No.' There's no point lying about it. 'I've never wanted power or control. I would be a terrible ruler.'

'But it's yours by right.'

'Is that enough, though? Shouldn't it be earned?'

Jax rubs his face in his hands. 'As if things weren't already complicated enough.'

'What does that mean?'

'Nothing, it doesn't matter,' he says. 'Come on, we should catch up with the others.'

But I'm not going to let him off that easily, not after everything I've just shared, and I grab his arm to keep him from walking away.

'If you want me to come any further, you need to tell me what's going on.'

He looks at Mordecai, as if he's willing his companion to come to his rescue. But Mordecai doesn't turn round and Jax sighs.

'We need you to fight for the throne. We need you to want it.'

'Why? You've done without a king or queen for centuries. Why's it so important for me to claim it now?'

Jax lowers his voice. 'Because the other Guardians got tired of waiting.' He glances around, making certain no one else can hear him, and I feel a worm of apprehension uncoil in my gut.

'They found someone else, Marianne. Someone else is going to take the throne.'

16

The night is still and gloriously black. A light spray is blowing across the deck and as it caresses my face I breathe in the salt air, realising how much I've missed the sea.

Mordecai's ship is a solid but small sloop, and she is wonderfully fast. When we first boarded, Mordecai was keen to show Olwyn and Rayvn how everything worked, and I couldn't resist joining in. For so long I've been their student, learning the ways of the mountain, but I grew up on a ship. Here, I am the teacher.

Intended to be sailed by one person, the sea-sloop is sleek and streamlined. She dances easily to the ocean's music, but is perfectly balanced, so with every lift and dip she never tilts dangerously. Below deck there are only two berths, so the rest of us will have to sleep under the stars, but though it's cosy, it's not cramped. My cousins are drinking in every bit of knowledge – from the sails to the rigging – with extreme enthusiasm. Even now they're practising tying knots under Jax's watchful gaze.

Mordecai is supposedly sleeping, but I doubt he's having any more luck than I am.

I'm sitting beside the rudder, forfeiting my rest time to steer this nippy little vessel. There's no point even trying to sleep when my mind is this busy, and with the wind strong behind us someone needs to keep adjusting the heading. I'm more than happy for it to be me – being on the water again is soothing my troubled spirits.

The rest of the journey from the mountain to the harbour was filled with intense conversation and I'm still not sure what I think of all I've been told. That the majority of the Guardians had decided the search for the direct line of descendants had gone on too long with no success, and decided to put their contingency plan into action. For while their main quest had been to protect and guard my family, they had also been watching offshoots from the line. Five generations after the slaughter, my great-great-great-great grandfather had a younger sister. Her descendants had also been monitored and now the youngest of that line is being prepared for the throne.

His name is Rafe. He will be King.

And it bothers me.

Though I've never wanted to be Queen, I'm surprisingly riled at the thought of someone else taking what's not theirs to take.

I look down at the dark waters and remember how I summoned water raptors from them before. Are they still there? Are they biding their time, waiting for my call once more? Would they return for this other king?

Would the snow mares let *him* ride them? For the first time I wonder how much the islands choose their ruler, and feel a tremor of both terror and delight that they might choose me.

I miss the power I felt that day I called the raptors. Ever since I have been fighting and failing, losing control over every part of my life. I long to feel that sense of invincibility again, to see my enemies cower and tremble in fear. And yet . . . didn't I tell Jax I had no desire for power and control? Why does magical power entice me so much more than the power of ruling?

My fingers reach towards the waves, the temptation to speak to the raptors almost irresistible, and I'm imagining them breaking through the surface, drenching the deck with spray, their cries piercing the air . . .

Mordecai sits beside me, shattering the illusion.

'Can't sleep either?' he says.

'Evidently.'

He responds with his most charming smile. 'I feel like we've got off to a bad start,' he says. 'Which is a shame, given I've devoted my whole life to finding and protecting you.'

Though I can tell he's trying to make amends, everything about his statement irritates me. I never asked him to do either of those things, and I never would. Do they speak this way to their new prince? Does *he* regularly get told they're there to protect him? Or do they feel that because I'm a woman I need protection? Should I be flattered by these supposed acts of devotion?

'There was a time when I needed protecting, and you weren't the Guardian who was there for me,' I say. 'Grace was the only Guardian I knew and trusted and she didn't trust the rest of you. So forgive me if I don't instantly fall for your honeyed words.'

Mordecai remains silent for a moment, realising he's on ground more dangerous than the mountainside. When he tries again, his voice is softer, less arrogant. 'Grace was my cousin, did you know? I trained with her and Jax as children, and we only separated when Jax and I returned West and she did not.'

I look out towards the sea, so he can't see my rising tears. 'You should never have left her.'

'No, we shouldn't have.' And I hear grief in his words. 'Grace always was the smart one. The best thinker, the best fighter. When she said we should look in the East, we should have listened.'

Neither of us speak for a while and I know it's time to move the conversation back to the present; I can't keep dwelling on the past.

'So, what's wrong with this Rafe then?'

Mordecai also seems relieved to move on from the painful topic of Grace. 'I think you'll find he goes by *Prince* Rafe, thank you very much. And who says there's anything wrong with him?'

I give Mordecai a small smile. 'You'd hardly have come all this way to find me if you were happy with your new king.'

He sighs. 'I guess some of us weren't ready to give up on our true calling. We still believed the real heir was out there to be found.'

'And what did *Prince* Rafe think about you continuing to search for me?' I emphasise the word 'Prince' with all the sarcasm it deserves. When Mordecai hesitates, I groan. 'He doesn't know, does he?'

'The thing you need to understand about Rafe, is that he was taken in by the Guardians when he was only five years old. They've been grooming him to be the King his whole life.'

'Why now? What made the Guardians decide to reclaim the throne after all these years?'

'Gaius sensed the time had come.'

'Gaius?'

'The Mage we told you about. He's been allied with the Guardians for many years now. He's currently acting as an advisor to Rafe, though he knows about you, of course, as he was the one to feel your presence.'

My heart flutters with excitement. 'A Mage advising royalty?'

Mordecai nods. 'Just like the old days.'

Excitement gives way to jealousy. It should be me working with their Mage. 'Tell me about him. Gaius, I mean.'

'Well, he's old, had a hard life. Like you, he's a descendant of one of the lucky survivors of that brutal annihilation, so he has a connection to the palace. It's destiny that he should now stand alongside the next monarch.'

'Apart from Gaius, who else knows about me?'

'Only a few of the senior Guardians. We thought it best to find you before revealing your existence to too many.'

The wind is changing direction now, and for a moment I have to concentrate on zigzagging the sea-sloop through the choppy waters. The boom swings from port to starboard, nearly knocking Olwyn overboard before Rayvn pulls her out of the way. When I've steadied the boat, I realise Mordecai is watching me closely.

'What?'

'Why are you here?' His direct question takes me by surprise. 'If you don't want to be Queen, then why have you returned to the West? Your life looked pretty perfect when I left you in the East.'

I chuckle humourlessly as I shake my head. 'You have no idea, do you?'

'Then tell me.'

He's right – if I want to work with them, I can't keep holding them all at arm's length.

And so I sum up what is happening in the East. All the conflict, all the starvation. While I talk, I notice the other three are straining to listen, so I lift my voice to carry. It's when I explain why I came West, what I was hoping to find, that I see the Guardians' faces drop.

'You came for help?' Jax sounds disappointed.

'She came for magic.' Olwyn on the other hand sounds proud.

'I came for both.'

Jax and Mordecai are sharing a troubled look and my spirits sink.

'What? What is it?'

Jax exhales a deep sigh. 'I'm not sure why you think anyone here would help you. Help the East? They destroyed us.'

'I know.' There's a bite to my voice now. 'Trust me, I understand all that's been lost.' I see Olwyn flinch slightly at my anger and force myself to calm down. 'Aren't you sick of it, though?' I ask, more softly this time. 'Of the separation? The bitterness? The turmoil? I know how these islands have suffered. Why not try to reunite East and West and seek peace again? Surely that's in everyone's interest.'

Mordecai looks sceptical. 'And you want to achieve that without being Queen?'

I rub my face with my hands, too weary to keep arguing. 'I don't know. I'm just tired of all the misery. I want it to end.'

'How bad are the other islands?' Rayvn asks Mordecai. 'We've been sheltered up in the mountains from the rest of the world.' I hear her resentment seeping through even in that simple statement.

'Bad,' he replies. 'Especially the Twelfth.'

'Great,' I say. Just what I want to head into.

Jax rests his hand on my shoulder. 'Look, we've taken an oath to serve you, whether you choose to be our queen or not. We'll help you however we can, but I can't speak for the rest of the Guardians. My advice is that we tread carefully when we arrive at the palace. Very carefully.'

'Agreed,' says Mordecai. 'I think you'll find many reluctant to acknowledge you at all.'

'Why's that?' It's Olwyn that asks, and it warms me to hear how defensive she sounds towards me.

'Because now their plan is Rafe. Not Marianne.'

'Fine. So we say I'm not there to challenge him, but to seek guidance from Gaius, the Mage.' Which is actually the truth – from my point of view anyway.

'All right,' Mordecai says. 'But please don't rule out the throne altogether. Restoring peace to the West will be even harder than achieving it in your beloved East.'

The most I can bring myself to do is nod. I don't want to commit to anything I'm going to regret.

'So how long until we reach the Twelfth Isle?' Rayvn asks, her impatience obvious.

'In this ship? Not too long,' Mordecai says. 'But we have to stop off on the way to get Astrid.'

This is the first I've heard of a detour. 'Who's Astrid?'

'One of us,' Jax says. 'Her father is sick and so we left her on the Ninth to visit him while we came to find you. We promised to pick her up on our return.'

There's something about the way he says 'one of us' that makes me realise he doesn't just mean one of the Guardians – he means one of the like-minded Guardians. There is clearly huge division growing among them about the future of their duty and of how to fulfil their promise to protect the royalty. My sinking feeling deepens; I've just swapped one political mess for another.

By the time dawn has broken the Ninth Isle comes into view. The sunrise seems to scorch the landscape in flame, but as we approach I realise it isn't the light creating the colours; it's the landscape itself: the cliffs are steep, exposed and rust red; clusters of bright yellow flowers burst like stars from the stone; and small orange birds flit in and out of nesting holes. And yet, for all its beauty, a strange sensation creeps over me, a feeling that I shouldn't be going there. The nervous flutters only increase the closer we get, and as Jax steers us into a fairly empty-looking harbour, Mordecai takes me aside.

'Can your cousins fight?'

I'm surprised by the question, because what does he think the protectors of the snow mares do? 'Of course. They're not carrying those spears for fun.'

'I just needed to check.'

'Why, are you expecting trouble?'

'On the Ninth Isle? Always.'

'Let me stay with the boat.' I say it almost impulsively and register his surprise.

'I wouldn't have thought a little danger would scare you, Viper.'

'It doesn't,' I say, trying to hide my irritation. 'It's just a feeling that's all. That if I go on land, nothing good will happen.'

'Is this one of your magical feelings?' I can tell he's only teasing, but it irritates me nonetheless.

'Listening to my feelings has kept me alive this long.'

'All right,' he says, stepping back slightly. 'I didn't mean to offend.'

'I'm sorry.' I'm being unfair to him. Maybe it's something to do with how he reminds me of my wedding, of Torin and Bronn and all my uncertainty regarding their well-being.

'Don't worry,' he says. 'We'll fetch Astrid, grab some supplies and be back before day's end. You can stay here and stop anyone stealing my ship.'

I raise an eyebrow. 'Is that likely?'

Mordecai laughs. 'Oh yes.'

When we pull up at port, I watch Mordecai press silver into the palm of the harbour master, and then stare with unexpected longing at their retreating backs as they follow the road up into the island. Perhaps I should have gone with them after all.

Instead I regard the harbour with a wary gaze. There aren't many people about; though, from the distant drone of noise, I suspect there are a fair few in the ramshackle tavern at the far end of the pier. I can't see any signs of danger, but then it's early in the morning. Perhaps everyone's still sleeping off last night's fighting and drinking.

I turn away to look at what lies beyond the cove and something catches my eye. Though I can't see properly with the rocks in the way, it appears as if the sand in the bay is pink. I lean as far against the rail as I can, stretching for a better view, and, sure enough, the ground is shimmering like a shoal of rosetails.

But pink sand is not the only thing the improved view reveals. I can also see a group of men, crowded round something, their arms swinging back and forth, raining blows down on whatever lies among them. Narrowing my eyes, I manage to catch a glimpse of a body on the ground before it's concealed once more.

Cursing with frustration, I jump off the sloop on to the harbour. I'm sure the boat will be fine without me, and I have to put aside my own misgivings about landing on the island, because I can't sit and do nothing while someone's in trouble.

Running towards the hidden cove, I scramble over rocks and drop down on to the sand.

'Leave him alone!' I shout at the men, who are still beating the life out of their victim.

They look round at me in surprise but deem me so little threat that only one man breaks from the pack to stroll towards me, and he stinks of rum and piss. I easily dodge his slow attempt at a punch, and then grab his arm, twisting it hard until it snaps beneath my fingers, and hold it while he screams.

That gets their attention.

'Leave that man or I'll kill you all,' I say and this time they believe me. They run away from me, away from the beach, and I hurry towards the body lying on the ground.

The man they were beating is old, frail and unconscious. I kneel beside him, but can tell in a moment there's nothing I can do. Even as I try to staunch the bleeding coming from his head, he's slipping towards death. They've robbed him of everything, and that includes his life.

Stepping away, I sink into the sand, curling my fists into balls. Anger seeps out of me as I swear into the wind. Always I'm too late – for this stranger, for the islanders on the Sixth Isle. I cannot afford to keep being one step behind. Not when the lives of the people I love

301

are at stake. So many promises I've made – to Torin, to Bronn, to Raoul and Lilah, to the islands themselves. If I'm to keep them, I have to do better.

I wonder whether to go in search of my friends, but know I'll probably end up lost. So I decide to stay with the dying man, to make sure no one disturbs him in his final moments. I run my fingers through the pinkish sand, softer than silk, wondering what could make it this colour. Pigment from shells crushed into minuscule pieces perhaps?

There's a movement further down the shoreline. Sitting up, I squint to get a better look and realise there are three people walking in my direction. I rise quickly to my feet and rest my hand where my knife sits in my belt, in case it's the thieves returning to strip even the clothes from the old man's back.

But I can soon tell it's not. Two men and a woman, all three dressed in rags and looking undernourished, are approaching me, confusion on their faces. There is a wild look about them that unsettles me and my hand twitches towards my dagger.

'What are you doing here?' It's the woman who shouts over at me, her eyes piercing, her face leathery. The anger in her question throws me.

When I don't answer immediately, she continues. 'Don't you know where you are? Don't you know what this place is? This is the Blood Isle. You shouldn't have come.'

Though I have no idea why I'm on the receiving end of her anger, her words don't escape me. Blood Isle. I look at the pink tinge to the sand, remember the red cliffs, and feel my own blood run cold.

'That's right,' one of the men says, noticing the direction of my gaze. 'There's as much blood in the ground here as there is rock.' Then his voice changes. 'Why did you come?' Now he sounds desperate, as if my presence has caused him pain.

I open my mouth, without knowing what I might possibly say, but before any sound can spill from it, something moves behind me. Spinning round, expecting danger, I see the old man I'd given up for dead struggling to his feet. He stares at his hands for a moment before looking up at me.

'You're alive,' I say, relieved to have been wrong about his fate. 'Are you hurt?' But he just continues to stare and a sense of foreboding passes through me, raising the hair on my arms.

And then the shouts start.

My head whips towards the harbour where the sound is coming from, my heart beginning to race. I turn briefly back but there's no surprise on the others' faces. They look sad, as if they expected nothing less.

Sensing I will get no answers from them, I race towards the settlement, pulling my knife free as I run. Once I've scaled the rock separating the cove from the harbour, I see men fleeing from the tavern, stumbling in their haste and looking all the more fearful for their delay. As I draw near, I grab the arm of one man, recoiling when I see his terror.

'What is it?' I ask, unsettled by the chaos.

He stares at me as if he doesn't really see me. He just points frantically at the tavern, before spinning on his heel and running away as fast as he can.

I frown, wondering what could possibly have caused such a reaction, and resolve to find out for myself, but as I weave through those fleeing, more screams reach my ears. More distant screams. Coming from the direction my friends went. And as I hear other sounds too – the clink of steel, the crack of pistols firing – I abandon my thoughts of the tavern.

Sprinting towards the town, my only thoughts now are of Olwyn and Rayvn. Though I know they're skilled fighters, they've also never left the relative safety of the mountains and, having encouraged them to leave, I feel responsible for them.

As my fear increases the nearer I get to the main settlement, I realise it's more than that. I've grown to love them. They're my family. The thought of anything happening to them is too much to bear.

The road I'm on leads straight from the harbour to the settlement, a snaking incline flanked by crimson trees, their trunks twisted, their long feathery branches sighing mournfully as they sweep the ground. Those running from the harbour like myself are soon met by a wall of other people coming towards us – fleeing the settlement. It's mayhem, the reek of fear unavoidable. The two opposing crowds meet each other and more shouting commences; it's mere moments before the first punches are thrown. I try to overhear what people are afraid of, but only get snatches that make no sense. The best I can decipher is that there's been some sort of invasion. I run faster.

Dodging through the crowds, I finally reach the settlement and grind to a halt – partly because I have no idea where I'm going, but also to take in the sight before me. There are people everywhere and they can easily be divided into two categories. Those who look confused and those who look afraid. Pistols are being fired, but no one is falling to the ground and I can't understand what's happening.

Someone grabs my arm, and I spin to defend myself, but it's only Olwyn. I pull her into an embrace.

'I was coming to find you,' she says and I hear her relief that she's managed it so quickly.

'What's happening?' I ask her, alarmed by how pale she looks.

'It's Astrid's father,' she says. Though she's clearly scared, I can see a glint in her eye. She's also excited. 'He's alive.'

'So?' I'm still struggling to understand.

'He wasn't. Astrid was mourning for him. But now he's back. They all are.'

'Who are?'

'The dead, Marianne.' And her eyes dance with wonder. 'The dead have risen.'

It's not possible. I know it's not. And yet I believe Olwyn completely, as if it's the only conclusion anyone could possibly reach. My eyes scan the scene again and this time it makes sense. People are seeing ghosts and in their fear are shooting them, trying to return them to their graves. When they fail, it only makes them more afraid. The dead, on the other hand, simply seem bewildered, uncertain why they are here, confused by the response.

Olwyn is tugging at my sleeve. 'Come on, we have to get back to the others.'

I let her take my hand and lead me through the street, ducking and weaving to avoid the chaos.

'Moyra?'

Something about the voice cuts through me, and though it's not my name being called, I know it's directed at me. I turn to see who's spoken, my hand slipping away from Olwyn's. The woman is staring at me like *I'm* the ghost and I step towards her, suddenly oblivious to what's happening round me, drawn to the unnerving familiarity about her.

Standing directly in front of me, searching my face, the woman cries out, her hand flying to her mouth. 'Oh!

You look so like her,' she says, and I'm stunned to hear the dead speak.

'Like who? Moyra?' I think I already know the answer.

'Yes. But you have a look about him too, mind. You're their young lass?' And the woman's face is full of love and sorrow.

Tears spring all too quickly to my eyes. 'You knew my parents?'

The woman nods. 'Oh yes.' And then she smiles. 'I loved your father his whole life.'

I realise why she looks so familiar. I've seen that nose in the looking glass. The angle of her brow is the same as my own. 'You're his mother?'

'I am.'

'My grandmother.'

A radiant smile spreads across her face, matching mine.

Olwyn has doubled back to see what's delayed me and is staring at us in confusion. 'Marianne?'

My grandmother tilts her head. 'Marianne.' She echoes my name.

No. I want her to know the truth. Want her to know the name my parents chose for me. 'They called me Mairin. That's my real name.'

My grandmother smiles at me. 'I'm Baia. It's so wonderful to meet you.'

Olwyn looks more than a little unnerved that I'm talking to a dead woman, and reaches for me. 'We have to go.'

There's no doubt it's dangerous out here on the streets, but if Olwyn thinks I'm going to walk away from the closest family member I've ever met, she's sorely mistaken.

'Come with us?'

Olwyn doesn't look best pleased that I've invited a ghost to join us, but I don't care and feel a great sense of relief when my grandmother nods.

'We must hurry,' Olwyn says again, and this time I go with her, checking Baia is following behind.

Despite the madness devouring the island, I find myself impressed with Olwyn's sense of direction as she leads us swiftly through the narrow, cobbled streets to a small cottage, where we bang on the door.

Mordecai opens it, and his already pale face grows whiter when he sees we've brought company. He ushers us in before slamming the door shut, barricading it with a heavy table.

The small room is fit to burst with people, all of whom look equally spooked. On one side all my friends are hovering, Jax's arms round the woman I presume is Astrid. Her eyes are locked without blinking on the man she recently buried, who now sits in a chair on the opposite side of the room.

'What's going on?' I say, hoping someone has some answers.

But everyone looks equally blank – apart from my grandmother.

'Don't you know?' she says to me. 'You did this.'

I stare at her, my face beginning to burn as I realise everyone's looking at me. 'No I didn't.'

It's Astrid whose eyes widen as she understands what Baia is implying and she pulls away from Jax, her attention now directed solely at me. 'They said you were staying with the ship. Did you come on land before this started? Did you go to the sands?'

'Yes,' I say. 'I went to the cove beside the harbour. There was someone in trouble.' My voice is too defensive, but it's strange to meet someone for the first time and have to convince them you aren't responsible for the reappearance of their recently deceased father.

Astrid glances at Baia who nods, as if confirming Astrid's unspoken theory.

'What is it?' Mordecai says.

'You don't know the legend?' Astrid looks from Mordecai to Jax, but they both seem none the wiser. 'How a child of the bloodline could call forth the island's spirits through the blood in the ground?'

I remember sinking into the sand, channelling my anger, my regret for the dead I have failed, into it. I shake my head. 'No. Please no.'

Rayvn narrows her eyes. 'Is that even possible?'

Astrid gestures to the outside. 'Do you have another explanation?'

Sickness rises inside me. The old man from the beach. He didn't recover; he was dead. I brought him back. It was me. It was all me.

'I didn't know!' The words come out like a gasp. 'How could I have known? What kind of island is this?'

Astrid looks at me through her dark lashes, wild curls of hair not unlike my own framing half her face, the other half of her head shaved close to the skin. 'A cursed one. One where your magic is connected to its very roots. Long ago, there was an uprising on the Twelfth Isle. The people were starving, and the fault lay entirely with the King, who only cared about smoking billo-weed day and night. The King demanded the people from all islands fight for the crown against the rebels. But the Ninth refused their help. After much bloodshed, the rebellion failed, but once he had revelled in his victory, the King turned his wrath on the Ninth. Outraged by their betrayal, he used what little magic he possessed to tie the spirits of our ancestors to his descendants. Those that died on this land could never know peace, always waiting should the royalty summon them, bound to obey them for ever. But the dead have slept for centuries, the legend passing from generation to generation our sole reminder of the blood curse. Until today.'

'I'm sorry.' What else can I possibly say?

'There must be some other way to stop this.' Olwyn remains ever practical.

My grandmother comes to rest her hands on my shoulders. 'There is. You simply need to leave these shores and we will return to the place you summoned us from.'

'Then we must hurry,' Mordecai says. 'Before this island tears itself apart.'

'Wait.' Though I'm sorry I've disturbed the dead and terrified the living, I'm not ready to bid farewell to my grandmother just yet.

Ignoring the others, I face Baia once more and see understanding in her eyes. She knows I have questions only she can answer.

'You have magic in you,' she says, and she sounds proud. 'Do not be afraid, Mairin. Of yourself, or of it. Learn instead to embrace who you are.'

'Did my mother have magic?' I'm thinking of what Mama suggested, that perhaps my mother had sought out Esther for the very reasons I had.

'Oh yes.' Her smile fades. 'Do you know nothing of your parents?'

'Only that they were murdered.'

If the dead can feel pain, then I've just stuck a blade through my grandmother. It's clear she hadn't known their fate before she died and it takes her a moment to gather herself. 'I wish we had more time,' she says. 'There is much to speak of. But your friends are right. Our presence here is only causing harm.'

Mordecai looks grateful and motions to move, but my grandmother holds up her hand.

'But this you must hear – all of you.' Though she's speaking to the room, her eyes lock firmly upon my own. 'Your father was a Guardian of the Royal Bloodline. That's how they met. He devoted his life to protecting Moyra and, though it was forbidden, they fell in love. But they were being hunted and they fled here, afraid. They wouldn't tell me what troubled them, but nothing had ever scared your father before. Moyra wanted to learn how to protect herself and so they were seeking the Mage on the Eighth. Clearly they were too late. I don't know what evil pursued them, but be warned: it may still be looking for you. Be careful, my child.'

It's a lot of information to absorb. My father was a Guardian? I had always wondered about him, but I'd never considered this possibility, though I don't know why. It makes more sense than anything else. It would seem I inherited my fighting skills from my father, my magic from my mother. I've never missed them more than right now.

'They were fleeing Adler,' I say, my voice flat. 'He's no longer a threat to me.'

But my grandmother doesn't look convinced. 'I perceive the danger to you most acutely. Trust no one.'

Mordecai touches my arm. 'We have to get you out of here. Please.'

I glance over at Astrid, who's moved to kneel beside her father, savouring these stolen minutes together. Her grief is an open wound and I can't keep her in distress any longer.

'One last thing,' I say to Baia. 'Can I . . .' I struggle to put my question into words, but she knows what's in my heart.

'Can you raise the dead on other islands?' she guesses.

We both know I'm thinking of my parents. I would do almost anything to have the chance to meet them, to speak with them.

'I'm sorry,' she says with a shake of her head. 'Only those who've bled into this rock are yours to raise. But while I shall always be here for you, do not call me lightly. It was a cruel act of the King to bind us to the living. Souls should be allowed to rest with the earth.'

I nod, even as tears prick my eyes. I don't want to lose her so quickly after having found her.

Though everyone's itching to go, I don't move, looking up at my grandmother through misty eyes, thinking of Old Tatty's prophecy, which never truly leaves me. 'Does it hurt?'

Baia's eyes are full of sorrow. 'To die? Yes. To be dead? Not at all.'

314

The tears spill now as I say, 'Goodbye.' The moment the word escapes my lips, Mordecai seizes his opportunity and unblocks the door. Astrid bids a tearful farewell to her father and together our group of the living run back into the hectic town.

We sprint hard towards the harbour, and as my feet pound along the track I curse myself for not listening to my own internal warning to stay off this island. And yet I can't regret meeting my grandmother – even if she is dead. To have learned about my father is a gift I wouldn't trade for anything.

But as we reach the harbour my heart sinks. In their desperation to flee the island people are trying to take any boats they can – including ours.

'No, no, no,' Mordecai shouts when he sees a group of men boarding his beloved sloop.

Roaring with aggression, we cut through the frantic crowds, our determination far outweighing theirs. Though the men have successfully untied Mordecai's ship and are starting to pull away from the port by the time we get there, the boat hasn't gone far enough to stop us all from leaping aboard.

The second my feet leave the land, the change is noticeable. I can almost hear the island breathing a sigh of relief.

Rayvn and Olwyn are able to knock several of our unwanted passengers into the water with their spears, while the rest of us resort to our fists. It's not far for the thieves to swim once we've sent them overboard, and only when we're alone do we all relax.

Jax is the first to laugh – a noise filled with nervous tension. 'Astrid, meet Marianne. Our rightful Queen and apparently the bringer of nightmares.'

Despite having every reason not to like me one bit, Astrid comes and gives me a warm embrace. 'It's so good to finally meet you.'

'I'm sorry,' I say, feeling more than a little awkward. 'For your loss.'

Her eyes swim with tears. 'Thank you. You know the pain of losing a father.'

I squeeze her hand, but say nothing. I never knew my real father to grieve for him, and I took the life of the cruel man who raised me. I can only ever mourn for what might have been.

As we settle down to our journey, I notice once more how Rayvn sticks closely to Mordecai's side, asking him endless questions about sailing, the mechanics of the ship, the sails. Her thirst for knowledge makes me smile. She's like a bird who's been kept in a cage her whole life and has finally been shown the open sky. Her wings are stretching for the first time and she's realising how far they reach.

Olwyn comes to sit beside me with a mangwyan fruit sliced for us to share.

'Hungry?'

I'm not, but I take a piece anyway, because I want her company.

'Rayvn likes the sea,' I say, nodding in her direction.

Olwyn smiles, but there's sadness there. 'There'll be no return to the mountains for her.'

I chew the sweet flesh without tasting it. 'Why do you say that?'

'Because I've known her all my life,' Olwyn says. 'And I've never seen her so . . .' She searches for the right word. '. . . alive.'

'How about you?' I ask. 'Do you feel alive?'

Olwyn takes her time before answering. 'I'm glad to have the opportunity to leave the mountains, to see the islands. But I feel like a child taking her first steps. Like I could fall at any moment. There's so much I don't know, and an overwhelming amount to learn. It feels like I can't quite get the air into my lungs quickly enough to breathe properly, that I might blow away like dust on the wind.'

I watch her closely, the way she stares out to sea, letting the breeze cool her skin, and for a moment she seems so fragile. But I know her better than that. Olwyn is the calm to Rayvn's storm. Where Rayvn burns with fire, Olwyn runs deeper than the ocean. Her wisdom is her strength, her steadiness an anchor. The more she doubts herself, the more I trust her.

'Today I watched the dead walk,' she says, turning away from the water now. 'I don't know the rules any more.'

I lean my head on to her shoulder. 'Neither do I.'

Olwyn starts to laugh. 'We're in so much trouble.'

'Walking disasters,' I agree.

'But not Rayvn.' Olwyn's sigh swallows her laughter. 'She's never been surer of herself. I envy her.'

I look at Olwyn, and see her happiness and loss all at once. Grace may not have shared my blood, but she was my sister. I know what it is to be separated, to live with the empty space where she should be. I don't wish such a fate for my cousins, but it's clear that Olwyn already foresees a time where she and Rayvn will take different paths. Paths that may never lead back to each other.

And I squeeze her hand.

Over the next few days, I find myself watching Rayvn closely and I can see why Olwyn envies her. She's blossoming with every passing minute. Her strong physique grows tighter as she adapts to living on the water. Her balance is extraordinary, and during stormy weather she is entirely unfazed by the rocking motion of the ship, bounding about with ease, shimmying the mast as if she'd been doing it her whole life.

I'm now entirely certain about what I've long suspected: Rayvn is a born Snake.

I think she feels it too, because as the days pass and our destination grows closer, I sense her mood dampen at the prospect of leaving the sea.

So early one morning, I rise to scrub the decks with her, wanting a chance to speak without anyone overhearing.

We work for a while in silence. Rayvn may hold a grudging respect for me since she saw me fight, but our relationship is still cool, if no longer frosty.

'We'll be arriving at the Twelfth the day after tomorrow,' I say eventually.

Rayvn says nothing, only scrubs harder at the plank of wood beneath her.

'I wonder what it's like?' I'm more musing out loud now, because I don't think Rayvn's going to answer, but she grunts out two terse words.

'Who cares?'

I hide my smile. She's talking to me.

'Aren't you excited?' I ask with mock surprise. 'A whole new island to discover, the home of the royal family?'

Rayvn shrugs. 'It's just another landmass, full of people who hate each other and will hate us. What's there to be excited about?'

I let the question hang in the air, wondering if I really dare set my idea in motion. 'Something's bothering me,' I say, choosing my words carefully. I flick my eyes over to see if she's listening. I have her attention. 'My friends back in the East still think Mordecai is responsible for the attempted murder of my husband. They're searching for the wrong man.' I pause again, letting her take this in. 'I need to get word to them that they should be looking for someone else, to rethink their strategy.'

Rayvn stops scrubbing and sits up on her knees. 'You want to send a bird?'

There's only one bird I'd depend on for such a message and I don't want to dwell on what might have prevented Talon from returning to me.

I look her firmly in the eye. 'I would rather send someone I trust.'

I can almost hear her mind turning this over, as she processes what I'm really saying. She clearly isn't sure whether she can believe it.

'Who?' she asks suspiciously.

'You seem happy at sea,' I say, my voice quiet but warm. 'I would trust you to take my message to Bronn. He would like you.'

'You want me to travel east? And find your ship?'

I nod. 'If you wish to go.'

We hold each other's gaze for a moment – an understanding passing between us.

'Yes,' she says eventually, her eyes burning with excitement. 'I'll deliver your message, if that's what you want.'

'Thank you,' I say and stand up to leave, our business complete.

But, as I do so, she calls out to me. 'Marianne?'

When I look back, I see the rarest thing. Rayvn is smiling at me. 'Thank you.'

The words are barely a whisper, but they dance on the sea air and wrap themselves round me like an embrace. It's the closest to a hug I'll ever get from Rayvn, but it's enough.

It's enough.

18

We arrive at the Twelfth under the cover of night. Mordecai sails us round to a hidden nook in the cliff that he's clearly used a thousand times before and we prepare to go on land. All of us that is, apart from Rayvn.

She will take the boat East and find the *Maiden*, ostensibly so she can inform Bronn of Mordecai's innocence, but I think we all know she won't be coming back. Olwyn has been predictably supportive, though I see how it grieves her. Mordecai is less enthusiastic, not wanting to give away his boat, but Rayvn promises him she'll return it. It might take her a while, but I'm certain it's a promise she'll keep.

I was concerned such a small sloop might not be strong enough to navigate the open ocean between the West and East, but when I expressed my concern Mordecai had given me a crushing look and said, 'Well, it got me to you before, didn't it?' and that was that.

We've talked through charts, Jax has advised where she can stop for supplies before venturing into the open sea, and finally there really is nothing left to do but say goodbye. When I lean forward to give Rayvn an awkward hug, she pulls me tightly towards her, much to my astonishment.

'Have you any other message for Bronn?' She whispers it so no one else can hear, and I realise that for all I've not talked about him, she's heard what I've left unsaid. She's continued to surprise me to the very end.

What would I like her to say to him? That I'm sorry? That I miss him? That I wish he was here with me so I didn't feel so alone, so incomplete? What purpose would any such message serve? I move slightly away and shake my head. 'Thank you, but no. Only what we discussed. And, Rayvn? You can trust him, no matter what he says or does.' I don't know why, but it seems vital that she knows that.

'You all be safe,' Rayvn says, after we've climbed on to the narrow path leading up the cliff, leaving her in the boat. She looks directly at me. 'Go raise that army, Viper Queen.' And with a half-mocking, half-sincere bow, she takes the rope from Mordecai and pushes the boat away from land.

Olwyn waves at her for a long moment, before turning briskly away. 'Come on,' she says, her voice shaking slightly with emotion. 'Let's go.'

None of us argues with her, and together we traipse up the cliff side, our cloaks wrapped round us, our daggers drawn, silently disappearing into the night.

We don't want to be seen – by anyone – and so we move like shadows across the grass that takes us from the cliff edge further inland. It's a shame I can't see much of the scenery but as darkness hides the island so it obscures us. When the sun begins to rise, we rest for an hour or so, in a damp woodland full of trees with drooping leaves that occasionally float to the ground like tears. It's so dismal I have to hide my disappointment.

'It's like the whole island is in mourning,' Olwyn says to me under her breath and I nod in agreement.

Astrid, who's sitting beside Olwyn, overhears. 'You have no idea.' She moves round so that we're sitting in a triangle.

'What do you mean?' Olwyn's voice is barely a whisper.

'This place is pure darkness and death,' Astrid says. 'There is no happiness to be found on the Twelfth Isle.'

But before she can continue, Mordecai gestures for us all to be silent. 'Something's coming,' he says.

An eerie silence descends, the rustle of leaves making us all tighten our grip on our blades. And then the branches part, as a huge bird swoops down, screaming out a greeting, and the others all brace to attack even as I hold out my arm.

'It's OK,' I say, relieved and trying not to laugh at their shock. 'It's just Talon.'

Mordecai shakes his head in disbelief. 'You have a sea vulture?'

'I don't think anyone owns Talon,' I say, stroking his feathers as he nips my fingers. 'You found me then?' I say to my friend. 'I thought I'd lost you too.'

'Is there any chance he can go back to wherever he came from?' Mordecai asks. 'A massive sea vulture doesn't really help the whole being inconspicuous thing.'

I ignore him, and step away from the others, not wanting them to hear what I say to Talon. 'Have you been back East?' The bird bobs his head in way of answer. 'Is Torin still alive?' I hold my breath until Talon nods once more and I rest my head gently against his. 'Thank goodness. And Bronn?' This time the bird tilts his head, and I know what that means. 'He's not doing so well?' Talon makes a small squawk in response. 'Things are that bad?' This time he flaps his wings, and I have to duck to avoid getting hit in the head. 'All right, I need to hurry, I understand. I'm doing my best.'

I glance over to where the others are waiting, pretending not to watch what I'm doing and failing miserably.

'My cousin is sailing back to the *Maiden*,' I say to the sea vulture. 'She's alone and on the ocean. Will you watch over her for me? Let me know when she's safely there?'

Talon nuzzles into my neck. It's not simply affection. He wants payment. 'Fair enough,' I laugh, and take some mangwyan fruit from my bag, which he gratefully devours. 'Be safe,' I say to him, and giving me a withering look that says I should worry only for myself, the sea vulture takes to the air and disappears beyond the forest canopy.

The moment he's gone, a cloak of loneliness wraps round me. I wish he could have stayed; the reminder of home was comforting. But at least I know Torin still lives, even if the rest of his news wasn't so welcome.

'We should keep moving,' I say to the others as I rejoin them. They exchange glances, but say nothing as we resume our journey.

Astrid stays close to Olwyn and me as we prowl through the trees, constantly alert to our surroundings. Once we emerge from the forest, we are more exposed and we detour off the path to avoid travelling through a settlement. But as we pass over the brow of a hill we see – then smell – the smoke rising.

'What's that?' I ask, readying myself for action.

'Just your average civil unrest,' Mordecai says, holding my arm. 'Nothing to concern us.'

I stare at him with astonishment. 'Nothing to do with the heir to the throne and her protectors? Are you kidding me?'

'Slow down,' he says with a grin. 'Let's get you crowned first, and then you can get to work fixing the Isles.'

I don't return his humour. 'There could be people in trouble.'

'There are always people in trouble. You won't help them by storming in there. That's how you get yourself killed. You help them by coming with us.'

Maybe he's right. Maybe I shouldn't keep rushing into danger. Maybe I should start thinking with my head, not my heart. But that's just not who I am.

'I don't plan to storm,' is all I say, before I turn my back on him and start running towards the settlement, taking my dagger firmly into my hand as I do.

I proceed with caution, not knowing the terrain or what I might possibly find. All I know is if I walk past and do nothing, I have no business asking the people here for help.

The settlement is quiet as I approach, the air thick with smoke, as buildings surrender to the flames. I'm too late. The fight is over, only the spoils remain, which means it'll be more dangerous for those who have survived – *if* any have survived. Positioning myself behind a cluster of rocks, I survey the situation.

There are many bodies scattered on the ground. The attackers roam between them, checking the corpses for anything worth stealing, and the blatant disrespect they show for the victims makes me want to leap out and slit their necks. But I wait. For now. I want to be sure how many there are.

A slight movement behind me causes me to swing round with my blade raised, but it's just Jax.

'The others are surrounding the settlement,' he says. 'What do you want us to do?'

I smile at him, grateful for their support. 'Who are these people? Bandits?'

Jax watches the scavengers for a moment, frowning. 'Probably. Do you think there are any survivors?'

Before I can answer, a scream pierces the air and we look at each other.

'Come on,' I say, already running towards the desperate sound.

The people in our path look up in shock at our appearance, and they barely have time to blink before we strike them down. And then my other friends are there, joining the fight, and I slip past them to follow the sound of screams.

The cries guide me to where I'm needed, and I see a man ripping a woman's top from shoulder to waist as he pushes her against the wall. I can smell her fear even through the smoke, and my dagger leaves my hand immediately, landing firmly in his back.

He staggers forward, confused, trying to reach for the blade. But I get there first, and pull it from his flesh, before bringing it round to his neck and pinning him against the wall.

'You're going to die anyway,' I say to him. 'But if you tell me who you are, I'll make it nice and quick.'

He grins at me in a way that makes my blood chill.

He doesn't care. 'You're too late. Your clan is finished, your lands taken. They belong to my people now.'

I frown at him, piecing things together. So this is a warring territory situation. But while I'm figuring this out, the woman he attacked has found a sword lying on the ground and she drives it hard through her would-be rapist's stomach, twisting the blade until the light slips away from his eyes.

She's shaking and I gently prise her hand from the bloodied hilt.

'Are you OK?' I ask, though clearly she's not.

'He killed her; he killed my wife,' she says, choking back tears.

I rest my hand on her shoulder. 'I'm so sorry. Are there any other survivors?'

She shakes her head. 'I don't know.'

My friends have joined us now, and, like me, are spattered in blood.

'We've not found anyone else alive,' Mordecai says.

'I think some people may have fled,' Astrid says. 'I saw tracks heading east.'

The woman nods, holding her torn shirt up to protect her modesty. 'We have friends that way. I hope they made it.'

'You know these people?' I ask her, gesturing to the dead man now slumped at our feet.

'Yes,' she says. 'A rival clan from across the river. They've been trying to take our lands from us for years.

We've always managed to defend them, but tonight everyone was celebrating our wedding, and we were distracted. It was meant to be a joyful day.'

None of us knows what to say. She's lost her wife, her village and her people all in one night. Olwyn shakes off her cloak and gently places it over the woman's shoulders.

'Let us take you to the next settlement,' I say. 'Hopefully you'll find others who have survived.'

I can see Mordecai shaking his head at me. He wants to get going, not delay any further. I ignore him.

We walk beneath the stars, stinking of smoke and blood, until we deliver the woman to safety. Having reunited her with a handful of surviving kin, now being cared for by their neighbours, we bid her farewell, and much to Mordecai's relief, finally resume our own journey.

We travel in silence now, the taste of misery in the air. We're all filthy from the fight, and a sudden weariness grips me as I realise I never asked the woman her name. Perhaps seeking comfort of her own, Olwyn appears beside me, and slips her arm through mine. It occurs to me that such violence is still a new sight for her, and I squeeze her close to my side.

The night feels endless, the open jaws of despair waiting to swallow us whole. It seems like for ever before Jax slows down, warning us all to be careful.

'There's a drop ahead.'

'A drop to where?' My curiosity is a welcome distraction.

'To your death, that's where.'

Mordecai cocks his head to one side, noticing my interest. 'You want to take a look?'

'Am I allowed?' I don't bother keeping the sarcasm from my voice, but he just rolls his eyes.

'Watch your step, all right?'

We stand on the edge of the cliff and peer over. Jax wasn't kidding. The ground gives way to a sudden and sheer decline, which plummets all the way down to a deep valley that stretches out beneath us. Bathed in moonlight, the ground below is bone dry, covered in grey ash and scarred by deep fissures, which periodically emit violent bursts of gas high into the sky. At the far end is a vast tree that's been mutilated – nothing remains but a charred trunk that's split into three lethal-looking points. The whole valley simply dares you to attempt crossing and try to survive.

'The Fire Fields,' Astrid says, watching my expression closely and frowning. Perhaps she can see me being drawn to the deadly challenge like a gnat to water.

'Why are they called that?' Olwyn asks.

'They're dormant now, but you see the gas vents? They used to spit out flames. As the route through the valley is the easiest way for an army to approach the palace, they served as a perfect defence.'

'What happened to the tree?' I can't take my eyes off it – broken but more powerful than ever because of it.

'It's called the Lightning Tree,' Mordecai says. 'So I'll give you three guesses.'

And in the chill of the hostile night an excitement grows inside me, one I've never experienced before. There's magic here; there's beauty. There's death and there's history, and somehow I feel like it all belongs to me. And there's more than a little taste of destiny in the air.

'So how do we get to the palace?' I could be wrong but I think Olwyn is as keen to drag me away from here as Astrid is, both of them troubled by the possibility that I might actually like this vicious terrain.

'This way, come on,' Jax says, and reluctantly I follow them away from the cliff edge and along the track that runs parallel to the valley.

Resisting the urge to keep peering over, I instead focus on what lies ahead. We're on a gentle downward slope now, winding our way to the safe end of the valley, and as the sun begins to creep over the horizon, I catch my first glimpse of the royal palace.

Wrapped in gloom, the vast black stone building looks cursed. Walls have fallen, plants have taken over, the water surrounding it is murky. The trees seem perched precariously on the hillside beyond it, their roots clinging like talons to the ground.

It's magnificent.

As we approach, my nerves shimmer inside me like light on the sea, even as I'm aware of the tension rising in my Guardian friends.

Mordecai, Jax and Astrid are recognised on sight by the guards at the palace gates and we're quickly granted admission. Olwyn and I are watched more closely as we pass over the threshold, but while Olwyn seems fascinated by our surroundings, the weight of history hits me like a wall.

It feels like I've been here before.

Like I was always meant to come.

Like I should never have returned.

'You all right?' Astrid asks, tucking in beside me.

I nod. But I'm lying. I feel as though the dead are watching me.

Up close, it's even clearer that the palace is utterly dilapidated, ravaged by nature over the centuries. Mordecai leads us through hallways where the windows have long since lost their glass to ivy, tendrils clawing their way inside. Stone crumbles away from the roof and light bleeds in through the cracks in the walls. Thick tree roots have invaded the floor, and, like a shadow squid enveloping a ship in its mighty tentacles, seek to sink the ground beneath our feet.

We reach a set of vast double doors guarded by two men who greet my Guardian companions with a warm embrace, before giving Olwyn and me more tentative looks.

'You were successful?' From the sound of the man's voice he hadn't been expecting them to return at all.

Mordecai's smile is so wide it's infectious. 'Oh yes.'

'Good luck then,' and they push the doors open.

Jax and Astrid fall naturally but noticeably to my side, and I sense they're trying to protect me. It doesn't feel patronising or irritating – it feels caring and loving and I've never wished Grace was alive more. She would have been so proud of this moment.

This throne room makes the Eastern King's look minute. Massive stone slabs – now invaded by moss and weeds – pave the floor, while the ceiling – home to birds nesting in the beams – towers above us. Two thirds of the way up the room is an impressive archway, where a pair of trees have been planted, presumably for decorative effect. But left to their own devices for centuries, the trees have taken over, their roots sprawled and intertwined across the ground and up the archway, hanging from it like thickest rope. They've climbed up and pushed through the roof so that I cannot see the tops of them. And still even they cannot make the room seem small. It's awe-inspiring.

What's not so appealing is the group of men and women watching us approach from the throne end of the room without a great deal of excitement. In fact, they look distinctly dismayed at our arrival.

The boy who sits at the foot of the throne must be Prince Rafe – and he is a boy, with to my eye no more than fifteen winters to his name. And while Bronn was already a man by that age, having lived a hard life as an apprentice assassin, this Rafe looks as though life has treated him rather too kindly. There's ample flesh on his bones and a childish petulance in his eyes. It appears he's not yet permitted to actually sit on the throne, which is an unexpected relief.

My throne.

I shake away that unwanted thought and try to focus on plastering a winning smile on my face. I suspect what I achieve is more like a threatening scowl.

'Mordecai,' an older man says, stepping forward. 'We did not expect your return so soon.'

'Or indeed at all?' There is no malice in Mordecai's voice, only a gentle teasing tone that implies he's aware of how things are, but doesn't care.

'You found her then?' And the older man glances from me to Olwyn, wondering which one of us is the woman he should be kneeling before. From the look on his face he finds us both lacking. It occurs to me that in our bloodstained clothing we look far more like warriors returning from battle than royalty seeking the crown.

Jax touches my elbow. 'Yes.' He gestures to the man before us. 'Let me introduce you to Arlan, the Master of

335

Guardians. Arlan, this is Mairin of Vultura. Our one and only true heir.'

Again, though the point is made lightly, it is made firmly.

'Call me Marianne,' I say, extending a hand of friendship.

But Prince Rafe jumps to his feet, coming to stand beside Arlan. 'Forgive my scepticism, but what proof do you have of such a claim?'

Astrid gestures to my neck. 'May we?'

I nod, and turn round, sweeping my hair away to reveal my birthmark. The intakes of breath make me suspect it's a lot sharper than anything Rafe possesses.

'That alone is hardly conclusive,' I hear Rafe protest, and I will him to stop. I didn't come here to challenge him but calling me a liar may just tempt me to change my mind.

'She rode a snow mare,' Olwyn says. That gets everyone's attention.

Mordecai capitalises on it. 'She summoned the water raptors.'

'She raised the dead on the Ninth.' Astrid's voice shakes slightly, her grief ever close to the surface.

'There is no doubt,' Jax says. 'Marianne is the direct descendant we've been seeking all these years.'

Even Rafe has no answer to this, though I see him looking desperately at his advisors for some assistance. But they seem to have been rendered speechless.

'I haven't come to cause any trouble,' I say, which is true, though I neglect to mention that trouble seems to follow me everywhere whether I want it to or not. 'I came to see if there was anyone in the West willing to help me.'

Arlan frowns. 'What help could we give you?'

'I need an army.'

It's Rafe who laughs first. 'And you think I'll give you mine?'

I force myself not to glare at him. 'I thought there might be some willing to stand with me to bring peace to our Isles once more. I was led to believe the Guardians were brave and strong.'

'We are,' Arlan says, clearly affronted. 'But our role is to restore the crown, not fix all the problems of the world.'

'A role you're apparently willing to bend the rules on.' I fail to keep the bite from my voice. 'Perhaps it's time to do things differently.'

Astrid attempts to diffuse the rising tension. 'We all took oaths to protect the bloodline. Marianne therefore requires our loyalty.'

A woman with greying hair steps forward, and her features are similar enough to Rafe's for me to suspect she's his mother. 'I would say she seems capable of protecting herself. And protection is all that is owed.'

We're rapidly heading to a fight, much to my dismay, and I can feel everyone tensing for battle, when a door off to the right flings open, demanding our attention.

337

An impossibly old man enters the room, dragging his feet across the stone floor. With every pained step his robe pulls back to reveal the cause: both feet are missing all their toes. The stick that aids him pounds the ground like a tedious drumbeat. But what I notice more than anything else is the magic radiating from him.

'Gaius?'

His ancient features break into an expression of sheer joy as he reaches a clawed hand towards me, stopping just before he actually touches my face. 'You've come at last. I knew you would.'

Seeing their Mage greet me with open arms clearly unnerves the other Guardians and their boy-prince. Perhaps they were counting on him to advise me to leave, or dismiss me as an impostor, but one thing is certain – his opinion holds more weight than most and my dwindling hope is rekindled.

'May I see your mark?' Gaius asks me, his eyes bright flames set in withered skin.

Once more, I lift my hair to reveal my neck and he reaches his misshapen fingers towards it, but again he refrains from touching me.

'There is no doubt,' he says, loud enough for everyone to hear. 'She is our heir.'

'And what of Rafe?' The woman I've guessed to be his mother is incandescent with rage. 'You have been advising him all these years, training him to be King.

Would you dismiss him now for this stranger? This *girl*?'

She emphasises the word 'girl' with contempt, which I think is rich considering Rafe is not only younger than me, but more importantly lacking any life experience to aid him as a ruler.

'Eena, I'm merely confirming she is the descendant from the bloodline,' Gaius says with what sounds like forced patience. 'But . . . as to whether she wishes to claim the throne, that is a question still to be answered.'

Everyone looks at me, and I wish they wouldn't. Always people want answers to impossible questions. I attempt to be as non-committal as possible. 'Like I said, I came for help.' I won't be pushed into making a decision about the throne as if I were merely playing dice. Too much is at stake. 'Help taking down the King in the East.'

'We will never aid the East, not after what they did,' Arlan growls.

'That was two hundred years ago.'

'They came here,' he says. 'They murdered our people.'

'They murdered *my* people.' My temper is fraying now. 'Don't tell me what the East did to the West. I've spent my whole life paying for it. But we have a chance now to put things right. My mother was a royal, my father a Guardian. I am the Viper. I am the one who will unite East and West once more.'

I didn't even know that's what I was going to say until I said it, but the words fill me with bubbling excitement. That *is* what I intend to do, by whatever means are necessary – even if I have to die.

Eena wraps her arm round Rafe's shoulders, but I can tell the gesture isn't to comfort him; it's to silence him. 'You are a stranger here. You know nothing of the West and its trials. We have enough problems of our own to contend with and don't have the resources to help our enemies.'

But before I can ask her to expand, Gaius stabs his stick on to the floor. 'Enough,' he says. 'Our guests have had a long journey and must be allowed to rest. I suggest we convene on the morrow to discuss further how we should proceed.'

His words carry weight and it is agreed our talk will resume in the morning, though I have no doubt many conversations will be taking place before then. Knives are about to be drawn.

Gaius beckons to me. 'Perhaps we could have the chance to speak alone for a moment?'

I turn to Jax, who nods his approval. 'I'll come and fetch you in a while,' he says.

I can feel many others frowning, though, as we leave the room together, and I gain a little more insight into how influential the Mages were – and still are – to the royalty. I remember what Mama warned me, of how those with power don't like to share, and a sense of dread grips me.

Gaius shuffles slowly down a corridor off the throne room and leads me into a far smaller, pokier chamber, which couldn't be more cluttered. Books spill from overcrowded shelves on to the floor, and papers are strewn across every surface. Gaius gestures for me to take a seat, and he positions himself in a chair behind the desk.

For a moment he simply catches his breath, the exertion of the walk taking a toll. In addition to his toeless feet he's missing three fingers on his left hand, and I'm certain the misshapen fingers on his clawed right hand were at one time all broken, and left to set poorly. I wonder what has happened to him to cause such injuries.

'So,' Gaius says after a while, fixing an unnervingly intense stare on me. 'Now that we are alone, let us talk freely. I believe I know why you are really here and it's not the throne you seek.'

I shake my head. 'No. Not the throne.'

We hold each other's gaze for some time, weighing the other up. Trust is essential, yet so hard to gain.

Gaius speaks first. 'Magic is not something that can be taught. You either possess the gift, or you don't.'

'And if I do?'

Now Gaius smiles as if I've confirmed what he already knew. 'Then I can show you how to master it. How to enhance it.'

Excitement spreads through me like fire, my smile bright like flame. 'That's why I'm here.'

'Royals and Mages have long since ruled together, but to have someone who is both?' he says, his voice full of wonder. 'You would be unstoppable.'

'I'm not interested in power. I simply want peace.'

Gaius laughs, but it sounds more like a cough in distress. 'Liar.'

'Excuse me?'

Now he leans forward, knocking a precarious pile of books to the floor. 'You came here with one desire: to become a Mage. Am I right?'

'Yes, but—'

He slams his hand down on to the desk. 'Foolish girl. You cannot believe that the ability to wield magic is anything *but* power. Stop lying to yourself. Admit the truth. Revel in the freedom of honesty. You. Want. Power.'

His forthright manner is jarring and yet liberating. I've never spoken openly to anyone about the depths of my yearning for magic – not even Bronn. He never really understood the pull it has over me, saw only the danger it posed. But now here's someone who shares my love of it and is drawing something I've been unwilling to admit out of me. I do want power. There's nothing more exhilarating than bending the laws of nature to my will, to alter what shouldn't be altered. But therein lies my conflict. Balancing the power with the darkness lurking always behind it.

'How do you resist giving in to the magic?' I ask him, the words escaping before I have a chance to consider the wisdom of asking a stranger this. I've revealed my fear without meaning to.

Gaius leans back now, content to have broken my defences. 'It isn't easy, but it can be done. You just need to focus on what you want to achieve. Then you can master the magic, not the other way around.'

His words are as seductive to me as any I've ever heard. 'And you'll teach me?'

He stretches his arms out in submission. 'You are the rightful heir. It is my duty to obey any order you might give.'

Now I'm the one to lean towards him. 'No. I don't want you to do this because you must.'

'You will be obedient to me?' He raises his eyebrows in surprise.

'You are the Mage, are you not? I am merely a student. I wish to learn all I can.'

Satisfaction glimmers in Gaius's eyes and I wonder how long he's waited for an apprentice to show up.

'Then we have an understanding,' Gaius says. 'It will certainly be a relief to young Prince Rafe to hear you wish to be a Mage, not a queen.'

The thought makes me squirm. Apparently some part of me is not entirely ready to relinquish the prospect of ruling altogether just yet. 'He should concentrate on being the best the Western Isles deserves.'

Gaius sighs. 'If you think that boy is capable of ruling, then you have more to learn than I thought.'

'Why?' I've already made my own judgements about the boy, but Gaius has been advising Rafe since he was five. His opinion matters.

Gaius gives a mirthless laugh and shakes his head. I'm going to have to earn information. There's something he wants to hear from me first. 'Do you want power?'

Taking a deep breath, I lift my eyes to meet his. 'Yes. I want power.' The words are barely audible, but Gaius hears.

'Then shut the door.'

The meeting is called before the sun rises. Perhaps the Guardians think that I'll oversleep and miss it, but as I barely slept anyway I'm ready the moment Mordecai knocks on my door.

I've tossed and turned all night, unable to stop thinking about what Gaius said to me alone in his cluttered chamber.

'The first rule of magic is that there are no rules,' he'd said. 'It is everywhere: in nature, in the elements. The wild energy within every living thing. It is chaos. It is savage. And you, my dear, are one of the rare few who can communicate with such a force.'

Even now those words thrill me.

He'd gone on to explain how magic manifests differently in every Mage, that every individual has a talent unique to them. That I must discover where my gifts lie.

But it was what he'd said right before I left that had kept me awake through long and lonely hours.

'I can teach you all I know, guide you towards your potential, but to become a Mage you will face an ultimate test, one not of my choosing. I cannot tell you what it will be. Each Mage endures their own, a trial that will challenge you and your magic to your very limits. You alone must understand what is required of you, and if you should pass . . . well, then you will finally have embraced the power inside you.'

It sounds an awful lot like a Snake Initiation to me – something I failed. And those that passed? Well, Bronn certainly paid a high cost. I can't shake the feeling that this magical equivalent will be no different.

I have to remind myself that I need the power being a Mage will bring. Not to rule. Not for a throne. But to protect myself and the people I love.

It doesn't unknot the coil of fear snaking inside me, though. And Old Tatty's words whisper louder than ever.

I have seen your death.

I follow Mordecai through the labyrinth of corridors, until we reach our destination. In a damp room, where the fire struggles to spit out sufficient heat, is a long, thin table. Gaius, Arlan, Eena and, of course, Rafe are seated round it, as are another man and woman whose names I don't yet know. I'm dismayed not to see Astrid and Jax, but I'm furious not to see my cousin.

'You can't exclude Olwyn,' I say, before anything else can be discussed. 'She's a Protector of the Snow Mares, and her links to the bloodline are arguably as strong as Rafe's.'

There's an intake of breath at my lack of respect, but I refuse to give Rafe a title he doesn't deserve. He can call himself Prince to his heart's content, but I won't do so.

When I refuse to back down, Gaius clears this throat. 'Perhaps it would be wisest to fetch the young woman? What harm can it do?'

Glances are exchanged and Arlan nods, issuing orders that a guard brings her to join us. We sit in silence while we wait for our group to become complete.

I look over at Gaius, remembering something else he told me yesterday, that Rafe is to all intents and purposes Arlan's puppet, groomed from an early age to do whatever Arlan suggests and give him the power he craves. According to Gaius, there is deep corruption within the Guardians – many of whom believe that after all these years they are the ones who deserve power. Those, like my friends, who wish to remain on their true path, are outnumbered, and it's only a matter of time before the two factions go to war with each other.

His advice sits at the front of my mind: focus on the magic, leave them to destroy themselves and pick up the pieces later.

The prospect is a tempting one.

Olwyn joins us before I can contemplate the idea any further, throwing me a quizzical look as she takes the empty seat to my left.

'Happy now?' Eena's manner is less than welcoming.

I smile sweetly. 'Ecstatic.'

'So, shall we begin?' Gaius asks, and I'm glad he's asserting himself firmly as overseer of this meeting.

'I don't see the point of this gathering at all,' Eena says, her animosity from yesterday in no way diminished. 'What is there to say? She wants an army; we won't give her one. She should leave and slither back to whatever cesspit she crawled out of.'

'Apart from the fact that this is her palace,' Mordecai says, and I notice his friendly manner is all but gone today.

'It's not hers, it's mine,' Rafe says, and everyone looks at him. I think even my opponents are surprised at his adamant declaration. 'I've lived here my whole life,' he says, glaring at me. 'She can't just walk in and take it.'

'Everybody, slow down,' I say. 'Why don't you start by telling me about the problems you're facing here?'

Arlan sighs, realising Eena isn't going to give me the satisfaction of a conversation and that it'll be up to him to make their case. 'You must realise, surely, that these Isles are out of our control? Lost to lawlessness and violence?'

I think of the woman we helped, of her home and family destroyed, and frown. 'I understand that many generations ago the royal family were wiped out. But someone must have risen to take control.' In the East it's been the bandits who have taken advantage of unrest. There's always someone waiting to take power if it's left exposed. As perhaps Arlan himself knows only too well.

It's Mordecai who answers. 'Yes, and they rule with terror and without mercy.'

'Who are they?'

There is an uncomfortable silence.

'We don't know,' Arlan says.

I stare at them all in astonishment. 'You don't know? How is that possible?'

'Because no one has ever caught them,' Mordecai answers. 'They slip like shadows into homes and take whatever they want and then disappear. They call themselves the Hooded.'

Olwyn and I share a look. I certainly don't need reminding of the last time I heard that name, when I was nearly offered as a sacrifice to keep them away.

His tone prompts my next question. 'And what do they want?'

'Children.' His voice is so quiet it's almost a whisper.

It's like my blood runs cold, only to burst into flames seconds later. 'Children? Children are going missing and you're doing nothing to stop it?' I stand up so abruptly my chair falls over. Mordecai reaches for my arm, but I pull it away. 'Who are you people?'

'Your hosts,' Eena says, her voice pure venom. 'Sit back down.'

I don't want to. I want to storm out, find a ship and flee this place. But then what? I'd be abandoning both the West and the East to ruin. I cannot save Torin if I run.

Though it pains me, I do as I'm told. Gaius catches my eye and nods his approval. I need to bide my time if I want to help the Western or Eastern Isles.

'The Hooded are clearly working for someone,' Arlan continues as if my outburst never happened. 'But we don't know who.'

I doubt they've tried too hard to find out.

'On my travels I've asked about them,' Mordecai says. 'One name I keep hearing is Greeb. I think he's the one behind them.'

Arlan sighs as if he's heard this a thousand times before. 'There's no evidence such a person exists, let alone that he controls the Hooded.'

'But don't you see now?' Eena asks me. 'The Hooded go after children and Rafe is a child. It's vital we protect him from these monsters. That's why we can't spare the Guardians.'

I understand. She's a mother who wants to keep her son safe. But she's prepared to sacrifice all the other children of the islands for him, and that I cannot condone.

I try appealing to him directly. 'Don't you care if the land you are to rule over is at war? Doesn't it break your heart that people are being killed?'

Rafe glances uncertainly up at his mother, before looking back at me. 'But we're safe here, aren't we?' He's afraid – but only for himself.

'Of course,' Arlan says. 'You have all of us here to protect you.' He glares at me. 'That is our duty. To serve the King.'

Fury bubbles hot beneath my skin. *He's not crowned yet.* 'So you'll use your army to help no one but yourselves.'

Not one of them so much as meets my eyes, giving me their answer.

Swallowing back my anger, I make a decision. I won't abandon the West to this savagery, but I can't afford to turn the Guardians against me – yet. Instead I shall train with Gaius. I shall gain my own power. And then we'll see about putting things right.

'Then there's nothing more really to say is there?' I try to bring this session to a close, wanting to go before I say things I'll regret.

'So you'll leave? You won't contest the throne?' Eena asks, more than a little confused.

'I think there must be a way to protect the islands from the Hooded, while still ensuring Rafe is safe.' I choose my words carefully, being deliberately vague.

'Well, I for one welcome the help,' Mordecai says. 'Marianne should be allowed to stay here for as long as she wishes, and be treated with the respect she deserves as our *true* heir.'

Arlan's whole face burns with disapproval, though he bows his head in agreement.

I nod my appreciation and then walk out of the room without looking back, and though I can sense Olwyn and Mordecai right behind me, I desperately want to be alone. Rage and sorrow crush at my throat and chest, suffocating me – I have to get out of here. So I run. I hear Mordecai call after me, and I fly straight past Jax and Astrid who were waiting to find out what happened. I race through the crumbling corridors, and out into the overgrown grounds. Long grasses brush against me, rampant brambles try to catch me, but I keep running until something looms before me, and I slow as I realise what it is.

A grave.

Marked by a rough-hewn piece of stone that's been claimed by moss and lichen, it's clearly old. Very old. I brush it with my fingers, and sense a buzz of energy, a memory of the lives once lived. There is more than one body beneath the ground.

'Your ancestors are buried here.'

I turn to see Astrid and Olwyn walking towards me.

'All of them? With only one grave?'

Astrid shrugs. 'There was a war. There wasn't time to honour the dead properly.'

Olwyn steps forward, until she's close enough to take my hand. I shut my eyes and will her not to ask me how

I'm feeling. I don't want to talk about what just happened. I don't want to think about what to do now. I came for help and instead have discovered a new enemy. The Hooded are yet another front on which to fight. How do I face the choices before me? Who do I want to be? What matters most? Viper, Queen or Mage? Which path will lead to victory?

'Do the islands in the East have different names like ours do?' she asks, and I'm so surprised by the question that I look straight at her. Olwyn smiles, and not for the first time, I'm swept with gratitude for her. She's giving me something else to think about.

'Yes, they do.' But I don't want to think about the East. 'Tell me yours – apart from Blood Island, I already know that one.'

Astrid shoots me a slightly withering look.

'And you know about the Seventh Isle,' Olwyn says, ignoring Astrid.

Ah yes, I remember Rayvn's words about Shadow Island, home to all manner of spirits and demons. It sounds mysterious, sinister – but I'd be lying if I said it didn't intrigue me.

'If it's cast in shadow, what grows there?' I ask.

'Not a lot. It's a swampland, humid, dank and murky. Lots of vegetation. I've heard a certain type of tall tree grows there, one with many strange roots that grow out from high up the trunk. They call them drowned men's hair.'

An involuntary shudder passes through me. 'What about your island? Let me guess – Crystal Island? Shining Island?' It would make sense for it to be known for its diamond-like sand.

'Good guesses, but no,' Olwyn says. 'It's named after the mountains and the mares. Snow Island.'

For a brief moment her smile fades, as she's reminded of Mama and Pip. I understand. My smile has faded too.

'The Tenth Isle is called Fire Island,' Astrid carries on, noticing the shift in mood. 'Virtually uninhabitable. Imagine the Fire Fields we passed, only covering the entire island.'

I remember the incredible sense of excitement I had gazing down at the barren valley spewing gas intermittently from the vented ground, and imagine it on a vast scale. So much power.

So much magic.

The thought comes from nowhere, but I wonder if it's true. 'Is it safe?'

'Well, the fields are dormant at the moment,' Olwyn says. 'Nothing more than a smoking presence on the horizon. But it hasn't always been that way, and it won't stay like that for ever. One day the fires will burn again.'

'And the Eleventh is Song Island,' Astrid says. 'In part, because those born there are naturally gifted musicians, and partly because the island sings.'

I'm mesmerised. 'It sings? How?'

'No one really knows. The way the wind passes through the grasses, the way it echoes through the valleys. I've been there a few times; it's quite beautiful.'

'Lastly, there's this one,' Olwyn says. 'The Jewel of the West.'

'Or it was once.' Astrid's sadness is unmistakable. 'I've seen paintings of when the land was lush with colour, wild animals grazed and life thrived in every way. The settlements shone with happiness. Contentment. Those pictures look like a dream. Or a lie.'

I look up at the palace, a forgotten relic of a prosperous time, and realise with some surprise that I feel a need to restore it – restore the island – to its former glory. I can't do that hiding away.

Taking a deep breath, I squeeze Olwyn's hand. 'Come on, we should go back.'

Olwyn and Astrid slide their arms through mine, and together we return to reality, their presence softening my anger and strengthening my resolve.

When we reach my chamber, Mordecai and Jax are waiting for us.

Mordecai wastes no time. He takes one look at me and says, 'So what do you want us to do?'

I clench my jaw and speak through gritted teeth. 'We're going to find out who the Hooded are. And then we will end them.'

I scan their faces and see only support. They hate this situation as much as I do.

'Leave it to us,' Jax says. 'You keep your head down and don't give Rafe any reason to withdraw his hospitality.'

'There may be others willing to help us,' Astrid adds, her voice low. 'I'll see what I can do.'

'Be careful,' I say. 'I don't think I'm well liked here.'

'Which is strange given your return should have been cause for celebration . . .' Mordecai says, before trailing off. He's looking behind me, and I turn to see what's caused him to fall silent.

Gaius is standing at the end of the corridor, waiting for me. A shiver of excitement runs up my spine. It's time. Finally, it's time.

'I have to go,' I say, already moving towards Gaius. 'Find me later. We'll talk more then.'

When I reach Gaius, he says nothing, simply turns and hobbles off. I assume he wants me to go with him, and so I follow him along the dark hallways, venturing into a part of the palace I've not seen before. He struggles down a winding staircase, but I sense offering to assist him would cause great offence and so I merely continue to be his silent shadow until we reach a strangely-out-of-place little door in the stone wall.

Acknowledging my presence for the first time, Gaius gives me a grin that tells me I'm going to like what's behind this door, and he opens it wide.

Though it's far larger than yesterday's room, it's equally untidy – like some sort of magical explosion took place. Benches are covered in everything you'd expect a Mage to have: pots are surrounded by bottles and jars; a fire burns in the corner, a concoction brewing in a cauldron over it; acrid smoke fills the air so that my eyes burn. The smell is strange, like a mixture of earth and rainwater, but with an underlying sourness I don't recognise. Any spare space is covered in books and papers, while ink stains the floor, along with other substances I can't identify. Clearly Gaius is not one for order.

'This,' he says, moving to the nearest bench and brushing papers out of his way, 'is where I work. It's where you will learn. And given Arlan and Eena are already scheming to get rid of you, I don't think we should waste any time, do you?'

I run my finger along the bench, picking up a trail of dust. 'Short of surrendering all my rights, nothing I do will please them.'

'Why is it you seek power in magic, but not in ruling? You could have both . . . have it all.'

It's a good question, and for a moment I have to consider my answer. Do I simply want power without responsibility? Is that why I left Bronn to captain the *Maiden*? Does wearing a crown mean I can't run when it becomes too hard?

'Kings and queens fall,' I say, and I'm telling the truth, even if not in its entirety. 'Their power is finite, fragile. It can be taken from them, as history has shown us time and again. I want power that cannot be so easily stolen from me.'

Gaius's eyes shine, and I can't read his reaction. If he suspects my other fears, he says nothing.

'Well, it's not my place to tell you what to do in that regard,' Gaius says. 'In matters of state my role is only to advise.' His expression changes from meek servitude to one so cunning it takes me by surprise. 'But in magic? Now that is a different thing altogether.'

'So where do we start?' I'm almost giddy with excitement.

'Why, at the beginning of course. Tell me what you already know.'

That seems fair enough, and I perch on a stool as I tell him about my childhood studies with Milligan back on the *Maiden*, my long-seated thirst for knowledge on how to heal. I tell him of the books I've read, the way I can see life leaving a body and what I did for Lilah. As I talk, something inside me settles. I'm remembering why I want to be a Mage. Not for power – though I can't deny the temptation it holds – but to mend. Olwyn was right – in my heart I'm a healer. Whether it's an injury in the body or the unrest on the Isles, my desire is to fix and to restore. That knowledge brings me peace as I talk. Old

Tatty told me that if I didn't want to lose myself to the magic, I had to know who I was and this is something I can cling to. It's how I'll fight the darkness.

When I finish relaying all I can think of, Gaius sits there for a while, nodding his head while he ponders my words.

'Interesting,' he says. 'These books – you didn't happen to bring them with you, did you?'

'I'm afraid not. But I made notes,' I say, wishing I hadn't left them behind in my room.

'I would very much like to see them some time,' he says, and I'm more than happy to agree.

Gaius continues to mull things over, what fingertips he has remaining pressed together. 'Very interesting indeed,' he muses. 'You are clearly drawn to healing – what we must do now is discover whether that skill is aligned with your magic or simply a coincidence.'

He struggles out of his chair and walks over to the fireplace, resting against the hearth.

'Show me how you would treat a burn. Use whatever you wish,' he says, gesturing to the room.

Ideally I would use a generous amount of second-salve to soothe a burn, and instinctively glance down to the scar on my wrist caused by molten metal. But I suspect that Gaius doesn't have a large supply of ingredients from the East. I shall have to mix an ointment of my own and search through the scattered bottles until

359

I find one labelled 'powdered moonflower', and one branded 'fyre'. Pouring equal amounts of both herbs into a mortar, I grind them together with a pestle, adding a little water into the mixture until slowly it forms a dark paste that is mostly brown in colour with streaks of orange.

I take it over to show him.

'Let's see how effective it is, shall we?' And, to my horror, he thrusts his hand into the flames beside him.

'Gaius!'

'Go ahead,' he says, removing his hand from the fire, and sucking his breath in with pain. 'Treat it.'

I stare at him for a moment, stunned by his action, but get to work, smearing the paste liberally over the angry red skin, wishing I'd made more because the burn covers a large area. This hand is already missing three fingers; it doesn't need to be scarred too.

When I'm done, I look up at him uncertainly.

'Good,' he says. 'You've treated it just as I would hope any good healer would. If I keep this bandaged for several days, I should end up with a clean scar.'

I wait for him to continue. Because I'm certain this isn't the end of the lesson.

'Now, would you be so kind as to make another batch of your ointment?'

Doing as I'm told, I repeat the process, watching him closely for fear he'll plunge his other hand into the fire.

He does not. Instead he takes a cloth and wipes off my first remedy, taking some of his blistering skin with it too.

I hurry over to him, my second batch of medicine ready. 'Now what?'

With his uninjured hand he passes me a small bottle filled with fine white fragments. 'Now add a pinch of this.'

I take it and open the lid. 'What is it?'

'Shavings. Of animal bones.'

Glancing up at him, I see the challenge in his eyes. If he thinks me squeamish, he doesn't know me yet. I add the grains of bone and mix it in well, looking at him for approval when I'm done.

'And now for the most important part,' he says. He pulls a small book from his pocket and hands it to me. I open it to see pages filled with the ancient language of the Mages. 'It is the incantation that takes a potion from ordinary to extraordinary. The words are nothing in the mouths of people without magic. You are the vessel. Let's see if you truly have the gift or not. Choose what words seem right to you.'

My heart beats a little faster. I can feel the magic rising inside me; my blood starts to heat and my skin burns from the inside out. I stir the remedy again and this time whisper the word, '*Vellja*' over it too. If I've remembered correctly, it means 'heal'.

Gaius offers me his burnt hand, and once again I rub the paste over the raw skin, but instantly know something is different this time. Before it was an unremarkable act, the simple appliance of ointment to wound. This time I feel the crackle of skin, a pulsing energy, and I think he does too, because he pulls quickly away, giving me a slightly suspicious look. He immediately hides it, but I wonder what I've done wrong.

'I'm sorry,' I say, my confidence shaken. 'Did I make a mistake?'

He is staring at me now, and I know something's not gone to plan. Once more he wipes his hand clean and holds it up for us to look at.

I have to blink several times before I'm certain what I'm seeing is real. The skin shows no sign of any burn – not even a scar.

'How did you do that?' Gaius almost sounds like he's accusing me of something.

'I just did what you asked. It's good, though, right? Your skin is completely healed.'

'What I wanted to teach you was the difference between a remedy and a potion. That a potion is faster than a remedy. I expected to see noticeable improvement, not a complete cure.'

Our eyes meet and I see my own uncertainty reflected there.

'It would seem your magic is indeed aligned with healing,' he says eventually. 'In fact, I would go so far as to say you appear to have a link to the life force itself. It may even be possible one day for you to heal with a single touch.'

It seems unimaginable to think I could ever wield such a power and I'm about to tell him so, until a memory nudges at my mind. A memory of holding a broken little moonbird in my hands on the deck of the *Maiden* and willing it to survive. Of seeing it recover and assuming I had been wrong about how close to death it was. Is it possible my touch *did* heal it after all? That the magic within me answered my deepest plea without my knowledge?

I share the story with Gaius and his dishevelled eyebrows twitch upwards. 'You have a gift. What we must do now is teach you how to use that power on command. That is the challenge before us. Are you prepared to do all it takes to harness your abilities?'

'Yes, as long as you don't do anything like that again. What if I couldn't have cured you?'

'Marianne, do not make the mistake of thinking what we do in this room is safe.'

While my tone was playful, his is deadly serious and the mood in the room shifts.

'Magic isn't safe,' he continues. 'It's wild, unpredictable. Trying to harness it is dangerous, both for us and those we wish to use it on. You must understand the sacrifice required of you to become a Mage. Are you prepared to take the risk?'

His words are meant to warn me, possibly even scold me, but they thrill me.

'Yes.'

And his smile returns. 'Good. Then let us continue.'

20

I barely leave the sanctuary of Gaius's potion room for the next few weeks. My eyes have been opened to a vast new world of possibilities and it's staggering to realise how little I knew before.

My mornings are spent in study, reading through his papers and understanding the properties of plants and herbs in greater depth. I spend hours memorising incantations and experimenting with different ingredients in the many cauldrons Gaius provides.

He works me hard, demanding perfection from me and my craft. Though he can be gruff at times, I know he's pleased with me when a smile twitches at the corner of his mouth.

In the afternoons everything changes. Gaius brings me rats from the kitchens, still hanging from the cook's traps. He lays them out in front of me, like a cat delivering a gift, and I attempt to heal them with nothing more than my touch.

Every time I fail.

Though I've started to recognise the various sensations magic creates in my body – some harmless, some curious, some almost painful – I cannot get close to commanding it.

And I try hard. The pitiful noises the rats make with their bodies half crushed by the cruel traps distress me, as does the sight of them trying to twist free from their torment and failing, their spines snapped by the lethal bar that's imprisoned them.

Again and again I focus on the need to save them, trying to replicate the instances before when the magic has come so willingly to my call, but it remains silent. Unreachable.

It's frustrating Gaius, I can tell, though while I work he never speaks. Only watches. Sometimes he takes pity on me and allows me to try a potion on the rats, but I'm yet to discover one that can mend bone and repair organs.

When the creatures inevitably die from their injuries, I resume my practice of autopsying, something I started doing when I was living aboard the *Maiden*. Now, no longer needing to keep it secret, I can undo the body in a more methodical way, peeling back flesh, removing organs and laying them out on the benches to understand how they connect. Gaius has even helped me boil the flesh off several carcasses, so I can study the skeleton more closely. I can see where the small bones have broken or been crushed, sometimes just the backbone, but sometimes the ribs too. The occasional poor rat has had his skull crushed and was already beyond my help.

For all my failings Gaius doesn't chastise me.

'You must simply keep trying,' he says. 'We know you have it in you.'

He asks over and over about my ability to see threads of energy rise from a dying, or even dead, body. It's not something he's come across before, and though he speaks of it as a wonderful gift, something deep inside me wants to reject his praise. So far it's done nothing good.

'Only because you haven't harnessed your ability properly,' he says during one of our many discussions on the topic. 'As you're discovering, all skills must be practised, even ones you're naturally gifted at.'

I give him a withering look, as I peel redroot. 'What do you suggest? Would you like to stab yourself and see if I can fix you in time?'

He scoffs at my sarcasm and flicks some seeds in my direction. 'Of course not. But maybe we should forget about trying to heal the rats while they live, and should instead concentrate on bringing them back from death.'

I shake my head. 'A boy far wiser than his years once told me I shouldn't try to, that it can do no good. And after what happened to Lilah I'm inclined to agree with him.'

'But that was only your inexperience,' Gaius argues. 'Listen to what you're saying. No good? You could raise the dead, Marianne.'

I remember what happened on the Ninth Isle and think that perhaps the dead might not want to return.

'I want to heal. Raising the dead isn't natural.'

'Well, then the dying. You could bring them back from the brink.'

'You assume there are always threads there to restore. None of the rats have had any.' A fact I find fascinating. I don't know why some deaths offer the chance to be undone, while others don't, but I wonder if it has something to do with the suddenness of the demise. Too quick and all trace of life is immediately extinguished. Too slow and prolonged, and there is not enough energy left at the very end to salvage.

I gesture to the ingredients laid out in front of us. 'Besides, you're teaching me the power of potions. Firewort can stave off death, I've seen it.'

'Why would you want to settle for such limited abilities? What if you don't have access to the ingredients you need? Another Mage might have to resign themselves to that situation, but you have the potential to go beyond, to summon the magic within.'

And to prove his point Gaius grabs the stick of redroot from me and places it before him. Raising his hand and closing his eyes, he mutters words under his breath and I watch the redroot burst into flames. I grab a jug of water and throw it over the burning mass before it can spread to the very flammable contents of the room.

'You see?' he says. 'There's so much more than potions.'

He's right of course, and I double my efforts in my

368

attempts to heal the rats – for what good it does me.

What little time I'm not with Gaius is spent in the company of my friends. True to their words, Mordecai and Jax have been out travelling around the settlements seeking information, but to their frustration the Hooded remain as elusive as ever.

Astrid and Olwyn meanwhile have struck up quite a friendship, which pleases me no end. In between teaching Olwyn the skills required to become a Guardian, the two of them have subtly been speaking with other people, trying to find out where loyalties really lie.

'Part of the problem,' Astrid says one evening, as we sit in Mordecai's room together, all catching up on the day's events, 'is that virtually no one has met you. How can they support a potential Queen they've never even seen?'

'All right,' I say. 'What do you suggest? Arlan's hardly going to parade me through the palace.'

'How about you come and train with us tomorrow?' Olwyn says. 'You won't meet everyone, but the courtyard's always busy, and word about your skills will spread. You don't have to do anything, just be yourself.'

'That's not a bad idea,' Jax says.

I agree, but it means disturbing my work with Gaius and I'm reluctant to risk any progress I might be making with the rats.

'I suppose so.' I could hardly sound less enthusiastic.

'I know you're enjoying your studies,' Olwyn says. 'But I've barely seen you in weeks.' She hesitates. 'It might be good for you to do something different.'

With a pang of guilt I realise why I've felt so pleased she's grown close with Astrid. It means I don't have to worry about being responsible for her. I check myself quietly. I mustn't forget who my true friends are.

'You're right,' I say, stretching to clutch her hand. 'I've missed you. It'd be nice to spend some time together.'

'And meet your loyal protectors.' Mordecai sounds bitter. He's really growing to hate his own people.

There's a knock at the door and we all glance up in surprise.

'Expecting anyone?' Jax asks as Mordecai gets to his feet.

'No,' he says, and I notice his hand rests on his dagger as he goes to the door.

He opens it a fraction and exchanges words with the person on the other side, before closing it and turning to us all.

'We'd better go,' he says. 'There's something happening in the throne room.'

As we hurry down the corridor, Mordecai reaches for my arm. 'Gaius sent someone to alert us. Whatever's going on, our presence isn't wanted.'

'Do we know what's wrong?'

Mordecai shakes his head. 'No, but whatever it is, I

don't think you're going to like it.'

He's warning me to keep my temper and hold my tongue, but I won't make any promises I'm likely to break.

As we walk into the throne room, I quickly take in the scene. Rafe is sitting on the throne – actually on the throne – and instantly my blood boils. How dare he? There are at least thirty Guardians in the room, most of whom seem to be there to protect him, but there are a handful storming angrily away from the throne towards us, and there's a definite atmosphere of mutiny in the air.

As one of the men pushes past us, Mordecai grabs his arm.

'What's going on?'

The man points at Rafe. 'Ask him.'

I can feel my opportunity to find out what happened slipping away and decide I'm going to have to act before these men leave.

With as much authority as I can muster I stride towards the throne, my eyes locked on the boy upon it and the two people either side of him.

'What is happening?' I demand to know. 'Why are these men so angry?'

Arlan narrows his eyes when he sees me, but it's Rafe who answers. 'What is she doing here?'

'A good question,' Arlan says. 'Your presence was not requested.'

'It doesn't have to be.' I see everyone flinch slightly at

my tone of voice and satisfaction creeps in. I'm sick of them treating me like a nobody in my own palace. 'You seem to be under a misapprehension that I've granted the throne to Rafe, but I have done no such thing. Until such time as I do – *if* I do – he has no right to sit there like a king, nor does he have any right to exclude me from matters of importance. So you will answer me. What is happening?'

For the first time since I've arrived I see a glimmer of fear in Arlan's and Eena's eyes. They had completely underestimated me.

When they don't answer, the man Mordecai spoke to decides to do me the courtesy.

'We've travelled from Arbner,' he says. When I look blank he adds, 'A nearby settlement. We were only passing through, but found a town filled with grief, a wailing like I've never known.'

'The Hooded?'

He nods. 'They took all the children.'

'All of them?' I can barely say the words.

His jaw clenches. 'All of them.' For a moment he composes himself before spinning on Rafe. 'So we galloped here with every haste to rally help. But it seems our hands are tied and we must stand by while atrocities are committed.'

'You have to send help,' I say to anyone who will listen, almost speechless with shock. 'We may still be able to catch up with them.'

Arlan fixes his most steely gaze on me. 'The Hooded are masters of disappearance. We'll never find them.'

'They won't find it so easy to hide in shadows with a settlement full of children in tow.'

'Has it occurred to you this might be what they want?' Eena says. 'For us to send out our best men and leave Rafe exposed for them to swoop in and kill?'

The fire of my rage is burning bright now. 'You have hundreds of men! Send half and you'll still be well protected. These are children we're talking about.' I manage to stop myself before I say that I doubt the Hooded care about the life of Rafe. What threat does he possibly pose to them?

'The decision has been made,' Arlan says. 'You will not challenge the Prince, nor will the Guardians disobey his orders.'

Only a calming hand on my shoulder stops me from rushing forward to punch his arrogant face. Olwyn knows my temper is about to erupt.

'Perhaps we should ask the Mage what he advises,' Eena says and I feel a wave of relief. Gaius will help. Gaius will make this right.

Stepping out of the shadows, Gaius avoids looking at me. 'I agree with the Prince. It is unwise to pursue them when we have no knowledge of where they've gone. It would be a hollow endeavour.'

The betrayal stings. I've lost this battle as I have every other since I arrived.

'If you let the West burn, then what will be left for you to rule?' I say softly to Rafe. 'Listen to your own heart, not those around you. And don't let fear paralyse you. There's always something you can do.'

And with that I leave, emptiness growing like a chasm in my chest. I want to be alone and so I don't wait for my friends, but when I reach my room Gaius is there. I don't know what secret passage he must have used to get here so quickly from the throne room, and right now I don't care.

'Marianne—' he begins, but I cut him off.

'How could you? I thought you were my friend?'

'I am your teacher,' he says with restraint. 'But I advise the royalty, and as you haven't claimed the throne that still means I have to counsel that little imbecile. And whether you like it or not, charging out into the unknown is not a good plan. It's an impetuous one, one that will get many people killed. Your impatience does you no credit. Sometimes you still act very much like a Snake.'

My anger flares up at the insult, but I fight it back. I don't want to quarrel with Gaius. Instead I lean my head against the cold stone and close my eyes.

'Do you know what you need?' he says. 'Some air.

I've had you cooped up inside for too long. There's a small doorway in the west wing that leads on to an external staircase. If you were to slip out that way, no one would see you go. Why don't you go and clear your head?'

I frown. 'I thought it was dangerous out there?'

He smiles as he starts to walk away. 'And here I was thinking you lived for danger.'

The prospect is too appealing to resist. The walls of the palace feel like they're closing in on me and I can hardly breathe. Pausing only to grab my cloak, I follow his directions, creeping along the hallways until I find a little door that looks so much a part of the wall I almost miss it. I have to shove it hard, but when it opens a blast of cold night air hits my face. I'm outside.

I hesitate for a moment. Perhaps I should tell one of my friends where I'm going, but then I decide against it. They'd only want to come with me, and right now I need to be on my own. I'm too angry for company. Besides, Gaius knows where I am.

Stone steps jut out from the wall and I run down them with such speed I feel like I'm gliding. Almost flying. It's good to be out, even if there is menace in the air. The stairway leads to a lower part of the wall and it's easy to scramble over and escape the confines of the palace. Keeping low, I prowl beyond the ramparts towards the small settlement in the distance. My mind is muddled with conflict. Am I really going to stand by and let that boy be manipulated by Arlan and his mother to make unconscionable decisions? He can't rule the Western Isles; he just can't. And yet . . . I don't want to either. For all the sense of responsibility I feel towards the throne, the possessiveness I experience whenever I see Rafe on it, I still don't want to be the Queen. I just don't want someone worse to take my place.

Yet the problem is I am the Queen. I am Mairin of Vultura. Whether I like it or not. Whether Rafe is crowned or not. There is no pretending otherwise. And when I think of all I'm prepared to do for the East, then surely I should be willing to do more for my own land? And here lies the cause of my anger. What *can* I do? I came to find help for the East and instead stumbled into bigger problems. I was arrogant to think I could fix this. Perhaps Old Tatty was right. Unbidden, her words come back to me like a warning.

Time is running out for you. For all of us. Your enemy will destroy you and everything you love. We will all be destroyed.

Maybe some prophecies just have to come true, no matter how hard you try to fight them.

I've come further than I intended and am about to head home when I hear raised voices. I pause, listening intently. A scream quickly follows, and another, and I know someone's in danger.

All my experience tells me I should walk away, that every time I try to help it only gets me into trouble, but I still pull out my dagger and run forward.

The cries grow louder now and I pull my hood up as I creep through the shadows on the outskirts of the settlement. I peer round a crumbling brick wall and take in the scene before me. A group of five armed men are terrorising a young family with a small child.

The man and woman look like travellers, perhaps returning home, and are begging the gang to believe them when they say they have no coins to give. Sickness stirs in my belly. These men don't want money; they want violence. I know because I recognise it from the days when Adler and his men would pick fights simply because they lusted after blood. My rising rage turns feverous.

One of the group reaches for the woman, who flinches away, shielding the child with her body. Her husband steps forward to protect them both and receives a wallop to his chin that sends him flying. The woman rushes to his side, and I can see her pleading with the men to leave them alone and let them pass in peace.

I'm no longer watching with any sense of detachment. I'm seeing another man and woman, another child, being attacked years ago by violent men. My mother fought to the death to protect me and failed. I can't stand by and watch another family be ripped apart like mine.

The child's screams tear through me like a blade and I charge forward, without thought or strategy, launching myself at the nearest attacker.

It's chaos. My assault is wholly unexpected and takes the gang completely by surprise. I manage to floor a couple of big guys before they regroup and forget the family sprawled on the ground who are staring at me like a demon saviour. These men wanted a fight and now they've got one.

All my anger, all my frustration, is directed furiously at these strangers and I punch, kick, lash and bite with wild abandon. At some point I scream at the family to flee, but as soon as I see them safely escape I completely lose myself to the turmoil in my head, bitterness and hatred turning me into a violent mess of limbs.

It's only after a while that it occurs to me that for every man I defeat, another comes at me. They've got reinforcements and I'm increasingly outnumbered. I'm even more surprised to realise I don't care. I'm tired of everything. I'm sick of trying to put right other people's wrongs. I can't fix the Twelve Isles, that's the truth of it. I've destroyed the man I love; I've abandoned the man I married. I miss too many people I can never get back, grief a weight constantly crushing me. It's all too hard.

I can't fight life any more. And so I just fight. If this is it, then I'll fight to my death.

Slowly they close in on me, taking advantage of their numbers, but I barely feel the blows as they land on me. I keep swinging, I keep lashing out, though deep down, I'm giving up.

And then another shadow emerges from the night to join the fight. My fight. It moves with spectacular fluidity, like it's performing a lethal dance. For a moment I think it's Grace's ghost come back to save me, but this person is definitely alive. The dead don't bleed.

Astrid.

Something snaps awake inside me, the strange trance lifting. Where moments ago I was ready to give up, now her presence revives me. There are too many for her to fight alone, just as there were for me. But for both of us together?

I position myself at her back, and wordlessly we adapt our fighting style, moving as one dangerous cloud of savagery. Together we dispatch the gang with deadly efficiency, and when it's done we turn to face each other.

'How did you know where I was?' I can taste blood when I speak.

'Saw you leaving the castle. Come on, we'd better hurry,' Astrid says, glancing around vigilantly. 'It's not safe out here.'

But with the fight now over, and the family out of harm's way, pain is sweeping in. I hurt and it must be obvious, because Astrid wraps her arm round my shoulder and supports me as we head back towards the palace. Not once does she lose her focus, her sword drawn, attentive to our surroundings, and I allow her to guide me home. I can't remember the last time I trusted someone enough to let them lead, but as the palace grows closer I practically shut my eyes and follow her steps. The relief of not being in charge is immense.

I must lose consciousness because I don't entirely remember making it back to the palace, or how we get to my chamber, but somehow we do, and then Astrid is lowering me into a chair, before lighting the fire and fetching me a goblet of wine.

My hand shakes as I raise it to my lips, relishing the burning sensation as it glides down my throat.

'Thank you,' I say, as she passes me a cold, damp cloth to press to my split lip. I wonder how much of a mess I must look.

Astrid leans against the fireplace, and her face is full of reproach. 'What were you thinking?'

I shrug, not wanting to admit how badly I lost control of my emotions. I nearly lost more than that.

'You could have got yourself killed.'

'They were going to kill a family.' My voice is flat, emotionless.

Astrid says nothing but takes the cloth from me and rinses it clean in a bowl of water, before handing it back and gesturing to my eye. I hadn't realised it was throbbing, and the cloth simultaneously soothes and stings as I press it there.

'You're unhappy.'

I'm grateful that she doesn't ask it as a question, just presents it as an observation that doesn't require an answer.

'I'm angry. All the time.' I look up to see her sad eyes staring at me. 'When did everything get so twisted? When did everyone start hating each other? Why can't . . . ?' I trail off. What's the point? Astrid can't answer these questions any more than I can.

She comes to sit beside me and takes my hand. 'I understand,' she says. 'You've been fighting your whole life. But the thing is, you can't give up.' Her eyes burn with sincerity. 'You're our leader, our general. Our Queen. You can't escape that, no matter how much you want to. And I know it's hard – painfully, excruciatingly hard – but you can't give up. You can't. We need you.'

Tears spring mercilessly to my eyes. 'I don't know what to do. The world is burning and I don't know how to stop it.'

She tightens her grip on my hand. 'You face one fire at a time. And you don't have to do it alone. I've sacrificed my whole life to finding you, in the hope that one day I would have the honour of serving at your command. So have Mordecai, and Jax. You have friends, Marianne.

And for all the enemies waiting to strike you down we are ready to hit back. We're not giving up on you, so please don't give up on us.'

Her words are a balm on my bruised soul and slowly I can feel my pulse steady once more. I was wavering on the precipice before darkness and Astrid has pulled me back. I nod, reassuring her I'm going nowhere, and wrap my free hand over hers. Her shoulders drop. She realises she's got through to me and her relief is palpable.

When the moment passes, she stands up and refreshes my cloth once more.

'Where did you learn to fight like that?' I ask her, thinking of the ease with which she stormed into the threat of so many.

Mischief dances on Astrid's lips. 'You can see when you join us in the morning. We train early – if you think you can keep up.'

'I'm not sure I can,' I say with a smile, but a nagging thought claws at the back of my mind. Something about the way she fought is tugging at a memory I can't quite seem to grasp.

'Well, you have a good excuse,' she says and gestures to my bruised and battered face. 'For now get some rest.'

I thank her once more and then she's gone, leaving me alone with my pain and wounded pride. I made a mistake tonight and it nearly cost me everything. Since I've been here my anger never seems far away, my frustration always bubbling under the surface ready to strike. I don't like being this way.

I drag myself out of the chair to see how bad my reflection is in the looking glass. It's worse than I expected, and the prospect of tomorrow trying to convince other Guardians I'm their Queen with these injuries seems futile.

I creep out into the hallway and wind my way down to Gaius's potion room. To my relief, he isn't there. I set to work, boiling some water and adding silverbud and swampnettle to it, my usual ingredients for healing cuts. Then I add wildroot and a pinch of dirt for extra potency – again, a known addition to speed the healing process. And then I deviate. Where normally I would stop and drink the tonic, now I search through Gaius's vast store of ingredients until I find what I'm looking for. I add a spoonful of powdered hoof and a sprinkle of ash, before leaning over and squeezing in a drop of blood from my split lip. I stir the brew, whispering the same incantation I used for Gaius's burn over it, and finally remove it from the heat.

The smell is vile, but I hold my nose and drink the potion down. My body burns from the inside out, but in a good way. I can feel the magic taking hold. And when I return undetected to my room, I look once more at the looking glass and smile.

All traces of the injuries I sustained tonight are gone.

I rise with the sun, feeling more invigorated than I have in a long time. My potion seems to have given me a new lease of life. Wanting to keep my word to Olwyn, I head towards the large courtyard where the Guardians train multiple times a day.

To my surprise there are already at least sixty people filling the space, working hard on their skills. They're performing a range of different drills – everything from sparring to sword practice – but they have one thing in common.

They're all blindfolded.

Once I've spotted Olwyn, I weave carefully round the edges to reach her. She's sitting with Jax and together they're watching Mordecai and Astrid fight.

'You came,' Olwyn says, and I can hear both her delight and surprise at my presence.

'Of course,' I say, as if there was ever any doubt. 'Who's winning?'

'You tell us,' Jax says with a smile.

He's right to be amused. Astrid and Mordecai are both excellent fighters and it's mesmerising to see them. Once again I feel I'm watching a dance. Once again a nagging feeling bothers my brain. There's something here I'm missing.

When Astrid manages to knock Mordecai to the ground, she pulls off her blindfold and laughs. 'I believe that's two–one to me.'

Mordecai gets to his feet, brushing the dirt from his legs. 'You got lucky.'

Then they see me. Mordecai smiles and runs over to give me a friendly hug. Astrid, however, looks slightly shocked.

'You've come to train?' Mordecai says.

'No, just to watch the experts,' I say.

'You should join us,' Astrid says, though she's still frowning at me. 'Nothing sharpens your reflexes like fighting blind.'

I suddenly think of Sharpe, and want nothing more than to bring him West, so he can train with the Guardians, regain his confidence and be Torin's official bodyguard once again. I miss them both with unexpected longing.

'I suppose I could try,' I say, though I'm hesitant. I really don't want to make a fool of myself in front of so many people.

Perhaps sensing my caution, Astrid comes over to me. 'Fight Mordecai. We all know you can kick his ass.' And she winks at him.

'Charming,' he replies, but he's not offended. I can tell he's desperate to get a chance to try out his skills on me.

Under the cover of tying her blindfold around my eyes, Astrid leans close and whispers in my ear. 'What happened?'

I realise the reason behind her shock upon first seeing me. She was expecting to see a black eye and swollen lip.

'My studies with Gaius are going well,' I say, grinning, but despite not being able to see, I can tell she doesn't return my smile. All I can sense is concern.

'Fighting blind is all about focus,' she says, ignoring my miraculous healing. 'Trust yourself and your instincts and you'll unlock all your potential.'

And then she's gone. I'm alone, in the dark, with nothing to go on other than the assumption Mordecai is opposite me.

His fist strikes me without warning, right on my shoulder, and I stumble backwards. I'd completely misjudged his position and feel disorientated.

Mordecai hits me again, this time on my thigh. I can feel he's not using much force behind his blows and his manners spike my competitiveness.

'You taking it easy on me?' I taunt him.

'Well, it is your first time,' he replies.

Got him. His voice gives away his position and I lunge forward, landing a successful punch to his guts.

Behind me I hear Jax laugh and I start to relax. Once I do, my fighting instincts kick in.

All the other noise disappears. I listen only for the sound of Mordecai's feet, the heaviness of his breathing, the pounding of his heart. Every footstep, every breath, every heartbeat betrays his location so that I can attack, and with each successful hit I make, my own pulse steadies, my nerves calm. I'm in control; I know what I'm doing. I was taught by a Guardian. I can hold my own alongside them.

The thud of Mordecai smashing to the ground brings the fight to a close, and I pull off my blindfold, only to see that it wasn't solely my focus on Mordecai that had made all other noise disappear. Everyone else has stopped fighting and is watching me.

I walk over to Mordecai, who's taken his blindfold off too, and offer him my hand. 'You OK?'

'Have you done that before?' he says with a slight frown.

'No. Why?'

'Because you're good, that's why,' he says, and the frown turns to a smile. 'Too good.'

'Well, I still think you were giving me an easy fight.'

He laughs. 'Maybe at first. But not at the end. I was doing my best just to stay upright.'

'Sorry,' I say, patting him on the back. 'What can I say? I'm a Snake.'

'That was amazing,' Olwyn says when we return to them. 'And look,' she adds in an undertone, 'if they didn't know who you were before, they certainly do now.'

She's right, the other Guardians have definitely noticed me – though whether in a good or bad way, I'm not sure.

After that I opt to watch rather than fight more. Olwyn's taken well to her training, and I'm seriously impressed. Her fighting reflects her personality – thoughtful and patient. She bides her time before she strikes. I miss being with her, I realise. Of all the people I know she's the best antidote to my anger. She calms me when others can't, makes me laugh when I need to break free from despair. In truth, with her quiet strength and kind compassion, she would make a better queen than me.

I stay a while longer, but eventually the lure of the potion room grows too great and I make my excuses to leave. I'm not sure what mood Gaius will be in today after last night, but between the thrill of healing myself yesterday and winning the fight just now, I'm too excited to care.

'You're late,' he says when I walk into the room.

'I joined the others for some training.'

It's only when he turns to face me that I realise how much my absence has displeased him. 'You don't train with them. You train with me.'

Slightly taken aback, I make my apologies. 'I'm here now, though. Ready to learn.'

'Do you mean that?'

His coldness is unsettling me. 'Of course.'

'Good. Because after you threw your weight around last night, Arlan is more determined than ever to be rid of you, so we have no time to waste.'

He moves over to the store cupboard and opens the door, revealing, to my shock, a bound and gagged man.

With surprising force Gaius shoves the man in front of me. 'Kill him.'

I stare at Gaius, unable to comprehend what's happening. 'Excuse me?'

'You have so much potential,' he says with forced patience. 'It's time to forget the rats. Healing is fine, but restoring life is the most powerful thing a Mage can do. You've been given a rare gift, one I've never known a Mage to possess. But unless you practise, then you will never fulfil it.'

'I'm not going to kill someone!'

'He's going to die tomorrow anyway,' Gaius says, as if what he's asking is nothing. 'I took him from the dungeons. He's a murderer, scum, whose execution is scheduled for dawn. Besides, if you succeed, he won't be dead anyway, and your guilt will be redundant.'

'You think because he's a prisoner that makes it all right to experiment on him?'

'You have to hone your skills. I told you there would be a challenge you must face to become a Mage – this is it. This is your test, Marianne, the art you have to master to step beyond what you currently are into something greater. *This* is what you need to be powerful enough to save your people and fulfil your destiny.'

His words find their mark. Such power is within my grasp. Maybe the sacrifice doesn't have to be mine, but another's. I can stop spending hours failing to heal broken rats and focus on the bigger picture. I can become the Mage I wish to be, all it would take is a stab to this man's heart. Surely that's a cost worth paying to save the East? To return home and free Torin? This man, this killer, is nothing to me. Those I wish to protect mean everything.

'If I succeed in restoring his life, I will unlock my powers?' I have to be sure I've understood.

'Yes. I'm convinced this must be your test. And once you've succeeded, you never have to do it again, unless you choose to. You simply have to confront the task that will take everything you possess and complete it. That is how you – how anyone – transcends their limits to become a Mage. What you do with your untapped reserves of magic afterwards, is entirely up to you.'

I know exactly what I would do. I would demand the Guardians obey me or face my wrath; I would crush the King like the parasite he is; I would destroy everyone in my path. The magic rushes to the surface at the mere prospect, urging me on, whispering for me to do it, to fulfil my destiny. I can pass this test and finally the magic can be free. Can be mine.

'What test did you have to pass?' I ask Gaius. 'What sacrifice did you have to make?'

But Gaius shakes his head. 'My choices were my own. As are yours.'

My eyes meet the prisoner's and I see his fear. And then my own rushes in. I'm terrified – not of him, not of magic, not even of Gaius – but of myself. Did I seriously just consider this? Have I lost sight of what matters so much that I would kill to pursue my own gains? Bronn was right all along. I cannot be trusted with magic. I desire it too deeply; I need it too badly. If I cross this line, there's no coming back. The magic will consume me, and anything I say to persuade myself otherwise is simply a lie.

But I can hear it howling within me, outraged to be denied freedom.

'No. I won't take a life for no reason.' I feel just like I did all that time ago, refusing to kill at my Initiation. But then I immediately knew it was something I could never do. How far I've fallen. Still. I wouldn't kill for Adler. I won't for Gaius.

Gaius doesn't even try to hide his disappointment. 'I thought you wanted to be a Mage. You're the Viper – surely you have the stomach to do what's necessary?'

His comment hits a nerve. He's not the first person to accuse me of cowardice. But killing this man serves no purpose beyond furthering my own selfish desires. I won't do it.

'I do want to be a Mage,' I say, an edge to my voice now. 'I killed the man who raised me, so don't tell me I can't do what I have to. But I could kill this man and a dozen more and fail to bring a single one back. That's needless death, for what? For me to experiment?'

'Exactly! How else are discoveries made? You were happy to test your abilities on the rats.'

'You cannot compare kitchen rats to a person's life!'

'Why not? It is simply the natural progression. Always there are sacrifices, Marianne, always. It's time for you to make yours.'

Sacrifice. Every time I hear that word, my skin prickles in pain. I know a time is coming when I must make more. But this isn't it.

I shake my head. 'I'm sorry, Gaius.'

He sighs. 'I'm sorry too.' And without warning he swiftly raises a knife and slits the man's throat.

Blood pours instantly to the floor. The man's eyes are wide with terror, as the life quickly drains from his body. I look at Gaius in horror. 'What have you done?'

'I'm teaching you. Now save him.'

He thrusts the bleeding man towards me and, forcing down the rage that's rushing up like bile, I help lower him to the floor and focus all my attention on saving him.

His life is passing now, almost gone, the cut inflicted deep and fatal, and I watch the dance of the threads of energy rise up from the body, weaving among each other as if for comfort. The tangled net I must repair. I tried to do it for Lilah, and only half succeeded. I must learn what I did wrong. But for the first time I'm afraid of the magic. Afraid to release it, afraid of becoming the monster I now know for certain lurks within me. Breathing deeply and feeling the pulse of magic in my fingers, I raise them towards the strands, moving the threads back towards the body with surprising ease. I find myself muttering, '*offuggr*' under my breath, the ancient word for 'backwards'. I want to undo the damage done, the violence, and put things back the way they were. But though I'm working fast, my fingers nimble, part of me is still scared, hesitant, and already the threads are starting to fade, my eyes struggling to see them any more, the colours diminishing.

No, no, no. I try to move faster, knowing time's running out, but the energy dissipates and soon all that remains before me is a limp carcass. Death has defeated us both. I've failed.

I direct all my anger at Gaius. 'You killed him.'

'No, you did. You failed, not me. And I will not apologise for pushing you to greatness. I will slay a thousand men if that's what it takes for you to learn this art.'

Watching his face twist in anger, I no longer recognise him, and would weep if I weren't so furious. This cruelty is at odds with the kindness he's always shown me. It's like looking at a reflection of what I saw inside myself. 'Why does it matter so much to you?' I manage to ask, through my rage.

'Perhaps I haven't been clear enough.' His voice is tight with forced patience. 'Perhaps the word "test" has been misleading. It is a trial, a torment, a barrier that must be battered and smashed until we lie broken and destroyed on the other side. A feat of endurance where we sacrifice everything we hold dear, all the most important things . . . where we leave behind the ordinary and transcend to brilliance. I am quite convinced that *this* is your test. Pass, and you will be a Mage. Fail, and you will remain as you are. Never quite enough.'

'Then so be it.'

My answer clearly isn't what he's expecting – he thought his speech would impassion me. It didn't. Magic is a part of me and I love its wild seduction – the way it makes my heart beat stronger, my blood run faster, my head positively hum. But I fear it just as much I crave it. And I won't lose myself to it. I can see now what Old Tatty meant – it demands everything and takes even more. If I go down this path, slaughtering innocents for my own gain, I will never come back. Maybe this is the sacrifice I'm meant to make. Giving up magic to protect my soul. If so, I'm prepared to make it.

Gaius, on the other hand, is struggling to make peace with my decision. His eyes and nose are twitching with barely concealed rage. 'You're walking away? After all the training I've given you?'

'I'm very grateful for everything you've taught me—'

'I see no gratitude in this,' he spits at me. 'You've wasted my time, you spoiled wretch. Is it the throne you want? Is that it? Because that power is *nothing* to what a Mage can wield. You're not fit to call yourself Mage or Queen. You've long since left behind the title Viper. You've failed in this, as you fail in everything, and I can't bear to look at you any longer. Get out.' When I don't move, too startled to react, he starts to shout. 'Get out. Get out!'

I obey then, suddenly afraid. Gone is the teacher I've grown to trust, replaced by a monster. His words reverberate loudly in my head, echoing my own darkest thoughts – I'm not good enough. I never have been and now it's clear I never will be.

Though I'm shaken by my clash with Gaius, it helps clarify things for me. For too long I've allowed anger and frustration to paralyse me, allowed Rafe and his people all the power. I may have failed at magic, but there is one thing I'm good at. It wasn't a mistake to go out to the settlement and defend people – the mistake I made was going alone. So that night I sit with my friends and tell them what I think we should do.

'Will you come with me?' I ask when I've finished explaining my plan.

Jax and Astrid share a smile. 'Hell yes,' they say simultaneously.

Mordecai, however, is frowning. 'You want us to sneak out, with no one else knowing, to defend the settlements?'

I should have fought before, when I first learned the Hooded were taking children. Instead I wasted time being angry that I couldn't persuade the others to act. It's not a mistake I intend to make again. I think back to what Raoul said about me. It's time I was the storm.

'Yes, that's exactly what I want us to do. But if you don't want to . . .'

'No, I want to. I was just making sure I understood you right.' Mordecai grins at me.

'You sure?'

'Certain. It's time the Guardians did some guarding.'

'I think after your display this morning, there are others who will join us,' Astrid says.

'Then round them up. We go in an hour. If bandits are hunting tonight, we'll make them the prey.'

Within half an hour she manages to recruit ten more Guardians to join our cause, and soon we're creeping out of the palace the same way I left last night, only this time I'm not fuelled by frustration and fury, but by determination.

Mordecai falls to walk beside me. 'We need to talk about the Hooded,' he says, his voice soft in the still night. 'I've been studying the pattern of their attacks. At first glance they seemed random . . .'

'But you don't think they are.'

He shakes his head. 'I mapped them out. They're getting closer.'

I frown. 'To the palace? Is Eena right, are they coming for Rafe?'

Mordecai shrugs. 'I don't know, but something's pulling them this way.'

'In that case it's even more important we protect the settlements. We know there are already bandits here.'

Mordecai looks at me sideways. 'Do we?'

I realise he doesn't know about what happened last night, but before I can say anything, Astrid has come up behind me. 'Yes, I told her. Heard rumours from patrol.'

Mordecai's not stupid; he knows there's more we're not saying, but before he has a chance to probe further a sound catches my ear and I grab his arm to silence him.

It's a cry, like the raw wail of grief I made when Tomas died. And I know it's not bandits here tonight. The Hooded have come for the children.

My legs move faster than I knew was possible as I race towards the sound. The settlement is quite large and well populated. With only moonlight to guide us and the streets filled with people – sobbing and desperately searching – it's hard to see what's happening.

As I run up, a man points urgently to his left. 'They went that way. Help us, please!'

I nod and head in the direction he indicated, my mind sharp and focused. I'm ready to fight. I can hear the steady sound of breathing just behind me, and know Olwyn has my back.

And then I see one: a hooded figure – face hidden by their cloak – carrying two children, one under each arm.

'There,' I whisper to Olwyn, who has come up beside me.

The Hooded reaches a barn and goes through the door.

'That's where they're taking the children,' I say. 'Go round to the back, make sure there are no other exits.'

Olwyn nods and disappears into the shadows.

If we can trap them in here, we can end this once and for all. The stories that have grown around the Hooded have made people think they are unbeatable. But they're just people. Anyone can be stopped.

But as I creep towards the barn the weight of a body leaping from the rooftops sends me crashing to the ground. Both my attacker and I are on our feet instantly, and though his hood is up I can see the glint of cruel eyes.

Hatred rises inside me, and I pull my second dagger from my belt, so I have a knife in each hand. And then I attack.

He parries with equal speed, our hands moving furiously fast, so that sparks fly as our blades meet. His defences are strong, and it's hard to find a way to break through, but I keep going because there is no alternative. One of us will fold first, and it won't be me.

When it comes, the slip is small, but any error in this fight is costly. He simply doesn't move his hand fast enough and my blade cuts across his thumb, slicing right through the bone and leaving the top half of his thumb dangling by a few threads of muscle and sinew.

The hooded man recoils in pain and I kick him hard in the guts, wanting to end this, to finish him. But to my surprise he turns and runs.

For such fearsome warriors I wouldn't have expected the Hooded to be cowards, but push the thought aside as I chase. He's heading for the barn, but if he thinks he'll be safe there with his fellow Hooded to protect him, he has no idea who's pursuing him.

I fling the barn door wide open, ready to fight anyone waiting for me, only to skid to a halt. The barn is empty. There is no one in here.

There are few places to hide – the harvest clearly hasn't been bountiful this year – and I look behind every barrel of grain, every stack of crates, under every pile of empty sacks in the loft. I check the floor thoroughly for trapdoors or secret compartments. Nothing. The only way in or out is the door I came through.

They have simply vanished. Gone like smoke in the night.

We return to the palace dismayed and disbelieving. I hadn't truly believed the Hooded were an enemy we couldn't fight, but how do you destroy what you can't see? Though it's early when we arrive home, I head straight for Eena's quarters. Perhaps if she knows how close the Hooded are to her beloved Rafe, she might be willing to offer us the army we so clearly need.

I knock on the door, and Eena calls for me to enter. But as I go into the room someone's coming out. His head is down as he brushes past me, but I would recognise those amber eyes anywhere and my heart leaps into my throat, momentarily choking me. The last time I saw this man he was leaping from a window after plunging my knife into Torin's chest.

'Can I help you?' From the tone of her voice I think the only assistance Eena wants to give me is a sharp push off a high cliff.

Thinking quickly, I erase any trace of my increasing alarm at seeing the assassin here. The last thing I want to do is let on that I recognised him.

'Sorry to disturb you,' I say with friendly warmth. 'I was looking for Gaius.'

Eena looks with exaggeration around the empty room. 'Well, as you can plainly see, he's not here.'

'You're right, I'm sorry.'

And I shut the door quickly behind me, looking up and down the corridor to see if there's any sign of my would-be assassin. He's disappeared as quickly as he did out of Torin's room that fateful night.

My heart is racing and I start to run. I find my friends returning to their quarters and their expressions fall at the sight of my panic.

I pull them into Astrid's room and tell them what I saw. There's silence.

'Are you sure?' Jax says, exchanging concerned looks with Mordecai.

'Yes,' I say, cursing my own stupidity as everything comes together in my mind. I'd seen the clue in Astrid's fighting style, in all the Guardians' fighting. It seemed familiar because it reminded me of how exceptionally skilled the assassin had been. 'The assassin was a Guardian. He was there to kill me.'

'Then someone else must have known about you,' Mordecai says. 'I swear, I knew nothing about him. I came East alone.'

I believe him completely. There's no deception in his shock.

'Rafe found out then. Or Arlan. Or Eena. One or all of them knew and sent someone to kill me to eliminate any threat to the throne.'

'When he failed, he must have thought your incarceration was enough to prevent you from being a problem,' Astrid says as Olwyn stands up to give me a hug.

'He didn't know who he was dealing with,' she says with such fierce loyalty it hurts.

'So what do we do now?' Jax asks.

'Nothing,' Mordecai says and everyone looks at him in surprise. Apart from me. I think I know what he's planning and agree completely.

'Nothing?' Jax clearly doesn't.

'Look, at the moment we have an advantage,' Mordecai explains. 'They don't know we're on to them. If we show our hand now, we lose. We don't have the support yet. But we can get it. More and more of the Guardians hate how we're trapped inside these walls while our people are suffering out there. When we tell them what happened last night, even more will join us. More importantly very few of them like Rafe – they only support him out of loyalty to Arlan. If we can build a convincing case of how they tried to have Marianne murdered, we can finish them once and for all.'

'Then we wait, lie low,' Astrid says. 'Time to raise that army after all.'

I manage to give them a grateful nod in agreement, but the truth is I can't stop thinking of Torin, of the look on his face when he was attacked, of everything he's had to suffer because of me. It's all my fault. I've never wanted to be by his side more than I do right now.

I realise I haven't mentioned my argument with Gaius to them. It doesn't seem as important, though, given the enormity of this new revelation. Besides, putting aside my dreams of becoming a Mage means I'll have time to meet other Guardians and try to win their support.

Because I'm no longer under any illusions. The Hooded aren't the only ones I need to fight. I am at war with Rafe. I have been for months. I just didn't know it.

We spend the rest of the day together, devising strategies. But for all the seriousness of our conversation I can't help but notice Mordecai smiling to himself.

'What's so funny?' I say eventually, exasperated that he can find humour in this situation.

'Oh, just you.'

'Me? What did I do?'

His smile widens. 'You've decided to be Queen.'

'Finally,' Jax adds.

I prickle defensively, but realise what he's said is true. At some point during the day, I did make my choice. After all, I've turned my back on being a Mage, and Bronn is the better Viper. Being Queen might be a fragile power and others may seek to take it, but I can at least try to use it for good. 'Well, there's no way I'm going to let him have the throne now, is there? He tried to have me killed. For all I know he has succeeded in killing Torin. He's not fit to call himself King.' I'm referring to Rafe, but I hold Arlan and Eena equally responsible. 'And if I'm going to stop the Hooded, I need the throne.'

'Good,' Mordecai says. 'It'll be easier to recruit numbers if you're decided.'

As evening draws in, Jax and Mordecai have to leave to fulfil their duties, but the rest of us stay, not wanting to be alone.

I watch as Olwyn and Astrid sit next to each other, shoulders touching, knees brushing, and smile to myself. I knew they had grown close, but there's a glimpse of something more. A deeper affection. It gives me a sense of hope that even in dark times, when everything seems so bleak, love still finds a way to bloom.

It is a night for distraction, so we talk of everything and nothing, our voices mere whispers on the air, until we can't keep our eyes open any longer and decide to snatch some sleep before heading out on our next patrol. But after Olwyn leaves, I linger to speak to Astrid.

'Listen,' I say. 'If anything happens to me, then keep Olwyn safe. If I die, she gets the throne, understood?'

Astrid can't hide her surprise – or her concern. 'Nothing's going to happen to you.'

But my death has been prophesied and I know who's trying to kill me. It's only smart to have a back-up plan. 'You're the one that told me I'm not doing this alone, and you were right. It's going to take all of us to bring peace. If I'm gone, I need to know you'll carry on without me.'

Astrid sighs, but finally agrees.

'And you know as well as I do that Olwyn would make an exceptional Queen,' I say.

'I don't think anyone will argue with your choice,' Astrid says. 'But nothing's going to happen to you, OK?'

I smile, mainly to reassure her. 'OK.'

But as I walk back to my room I wish I could believe my own words. I'm uneasy and can't shake the feeling that I'm missing something important.

The sight of the body sprawled on the floor outside my room sends all other thoughts out of my head.

'Gaius!' I run to his side, not certain whether he's alive.

To my great relief he stirs, though when I reach him I see he's bleeding profusely from his stomach.

'Gaius, what happened?'

'I was coming to see you,' he says, groaning in pain. 'They were already here ... they were fighting and he stabbed me.'

'Who was fighting?'

'Mordecai. Is he alive?'

I stand up and hurry into my room, which has been ransacked. Beyond my bed Mordecai is lying on the floor, face down, and I run to him.

'No, no, no,' I cry as I reach him. Turning him over, grief crushes my throat as I see his glassy empty eyes, his expression still shocked that someone had bested him. My fingers touch his chest and come away bloodied. He has been stabbed straight through the heart.

'I'm so sorry,' I say to him, brushing the hair from his face, willing him to wake up, to smile at me, mock me for falling for his joke. But there is nothing left, and his loss is a coldness that's spreading through my veins.

There is nothing I can do for him, but Gaius is still alive so I force myself to leave my friend and return to my teacher.

'Mordecai is dead. Here, let me help you,' I say, but he pushes me away.

'No, I can take care of myself. You have to stop him, the one who did this. He fled the palace; if you take our path, you can cut him off. Please, you have to catch him.'

It has to have been the assassin. Perhaps he knew I recognised him earlier and came to my room, though I can't imagine what he might have been looking for, or why Mordecai was there. Had he been checking I'd made it safely to my quarters? Or had he wanted to talk to me about something? How is it possible I will never be able to ask him?

I hold Gaius's hand tightly, not caring about the blood. 'I'll get him.' And, the vow made, I race off into the night, determined the assassin won't escape me again.

Once I'm outside, I wish I'd brought my cloak. The air is cold tonight, but there's no time to let it bother me. My eyes are searching the area for any sign of movement. For a while I see nothing, and I begin to despair that I've been eluded once more, but then I see it, a shift in the shadows scrambling up the wall, and I set off in pursuit.

The assassin quickly makes it over the ramparts and heads towards the nearby settlement, and I sprint after him, ignoring my burning lungs as I push my body as fast as it's ever gone.

But then I lose him. Slowing down, I listen carefully, trying to pick up his trail. He's disappeared. I creep along, always watching, but he really has vanished. Just like Mordecai did when Bronn was tracking him. Just like the Hooded did.

The realisation comes too late, my brain only now comprehending what should have been horribly obvious. I wasn't meant to find him. I've just been led into a trap.

The blade is at my neck all too quickly.

'Don't try to fight.'

I raise my hands in surrender, before throwing my head backwards hard into my captor's face. I hear his nose crunch as I land a blow on his wrist, disarming him. I spin round to confront him, but he's vanished. Before I can collect myself, someone punches me in my back, causing me to stumble forward. A hefty kick knocks me to the ground. I roll over in time to intercept the fist aimed at my chest and grab the man's hand, pushing on it with all my weight as I jump back to my feet. Now he's the one who's unsteady, and I hit him hard – his jaw, his ribs, his guts.

'Enough!'

The shout causes me to pause in my attack and look over my shoulder. Emerging from the shadows are half a dozen people. The Hooded. One of them holds a child in front of them, a knife positioned against her throat.

'One move and the girl dies.'

This time when I surrender, it's genuine. 'Who are you?'

'What a disappointingly boring question,' the man behind me says and that's the last thing I hear before I'm beaten round the head and black out.

When I wake up, my hands are tied behind my back, my feet are bound and I'm being slapped across the face by a startlingly beautiful woman.

'Finally,' she says, when she sees my eyes blink. 'You're no good to me dead.'

I take in my surroundings, trying to figure out where I am. The building I'm in has a high ceiling decorated with carved beams. More candles than I've ever seen in one place illuminate the space, their light bouncing off the huge piles of gold and crystal on display. It's as if all the wealth of the entire island is in this one room. I think we might be inside a temple. The six Hooded figures are positioned around the room, blocking every possible escape.

'What do you want?' My head is still pounding from the blow it received, my thoughts a little disjointed.

'With you? Nothing.' And she smiles, sitting back like we're old friends. 'I'm simply a trader.'

I scowl at her. 'Of what?'

'Anything. Everything. Artefacts, treasure, people.'

My brain struggles to work. 'You're Greeb?' Typical – the Guardians had assumed she was a man.

'Yes, and you're Marianne, so that's the introductions out of the way.'

'So you've been acquiring children . . . for someone else?'

She smiles. 'I'm glad to see Vorne didn't knock your brain clean out.'

He may as well have done, the difficulty I'm having making sense of this. 'What would anybody want with so many children? Slaves? Who do you work for?'

'For anybody willing to pay enough. But as it happens the man I take children for is the same man who asked for you.' Greeb laughs. 'Oh, don't worry, he'll be here soon enough. Don't trouble your pretty little head.'

I test my restraints, but they're holding fast. Greeb sees me and clicks her tongue with disapproval.

'Don't insult me, please. Every precaution has been taken to ensure you can't escape. I'm sure you've been underestimated before. I understand. Even when they see it, no one truly likes to believe a woman can be so capable, so intelligent, so fierce. They're always shocked when we bite back.' She laughs again. 'But I won't make that mistake. I know what we can do. And I don't get paid unless I deliver you. Alive.'

'I can pay you more,' I say, appealing to the mercenary in her. 'If it's gold you want, I can get you gold.' Right before I cut her heart out. If she even has one.

Greeb purses her lips, as if she's considering my offer. 'Tempting, but no. I like this man. We work well together. He requires many things and the rewards are more than satisfactory. Besides, I have a reputation to maintain.' She stares at me for a moment, and then leans forward. 'Though I will take this.' And she yanks Torin's necklace off my neck. 'Worth a lot, I reckon.'

'Give that back,' I growl.

Greeb smiles. 'It is pretty, I agree. Perhaps I'll keep it for myself.'

'People will be looking for me,' I say, trying to ignore her taunts. 'And when they find you, they'll kill you.'

'You never cease to disappoint me.' The voice comes from the entrance, and my blood runs cold. Of all the people he's the last I expected to see. Gaius is hobbling towards us, no trace of his earlier wound. 'Your friends won't find you, any more than they could ever find the Hooded.'

'Gaius?' My heart breaks as I realise how blind I've been. All this time it was him. Why didn't I see? Of course it was him. A puppetmaster manipulating us all. He even showed me – he didn't bother to hide his lust for power. I was so absorbed in myself that I didn't see. 'They have talismans, don't they? Like Mordecai had. And the assassin you sent.'

'Well done,' he says, licking his lips free of spittle. 'Almost right. Apart from I didn't send the assassin to the East. That was all Arlan's doing. I don't want you dead. I did use the assassin tonight for my own purposes, though.'

'*You* had Mordecai killed?'

'Oh, Mordecai was simply in the wrong place at the wrong time. No, the assassin was required only to lure you into my trap. I knew once you saw him, you'd run to your friends, which would give me time to search your room. I also knew you'd hunt him down when you'd thought he'd harmed me. You're very predictable. How was I to know Mordecai would come to your room just as the assassin and I were tearing it apart? He saw too much and had to be disposed of. Whatever he wanted to say to you, I suppose we'll never know.'

I swallow back my grief. 'And your own injury?'

'Hog's blood. A mere distraction.'

My stupidity makes me want to scream. 'What do you want with me?'

'There's a lot we need to discuss,' Gaius says, and he's pulling a bottle from his robes and handing it to Greeb. 'But now really isn't the time, or the place. Let's adjourn to somewhere a little more comfortable, shall we?'

The Hooded sweep in on me. I fight with every ounce of strength I have against my restraints, so that it takes all of them to pin me down. Someone holds my head back, another pinches my nose, while my mouth is forced open and the potion poured down my throat. The taste is repulsive and I would throw it up if my jaws weren't being tightly clamped together. The last thing I see before the world turns black is the man I trusted, smirking with delight.

The cavern is cold and damp, and the smell is poisonous. Though I'm barely conscious, I'm aware of being dragged into the foul pit and, as I lift my throbbing head, I see row upon row of cages. Birds, animals, plants. I don't quite understand what I'm seeing, but I don't need magic to sense the despair and misery filling the air.

Deep in the heart of this hell is a cage waiting for me. I'm thrown in, the key quickly turned in the lock, and then I'm left alone, my mind fighting to wake up from the drug Gaius gave me.

I can't stand up, not fully. The cage is only tall enough for me to stoop, so I sit down on the hard ground, which is wet with algae. There's not even enough space to stretch my legs so I'm forced into an uncomfortable curled position.

I'm angry – mostly with myself. If I couldn't trust Bronn, a man I love, and who loved me, what made me think I could trust Gaius? How could I not have seen he was my true enemy? I was so blinded by my desire to learn, it didn't occur to me what his motives might be.

I suspect I'm going to find out what they are soon enough.

He comes eventually. After leaving me for several hours – enough time for my body to burn with discomfort – Gaius arrives in the cavern. I notice how the creatures cower at his presence. Even the plants seem to wilt to nothing.

'What do you think?' he asks, pulling a stool towards my cage and sitting upon it to rest his deformed feet. 'Like my collection?'

I have no intention of chatting with him. 'What am I doing here?'

'You're my guest, Marianne,' he says with a soft smile. 'You should be honoured – very few see my cavern. Only the chosen ones.'

'I'm your prisoner,' I point out, not interested in his honeyed words. 'What do you want with me?'

'You could have been here as my equal,' he says, and for a moment I hear genuine disappointment in his voice. 'But once you showed me your true colours, I realised you weren't what I thought. You're here so I can make sure your potential isn't wasted.'

I have no clue what he's talking about.

He reaches into his robes and pulls out a familiar notebook. My notebook. So that's what he was after in my room. 'This makes for very interesting reading,' Gaius says, flicking through the pages. 'But I was hoping there might be more about your ability to restore life.'

'Is that what this is all about?'

Gaius leans forward a little, ignoring my question. 'I have something to show you. Will you behave if I let you out?'

'No.'

He laughs and calls for assistance. Two Hooded appear, and Gaius gestures for them to open the cage.

'I think you'll find the drug hasn't left your system yet. You couldn't fight even if you wanted to.'

I'm pulled out by my hair and supported under each armpit by the Hooded, who drag me into a tunnel leading off the cavern. I have no idea what he wants to show me, until the tunnel widens, opening up into another pit, and I see the sight before me.

Row upon row of cages. Filled with children. Like me, they have no space to move. They make no noise. They've given up. They expect to die here.

I scream at Gaius, lunging towards him, desperate to kill him, but I'm weaker than I realise. I stumble, my legs collapsing under me, and slump to the floor in a raging heap.

'You bastard,' I shout until I sob the words.

Gaius simply chuckles as the Hooded haul me back to my feet.

'Always the defender of the innocent,' he says, still laughing. 'They're alive, are they not? They're fed and watered. What more could they ask for?'

'What are you doing to them?'

'Like you, they are my guests. Not quite as special as you, but important nonetheless.'

I may still be drugged, but this time when I lunge I manage to reach him, and smack him hard across the face.

The instant my skin brushes against his, it's as if a fire roars up between us. Like when I healed his burn, the crackle of heat rises – only this time when he tries to pull away I cling tight. A connection is forming between us, and I can sense Gaius desperately trying to break it. I can see into his past, but as him, from his point of view, as if I were living it. It grows stronger and I refuse to let go, wanting to see into his memory, wanting to discover what he's hiding.

I'm walking through the palace, only it's not the dilapidated ruin it is now, it's in full glory. But there is panic and urgency. I hurry along an empty corridor until I reach a door, pushing it open. Inside is a woman – regal and beautiful, poised with defiant dignity, two young children clinging to her skirts. Her fear is unmistakable, but she relaxes when she sees me. There is no doubt this woman is the queen.

'Gaius,' she says, her voice trembling. 'Are we lost?'

'Never,' I say, and the voice is different from the one I know. Higher, younger. 'I'm here to take you somewhere safe.'

The queen reaches forward and clutches my hand. I look down and see all my fingers are intact, the skin healthy and complete.

'Thank you,' she says, and I can tell she means it with every fibre of her being.

I bow. 'Ever your servant. Now come, we must hurry. They've taken the palace.'

Scooping her two children close to her, the queen sweeps out of the room, and together we race down the abandoned hallway. I can hear fighting nearby and the children start to cry.

I lead them down a flight of stairs and along a dark passageway. 'Nearly there,' I say, ushering them in front of me.

At the end of the corridor there's a door. It's a secret way out of the palace, but when the queen tries it, it's locked. She tries again and again to turn it but to no avail.

'We're trapped,' she says, her voice a frantic whisper.

'It'll be over soon,' I say, and the queen falters. She can see something in my face that alarms her.

'Gaius?'

Behind them another door in the hallway opens and a dozen men stride out from it. Men dressed in black clothing I would recognise anywhere.

'Don't struggle, Your Majesty,' I say. 'You'll only make it worse.'

And then I turn my back on her, the children and their desperate screams for help as I walk into the room the men came from and shut the door.

Even when the door closes behind me I can still hear the screams, but I ignore them, standing before a tall man dressed in the Snake clothes I know so well.

'Where is the boy?' The Viper is not pleased.

'I have men looking for him as we speak,' I say smoothly. 'Don't worry, we'll find him.'

'You'd better. My orders are to wipe out every living member of this family.'

'I understand your orders,' I say with sudden ferocity. 'You wouldn't be carrying them out at all without my help. Remember that.'

To my astonishment the Viper cowers a little. I've never seen a Viper scared. 'You will be well rewarded for your assistance. Payment shall be precisely as you requested.'

'I'll need the blood fresh, and any body parts you can spare.'

The Viper nods. 'My men will see to it. Can I ask what you intend to do with them?'

'You wouldn't believe me if I told you . . .'

*   *   *

The connection is severed abruptly, as Gaius finally manages to break my tie with his mind. But I already know exactly what he planned to do with them.

He's staring back at me, and I wonder how long we were linked and what he saw in *my* memories.

'You betrayed them,' I say, the strength leaving my legs. My gaolers catch me before I fall, and Gaius shouts at them to return me to my cage.

As I'm dragged back across the cavern, I seethe as the reality of what he's done sinks in. He isn't descended from the Mage who served the Western royalty – he *is* the Mage. He helped the Viper murder the royal family – my family – and in exchange took their flesh and blood. I once wanted magic instead of a throne because I thought magic was a power that couldn't be taken. Now I realise I was wrong about that too. The only reason Gaius would want their bodies is for the magic that ran through their veins. To strengthen himself. To become more powerful. And he's lived for centuries since on stolen power.

I'm so lost in my despair that I don't even realise we've returned to the original cavern until I'm pushed back into my cage. I look around me at the flowers and the animals in a new light. I think of the children in the adjoining cavern. He's draining life from all of them to feed his need. There are no limits to his depravity.

Gaius comes to sit with me, and I close my eyes. 'You let them die.'

He doesn't deny anything or ask me what I'm talking about. He knows exactly what I've seen. 'They deserved to die,' he says with undisguised contempt. 'What right did they have to rule? They were fools, the lot of them.'

'They trusted you.'

'Just one of their many mistakes. You see, for centuries Mages told royalty what to do. We were the wisdom and sense behind everything. But still we were treated as inferior, as disposable. Less than them.' He spits the words with malice. 'Summoned when it suited them and dismissed when it didn't. Always my advice became the King's words. What credit did I ever get?'

I stare at him, disbelieving. 'Credit? You killed them because you wanted credit?'

'I wanted to exist!' He's shouting now, bitterness still quick to flare even after all these years. 'I was invisible to them, and yet who enabled them to rule? Me! It was all me.'

'You were their advisor.'

'And that's exactly the problem. For too long we Mages were relegated to the sidelines, kept in our place, when all along *we* should have had the power – *we* should have ruled. I vowed I would change things and have devoted my life to the rise of the Mage.'

'But you've failed,' I taunt him. 'You're still just an advisor.'

'It's a funny thing, power,' he says. 'Over the decades I've learned that sometimes you can have more from the shadows. You think Greeb or that imbecile Prince are running things? They were my puppets, my cover until I was ready to rise. And when you arrived I thought our time had come. Finally a fellow Mage, one with royal blood no less. Together we could have ruled all Twelve Isles, Marianne. No one would have been able to stop us. But you fell short of what I hoped. You are too weak to rule. Now I will have to make other use of you.'

'You want my blood?'

'I want your magic.'

A sickening pressure tightens in my stomach. I don't think he's going to ask nicely for it.

'We're almost the same you know,' he says. 'We both have a connection to the life force in all of nature. But I see it for what it is – a valuable resource. While you wish to restore it to others, I seek to possess it for myself.

'You asked me once what test I had to pass to become a Mage? I always knew what it would be. Knew what had to be done. My mother was a weak woman who feared my magic. Thought a strap would beat it from me. It pleased me that she should be the one to help me unlock my power for good, as I drained her of her energy, her dormant magic, her life.

'Death held no interest for me, my plans needed time it wouldn't allow for, and so I used my gift to extend my life, taking others' energy for myself. The magic I extracted from your ancestors' blood made me more powerful and kept me alive for a long time. But once it ran out I had to find other ways to build my strength. I discovered my own fingers and toes could fuel the magic for a while, but eventually I ran out of things to cut off. Stealing a bird's voice or a flower's colour isn't enough to increase my power – it barely sustains me. So I had Greeb fetch me children. Their youthful souls are a more substantial nourishment. But what I really need if I'm to destroy my enemies once and for all is real power. And you, my dear, are brimming with untapped reserves.'

'You're going to kill me?'

'Eventually. One thing I've learned is that taking energy from the living is more potent than the dead, so your magic is distinctly more valuable to me while you still breathe. But ultimately I will outlive you, having stripped your magic from you like flesh from bone, and then you will die. But don't worry, that's years away.'

How comforting. If Gaius was willing to butcher his own body, I hate to think what he'll do to mine.

'Let the children go,' I say, my voice breaking with desperation. 'If I'm that much more valuable to you, then let them go. You don't need them any more.'

'Why is it you care one way or another for strangers?'

'It's just human decency. Perhaps you've lived too long to remember what that is.'

'As you so astutely pointed out, you're my prisoner. You don't get to make requests. I, on the other hand, have some things I'd like to know from you.'

Clearly my notebook wasn't the only thing he was after.

'Where is the Mage?'

That wasn't what I was expecting. *He's* the Mage. 'Who are you talking about?'

'The woman. The one you came here to see. When we connected, I saw your memory of her cocooned underground. Only a Mage could cast such a hibernation spell. Where is she?'

Esther! All that time I kept thinking of the cocooned woman it was *Esther* I was seeing? Finally it makes sense. If Gaius is looking for more ways both to keep himself alive *and* gain more magic, then another Mage would be the perfect source. She must have felt some warning and gone to ground.

Now it's my turn to laugh. 'That wasn't a memory. Simply a dream. I have no idea where she is.'

His face curls into a scowl and he grabs the thing closest to him, which happens to be a bowl, and flings it at my cage. I recoil, though the bars keep me safe. 'Then where are the books?'

I watch his rage and wonder how long he's been trying to figure it out. Since the day I first mentioned all the manuscripts I discovered in the East? Given that a fair few of them are with Bronn, there's nothing he can do to me that would make me reveal their location.

'Why do you want them? What do you hope to learn?' Even as I ask the question, I comprehend the answer. My gift. It always mattered too much to him that I master it. Is it simply because it's a rare talent that he wishes to possess it? Or are there even darker motives to his obsession with restoring life?

Gaius's lip is trembling with the effort of controlling his temper. 'You will tell me where they are.'

I match his determination. 'No. I won't.'

His eyes narrow. 'He'll die, you know.' He smiles when he sees my frightened reaction. 'The Prince you abandoned? The blood moon is close at hand, only a few cycles away, and with it comes his death. I've seen it. You can no longer save him in person, but if you tell me what I want to know, I will see to it that he lives.'

Oh, Torin. This is all my fault. I have failed him. But I will not place his life in the hands of this murderer. I'm done trusting the wrong people. From now on it's Bronn I'll trust. If anyone can save Torin, it's him.

'You think I'll believe any more of your lies?' I say. 'I'll tell you nothing.'

Gaius watches me closely and a menacing smile stretches across his face. He has another plan. 'Then I'll have to discover your secrets the hard way, won't I?'

He takes my first finger three days later. Before this he's made me watch his experiments, forced me to witness him bleach the colour from the most vibrant flowers, and, worse, silence the song in a bird's throat. He has serpents whose venom he milks like an act of humiliation. Every time, the exchange of energy causes him to swell with life, while his victims fade away. I've yet to see him

425

do his magic on the children, which is the only thing I'm thankful for right now.

I try to use my magic to escape, try to summon it back, but nothing happens. I can't even feel it within me any more.

'As long as you fear who you are, you cannot possibly hope to use it,' Gaius says derisively, when he finds me collapsed after one such attempt. 'Fortunately for me I have no such limitations.'

The removal of my finger hurts more than I imagined it would, an agony I couldn't prepare for, but still I don't tell him where the books are. He has his men hold me still so he doesn't have to touch me. He clearly doesn't want a repeat of our connection; though he could try to learn where the books are through my memories, apparently he still has secrets he is unwilling to share. Through tear-filled eyes I watch as he takes a part of me and adds it to a cauldron, then spends hours working on his incantation. When finally he drinks it the effect is immediate. I can see ripples beneath his skin, the magic burrowing like worms through his veins.

I hate him more than ever, as I watch him consume what belongs to me. Not just my finger, but my magic. It's not his to take. That he's making it part of him is the worst violation.

Apparently, though, he likes the taste of it, for over the next few days he removes another two fingers and four of my toes, choosing to store them in jars for future use.

'In case you die from infection,' he says to me as he wraps cloth round my stumps to stem the bleeding, taking care to keep material between our skin at all times. 'I want to have some of your energy preserved.'

I think that's the worst of it, but I'm wrong.

One morning, Gaius comes to visit me. The far end of the cavern appears to be open to the outside, and I can tell the time by the light and shadows that move across the floor. It's a form of torture in itself to count the days passing, and know the chances of my friends finding me fade with each one. Not that I really expect them to – Gaius is far too clever for that – but I cling desperately to this scrap of hope.

It's become his custom to sit with me as if I'm his pet. He holds up his clawed hand. 'Now I know you've been wondering how I did this. You're far too nosy not to.'

I can feel myself cowering slightly.

'I've taught you about sacrifice, Marianne. It wasn't your strongest subject, let's be honest. Long before I met you, I wanted to master the art of healing. I told you experiments had to be undertaken to learn more about magic, and my hand was just that. Could I break my bones and heal them?'

He waves the claw and laughs. 'Clearly, I failed, just

427

as you did with the rats. But I think it's time we both revisit our studies, don't you?'

Two of the Hooded come for me again, just as they did when he stole my fingers and toes. I don't cry this time. I don't scream, or beg, or any of the things I did when he first sliced me up. I'm too empty to struggle.

'I wonder,' Gaius says, 'if you were unable to heal the rats with a single touch because you lacked the necessary incentive. I think perhaps I can help you with that.'

He brings the butt of an axe down hard on to my arm. I hear the bone snap and hot white pain blazes through me. I would fall to the floor if I wasn't being held up.

'Now heal yourself.'

I barely hear his words through the agony clamouring in my head, but he's broken more than my arm. My spirit is crushed and I'm too afraid to disobey him.

I press my other hand to my injured arm, and will it to mend. But just as every time I've tried to summon my magic to escape, there is no answer to my call. Only a hollow void inside me where my despair stretches endlessly.

When I start to sob, Gaius slaps me hard, offended by my weakness. It was an impulsive action, made without thought of the consequences, but he quickly realises what just happened. Our skin touched and there was no connection.

He looks at me with a cruel sneer. 'Interesting. It seems that now I possess your magic, you can no longer see into my mind.'

Through my tears, I glare at him. 'And you can't see into mine either.'

His eyes narrow with hatred. 'No matter.' And he rests his hands roughly on to my arm, smiling when I gasp in pain. 'Now. Let's see if I can wield your magic more effectively.'

He mutters his incantations for most of the day, but my bone doesn't heal. Eventually – mercifully – he gives up and has me thrown back into the cage to punish me for my failure.

Out of kindness – or so he says – Gaius waits until the pain isn't so raw before he tries again. This time, when he breaks my shin bone, I do lose consciousness for a while. Yet again, we both fail in our attempts to mend me. I expect nothing else any more, but Gaius is furious.

For all his power he cannot master the art of healing in any capacity and somehow, through the pain, that gives me a twisted satisfaction.

'You envy me,' I say, my head leaning against the bars of my cage. My voice is soft, drained of vitality, but I know he hears me. 'You've spent all these years acquiring power, but my type of magic eludes you. Even when you attempt to take it from me.'

'You think I envy you? Look at the state of you, you pathetic, worthless creature.'

'Which just makes you hate yourself even more. To envy something you despise.' And I start to laugh and cry at the same time, because we are both doomed to keep living this nightmare.

After that his visits become less frequent. Days pass without his presence, until he returns one morning, poring over papers, trying to find the answers he so desperately seeks.

'Are my friends looking for me?' I hate myself for asking, aware it reveals my vulnerability, but unable to bear not knowing.

Gaius glances up. 'No.'

'Why not?' All foolish dreams of a rescue disappear. *Not even Olwyn?*

'Because they believe you've run away.'

I lift my head as far as I can. 'Why would they think that?'

'Because Mordecai was lying dead in your room. I simply convinced everyone that he had become infatuated with you, that he came to see you wanting more than you were prepared to give, and that you killed him in self-defence. I told them you fled out of fear and guilt.'

'They'll never believe you.' My friends would hear the lie in such a story.

'Why not? You did. You trusted me completely – just as they all do. The Guardians belong to me.'

I stare at him. 'What do you mean?'

His eyes sparkle with glee as he sees my uneasiness. 'I *made* them. I had to keep an eye on your ancestors, after all.'

Misery consumes me entirely. 'You created the Guardians?'

'I knew the remaining boy lived after the massacre of the West. Had to hunt him down and finish what I started. Only, the thing was, I learned something from his family that I'd never realised before. The royal family do have magic in their veins – but it is dormant. The Isles themselves recognised it, but it was a rarity for a ruler to command it. That's why they needed the Mages; they could not wield the power contained within them. When I tasted their blood I felt its weakness, its impotency. I could have killed the boy, yes, but what then? I realised that to access the power I craved, I would have to be patient. Bide my time. Because I foresaw that one day a child would be born who would be able to control what pulsed through their blood, one rare ruler whose magic would burn brighter than the very sun. I desired that power above all else and so I waited.'

'That's why you needed the Guardians. To keep the bloodline alive.'

'I saw an opportunity. Encourage hope within the people. Let them fight for a future they could believe in. Obviously I controlled them from a distance, but they served their purpose over the years. To watch and protect the descendants until the one I needed was born.'

'Why keep the other lines alive too? Why Rafe? Does he have magic?'

Gaius scoffs. 'That imbecile? No, only the direct line has magic in their blood. The other lines were there only to be useful when I needed them. When I wanted to start my war. It really is terribly easy to twist people to your will with the promise of power. How quickly they believe that they deserve it, that they are more worthy than others, that no cost is too high to hold on to it.'

So there is a war coming. One that will destroy the Twelve Isles and force them into servitude to Gaius.

'I thought your mother was the one I'd been waiting for,' Gaius says. 'Her magic simmered under the surface and I watched it grow as she did. I had a plan, to destroy her world and then swoop in to save her. And then your father ruined everything.'

I think of what my grandmother told me on the Ninth, that my parents said they were being hunted. I thought she'd meant Adler. 'They were running from you?'

Gaius nods. 'But before I could catch them, you were born. And, Marianne, how the islands trembled. You think anyone else can do what you do? That anyone can summon water raptors? You are alive with more power than you deserve. I knew the moment you arrived on this earth that the true child of the islands was here at last. And so I sent the Viper to find your parents. My Eastern connections came in handy once more.'

'Adler murdered them . . . for you?'

'Very efficient, I thought. Unfortunately he was supposed to bring you to me but I guess it's true what they say. Never trust a Snake. Still, at least I knew where you were, all safe and sound.'

It's like the world is falling away and there's nothing left to cling to. 'It was you. It's always been you.'

Gaius's victory is complete. 'Yes, my dear.'

His absences grow ever longer, sometimes so my water bowl runs dry, and I think I shall die from dehydration and be spared more torture. But he always returns in time to save me. To condemn me. Then one time he leaves and it finally and truly dawns on me. I *will* die here in this cavern of despair. But not soon. I will rot here for years. I look at my mutilated hands and feel numb. Gaius will take me piece by piece and, as he grows in strength, I will weaken. I can feel it already, the shift in balance. There will be no one to stand against him and he will make all that has come before seem kindness. He will, as Old Tatty foresaw, destroy everything.

As the last dregs of hope ebb away, I sit in a darkness

I've never known before. It's cold and lonely. All is lost.

And then, in the emptiness, a small pale glimmer flutters before me. A starmoth has flown into this desolate place, its shimmering wings beating fiercely like sparks of light. It's so tiny but so alive. And an ember of fire glows in a distant corner of my spirit. I'd forgotten the beauty of life. The colour of it. The strength of it. *The magic of it.*

I want to live.

Though I still fear my magic, if I stay here Gaius will use it for evil anyway. I must try whatever I can, whatever the cost, to stop him.

I just don't know if there's enough of me left to succeed.

I rest my bloody, mangled hands on the lock of my cage and will the magic to the surface. If Gaius has taught me nothing else, it's that I'm capable of great power. He wouldn't want me otherwise. And knowing I'm so valuable to him gives me confidence.

Nothing happens. The hollow space where once my magic dwelled has spread and consumed all of me. My hope. My strength. My future.

'Please,' I beg it, as I try again to summon it. 'Please.' But all that happens is my skin slides in the blood seeping from one of my many wounds.

I close my eyes and think of those dearest to me. The

memory of Grace and Tomas. Torin and Sharpe. Bronn. I will never see them again. Hot tears spill down my cheeks. Love shouldn't hurt this much. Gaius may have tortured my body, but it's the thought of them, of knowing I shall never see them again, that delivers the fatal wound to my heart.

A scream escapes me, rage, frustration and grief all rolled into one sound, and I shake the bars with all the strength I possess. 'Come on!' I shout at them, at myself. 'Come on!'

Something stirs inside me, something forgotten, something familiar. From the deepest parts of myself the smouldering ember catches fire, heat spreading as the magic rises – slowly at first, then faster, as if it can't believe its luck in finally being set free.

I can't believe it either, and a tiny laugh escapes my lips as I grasp the bars tightly, terrified I might lose it once more.

'*Brena, hyrri*,' I say, repeating the incantations for 'burn' and 'fire' over and over, only they are no longer simply words. I *am* the words, I am the magic – it's all one. My blood soars through me, a furnace in my veins, and I watch as the lock starts to melt, the heat surging out through my remaining fingertips until the metal has utterly liquefied and the door pushes open. I gasp, wondering how to stop the flow, because it's as dizzying as if blood itself was draining from my body. I clench what's left of my hand into a fist, and the magic pauses, pulsing beneath my skin ready for my next command.

I'm free. Now there's just the question of whether I have the strength to stand, let alone move. But I have to – simply have to – or I'm worse than dead. If Gaius finds me now, he'll cut me up and keep me in a state where I'll be begging for death.

Filled with confidence, I turn my magic on myself. Resting my hand against my broken leg, I try again to heal my bones with my touch. But though I strain until my veins are bursting, I have to admit defeat. Such a skill is simply beyond my ability and I don't have time to waste in delusions.

I stumble out of the cage, pain shooting through me, but I ignore it. I'm the Viper. I'm a queen. I can't let pain stop me now. I know there's no point trying to escape the way I came in – it'll be guarded and I'm in no condition to fight anyone – but there's the far end of the cavern, where light and air have tantalised me with their proximity. That's my best bet and so I shuffle my broken body in that direction, silencing the voice in my head insisting I can't leave everything else behind. I want to save them all: the children, the birds, the animals. But I can't help them right now, and though it hurts I make the selfish decision to save myself. If I can live today, maybe I can save them tomorrow.

If. Maybe.

Neither seems very likely right now, as I can feel the effects of my torture destroying me from the outside in. It seems to take for ever to reach the cave mouth, and with every agonised step I dread Gaius returning and discovering me. And then I realise why Gaius has left this entrance unguarded.

The cave opens straight into the cliff face; the only way out is a sheer and deadly drop down into the ocean.

Panic rises quickly, I can feel my fear taking over and I sink to the floor in a messy heap as despair returns, taunting me for ever thinking I could be free.

But then a strong gust of sea air blows in, the salt stinging my face like a slap. The only alternative is to hobble back to my cage and wait for death and I will not give Gaius the satisfaction. I look down at the swirling waters below, crashing over jagged rocks, and begin to smile as a plan takes shape in my head. It's a plan of the desperate, a plan ridiculously unlikely to work, but it's something. I'd rather die in the attempt and deny Gaius his magic, than live for nothing.

There's no time to waste. I shuffle back into the cave as fast as I can, until I reach the cages housing the serpents. I've watched Gaius extract venom from all of them except one – a horned black snake, whose back is zigzagged with scars from where Gaius has bled him. For some reason Gaius has avoided this snake's venom, and I can only guess it's because it's so toxic. And Mama told me about a snake with such venom – a death asp. I'm making a big assumption, but I think that's what it is. I can't cope like this for much longer, my body is too damaged to keep going, so if I want to escape, I need help. I remember what Mama said about the old myth, that a death asp can offer his venom as a cure. One bite from this snake will either enable me to carry on, or will kill me where I stand. Either way, I shall be free.

The snake and I regard each other for a moment. I say nothing; we do not share a language, but there are other ways to communicate. As I did once, what feels like a lifetime ago, with the timber bear, I look into the serpent's eyes and share my pain, my desperation, as I poke my mutilated fingers through its bars. Slowly it extends its head towards me, its forked tongue flicking over my skin, my blood. And then, with considered precision, it sinks its fangs into my flesh.

Instantly my pain lessens, not entirely, but enough for it to be bearable, and relief floods through me. Though its effects are no doubt temporary, the snake has granted me its venom as a gift, one condemned prisoner to another.

When it releases me from its jaws, I extract my fingers and open its cage. Mine was the only one Gaius deemed necessary to lock. Offering the snake freedom is the least I can do, but I don't wait to watch it slither away, I'm too busy opening all the other cages, allowing the creatures to escape, if they have the strength. Birds flap weak wings and fly towards the air, rodents scuttle into cracks in the cavern walls, and serpents wind their way over the dusty ground, perfectly camouflaged. In the final cage is a small black gull. It chirps noiselessly at me, an eerie silence. I do my best to wrap my hands round the bird as I take it from its prison. It's thin and weak and its dull eyes plead with me for death.

'Not today, friend,' I whisper. I carry the gull to the opening and let it feel the wind ruffling through its feathers. It opens its beak but no sound comes out – it's pitiful. I let my outrage fuel my magic, relieved to feel it rising to the surface again – quicker this time – and I close my eyes.

'*Talla*.' I order the bird to speak, willing my magic to fill the void Gaius left. Heat bubbles under my skin, my blood boiling with power that glides over the gull, shrouding it with energy and restoring what was stolen.

Sweet music dances on the air. I snap open my eyes to stare at the little bird, now singing his heart out. I did it. But there's no time to waste marvelling at the wonder.

'I need your help,' I breathe into its ear. 'Find Talon and send him to me. Can you do that?'

The bird chirps, but it looks uncertain. It's a long flight and the gull's little body is empty.

'It's OK,' I say, stroking its fragile head. 'I'll help.'

And once more I focus on the energy still buzzing at my fingertips. I'm going to have to give the bird some life, and the only one I have to give is my own. I won't steal from others like Gaius.

'Take what you need,' I say, my voice lost on the wind. I feel my energy pass to the bird, feel myself weaken as it grows in strength. When the bird stirs restlessly in my hands, I stop the transfer. '*Flauga*. Fly, my friend. And good luck.'

I release my hold, sending the gull into the air. He soars upwards and away, twisting and gliding with delight, before turning east and disappearing from sight. I smile, but then realise quite how much weaker I feel. With a bitter pang I comprehend how closely magic is linked with life force. I've seen it, seen Gaius take for himself, but for the first time I've experienced the exchange of energy, and can't deny the sense of loss to my body. Can't deny how tempting it would be to want to replenish that strength, how easy it would be to justify it in order to survive. The line between right and wrong doesn't look so clear any more, and it terrifies me. But for now I will not let the magic consume me. Not today.

I bring myself to the edge of the opening and move my legs so they hang over into nothingness. Even with the death asp's venom I won't get down this cliff alive by myself – not even if I had all my fingers and toes left. I need more help. I won't demand it from anyone or anything. But I'm not too proud to ask.

'*Veitja.*' I speak the word into the air, hoping someone will respond. The rock, like it once did before, or the ocean perhaps. But I'm met with silence.

'Please,' I say, my voice breaking into a sob. 'Help me.'

A distant noise reaches my ears and for one chilling moment I think it's Gaius returned, roaring with anger, but then I realise the sound is coming from outside the cave, not within.

Searching for the source, I squint and see the sea moving strangely, like part of it has separated from the rest and is moving in a different direction. The noise is thunderous as it stampedes towards me, a tidal wave rolling *against* the tide. Only when it's close do I see what has come to my aid.

A sea stallion – half foam and water, half flesh and blood – calls out to me with a piercing whinny.

I don't hesitate. I push myself off the cliff and fall, the wind cradling me before the stallion rises up to catch me. There is no pain on impact, just the warmth of life beneath me. I reach my hand towards a watery neck and what I touch immediately forms as solid shape.

'Thank you,' I say, though I'm not sure I make a sound. Maybe I just think the words over and over, but I'm certain the horse hears no matter what.

'Can you take me to the Eighth Isle?' I know I merely

think that, too exhausted for anything more, but no sooner does the thought form, than the stallion is moving at staggering speed, galloping across the water so that his hooves throw up giant waves behind him.

I pass out after a while. I'm safer than I've been in the longest time and I sense the sea stallion will protect me a while longer. When I wake, I'm lying on the familiar white sparkling sands of the Eighth. The sea stallion is nowhere to be seen, the water now entirely calm, and though I'm far from feeling well I've regained some strength from my rest. Sending thoughts of gratitude out towards the ocean, certain my saviour will hear them, I drag myself up the beach.

I have no idea how much time has passed since I escaped, but I'm not safe yet. It's time to put the next part of my plan into action.

It's time to hide.

Esther's hut greets me with cold emptiness. Nothing's changed since I was last here, apart from one crucial detail: my understanding of what happened to her. She perceived the threat of Gaius and hid – and now I know what he's capable of, what he'll do to steal my power, I'm doing the same.

But I finally comprehend what I should have a long time ago. Esther hasn't abandoned me, any more than I've abandoned my friends. She's been reaching out to me in visions, trying to show me her location – not so I can find her, but to warn me to go to ground. More importantly I've realised something else. There's a reason this clearing feels so devoid of magic. Esther has put an enchantment on it to disguise it from searching eyes. From Gaius's eyes. Which means, for now at least, I'm safe here.

I need to write a message for Bronn. He's the last person I should be asking for help. But he's the only one I can. It's time to place all my trust in him.

There are no quills and no ink. I search high and low and when I find nothing I search the other huts for anything I can use. Fortune favours me slightly when I find an old book, from which I tear a sheet of paper, but as for ink I'm going to have to be creative.

I have no blade, no weapon of any kind, so I venture outside and find a stick, which I sharpen with a stone until I fashion a point. Then I stab it into my finger and watch the red blossom of blood bubble to the surface. And I start to write.

I keep it short, concise. Seeing my plan scrawled in blood makes me question whether I have truly gone mad. It's pure insanity. But it's all I've got. I squeeze fresh blood out and carry on writing, stating what I require of Bronn. I want to tell him I miss him, want to tell him how desperately I've felt his absence, but I don't. There's no room left on the paper.

I lie out under the stars, but I'm too tired to sleep and instead feel the magic rise and fall like the tide inside me. It knows what I intend to do and welcomes it. I simply must hold on long enough to see my plan through.

No one comes. I remain undisturbed, undetected, hidden in this clearing just as Esther knew I would be. I hope wherever she is, she's safe.

By morning the sight I long for comes into view. At first it's just a black smudge against a stormy sky, but within minutes a sea vulture soars down towards me, stirring me from my waking dreams.

Talon swoops to my shoulder, pecking my ear with undisguised affection, and I have to stop myself from crushing the bird in an embrace. I've never been more pleased to see him.

'Good bird,' I say, thanking him for his speedy arrival. 'I need to ask a favour, old friend. Can you take this to Bronn?' And I hold up the scroll of bloodied paper.

The great sea vulture shrieks in answer and I brush his wing with my stubbed finger.

'Is he doing OK?'

The bird tilts his head intelligently, and I see his sympathy glistening in those wise eyes.

'Better than me, huh?' I laugh. 'That wouldn't be hard. Give this directly to him, and no one else. And, Talon? Look after him for me.'

Talon gives a gentle cry and nudges my face with his beak as I attach the scroll to his leg. I don't want him to leave now that he's here; he's a comforting piece of the life I wish I hadn't left behind. But there's only one way forward.

'Fly safe. Fly fast,' I whisper into Talon's ear, and with a mighty flap of his wings the great bird soars into the air, bearing east.

Now I have to wait. And prepare.

Days then nights pass, while I rest my body and hone my plan. I know what must be done, but it all hinges on Bronn, and whether he's prepared to do what I've asked.

The mangled stumps of my fingers and toes begin to heal over. I think of Olwyn and my Guardian friends. Do they hate me for the crimes they've been told I committed? Are they safe? Will Gaius dare to reveal himself or will he continue his pretence a while longer? Fear for them threatens to undo me, but worrying serves no purpose. They can take care of themselves, and right now, there's nothing I can do for them.

I collect rainwater in leaves to drink, and chew on the woody stems of plantains that grow up through the sandy ground. It's not much, but with the remnants of the death asp's venom still sustaining me it's enough.

Eventually I decide the time has come to leave the sanctuary of the clearing. If Bronn set a course west as soon as he got my message, then he should be here soon. I want to be waiting.

My journey to the beach is painful, my body stiff from lack of use, my broken bones healing all wrong. And I feel afraid. I'm unarmed, I can't defend myself. I'm vulnerable and it's terrifying.

But there's no one here, this side of the island completely deserted. I idly wonder whether that is Esther's doing too – she certainly would have used whatever magic was at her disposal to repel intruders.

The sand greets me with the tingling warmth of magic and I nestle in its banks at the top end of the beach, hidden from anyone passing – on land or sea. I try to remember when I last slept deeply.

I wait for days, watching the rising of the sun give way to the moon's reign five times. Doubt plagues me.

What if Bronn ignores my request for help? Certainly, what I've asked for is more than most people would be prepared to give. But Bronn's not most people, and I have to believe he's not changed from the man I knew, despite all I've done to destroy him.

On the sixth day I finally see the *Maiden* appear on the horizon, a mere speck at first, but quickly she grows – as do my nerves.

He's here.

Since I escaped Gaius, weariness has been my only companion, but now I must shake it away. The time has come for my plan to be put into action – if Bronn is willing to go along with it.

I walk down the shore, feeling the diamond fragments bite into my feet and crunching them between my remaining toes. The rhythm of the waves rolling out, then racing forward and crashing on to the sand, calms my anxiety as I watch a boat filled with a dozen men row over.

They bank on the sand, and drag the boat up, and still I stand there, watching, waiting. Bronn has brought some of the crew with him, and my heart swells with painful delight to see Rayvn is among them. Snake blacks suit her more than they ever did me.

When they get closer, Bronn signals for the others to wait and then he approaches me alone. His hair is tied back so there is nothing to disguise his eyes from me, but today I cannot read them. It's been too long. All I know is my heart is screaming out to him, longing for him to hear that it still belongs to him, as it always did.

He's aged, I think. There's a hardness to his face I don't remember, and I wonder if I put that there, or if something worse has happened to him while we've been apart.

Then I see how he's looking at me, and remember I'm wearing my suffering for him to see too. His eyes miss nothing. He sees my slight stoop, my missing digits, my limp as I take a step towards him.

I wonder if I imagine the pity I see in his eyes. If it is there, it's only for a second, quickly hidden again by a man masterful at deception.

'Thank you,' I say, taking another clumsy step towards him. 'For coming.'

Bronn doesn't move. There's a cold air blowing from where his crew stand watching and I want to cry. I'm not one of them any more.

'You had no right to summon me like you did,' Bronn says, and his words are ice.

'But you got my message? You read what I said?' I have to know if he's going to help me. If he's prepared to do exactly what I've asked.

'I did,' he says. 'After everything you've done to me you thought I'd come to your aid? Thought I'd rescue you?'

Panic flares inside me. What if he won't do it? 'Why are you here? If not to help me?' My own voice is small, but he hears.

It takes Bronn a moment to answer. He isn't finding this easy. 'Because the *Maiden* needs a true captain.' He raises his voice loud enough for it to travel down the beach. He wants the Snakes to hear. 'The East needs a real Viper.'

Behind him I see a slight shuffle of discomfort. The crew clearly didn't know this was why they were here. I glance over at Rayvn, whose eyes flicker uncertainly. Ren is close to her, and he too is frowning at Bronn. The others aren't my friends and in them I see nothing but excitement. They sense what's coming.

'You've come to claim the title?'

Bronn swallows hard before he nods. 'I have.'

I raise my hands in surrender. 'Please, Bronn. I'm unarmed. I can't even hold a blade.'

'Then it should make this easier,' he says and without warning he charges towards me, his dagger drawn.

I dodge as best I can, but my unbalanced feet trip in the sand, so I topple to the ground. Bronn is thrusting the blade down and I roll out of the way before scrambling to my feet. Now I can do nothing but block and parry his blows, but he's in peak physical condition and I'm a pale shadow of the warrior I once was. I fight to defend myself as hard as I can, giving everything I've got, though my body is screaming in protest, as is my heart. I can hardly bear this. I must bear this.

The crew do nothing but stand and watch in amazement. This isn't a sight seen every day. Even Rayvn and Ren make no effort to help me and their loyalty to Bronn is another blow to my heart.

I'm struggling to stay upright, and Bronn capitalises on my weakness, flicking his foot behind mine so that I trip. With one arm he catches me and with his other he presses his blade to my neck. For a fleeting moment it's as if everyone else disappears. Just the two of us, our faces so close that I can see all the anger, all the doubt in his eyes. We are both breathless, both tired of this fight. I hate what I've done to him, what I'm doing to him.

'I love you,' I whisper like a spell on to his lips. It's still true, will always be true.

There's a flicker of emotion in his features and I can't bear to see his pain any longer. It's time to end this.

'It's OK,' I say, giving him permission to take what he came for. 'Do it.'

My order seems to give him resolve and, with swift efficiency, Bronn glides his blade across my neck.

Heat blazes through my whole body and though I was expecting it, I wasn't prepared. Wetness spills down to my chest, soaking my clothes, and for a second Bronn's arms are round me until I slide down away from them for ever.

The ground breaks my fall, and I gasp for air but choke on blood. I'm scared at how fast it's happening, how quickly I can feel life slipping away. Bronn is victorious, the title of Viper finally his; he and his men are leaving now, returning to their boat amid cheers and shouts, and despite everything I don't want them to go.

I'm dying alone. The sand is turning red, drinking down the sorrow, fear and hope as they drain from my body, my soul ebbing away to the care of the earth.

I'm afraid.

I'm so very sad.

I'm . . .

ACKNOWLEDGEMENTS

Once again, I am indebted to many other people who've got me this far:

My fabulous agent, Davinia Andrew-Lynch, who amazes me on a daily basis with her fierce tenacity and unwavering support.

My exceptional editor, Lena McCauley, who has guided me through each edit with her wise and kind insight.

All the amazing team at Hachette – you have gone above and beyond for me. Extra special thanks to Emily Thomas, Samuel Perrett, Naomi Berwin, Natasha Whearity and Becci Mansell.

To my nineteen newbie friends – how lovely to have shared our exciting debut year together. Special shout-outs to Lucy Powrie and Kat Dunn for keeping me sane.

My fantastic family, who are beyond incredible. My dad has now read *Viper*, and can legitimately call himself one of my biggest fans. Endless thanks to my mum for reading every single draft I've churned out, and for her spot-on advice.

My one-in-a-million hubby, Joe, who also reads draft after draft and points me in the right direction. And my gorgeous girls, Kara and Odette. Thanks for the laughs and hugs through a busy, mad year. Love you all.

And lastly, massive thanks to all the bloggers, booksellers, reviewers, librarians, teachers and readers who have supported me this year and made it so wonderful. I'm truly thankful to every single one of you. Yes, you. You're the best.

BEX HOGAN

BEX HOGAN

ISLES OF
STORM &
SORROW
VIPER

ISLES OF
STORM &
SORROW
VENOM

'A rip-roaring, swashbuckling
adventure that left me breathless'
Kat Dunn, author of Dangerous Remedy

COMING SOON
VULTURE

THE FINAL BOOK IN THE
ISLES OF
STORM & SORROW
TRILOGY

Bex Hogan was raised on a healthy diet of
fantasy and fairy tales, and spent much of her life
lost in daydreams. Initially she wanted to train as an
actress, but she quickly realised her heart belonged to
storytelling rather than performing, and soon after
started creating stories of her own. A Cornish girl at
heart, Bex now lives in Cambridgeshire with her family.

Follow her on Twitter @bexhogan
or visit her website at bexhogan.co.uk.